D0319615

The Big Music

THE BIG MUSIC

[selected papers]

Kirsty Gunn

ff

faber and faber

First published in 2012
by Faber and Faber Limited
Bloomsbury House
74–77 Great Russell Street
London WC1B 3DA

Typeset by Faber and Faber Ltd
Printed and bound by CPI Group (UK) Ltd, Croydon, CR0 4YY

This book was published with support from Creative Scotland

ALBA | CHRUTHACHAIL

AUTHOR'S NOTE: I am most grateful for a writer's bursary from the Scottish Arts Council –
now Creative Scotland – received in 2003 that made this project possible. I would also like
to thank all those whose patience and advice allowed me to polish and refine the final
version of this book: Lee Brackstone, Mary Morris and Kate Ward at Faber, my agent Clare
Conville, copyeditor Lorraine McCann, Merran Gunn and Stewart Bowman, and finally,
my family, David Graham, Millie and Katherine, who gave me so much time.

This book is a work of fiction. All people, places and facts may or may not
be a product of the author's imagination.

A CIP record for this book
is available from the British Library

ISBN 978–0–571–28233–3

FSC
www.fsc.org
MIX
Paper from
responsible sources
FSC® C101712

2 4 6 8 10 9 7 5 3 1

for my father

Contents

Table of Pipers at The Grey House

John Roderick MacKay Sutherland of 'Grey Longhouse'
('First John'); early scraps of tunes survive
b.1736 – d.1793

Roderick John Sutherland (a tacksman);
extended the holdings of the House; also known as Roderick Mor
b.1776 – d.1823

John 'Elder' Roderick Callum Sutherland
(possibly knew Iain MacCrimmon, the last of that great family of hereditary
pipers, who died in 1822); bought the 'corridor' from Sutherland Estates
b.1800 – d.1871

John Callum MacKay Sutherland ('Old John');
first formal lessons conducted in a Study or Music Room at The Grey House
that had been extended and renovated; also known as John Mor
b.1835 – d.1911

(Roderick) John Callum Sutherland ('Himself'),
always known as Callum; the great twentieth-century 'Modernist' piper;
established the famous Winter Classes at The Grey House and oversaw
further renovations there
b.1887 – d.1968

John Callum MacKay Sutherland of this book;
secretly built what he called the Little Hut for composition work and writing
b.1923 – d.within these pages

Callum Innes MacKay Sutherland, his son

'See how the names themselves seem to sound as notes that are repeated and echo throughout the tune, one placed upon the other as
though transparently, as though one man may be them all.'
from 'The Big Music', Crunluath movement

'The Big Music' – a definition of piobaireachd

Piobaireachd (pron. *pe-brohh*) or Ceol Mor, as it is also known, translates
into English as 'The Big Music' and is the classical compositional form
of the Highland bagpipe. It is music that is written to be played outside
or in a wide space that may best set off its sound and range and scale, addressing large themes of loss and longing, of recognition and salute and
farewell . . . And so is music that cannot make itself be small. Like many
formal classical compositions it is lengthy and involved, constructed according to an opening theme – the Urlar, or Ground – and subsequent
variations that build upon it, including the Taorluath, the Crunluath, or
Crown, and the Crunluath A Mach that will describe the tune's conclusion. These later movements extend the Urlar's opening ideas while dem-
onstrating both the dexterity of the piper and the composer's ambitions.
The piobaireachd ends, however, not with difficulty and reach but in a
return to the Urlar's opening simplicity. Then the piper will play those
same notes with which the composition began, walking away over the hill
as the sound of the music fades from the air and stillness takes up its
watch again upon the empty page.

Foreword

The story that follows — a narrative made up of journal entries, papers and inserted sections of domestic history that together become 'The Big Music' — first came to my attention several years ago when I was working on a piece of short fiction that was set in the Highlands of Scotland. While I was imagining scenarios and characters for that project, thinking of this person, then another, deciding where it was they might live, planning the background of their lives, there was presented to me a file of papers — well, several files, in truth, bound together as separate chapters or sections with paperclips or stapled in sheaves, and some that were in narrative order, others not — that seemed to hold within it all the world I had been previously imagining, delivering it to me as something already in existence.

The more I read into these pages, the more deeply involved I became in their provenance and meaning. Were the sections part of one journal? They appeared to be, a large portion of them, as the reader will come to see, with all of a journal's quality of the personal, of something direct and urgent that needs to be told. Yet other sections of the file were more like transcripts, or notes for stories, or finished stories, some of them. There seemed no way at first of plying the layers of the pages together to bring some kind of structure to the whole.

Then, as I came to move the papers around, arranging them in different sequences and patterns, I saw that in fact the idea of the piobaireachd as a determining form was governing the overall content. Here, in this way, did I find 'The Big Music' – for that is what piobaireachd means, as described in the definition on p. xi. And by finding a title, embedded as it were within the *millefeuille* of these pages that were in my possession, well then, so I was able to find a shape for something that could be . . . What? Not so much a story as a place, a world. Something that could be held between the covers of a book that might read in parts like a narrative, in others like a history or even a dream.

That shape is the shape of the piobaireachd itself: a concerto, a piece of music made up of separate movements that take an idea and build on it, as the movements themselves build to a conclusion – that, according to the terms of the composition, returns at the end to the original idea, to the moment of utter simplicity that was the outlining of the first few notes.

My arrangement of what follows, therefore, is nothing more than a suggestion along these lines – of a shape – although there are pages here of writing that show that the same shape was also intended. The notation and references that appear on the text are my own, and indicate areas of further reading that may be of interest to those who want to explore more fully the world of this book, its history and music and sense of place. It is, however, by no means necessary to go to the Appendices and material that is available while reading. Rather, consider these additional pages as a landscape that is at your back or a view through a window or beyond an open door – a place to be explored only if you want to go there.

In addition, I have included in that separate section a list of papers that were part of the original cardboard file – manuscripts, documents relating to the history of The Grey House, notes and entries from various diaries that may have been used by John Callum Sutherland and his forebears – including a fragment of the unfinished composition 'Lament for Himself'.

In all my endeavours, I have been supported helpfully and enthusiastically by colleagues and friends – at the University of Dundee and elsewhere. Professor Christopher Whatley provided an historical reading list and certain books; with Dr Gail Low I came up with the plan of creating an archive for the papers that were assembled in connection with this project. In addition, my colleagues in literary and creative studies, Dr Jim Stewart and Dr Jane Goldman – Woolf scholars and writers both – have provided endless inspiration and ideas as we discuss Modernism and its glorious implications upon the construction of written texts. It was Jane Goldman, now of the University of Glasgow, who reminded me of T. S. Eliot's introduction to Djuna Barnes's *Nightwood*, in which he informs the reader of the importance of meeting the challenges of another kind of fiction that is nothing like a conventional story, to understand that the novel need not be just a simple form of communication from and about the real world but, like a poem, can be intricately and fully 'written'.

Finally, there can be no doubt that none of the pages gathered together here would have been so gathered, into this particular 'novel', were it not for the support – both financial and intellectual – of Dr Gavin Wallace, Director of Literature at the Scottish Arts Council, now Creative Scotland. The work of Dr Wallace and his team in supporting literature – and this project – has been of utmost significance to me, and I doubt this book would have become realised as a finished piece at all were it not for the generous support of a Scottish Arts Council Bursary seven years ago when the papers around me were first being sifted together and formed into certain piles and formations, and ideas for 'The Big Music' were swirling around in my head.

I hope that what follows might gather the reader up in the way it did me – these curious sentences and half-stories sounding through the paragraphs in ways that reminded me from the outset of the beautiful music my father has always played. His musicianship, his sense of Ceol Mor, 'The Big Music' that sounds from his pipes, in its fine and ancient form that is reflexive and supple and strange, is the inspiration for me tackling this project here in the first place.

The errors I make, either in translating the sense of the mystery of that music in words or in the descriptions of it that I give, are mine alone and are no way to repay the hours of advice I have had from him and from piobaireachd specialists and musicians, both in person and in the reading they have supplied. Consider these shortcomings simply a result of my poor and most rudimentary understanding of this complicated musical form played on an instrument that is still broadly misunderstood.

If these pages go any way towards bringing to a more general audience the richness and depth of a great music that comes from what is surely one of the most lonely and inaccessible parts of the British Isles . . .

Well then, perhaps my poor attempts at drawing together a text from it will be forgiven.

Kirsty Gunn

FIRST MOVEMENT:
URLAR

one/first paper

The hills only come back the same: *I don't mind*, and all the flat moorland and the sky. *I don't mind* they say, and the water says it too, those black falls that are rimmed with peat, and the mountains in the distance to the west say it, and to the north . . . As though the whole empty wasted lovely space is calling back at him in the silence that is around him, to this man out here in the midst of it, in the midst of all these hills and all the air. That his presence means nothing, that he could walk for miles into these same hills, in bad weather or in fine, could fall down and not get up again, could go crying into the peat with music for his thoughts maybe, and ideas for a tune, but none of it according him a place here, amongst the grasses and the water and the sky . . . Still it would come back to him the same in the silence, in the fineness of the air . . . *I don't mind, I don't mind, I don't mind.*

Is what there is to begin with, a few words and the scrap of a tune put down for the back of the book in some attempt to catch the opening of the thing, how it might start. With this image of a man, born eighty-three years ago down out of these same hills, and how he might think now how the land doesn't mind him, never has. Here he is walking in up the strath towards that far bend in the river and the loudest note could sound in his head and him follow it with a sequence and still this country, his country, would keep its own stillness and only give back to him the louder quiet, like the name of the tune itself could be *I don't mind*, is what he'll call it, 'Lament for Himself'.*

~

It's early morning but the sun is already well settled in the sky and there is no cloud near to cover it. Only a thin wind comes off the hill and makes it cooler than it was a second ago, but then it stops and it's warm again. The man shifts the baby he's carrying in his arms. In the wrappings and the cloth she's quite difficult to hold. Still, he moves her again, lifting her higher into the crook of his elbow, and she doesn't cry or twist, the 'E' note coming clear all around her, high and pure and steady, even now with her eyes closed. She'll be all 'E' into 'G' notes just, the little theme he wants for her, a lullaby. So who cares if the cloths about her are flapping in the air? That carrying her's not like the taking up of a parcel as he thought it would be? He needs her for the tune, even so. For listen: the sequence going now, from the 'E' to 'G' to 'E' to 'A' and repeat, you hear it? Johnnie does. The tune that's new life coming out of old and the drone going heavy below . . .

Of course he needs to keep the child with him for the tune. And get that bit down he just heard onto a paper and quickly before it's lost – but no time for it now. For they'll be up by now, back at the House, going into his bedroom and realising he's gone, seeing in the child's mother's room the empty basket. So he'll need to keep walking, and faster if he can, with his good stride. Cutting down off the bank and onto the flat, heading westwards, no change of pace for a man practised all his life to show rigour in his walking, never idle on the grass. Take the stride on the flat just the same as on the steep hill, boy. Don't think about stopping. The

---

* 'Lament for Himself' appears in various versions throughout the Appendices attached to this book but in the first instance is represented here as opening 'remarks', that is, the outline of a sequence of notes that introduce the main theme of isolation. This is created by a set of open intervals 'B' to 'E', 'A' to 'A', 'B' to 'E', 'A' to 'A' etc. that appear to sit against the emptiness of the background of the drone, the baseline 'A' note. Appendix 10/i contains more details of this sequence, and manuscript.

pattern of the walk lays down your ground.* Just as the sage-coloured grass at his feet can't be anything than that colour this time of year, late summer by now you might say because of how warm it's been sometimes and the air so clear but in the month's heart is resting autumn, and just as that grass underfoot has that small bite to it still says a good summer's passed and the deer will be down right enough later in the month just for to tear at the sweetness and substance of the grass . . . So the tune will stay and you can't change it, the ground laid out for the deer to come down.

He glances around to get his bearings though he barely needs to. There's the river at his left, his ben** side, and he'll be crossing it in a second to strike over the flat towards the base of Luath, take the small path up the side of the east face where it forms protection. The climbing of that part will be the steepest and most hard, then he'll cut up the green face and over the top and down, and he'll be running then, he thinks, oh, Johnnie. For won't he then be free?

He looks down into his arm. She's awake, the child is, giving him that fixed look but not judging, deep and thoughtful as though she's from another world, as well she has been for she's been with her mother . . .

'Hush.' He whispers quietly like he's seen her do, the baby's mother, pokes in one of the little cloths to keep her from the breeze. 'You know fine' he answers her 'what I'm doing with you here.'

For it's a tune for her, is what it is. The smallest, gentlest song against the ground, against the broad and mindless hills. He can hear it in his own 'Hush' and in her soft way with him as she lies in his arms, just looking up at him, just looking. The whole little song of her coming in, the few notes, like a breath of breeze across the land and him settling her in close to his side again as though that will quiet her but she's not crying.

'And this is the only way' says John Sutherland then, clear into the

---

* The Gaelic word 'urlar', the first movement of a piobaireachd, translates as 'ground' and lays down all the musical ideas of what will follow. Appendix II has more details of piobaireachd structure and form.

** Common usage — 'ben', meaning at the back, or to the side, in this sense, it's the favoured side of the hill. The Glossary has a list of Gaelic words and expressions used in this book.

air. 'You understand me?' He stops and turns, as though to a friend. As though he has a friend there with him and is talking with him as though talking in a room, or across a table talking.

'The only way' he says again to the friend, to the empty air. 'You do understand me. How I needed to have her with me this way for the tune.' So 'Hush again, my darling' he sings, speaks the words, shifting her into his other arm and looking about him for the right place to cross the water. Where he won't slip. Where he couldn't possibly fall.

~

To get something down now about the shape of the strath, this part of Sutherland, this river the 'Dubh Burn' it's called, 'Black Water'. Yet there's nothing particular in that name either for there are many rivers in the Highlands called 'black water' that seem to run that colour, the peaty dark that's common this part of the world.

This 'black water', though, is set in the north-east corner of Sutherland so could be, one may imagine, somewhat darker than the rest for the way it starts so deep inland, so far, far away. It starts up there east of the Brora, from a little fall that feeds into that famous river, and the Naver too, and makes its way south-eastwards, widening out several miles north of Rogart and carrying on in the same direction all the way to the sea. So it's always been a river for the fishing. Less known than the Brora and Naver but near as good for the quality of the catch – and yet, for all that, the land that it runs through has little marked on the map to denote it and for the best part of a hundred years the place where John Callum MacKay Sutherland of Sutherland wants to take himself, into the set of hills that are provided at the head of a long strath, below the peaks of the 'Cailleachs', 'Old Sisters', Ben Luath and Ben Mhorvaig . . . Well, it has always been as though empty here.*

Yet this part of the land was populated once, before the Clearings** this

---

* Various maps at the back of this book describe the area in which 'The Big Music' is set; general, particular and historical.

** Appendix 3 relates to the history of the Highland North East region and includes details of the notorious 'Clearances', when many were forcibly evicted from their homes

would have been, and well populated too for there's the ruins of a school-house a couple of miles back and around it, scattered like stones, the remains of little houses and crofts. And that's a generous thing to think. How the place was laid out once, to be a grouping of people with days to fill and order. There's that schoolhouse, set up on a hill above a kind of beach that the river has formed, broadening out with a little strand of gravelly pale sand, and children would have played upon that once, would have stepped out from it to swim, perhaps after their morning lessons they might have — one can imagine that — on one of those endless high summer days, doing that, gathering up their skirts and tunics and walking into the water.

So, yes, the strath would have had the sounds of cries upon the air, once, children and their parents, coming down by the river, calling each for the other, to come in, to go home, to come back . . . And there would have been animals here too, some sheep and a few cows grazing on the green that's rich along each side of the river, drained off every spring so it forms pasture in the warm months. There are also, one can see, on the low foothills and there are more beyond, on the high moor behind Luath, stone walls set in circles, those sheltering places made for animals but a shepherd will sleep there too, some nights, and further back, scattered down the strath beyond, are the houses and dwellings of the people who lived here. Can you think on that? Imagine them? The families and the children and their animals? It's as though, if you were out here now in this place, you might see them. Like you might be able to smell the ghosts of their peat fires against the air, hear their voices, catch in the wisp of the wind a frail ribbon of their songs.

Fair to say, then, no lie or exaggeration of the truth, that this has been hospitable enough land in the past, to grow things and to live. That this part of the strath that stretches towards the west . . . That it's been fair. That the water has been good with fish, the salmon that have been coming through to spawn for thousands of years and fat and glistening with milk and eggs. And that up on the hills there have always been enough deer, so

---

from the late eighteenth to mid-nineteenth centuries and relocated elsewhere or abroad.

there's meat too, in addition to the animals grazing, and wool, that there's the fact of green here and it has been fair enough, that the fact of all these elements taken together seems enough, more than enough when you look at conditions elsewhere, this part of Scotland, the far North East, they seem generous to my mind, like this really is a land of — as it's been called in the past, by those who remember from their grandfather's and grandmother's stories — 'Milk and Honey'.

There are bumblebees droning in the heather, on a warm day. On a warm day, dozing yourself on the hill, you could hear them. There were hives here once. In the same way as there were walls. There were wheels to spin, looms. There was a place to make butter and cheese. There'll be papers later in the book to describe the life that went on here, and there'll be papers set into the story that show how the Sutherland family first came to be here and what they did with the empty strip of the country that lay further inland along the river, that they made into grazing land, how they put into the low rising hills a track that could take a cart and some horses.* But for now it's enough to record the sense of thick earth that lies under your feet here, in this sheltered place along the black water, that though it's lonely now, and you can read only about the one man who's about to cross the water and head inland into what seems all emptiness, still, there's richness all about him, too, in this place, in its history embroidered with the business of people's lives and families and their homes, the small flowers they may have picked and tucked into their clothes, put in square jars on tables by the window where they might be seen in the light.

~

Before Johnnie now is the passing place of the river and he approaches it, where the stones are flat and good. Even with a child in his arms he can manage it here, able to manage her, get over on the stones and he's at the

---

* Details of the Sutherland family and the history of the place where they have always lived appear throughout 'The Big Music', particularly in the Taorluath and Crunluath movements, and in Appendices 4–9 that relate particularly to The Grey House.

edge of the water now and stepping out with the bundle of Helen's baby. There's his foot on the first flat rock, so smooth but not slippery and there's the next. He'll have her safely over, fine, no need to worry. He takes another step and there's another. It's true, he can do this, the rush of the water all around him, one foot to find another stone and there it is and the next. The sure base note of the drone keeps him steady.

Therefore he does manage it, to get over the water and to the other side, and up ahead of him, bearing down, is the green face of the first hill, the way the rise of it will take him and over. After that, well, there's a different way of going and no one would know to take that direction for it's a path that cuts off to the right and will bring him round the next hill, on and up through what he calls the 'sligheach'* way, to another hill by a path he himself named for it's the word for secret, for the darkness of the shadows and flintiness of the ground. They'll never find him then, that way he'll be going. And at the end of it the Little Hut that only he knows about, only John Callum knows, waiting for him, and for the child.

He'll have her there, to that place. She'll be safe enough, away from them all who'll be following them, and from the weather. He walks smoothly, this part where the incline is gradual, up over soft heather and no wet underfoot after the dryness of the summer, thinks how this is easy walking and barely noticing at first how the steepness of the hill will get under your legs, try and keep you back. Thinks how he can go on and on.

So he proceeds, and the morning still lovely all about him, the fine sound of the skylarks coming through the air now and then like little strokes of colour, little High 'E' notes striking through the light.** It's fair. It's fair. And the hill coming under him now and strong, the peaty path underfoot and rocks stubbed into it here and there to make the steps where you need them. One there, just where he has to lift up his foot, and

---

* Some Gaelic words are in use that are also translated into Scots/English versions of the same that sound similar to but are different from the full Gaelic pronunciations – 'sligheach' is such a word, also pronounced by people like John Sutherland in the more anglicised form of 'sleekit'; see Glossary.
** 'E' is known as the 'echoing' note on the bagpipe scale. The Last Appendix gives a chart with a full translation of the notes' meanings and characteristics.

another, and another, holding the bundle of the child easy against him as he makes the sharp rise.

For she must be kept quiet, undisturbed in his arms. Though the weight of her, the sense of bearing her . . . Is getting more and more difficult with every step, with every mark of his shoe, with every breath. And for sure he'd had no thought of change or rest or stopping when he took her up, had no thought then that a swaddled thing of her size could become so heavy in the carrying . . . Yet now he's thinking, feeling, what it is to hold another human being in this way. And, no doubt he would stop now, if he could, put her down. Just to have a space from her, a bit of breathing without the carry. So how must they do it, then? The women mostly, who have to bear the weight of their children in this way? For there's a weight to them, and before they're born, when they're inside the women there must be the weight of them, the babies, that weight. And yet the women walk, and you see them running with their children inside them or carrying them. And he's never thought before how that must feel – but he's thinking it now. And thinking too that this one here, barely three months alive, a dot of a thing – and yet. That she could arrange herself to be so . . . sensible, somehow. In his arms. Full of the sense of herself is what he means, the comportment of her. So there's that, too, isn't there? In the carrying?

He's breathing hard now, and the sweat breaking out down his back, through his shoulders, his arms strong enough but – eighty-three years, that'll do it. And he's not a mother. There's a taste in the back of the mouth you get when the exertion's too fierce and he has the taste now, like blood, but he can't stop. He's at a part of the hill where they could see him, and they'll be on their way now, and if Iain's with them they'll have the dogs too, and Iain may have his gun. He stops for a second even so, has to, panting. Figures it: twenty minutes. To get to the top of the face and over where he'll be hidden and by then the rest of them will be round the corner and on the flat, following the river and their eyes casting across the hills, for movement, for the dot of white against the green that's the child.

Should have thought of that this morning, when he took her, of course, of the colour of her cloths, for white's the worst. If it could have been black or blue, the thing she's wrapped in, but he can't undo the white and have her cold, so starts again, up the path, higher and higher and keep the walking smooth, Johnnie, don't make yourself feel frightened, for it's the tune, remember, the only thing that matters here. The keeping of the baby in the tune.

Because she's the part, remember, that he needs. His new life out of old, the part of the music that's already in his mind come in fresh here and untried. It's all here, in the sound of her, the frank open gaze to that which is around her, the movement of the clouds and sky and light and air. That she could be so sure of who she is in the world and so open to it the way she is now, here in his arms with her eyes wide open in that lovely clear, unblinking way. She's got that from her mother, though, that quiet and the looking, from her mother and from Margaret before her . . .

And Margaret.

The way she just came in.

A certain note, high and clear, though he can't hear it now. Like Margaret is here looking out for her granddaughter now, out here on the hills, like she can see her, the white cloths in his arms. Her note will be sustaining, when it comes, holding, holding . . . And then slowly, but, after the held sound of the octave, descending. The big open notes coming off there at the base* and the high fineness of her like a memory . . .

He'll hear it, soon, won't he? That certain note? Have it in the tune along with the 'F' and all the little 'E' notes that are there beside?**

Because he can hear the 'F' note, fine, that's there, and the others but it's all Margaret now, sunk into the grass for a minute like he might have to lie down with the fullness of that sound yet to come, might have to lay the weight of the carry down before treading on and up and on, following the soft little part of the path the deer have made for him, cut into the heather and the peat like slices of cake left in your back pocket to sit on, just like.

---

* The base note is the 'A', also known as the Piper's note.
** The 'F' note, or note of Love, figures as a 'return' in both Margaret and Katherine Anna's themes in the Urlar and in 'The Big Music' generally.

For Margaret . . .

And the little path . . .

Just to have her here with him, if he could have her . . .

With this air, sky, all around him, this soft, soft flattened earth . . .

But no time for any of that. His heart jumps with the awareness of it. No rest now any more than he could have rest before. Because when was it? An hour? When he took the child? For sure it's not two. And listen:

'B' to 'E', 'A' to 'A', 'B' to 'E', 'A' to 'A', 'B' to 'D', 'G' to 'G', 'B' to 'D', 'G' to 'G' . . .*

He has those notes already down, he has them – the 'B' to 'E', the 'A' and 'A' – but that's them coming now.

And the sound of his taking of her, the 'A' and the drop from the horror of what he's done –

to 'G'

From High 'G' to Low 'G'.

That's in the tune as well.

With snatching a child from its mother, stealing the baby where it lies sleeping in a basket while the mother is not there.

---

* This sequence of notes is the opening line of the fragment of music known as 'Lament for Himself' and is reproduced in manuscript at the back of the book. These first bars indicate the main theme of John MacKay Sutherland; the later 'drop' from High to Low 'G' occurs in the second line, as part of the so-called 'Lullaby' sequence – see later in this Urlar for further details.

insert/John Callum

This part of Sutherland is lonely enough then, people get lonely coming here, they're lonely if they stay. You're far enough away from the little towns of Golspie and Brora and Helmsdale to feel gathered up by the interior of the place, that great space of land at the centre of the Far North, and though there are villages scattered and post offices and there's the pub at Rogart and the Spar, still it's not like there's a sense of a street or other houses close by to hold on to. At the end of the night you go back to your lonely home. You turn the light on in the dark.

John Callum lives in one of these places, in the midst of the emptiness – though luckier than most for he's people to look after him at The Grey House, the Ailte vhor Alech, it is also called, 'the End of the Road'.* He sits in his chair, or lies in his bed, and there are those who would hear him if he might call out, or if a dream took him in the night or a terror or unaccountable rage or despair. There are those who could come for him, Margaret would come for him, and soothe him or feed him, there are those whose voices he would hear, even as he kept

---

* The House is known as The Grey House throughout 'The Big Music' but occasionally it is referred to by the Gaelic that translates as 'the End of the Road', owing to its position and history as a stopping place for shepherds and black-cattle herdsmen en route to the West and South. A full history of The Grey House, itself a name deriving from its original architecture as a grey 'longhouse', is available in Appendices 4–9; see also various maps and plans.

to his room he'd hear them. Enough to know, you might say, that they are there.

But he does not cry out, and he takes little part in the life of those who live with him. In the work they do they remain separate from him and he barely knows anything now of the running of the House or its land, of the sheep and woodland to be managed, or of the guests who may still arrive in the autumn and the spring for the shooting or the fish. And in a way, did he ever know? From the old days when his father ran the School here, the Winter Classes, and pipers came from all around the country to be here? Did he know then how his home was lived in and loved and described? Though he's stayed so much of his life in this place, was born and brought up as a boy playing in the strath and hills that surround the grey stones of the House, in the kitchen garden and paddock nearby where he kept his lambs and his pony, sitting on the low wall that protected his mother's flowers all those years and looking up at the sky . . . Because he left it all, did he not? Left his father and his music, called out 'I'll not be back!' into the air as he went away down the road? So no wonder then it seems that the life here does not belong to him entirely. As though, even with the House and its land at his back or in the field of his eye all the time he was away, there was nothing here for him, nothing, though all of it was home.

Is why he lives now as though not fixed to the place. Eighty-three years, maybe, but he's still like the boy with his legs dangling over the wall, banging the backs of the heels of his shoes against the stone and thinking anything could happen, anything. Could as well be he's a traveller passing through, one of his own paying guests staying the odd night in the House that he himself inherited, while the others, the family who work for him here, Margaret and her daughter, and Iain, Margaret's husband . . . They're the ones belonging.

So who comes near John Callum, then? Who lives near? There's no one lives near. The estate road turns off another that's as little known, isn't drawn on many of the maps you might buy; the nearest farm marked well beyond the House, and the one beyond further still. If you wanted a neighbour to visit, to have a drink with maybe, to come to you for an exchange of the news, you'd have to be thinking an hour for that, easy, more like two, for the time it would take to drive down to where the road joins the back way that eventually leads into the road to Brora. You'd come to the first farm then, the Sinclairs, then the Gunns – but it's a fair distance and that was not a thing the Sutherlands ever did much: go visiting. It's where Johnnie got it from, you might say, the canniness to go seeking out another's company, from his blood. Because his parents, they stayed close in the house just as he does now and never went looking for company. Even when their son grew up and went off on his own path they made no effort to turn outwards to other people but only saw those who came to them. They still had their School to run, was their thinking. John's father his pupils, his pipers, to see. What need they then for any more companionship and interest in others' lives? When everything they wanted was already arrived, was here, invited?

So, in the same way he kept, their son did, to the same habits of home. Though as a young man living in Edinburgh, and in London, too, he had friends and later might ask them up to the House, for parties and to stay – still, he was alone in the midst of the parties, as his father had been, and his father before him. It was as if, all through the years, the habits of the place had kept him. As if the patterning of the place, its silences and empty spaces, its quiet House, were so deep in that it didn't matter where else he was, he could have been in Paris or New York, or married or not, with a woman, or with a son of his own, or in a bar, with men . . . Still those habits were fixed. To keep apart. Keep in. Eighty-three years but on these hills, for a Sutherland from Sutherland, it's a spit. It's a blink of sun on the grey grass. As though you've lived your whole life alone.

one/second paper

'B' to 'E' though, in the meantime. 'B' to 'E', A to 'A', all that's counting now. Coming up the green face of the hill and Johnnie takes a breath and feels the life in it, the music, as though this is the first thing he's done in a long time that's real and that he's a man and not just some shadow creeping about the place, doing as he's told.

And 'B' to 'E' the notes all right, and leading to the 'A', and they're getting stronger and stronger, and down on the paper, for the notes are down, he knows, they're already written,* but only now is the felt weight of the ground in them, the same ground that's spread out now below him at his feet —

'B' to 'E', 'A' to 'A', 'B' to 'E', 'A' to 'A'

'B' to 'D', 'G' to 'G', 'B' to 'D', 'G' to 'G'

'B' to 'E'

---

* The manuscript at the back of the book that shows the fragment that survives of 'Lament for Himself' is all the composer knew of his piobaireachd and so he would have been largely unaware of its full meaning and patternings. However, the fact that the Urlar had nevertheless been written by John Sutherland in full, some weeks and months prior to when the events of this and subsequent movements of 'The Big Music' take place, gives the reader, and, at times, the composer himself, intimations of the ideas that would have been developed fully were the tune to be completed. Here is the musician hearing his own music as though for the first time, with understanding, as though composing it now. This will continue to happen to him as the book progresses and the Lament comes to reveal itself in full.

— so that from where he stands, up here on the tops, all he can see is the wide cast of his own music unfurling across the bare grass and heather. From the broad flats behind there towards the house up to the north side where the river makes its way heading back to the sea. All his long life coming back to rest here amongst the hills.

He puts his head up. Breathes again deeply into the air. And sure there's a sound distant could be one of Callum's dogs that he can hear way back down behind him but he won't let that stop him now, he won't. Won't let stop any of the notes coming, not the 'B' to the 'E' and the spread of the theme that he's already gathered up and put down on the page that's waiting for him up there at the Little Hut in the hills, or the new theme that's also come into the tune, more and more, the separate phrases of it are there and gentle, like a song, his lullaby for the child.

For 'E' to 'G', 'E' to 'A', 'E' to 'G', 'E' to 'E' . . .

Is what it is, a lullaby.

He looks down at her. She is sleeping. Though the blanket's not enough to keep her warm and part of him registers that, deep in, that she's not adequately covered. And that there'll be other things she'll be needing, too, the things a mother would know about, would have answered for — still. No time for that kind of thinking now. He has to keep walking. Keep going. Not to let those other thoughts enter in. Like Helen, come flying out of the house with no shoes on and screaming into the hills for him to bring her baby home. Or the sound of dogs and the thought of Iain coming after him with the dogs and his gun for to stop him. Because there's nothing would stop him now. He just tightens his hold. He's the one needs her for the tune — not them. They can come after him all they want to and scream and cry for him to bring her back but he'll have none of it. None of it. And —

Anyhow!

'Ha!'

He's not frightened of them! Back there at the House. He's not! So he can see them at the table this morning, can imagine the looks on their faces as Helen's there at the door with her empty arms. So he can hear the clatter of the china as Iain rises from his seat, Margaret's cry. Still! He'll manage them all away, he will. It's in his plan. And they'll never find him, never! In the place where he's going. He whispers to the baby now: They'll not find Johnnie.

~

When he left the House this morning no one saw him go. He was a secret then to them all. Getting up as usual, washed, he made his bed – though Margaret always tells him to leave it, he'd not have her at that kind of work, of the intimacy of a bed – so he tidied it himself while the rest of them were sleeping. The sheets and covers and the room entire ... That was this morning. Peeping into the dining room and there were the break-fast things laid out on the table, the sun coming in and striking at the comer of the table's wood. Remember it? The feeling of it so quiet and peaceful with the others in their beds and he was up, he was dressed and moving about the place, planning, thinking. For the tune has been with him for a while – on his mind, the great shape of it – and the first part put down, already written,* but needing something else in it, to make it whole, and he didn't know what it was – but then, there she was, the child.

So the morning like every other morning, you might say – and he's managed to leave the House before, earlier, this summer he managed it, to get up to the place in the hills then and they thought he was just down to the river, or up for a walk in the strath – but only this time they don't know, Margaret and Iain and Helen, too, that this particular morning has all been thought about and planned for. That it's to be much more than that, him just taking himself off like he's done before. But this time it's been arranged. Flushing the tablets down the toilet like he's been doing lately and none of them can notice. Practising with the stairs, going up and down. Waking earlier and earlier in the morning so as to be used

---

* The Crunluath section – especially three/second paper – of 'The Big Music' shows John Callum at work on his composition earlier in the year, when, despite a series of earlier strokes and spate of ill health, he was still fit enough to be able to walk up to the Little Hut in the hills where he did all his writing and composing. After his death, the manuscript for 'Lament for Himself' was discovered on his desk there, beneath the window.

to it, the feeling of being alert enough then and nobody about him. All happening without them seeing a bit of what he's doing, that he's getting stronger, clearer – but quieter too. So that he can be up like he was and taking some cereal in the kitchen and some juice and early this was, this morning, looking in on the dining room and seeing the breakfast things laid out just so and the sun coming in, but none of those things will be for him.

Was all in the plan. The clever thought of it. That no one would feel the difference when they woke, that he wasn't there, would not have heard him move about, wouldn't know that he'd been up and off before Iain was out for the generator even and then going to see to the dogs. Up the stairs he was while they're all still sleeping, and there in the basket, she was sleeping too. He'd just gathered her up, had the blanket waiting. Then down the stairs again and away.

That was this morning.

And there would have been a time then, at the beginning of the day, when he was long gone, that all would have been quiet at the house. At six o'clock. At seven o'clock. He can hear it. Like a little sequence of time at the beginning of the tune. The minutes passing, the seconds. With the sun at the edges in the rooms, and on the dining table the butter laid out and the white bowls and the marmalade and the jam. Listen. There's the clock ticking in its place over the mantelpiece, and there Margaret comes in with the toast and the porridge and Iain takes a seat like they all sit there together in the mornings before Johnnie is up and sometimes Helen has the baby with her, while she herself eats a piece of toast or takes an apple and cores it – but . . .

*You took her away.**

---

* Here arrives in the text for the first time the sound of a voice we shall hear more of as 'The Big Music' continues, that enters into the narrative and remarks upon it here, in this line of what will become known as the Lullaby, 'A Mother's Song'. The music for this Lullaby appears in the second line of the Urlar of 'Lament for Himself' and its words and further details can be found in this and in the Crunluath movements of 'The Big Music', as well as in the List of Additional Materials at the back of the book, in particular see scanned material.

Something there not quite the neat little sequence of notes that sounded so pretty before.

You carried her off, young Katherine Anna.

For there are the breakfast things still laid out on the table and the sun
coming in, struck at the corner of the table's wood the bright sun, but the
things all scattered and no plates or cups or silver knives at peace because
of the way one man, himself, has gone and killed the morning, gone, and
made the baby's mother cry.

~

A cool wind comes in and ruffles at his clothing now. A thin jacket. Little
town shoes. John looks up. What is it? The light going bad? No. A cloud
passed over the sun's all it is, and there are no more clouds beside. The day
fair enough, it's fair . . .

But a change nevertheless. And it was there in the midst of his walking
before, he may as well confess it: contained within the very interval of
High 'G' to Low 'G' – that drop – another theme inserted in the crazy
reach of notes, in that awful space between them.

He pulls his jacket to, wraps closer about her the child's white cloth.

You took her away.

There it is, all right. The change.*

You carried her off, young Katherine Anna.

Coming in at those words.

Making it colder. Thinner.

You took her away . . .

The words of a lullaby but not a lullaby at all.**

---

* Here, another example of what was described earlier – notes written by John
Sutherland in manuscript before their meaning was grasped and understood – in this
instance the octave interval and the drop of notes described in the second bar of the
second line of the music representing the act of abduction that was to occur many weeks
after composition.

** These words of the composition 'Lullaby' that appears in sections throughout
this paper are shown in full on p. 466. John Sutherland's paper 'Innovations to the
Piobaireachd', contained in the List of Additional Materials at the back of the book
may also be of interest.

For they're nothing like a lullaby, those words. And Johnnie can hear that. He can hear. Those words for the morning and the words for what he did. How he took the stairs two at a time while the rest of them thought he was still sleeping. How he reached into the basket and gathered her up like she was fruit, the sleeping child.

'But for the tune I did it!' he says, hearing his own voice sounding out in the air. 'Only for the tune!'

But it makes no difference. Speaking out loud. Sounding so certain in the open air.

For though his own words are loud they're not louder in his mind than the other words, or the music for those words for what he's done. And though it may be a pretty tune in the way the notes came in there alongside the theme, gentling it, and softening the fall of the 'G' to 'G' . . . That doesn't change it. The meaning of it. Of the words. And he's stopping now, no longer walking, no longer able. For the loudness of them, those words, the sound of them all through his mind and getting louder and louder . . .

The sound of the morning and the words for what he did.

You took her away.

Filling everything up, the air around him where his own speaking was, the spaces in his head.

Getting louder and louder . . .

Those other words.

Though he can't be minding them. Still there they are . . .

(first verse)
In the small room, a basket waits,
A basket empty for no baby is there.
The mother is gone, left the room for a moment
– and in that moment he's mounted the stair.
(chorus)
You took her away,
young Katherine Anna,
carried her off, tall Helen's child.
You took her away, a baby sleeping
In your old arms, took her into the wild.

Completing.

So he's stopping. Listening. When he should be moving on.

To a lullaby that's no lullaby at all.

You took her away, a baby sleeping.

In your old arms, took her into the wild.

John breathes, holds. He can't be dealing with this now. What the song is. What it isn't. He needs all his energy for the last of the hill. And he can't be waiting now on the side of the path or go back on his plan and his intention just because of words. For it's over to the right he needs to go, to get to the little path that's the secret, the way in to a bit of the hill unmarked by the rest of the path or the ways that you might walk, unknown.

So –

'Think about that, instead' he says. 'Says Johnnie!' Out into the air again. Like shouting, say it.

'The little path!'

'His clever plan!'

And . . .

'Think about that, my Johnnie.'

He takes another breath.

'Yes!'

Because he can. Think about those words. For they're better words. The little path. The clever plan. They're stronger words. And –

'Ha!'

Think that again, too. That: 'Ha!'

'And be strong!'

~

For they don't have the smallest, faintest dreamed idea. Back there, with the sun in the rooms. With the breakfast all laid out. They don't know even yet what he's up to. Because he's away, he is! Long gone! By the time Margaret's up and in the kitchen, and Helen coming through to boil the kettle for a cup of tea and she's not even been into the baby's room yet. While he's already hours into the day! Out on the hills with the sun rising fair. Gone long before them with their baby and on his way to the secret place.

No one else knows.

For they don't know, do they? About it? The *sleeach*, sleekit way you turn off the path towards it? Where you come up this part of the hill and cut down to the right, turn in to a little valley that you can't see from the flat . . . No one knows? That you can't see from here on the hill even, but it's there in the dark lee, in the crevice.

And . . .

'That's where we're going. Where I'm taking you, my darling.'

To the little secret place he made for himself up there and long ago.*

So he starts up again, increasing his pace now, one foot there on the path, another on a stone that will lift him higher up the hill. Like a stair the shape of the path, cut chunks into the peat and bits of rock jutting out to form a step here, and there. Up and up and then to look for the dip in the heather that's like an indent by a big boulder, like the sort that marks the entrance for a path or a way – and that's where he'll turn off and go in.

And oh but he'll laugh at them again, then. Make that sound 'Ha!', like he wants to laugh now, out loud! At the craziness of it! This plan of his and the way to make a tune! To be taking the child into the secret like he is. Showing her to the Little Hut, putting her there, when no one else knows about it at all.

You took her away . . .

So yes, all right, yes. Those words are still there but fainter just because now he's feeling strong. Thinking about the boulder and the path. And maybe he set that boulder up, some time, he did, long since, as a kind of signpost, to indicate the way to go but no one knows about that either,

---

* Here is a substantial reference to the small bothy or shelter John Sutherland built for himself in the Mhorvaig hills soon after he returned to The Grey House following his father's death. Having what he always referred to in his private journals by the initials 'LH' gave him somewhere he could be entirely alone and could separate himself from that musical legacy he'd inherited from his father. There are further details about the significance of the building and the music and notes that were found there that will play out in the Crunluath A Mach movement, and there is also further information in the List of Additional Materials.

not even his own son and Callum is in London now and he'll never see Callum again.

So . . .

Katherine Anna, Helen's child.

'Don't worry.'

Because she needn't mind. He doesn't mind. In the end it's not important what they think. What they might say. For they don't know, the others. They don't understand. How she's to be in the tune, the little one. How she'll make sense of it, make the finish of this 'Lament' of his – the words of a lullaby can't describe it because she's more than those words, she's more in this than all of them, in this tune that has his ending. That his life has come to nothing, maybe, but that she may make sense of it in beginning with her here. A little man and she can be a spirit, a great lover and an artist and a woman, that he can be an old man out alone on the hills but holding in his arms a queen.

~

By this time the weather has fully turned. The clouds that were laid over thinly on the blue, taking out the sun's warmth, have thickened, darkened, the rain come in from the west.

And John has no coat on.

Johnnie has no coat.

Just the cotton jacket and the thin, silly shoes. The baby is covered in the white blanket and it is this, in the end, the others will see up against the grey when Iain strains to get a glimpse in his binoculars, casting across the tops, along the green face: There it is! This tiny fleck of white against the greyness of the hill, against the rain. Is what will bring him in. Iain sending the dogs up first, once he's got the Argo over the river and across the flat, and then coming himself at a run behind them, closing in on the old man, minutes and minutes getting nearer to him and the child.

But for now you wouldn't guess it. That the morning's to be saved this way. All you'd see is an old man with a baby he shouldn't be carrying out alone with her in the weather and the child moving in his arms, a good sign perhaps, for I worried before when she lay so still and quiet. But this is her awake now, and twisting enough in an old man's grasp for to make him think for a second he could drop her. Christ! For not like a parcel at all, remember, he thought that before – she's a baby, Christ! – and now she's shaking her head, starting fretting, and turning and harder and harder for him to hold and – No! Making that sound, like No! again. No! And wide awake and in a temper and twisting and moving and screwing up her face and now she's crying, pure crying out into the air and loud and he'd need a lullaby now, all right, a real lullaby,* to keep her still and steady.

But not the one he's been hearing for none of that is about comfort – and he has heard all the words of that tune and they're not his to sing. With the weather turning into heavy rain it seems as though the hills themselves could hear that the song, and the dark air too could hear it, down by the House and up by the rivers and the loch, like Johnnie's poor mind can hear it, down by the House and up by the rivers and the loch, like Johnnie's poor mind can hear . . . That the voice of the song is not his, it never was, though the notes may be formed for it from out of his own tune. Because it's a woman singing, the whole lullaby in place now within the theme and set in the first part of the music, in the ground, this small thing contained within it and never his part to sing the words at all.

When it's a mother's song. Not his song. Only listen:
An old man taken the baby away,
He's snatched her up in his arms for to see
Her life in his, to stay his dying
but the child's not his, her mother is me.

---

* Information about traditional Highland lullabies that really might sing a child to sleep is given in the Crunluath movement of this composition. It is unlikely that John Sutherland would have known any of these – hence the line here no doubt describes the voice we heard from earlier in this Urlar, not his. See following paragraphs also for further evidence of this.

narrative/1

The people at the House and what they thought of him

Iain

Thinks nothing. Sits cleaning his gun. Glass of Morangie set down on the floor by his right foot, eye on the barrel.

Why should I be thinking about him?

Of the three of them, he's the outsider here. Knows fine what went on between the old boy and Margaret all that time ago. And –

To hell with him.

Because he knows fine, too, that was in the past and he's the one married to her, not that other. So:

To hell again.

For look at him, when he last looked at him. John Callum MacKay. He's old.

He takes a sip of his whisky. And Iain's the young one. Feels like it. He's the one fit and strong. He breaks the gun and takes up a cloth that's full of oil. Rubs the gun down the long length, turns it in his lap, once, twice. So just make it that there's nothing to think about that other one. Nothing. He's only old. And all that business with Margaret, it's in the past and long before he came along, before Iain came.

And by now he's been here longer than that other, too, when that other only returned to the House after his father had passed. Iain the young one from the beginning, you could say, in place here already when that other returned, and always younger than him, always, and stronger.

So —

To hell.

And most women, anyway, when you meet them . . . Well, they're going to have something from before you knew them hidden in their skirts.

He drains the glass then, sets it down. Takes up the bottle and pours himself another. No point going back into that bit of time anyhow, the past, with women. You move on. You marry. And he's the one did that, took Margaret that way. She was a woman with a child and he was the one, Iain, who gave her a ring, a name —

All right?

A decency you could say, for people still care about those things, and she did, Margaret cared.

So all right again.

For she needed it, didn't she? Margaret did? For Helen back then? A marriage and a place for Helen in a family when Helen was just a child? For them to be together here, working at the House, to be a family of their own.

They all wanted that, the three of them.

And nothing to do with that other. Nothing.

So just think nothing, think —

To hell. To hell.

For just because people like old Johnnie always get what they want, have a certain way with them, with women, with people. Just because they have money and a bit of power, maybe, or so they think . . . Well.

He's not going to let that trouble him now, Iain's not. He's not going to let a single thing trouble him now.

So.

He takes another sip of whisky.

Good whisky, too.

And just . . .

Don't think.

For he's got his own run of the place here, and Margaret, and Helen
. . . They all do, they do things their own way. And Iain the one sorts it
all out, it's Iain they call for, with the animals and the land, he the one in
charge and not that other who thinks everyone's just here to do his bidding, swanning up from London like he used to, calling them from the
end of the road, like some king, from the old call box there: 'Bring the
Land Rover down for me, will you, Iain? I'm back!'

For who does he think he is?

Old man?

Nothing bit of a man?

It's Iain who has the power here. You can see it, he still has it. In the
strength of his arms, his legs. Like a young man is what he is.

And fit.

He takes another sip.

And strong.

~

Margaret

(transcript)*

I see a look, sometimes, in his eyes and yes, it is then like it used to be. As
though . . . Perhaps. Is what I see. That look, and only that, nothing more.
For it's been a long time now since we were together in that way, and him
married at the time but with Sarah all the way down in London.

Do you have feelings about him now?

I don't have any feelings about any of that now.

*But he was lonely. And you were lonely too. I'm like you were back then, that time in
your life, alone with a young child.*

---

* The Taorluath and Crunluath sections of 'The Big Music' show certain transcripts of
recordings of conversations between Margaret and her daughter Helen, and notes made
that describe their relationship and discussions. In addition, Appendix 8/i shows how
these transcripts were used in establishing a history of The Grey House that is now held
in archive and may be consulted at leisure.

I could tell you what the feelings were back then.

I could try and write it down.

(notes)

How I was then, and you will understand this, any woman who's had a child but without a man around her, who's been on her own, would understand. How a woman like that, after childbirth and alone, is aware of her aloneness, somehow more aware, I think, is my feeling, in a way that a woman within a marriage is not.

I could tell you, Helen.

About the gaping kind of open feeling from having had a baby but no man there in the bed afterwards. After you've let yourself wide open for the child . . .

But you already know. You're my daughter and with a child of your own. Of course you know. How, after birth, one is made to be all open. I can tell you about this because you know too what it is not to value marriage in the same way – once you've gone through a labour on your own. You just don't.

So it is if there's no man to be with you at the birth, or afterwards in the bed. You just learn early it's on your own you'll be managing, alone, and you do manage, you get on with it, you're the one taking care. Nothing else for me to do now than keep that habit. Looking after the House, the mealtimes, taking care of the bit of the garden we've got left, managing the place for the guests when the guests used to come.

I'm busy enough. And as for John, well, you could say I've always been the one to keep a look out for him, take care of him. And so I will continue.

Turning over his bed –

(though it's not the same bed)

– and his sheets, in his bedroom –

(though it's not the little room at the top of the House)

– taking care of that room –

(where we used to go . . .)

– cleaning out his bath. I lay the table in the dining room like we've

always done, using that room in the evenings even though it's only him
here and the visitors may love it when they come, sitting around the lovely
wood of that table, and the candles lit, and the patterned china laid out
that was his mother's. But for the most part it's just one man at the table.
Though Iain will go in there sometimes, I know, to sit in his same seat,
and he'll take a dram there. I've seen him.

(transcript)

It's always been this way.

Always?

For ease, yes, let me say. Certain ways, patterns of doing things. Like
his mother used to do before him, and the mother before her no doubt.
The time passing not noticed because the House stays the same, the way
we do things the same.

So, yes, because of that maybe, that feeling of no time at all passed
between then and now . . . I can still see that same look in his eyes. And . . .

Perhaps.

Is the look. Yes, I do know that. For it's been the same look all these
years, though I'm with Iain now for more than thirty.

A long time.

A long time.

So . . . ?

Yes, perhaps.

I understand the look. I understand that feeling, too.

~

Helen

Her part would be to say: 'I don't feel I have any more choices about being
here than the others.'

And she could say that. Claim inevitable. The being here. The being on
her own in this empty place. That her mother's right, she's like her mother.
That she understands that all of it's a thing of no choice in the end, and her
bringing a child into it, too. Could say she had no more will in that either
than her mother did all those years ago when she brought her own child in.

So, she could say: 'I don't feel I have any more choices about being here than the others.'

For it's like she's never been gone now she's back here at the House again. Though she's had all her travelling and her study, and all her friends and lovers and her life. In the end she's no different than Margaret and Iain, no more variation in her than they who've never lived more than sixty miles from where they all bed down now, eat, work, as rooted here, brought back to the place she belongs to, as a plant dug up waits to be put back in the same kind of soil. Just as the old man himself came back after years of being gone, came back for good.

So Helen and her mother found home here in the end. And . . .

Perhaps.

Perhaps, nothing. It's only yes. Is what her mother means. Of course her mother can't keep that from her daughter. Her daughter's seen the look.

The glow coming off the pair of them like a kind of heat when they're in a room together, not often in a room together, sure, but when it occurs – that he may be sitting there in his chair and she's banking the fire or she's brought him something on a tray – then the feeling holds and burns. Though neither of them will talk about it, or show it – of that feeling or that light, to others or each other or themselves – no, not for years. Not for long, long years . . .

Still.

A daughter can see.

A faithful daughter.

'And Margaret' she would say. 'Don't think that I don't realise how that might keep a mother. Might keep a daughter, too.'

~

Margaret

(notes)

I know he's not been swallowing the tablets. The doctor knows. When he visited last he told me. 'John wants to come to the end now, Margaret' is what old Ramsay said. And I can't force him. I can't make him take the medication if he doesn't wish it for himself.

And for me? I don't know what to wish for. Him alive the shadow of the man I used to share a bed with, lie down with, while somewhere else in the House, in my own room, my child and my husband were sleeping – am I not to remember those times? Or the way he and I were together at the beginning? The way being with him gave me my strength, the feeling, I mean, for being on my own, truly alone. So strong in my body after that time we were together that it meant I could take Iain as a husband when he came here. That kind of strength.

It only comes from a bed.

I wouldn't say any of this, of course, to the others. Only write it to you, Helen. When you come to read this sometime.

And I think you know in full anyway what it was John gave me. I think you know what it was I needed for you'll have something of those same needs yourself. That come with having a child and looking after the child. That we seek out ways of making ourselves strong. Keeping the things in our lives that are private deep in and holding secrets as a source of power – though here I am telling my secrets now, in writing them down.

(Though I wouldn't tell about the room at the top of the House, where we used to be together, I would never tell . . .)

And so for that, for private thoughts, for my memories of that time, would I let him slip off now into illness and into age?

Or try and get him back by standing with him, watching, to try and make him that way take the pills, watching while he swallows, watching with my eyes his eyes the way we used to watch each other, every movement held.

Of course I would try to keep him.

Even with me seeing the way he is now. And him not wanting to eat or sleep or take his proper medication, going off on his own for hours back there in the summer like he used to do in the past, taking himself off for days at a time and I never knew where he went, but now not doing anything much at all.

Even then I would wish him away? To have him be finished for himself here and all our past together gone then, with the present?

You don't answer questions until you need to, that's the problem. You keep holding out, waiting. You keep thinking, a few months it will be better. Or let the summer pass and then you say the winter, let another year go by . . .

And still we've not decided here what we'll do, when he's gone. And it won't be long now, with Sarah phoning up from London every ten minutes to see if he's taken another turn and how to get him away down there with her, to one of her hospitals, I suppose, where they'll lock him up, where she thinks he'll be safe.

I know I won't find another job. I don't want it. Too old now, anyway, to be working on an estate somewhere else and there'd be others to deal with there and not like here where it's just ourselves and we can be on our own. For with Iain the way he is and Helen with us now and her baby to look after — it's not as though we could at any other place be fitting in.

Besides, they'd know. In those other places. That we'd been working for John Sutherland and that not ever a piece of land managed like the others are managed. More a place for the piping always, it's been, than a proper farm or for the fishing or the deer. And they'd know, for sure, the other estates. That we wouldn't have worked here in the way that would be expected. And they would have heard about Iain, too. That there's nothing much for him on the hills, with the run of the few sheep that's left. That there's little here for him to do.

So it would all get out.

That we do things differently, not like the other properties in the area, the farms and the estates . . . And always have done so. And now that the Piping School is long over, and the students and the pipers gone. We're just on our own here. And we have been for a long time now, a long time.

Therefore . . .

(and such a lovely word to write, to say: *Therefore* . . .)

With everything I've laid down here on paper, of truth and love and intimacy, the wrap of the past around our lives . . . I don't claim it's as though any of us here would want John to finish it. Though the dark's closer for him now than it ever was. Still. We need him to be here, we all do, for our privacy and for things to stay the same, the place the way it is to continue, for all of us.

Therefore . . .

(John Callum . . . My John Callum . . . Always *therefore* . . .)

Though it may be that we're caring for a ghost here, is how it feels, and though it's like standing with your back to vacancy, so we do, we stand. And I confess I have feelings for the man even after all this time, for he took my body and he let me take his, at a time when bodies were all I was wanting. He understood that in a way I believe few men will understand it from a woman. And that I could have at the same time towards him both coolness of distance and great warmth? I would have the same coolness and the same warmth now.

~

Iain

Sits.

Does nothing.

The fire on though it's not cold.

But it burns. It burns.

For Margaret's told him all he needs to know. About herself and that other. She's told him long since so no reason to have it between them — but how it does rise up between them. What happened in the past not gone away, not over the years it hasn't, and sometimes Iain senses it in the House, a thing still existing between his wife and another man and it sickens him, like a poison you give animals going through his own veins, to think of the old man and his wife having been together in that way.

So don't think.

Is why he won't.

Think anything, not now.

Takes up the bottle, and sets it down. Won't. Not ever. And that's what he's done, too. Kept it all from his mind.

Though from the first time he met him here at the House, when Margaret came out of the House to greet him, it was like he could smell it, that something had taken place, was maybe still being enacted between the two of them. So he remembers when that other first returned, for the funeral of old Callum. And the way he was with Margaret then, greeting her. Remember? Well, there's always that. That they'd known each other before, he could see that, though neither showed it. But remember too, he always will, Iain, he'll remember . . . How Margaret greeted him also, greeted Iain, the first day when he came here for the job. That day when he came here to meet old Roderick Callum and his wife – and this long, long before that other's return. And he was a young man then, by God, Iain was, he was no more than twenty – and how Margaret was with him then, that day, with him, Iain . . . Remember that? Of course he'll always remember. For that's the important thing. How she looked at him, that day as she came out of the house to meet him, smoothing back her dark hair with a hand that she then put out to him. To him! To greet him! He was lonely all right. And it was as though she could recognise that in him, she could see it right away. Couldn't she? That he was lonelier than that other would ever be, that one who would want for nothing but who would always get more and more and more.

For in the touch of her hand . . .

Though he came to know later, would sense in that other, the way he was with Margaret, that there was something still going on between them . . . Even so he remembers, too, Iain does, that first touch of Margaret's hand taking his hand that day. When she'd been lovely to him, to Iain, right there from the beginning. How he'd noticed everything that day. How she had a speck of a kid with her, standing at her side – and he'd taken that in, Iain had, how the child was Margaret's child and there was not about her any father – Iain had noticed that, too, from the outset. Had come to understanding right away: that it would be Iain himself who would take on that role with her, with Margaret, to help her with the child. It would be how he would get her. How he'd be able to claim her, keep her for himself, and they'd be secure together then.

Man and wife.

All through the little girl. Through Margaret being a woman on her own without a husband and with a child to bring up – and he could be

the one who would help them. The father. The husband. He would be the
one who took care when that other had never been around, the one, Iain
could be, who takes care now and always.

For he is the lonely one. Iain is. No one else needed to be with someone like he needed. And Margaret was there from the beginning, coming
out of the House to greet him . . .

The touch of her lovely hand . . .

Just her.

Just Margaret.

And so she was a woman who'd been with other men? So she had a
child by one of them, and something there between her and old Callum's
son that had started long before he came along, before Iain came along,
and that he could sense when that other was around and could feel? Still
she had turned towards him that day, Margaret had, towards him, put out
her hand – she'd touched his hand.

He looks down at his same hand now, as though the mark of her press
might be there still upon his palm.

See?

And –

Look at me, Margaret. Look at me.

Is how he willed her to see him that day. As he takes another sip,
remembering.

Look at me.

For hadn't he so needed for her to see him? From the moment of their
greeting? So needed to make her understand along with him – that he
could offer her . . . Something. That might count just as much as love, as
feeling towards him. That by way of income and support for the business
of bringing a child up into the world . . . So he could help. Though the
child would never be his child, still . . .

They could be a family, the three of them together.

Because that was the kind of man he was. Iain was. Who would be
straightforward that way, not trying to be the big man if you had no
intention. The opposite of that other, then, the type who'd be standing
too close to Margaret whenever he came back here – but not here ever to

help in any kind of way that was real. And he's always done that, too, that other. He's always stood too close.

No wonder he's always hated him, then. Old Johnnie. Will always hate him. For how could you not hate the man who loved your woman? Though you tried not to let it matter? Tried to keep it all down? For that other was the one got to her first and he still has to live with that, Iain does – the memory coming in every day as they're here at this House together now the old boy's back to stay. Iain having to bear it that he came second in line, second. Even now having to watch his wife with him, to give him his medicine, attend to the making of his bed . . .

No wonder he hates the one seems to take it all.

Is what he thinks.

If he thinks.

And he won't think.

For who gives a hare's jump now about old Johnnie? Those people that he used to know – where are they now? They're not here. Not even his own wife, his own son. And Iain has that, he has a family around him. And it's Iain, himself . . . Who did that. Made them into a family here. So Margaret could be his wife. And Helen like his daughter, she could be his daughter. Because he was a man who always wanted children, and no children followed, so Helen is like his only child and it's how he thinks of her: 'My Daughter,' he says to himself sometimes, when he used to set the money aside for her schooling and her university in Glasgow, he thought it then. 'My Daughter, Helen,' he would say. Though the money went into Margaret's purse so she could be the one would give it, that Helen would think she was taking it from her mother, not him, for he had little part in her life other than that, he was not her father . . . But still he could say: My Daughter, to himself. Think he might be something to her in that way, of helping her with money for her schooling, that he could be a father to her then and she his daughter, and him helping her that she could get herself off to university and into the world . . .

And now she's come home again, the money spent.

With a child of her own. Her own daughter.

And still, even now, he could take care, Iain could. The three of them together like they used to be together, inhabiting the House as though it is their own, with Iain at the table and passing out the plates. In the kitchen, seeing Margaret with a baby in her arms.

My family.

But that other one has been back amongst them now, and for a while he's been and not leaving, so it seems, for he's too ill to go. And that makes it – not the same. As it should be. Not the same as when he used to come for the summers but then he'd go away. Come back here maybe, and staying longer and longer – but then he'd go. And now he's not going anywhere. Just sitting in his chair, or sleeping. And there's work to be done around him like there was always work to be done for him, all work, work.

Like in the past –

'Iain, we'll be needing the rods'

'Iain, some help here'

– and –

'Tidy up the place a bit'

– and –

'Tell Margaret, will you?'

All work. All his asking. And them all having to do his bidding.

And all right, maybe it's not the same kind of work now as then, with him old and sick and frail, maybe – but still it's changed here. The place become his, now he's here all the time. This House his grandfather built, and his grandfather before him . . . His House. You feel it – Iain does – with him permanently in it. You feel his presence. His ownership. Though the land is everyone's, is everyone's – and you could say he has no right. That this lovely place belonged to old Himself * no more than it belongs to them, to Iain, Iain Cowie or to Margaret MacKay or to Helen or Helen's child. Belongs to them more in fact for they're ones who stayed

---

* 'Himself' was the pet name given to John Sutherland's father, the great Modernist bagpiper who went by the name 'Callum' though he'd been christened Roderick and became 'John', after the death of his elder brother, according to the Sutherland family tradition of so naming the first-born. There are more details about this, and about family trees, genealogy charts etc. in relevant Appendices 4–9. For now it is enough to note that Iain here is using the name 'Himself' ironically.

here, not swanning up from London like the son used to do. Bringing up a party of his so-called friends . . .

'Iain, I'm back!'

Well, are you, Johnnie?

'So bring the Land Rover down for me, will you?' 'Get the dogs ready for the morning?'

To hell.

Is the one thing Iain can think about old Johnnie now, and smile.

As he turns his gun. And it's his gun.

Slips the cleaning rod down deep into the barrel and takes another sip of whisky that's his own.

For bring the Land Rover down nothing. He'll see him dead before Iain Cowie does another thing for old Johnnie.

one/third paper

By now it's as though all the hills can hear that song, and all the dark air.
Can hear too, as Johnnie's poor mind can hear, that of course it's the voice
of a woman singing, the whole lullaby is hers. The words of her song
insist upon it.

It becomes higher and truer in the air, in the man's mind, with that
knowledge. High and fine like migraine and no amount of rain on his face
will take the sting out of the tune, bring coolness to his skin.

You took her away.

And not just the one woman singing now, there in the chorus, but all
of them. All of the mothers. As though all the women in the world are
singing out to the dark hills, to the poor crying sky . . .

You took her away, young Katherine Anna,
Carried her off, tall Helen's child.

And then the one woman's song, coming in higher and finer above the
rest of them, singing out on her own and ringing in his head like pain.

Her mother is me.

'Hush' Johnnie whispers at the baby, as though to quieten her. 'Hush'
again, when she's making no sound and there's nothing he can do anyway,
nothing, to take the crying away. For that is in the tune too by now, of
course it is, the slanting tears, the weeping and the rain. As much as the
theme, all this Urlar* grey ground that's around him, it's there, and the

---

* The Urlar is the opening movement of a piobaireachd – as is clear from this section

terrible octave drop, the 'G' to the Low 'G', for the thing he has done.

You took her away.

And he can't leave any of it out of the music any more than loosen the bundle from his arms. So 'Hush' he may say but what's the use in that, 'Hush'? No use. No more than 'You took her away'. There's no comfort in it, no sense, how could there be? Of a calming or a peacefulness for the child out here on the open hills away from her mother? For an old man with a baby – it's all wrong, it goes against nature. And somewhere deep in himself John Callum must know that, I believe he does know . . .*

Still he keeps saying to the baby, 'Hush.'

Though she's not crying.

'Hush.'

It's the hills that are.

The sky.

The mother's song.

The weather now is fully down upon them. The fine'ness gone. Rain comes in long pieces and he has to keep strong, is what he's trying to think, Johnnie is: how despite the mothers with their babies and their songs he must be fit and cunning and fast and strong. For they'll be after him, down there somewhere on the flat, Iain and Margaret and the rest. They'll be coming up behind and wanting her back, young Katherine Anna. They'll be wanting her home with them and safe.

It would have taken them no time at all to fix it this morning that they'd be after her and fast. The minutes of that first hour would have ticked by rushed and livid from the very second they found out she was missing from her basket and that he, too, was gone. There'd be Helen

---

of 'The Big Music' – to be followed by three other movements. Details of all these – the Urlar, ground; Taorluath, stag's leap; Crunluath, crown; Crunluath A Mach, the showing of the crown – can be found in Appendices 11 and 12, along with notes on structure and meaning.

* Here again is evidence of a narrative voice that is placed outside the experience of John Callum and others in this book. Is it the same person noted earlier entering into the text this way? I think we are asked to consider here that this may be the case. Either way, the first person 'I' appears here, and with increasing frequency as 'The Big Music' continues – though will not always be annotated separately.

running outside, half dressed, in her bare feet, screaming his name into
the bare hills, and 'No!', 'No!', Iain up from the table, clattering the things,
and straight out to the hut for the Argocat and his gun. Unlocking the
dogs from the kennels and setting them off across the grass, already with
the binoculars' glass casting across the distance . . .

And –

'Steady, Johnnie. Steady.'

Cursing himself as he stumbles on a sharp rock.

'Steady.'

For can he see him now? Iain? Can he see that speck who is himself
against the grey green'ness of the hill? A scrap of movement on the distant stillness? Can he see him now, where he is? Standing here panting and
a bundle in his arms mustn't let fall?

'Steady.'

With Helen running, screaming his name out from there on the grass
for him to bring her baby home and only Margaret can catch her, hold her,
holding her back. Saying 'Iain will find him' and that voice of hers low and
steady, soothing her. Saying 'Don't worry, Helen. Be calm. For her, you
must be. And babies are strong. So get her things now that you can take
them, get some bottles, some blankets, milk. Some warm things for her' she
says, 'Quickly, go!' – but putting her hand up to shield her eyes against the
sun the minute Helen's gone, for she too, Margaret, is straining to see . . .

Him.

'Johnnie. Steady.'

Where he is, where he's gone. Iain with an old jersey held at the dogs,
it's Johnnie's old fishing jersey and he's giving it to the hounds to pick
up a scent, so straight off they make a fast line to the right, towards the
river – and. . .

'Oh, John' says Margaret to him then, looking out towards the hills
where he may be. 'What have you done?'

~

Well.

Margaret.

No point in thinking about Margaret now. What she might say. How she may consider him. What she may think.

For Margaret . . .

He can have no thoughts about her now. No thoughts. Of that low and lovely voice of hers. Of the things she might say.

For 'Hush' is all he must think now, against her voice, against all the voices, all of them. And –

Faster. Further. Up the way, the path. To step again, and another step. On, and on and up again –

'For they're coming, Johnnie.'

They'll be close by.

Right up there behind him with the dogs and coming hard.

'Coming after you.'

From the first thing this morning when they knew that he was gone. With the glasses played across the hill and Iain's eye wanting, wanting to be upon him, and the gun at his side.

'So be faster than they are. Be further away.'

With every footstep. Every breath.

Because it doesn't matter, none of it, not to him.

'Old Johnnie.'

It doesn't matter.

Because they still don't know, do they? About the boulder and the path that's like a deer path going down into the crevice of the other hill, sitting in the lee of Mhorvaig and with a lost valley there and in it, tucked away, his secret. The private, private place.

'They still don't know about that, do they, Johnnie?'

And any minute, he thinks . . .

Any second . . .

Once the boulder's there, once he sees it, that'll be him. He'll be up and over where no one could spy him or follow. Not a mother with a scent for her child. Not a man with the dogs and a gun.

He turns, and heads now towards this last part, up the fast steep way across the high side. Because fast and fleet he can make these last steps, for this last climb, up and hard . . . And so he stumbles, a slide of fresh wet from the rain, and no coat on but just the thin shoes ... And so outcrops of rock are jutting and with the wet they could be like knives – and they're behind him now, behind him and they're close ...

The music's still counting for him, after all. And it will carry the story along even if he stumbles on the path. It will keep him strong. Despite them all after him, Helen screaming in the air and that tune of hers wanting to take him over to pull him back – still he's got his 'B' to 'E', that stubborn'ness of him and thrawn, and the 'F' to the 'G' and the 'F' to the 'A', that sequence too, he has that too, the music trying to release itself, to let something new come in, enter, one note, and another, and another, to climb back again into the theme as a lightness, a relief, but the theme he's laid down won't allow it, the scale won't allow it.

And Iain ...

Forget about Iain. He wasn't born here. Was not a boy here. He has no knowledge of the hill. For all his gun and his shot he has nothing of this place in him while Johnnie ... He's everywhere upon it. There's not a way or dent in the heather he doesn't know or plan for and remember. The very stones are like a path. And he can put more distance between himself and the House by imagination if he needs to, more than footsteps can do, for he's all-powerful here, he's all strength and knowledge and he's wise.

So move on!

Though the dogs might be coming, because there's the sound of them now ...

Quick footsteps on the beaten, shiny path! And faster again! Further again! And as though to hasten him this second the weather clears a little, opens up. The sky lightens. He takes a big step up the path, and clears it. Another few seconds and here's a patch of blue about him, a sudden bit of sun. The day thinning out, the weather, and it's fair again, it will be, and he'll look ahead and the boulder will be there and –

though the dogs are getting louder –

no one knows about his path, only him. Only Johnnie. It's his own secret from a long time ago after his father had died and he came back to his father's music then.

And so they're louder ...

The dogs ...

Still he will bring her, this one in his arms, to that same place, to finish it, the tune.

And the dogs ...

The dogs, anyway. They're his dogs. His own and Callum's dogs. They're not Iain's dogs. And so they're coming for him, so he'll whistle them in. He'll take them with him if wants to. He'll call them in for they're his dogs, Callum's dogs.

And he stops then. Just here, stopped, just now and he shouldn't have, with the weather clearing, second by second it is thinning and brightening and a new clean'ness, clarity in the air so he should be moving on by now – but he's stopped. With the sound of his own breathing, and the glass that's upon him now in the sudden sun. Hearing the sound of his own breath beneath the glass, in this clearing of the air. Though he should have found by now the place with the big stone. Though they could catch him out now while he's still out here and visible clear on the fresh hill. Though they could shoot him down.

He's stopped.

Waiting.

For it's Callum.

It is. It's Callum.

'Callum?'

And very close.

Up there with the dogs, for they're his dogs, they're Callum's dogs.

Callum.

'How are you, boy?'

And with him . . . He recognises who's with Callum here. Even from over on the hill, with the light in his eyes he knows him by that way of standing, his father. So his father's here, too.

Yes.

Come up with Callum, he must have, the two of them gone on up Mhorvaig ahead of him and now they're both here together, just over there where he can see them, and quite near, after all this time . . .

His father.

His son.

And he didn't think they were close at all, that they were just memories. For his father's been dead forty years and a long, long time since he's seen Callum by now but –

Here they are with him, just the same, and with the dogs, right here on the hill.

'My father' he says.

'My boy.'

They're together – and listen! You can hear it? How they have all come in? When first there was the one theme, and only Johnnie out here and on his own, but then the singling, and the doubling came in . . .*

With his father.

And Callum.

With the sound of Callum's dogs – and:

'Come in! Come in!' Callum is calling to them. The sound of their barking . . . Close . . .

And with those notes, these variations – first the one, then the other . . .

The hold on the awful drop, the 'G' to 'G' . . . It's broken.

With his father.

And Callum.

And himself standing here.

So the theme can be released now, he can hear the way it goes free –

all the extra notes of the variations let in –

with the singling and the doubling and the three of them together . . .

The music's hold on him broken with this change, this turn, that lifts him, like in a dream.

A lovely dream.

~

* The manuscript 'Lament for Himself' in its original form shows how the theme was to be developed within the Urlar, as two variations – first a singling (the insertion of a number of single gracenotes around the existing notes) and then a doubling (where these gracenotes are doubled from the 'top' to provide a sort of mirror image of the original tune). This is marked on the MS 'dithis' (pron. *zhitt-ee*), and note also the siubhal (pron. *shoo-al*), Gaelic terms meaning this particular musical development in bagpipe music.

Iain's hard behind him, though, and the sound of the dogs' barking is no dream. The whole day like a charge for him.

When Helen had let out that cry this morning, the sound of her, he'd never heard anything like it – when she realised what the old man had done. When she'd stood at the dining room doorway, saw them all at the table but that the baby was not there, was not with Margaret, or with them at all . . . How they'd rushed from the table to look through the House and realised that he was gone, too, the old man not in his bed. 'No!' she'd screamed then. 'No!' And Iain was out in the grounds in a second, and away looking down to the river, up the back paddock, but he's nowhere to be seen, the old man who's stolen their child, he's nowhere there or out beyond the green, past the stand of trees, the little burn – Iain's looking but nothing, nothing. So he's to the shed then straight away for the Argocat and his gun. Because Helen . . . She's like a daughter to him, his daughter, and of course he would protect her, do anything he had to do to protect her and her child –

As she ran screaming out onto the grass!

Flying out of the House, no shoes on her feet, like she was burning – screaming! That sound of her like a wound in the air, against the bright of the day. Like something he'd never heard before, her flying out of the House and screaming as she runs to be on the hill for to find him and to bring her baby home.

And only Iain can make it right. Bring the Argocat round, keep the engine revving on the grass while Margaret can talk some sense into her, that she must get some things and go with Iain now, to look for the old man who has her child. Only Iain can wait – while Margaret is gentle with her, calming her. Telling her that she must gather up her things, Helen must, to take with them. While he's keeping the engine running, found a jersey of the old man's so the dogs can get a scent. Staying there with the engine running until Helen is back with a bag, with the baby's things – but then they're off. Straight off across the flat towards the hill and the dogs up ahead already like a banner streamed out before them – and still, only Iain. Only Iain. For this is his family. They're his family. And they need him here. His wife. His daughter. His granddaughter. Though

Helen's not to be comforted and she's crying, there's that sound of her, but Margaret is managing to calm her even so and tell her that he, Iain, will make it right.

That he'll go after . . .

Him.

For whom he's loosened out the dogs. Had them smell the air. For he's like a criminal, the old man who's been living amongst them. Stealing out of the house with their baby in his arms.

A criminal. A thief.

So, yes, take a gun.

Take dogs and a gun as he would for any criminal, for any hunt upon the hill. If he may need it, to take a shot at the criminal's foot or at his knee. If he has to, to bring him down. He'll do anything he needs to do, Iain will. To make it right. To protect the child. And quickly pack the sack with a jersey and some blankets, the things Helen has got together, provisions, milk, and medical things. Throwing them on the Arogocat that's sitting running on the grass, the motor turning over, and he gets in, Helen beside him, and he manages to soothe her, too, like her mother soothed her, with low words. Like soothing an animal. Telling her that they'll get her baby home, the dogs have picked up a scent already, that she's not to worry. Chucking the motor into gear then and the tyres spin, catch. Increasing speed and increasing — and they're away. Keeping it to himself as the Argo ploughs down the hill towards the river that it's even crossed his mind for a second that he'd need a gun. That the idea of what an old man would want with a child, and a damaged man, a man with his mind not right and with his own family far away from him . . . Would occur to him at all, make him want to take it . . . Keep all those thoughts to himself. And keep the other simple fear in place instead: the simple fact that not enough's been provided for an infant out on the hills, carried any distance or cared for by someone who is frail and sick and weak. That she'll be hungry, frightened and very cold. A baby who is very, very cold.

That most simple fear perhaps the most dangerous part of all.

For the criminal has nothing with him, nothing.

To protect a child from the weather, to keep her from the sudden cold
– and though the dogs have a scent, he could be anywhere out there . . .

Anywhere.

But for the white blanket.

The white blanket that Iain will see.

The flag to bring her home.

~

And it won't be long now, though it will seem like hours to the mother –
after crossing the river and up the first hill's long side – Iain catching in the
glass the glimpse of white on the face of Mhorvaig and sending the dogs
ahead straight up in that direction. After turning the engine up a notch,
and they're up there and over, and they're starting to climb again . . .

So no time, it will take them no time at all then. Though it feels like
hours to Helen . . . No time. To get him, the criminal, to bring him in.
Rising up on the first side of the hill and over, down the dip and back
up again, the tyres taking the rock and the peat in one action. With the
weight of the gun at Iain's knee, the sound of the baying dogs . . .

And the temperature dropping, after that bit of rain before, and it's
much colder here than it was back down on the flat, but they'll get there,
Iain will, up the green face where he first saw the glimpse of white in the
binoculars' glass – 'There!' – and so fast over the tops and the baby alive
when he comes upon her, so he'll wrap her up in a thick blanket and have
her back to her mother, back into her mother's arms, Helen's crying, she
can't stop crying while she holds her daughter close.

'It's okay'

'It's okay'

'It's okay.'

And Johnnie?

Well, he won't get to his boulder. Won't manage the child into the valley like he'd been planning. Won't feel either the bite of Iain's bullet at his
knee – for Iain in the end would have no need to use the gun.

Only cut the motor and run across with Helen, to take the baby
from the arms of an old man standing there, talking aloud to no one, to

himself, out there on the hill, talking about nothing, pee running down his leg and tears in his eyes.

For Johnnie . . .

Look all around you, man, the air is clear and you can see for miles. The shadings of the green. Last of the heather's prime across the sides. The blue sky shining from edge to edge, and standing so still here to admire it all, out there against the hill, the spot of white so clear upon the empty landscape Iain didn't even need the glasses to catch sight of what he's been looking for.

'There!'

With the dogs starting up, leaping and wagging and spread out in a pack across the heather, and the sound of the Argocat can't put out the sound of their wild baying –

'Get him!'

Yet for Johnnie, at this moment, there's no sense of the glass's cast, or the naked eye. No sound of the motor getting closer, closing in. For he's just out here on a hill with his father and his son and the music singing for the three of them together in this lovely place. Three generations, three times for the Urlar to sound. Three. Three. Three. And no sense of what he's done – only his mind away and reeling out here in the air, the song in his head of a man at the close of his life and what words come into that, there are no words, or language or time. Only a tune.*

And he smiles, laughs then. Thinking how crazy he is and knows it, a fool and nothing to stop him now, nothing in his mind, no limits, no stops. For the ground's down, the music that he wrote, that has been writ-ten before and all filled with the darkness coming, the final sleep but then he'll have the next part to save him.

Because 'F' to 'G' he might have been singing to her before, and 'F' to 'A', like they were his notes to sing, but it was her, all strong and round and

---

* There is information about the structure of 'Lament for Himself' in Appendix 10/i, ii and iii, and about piobaireachd structure generally in Appendix 11. Also the Crunluath A Mach movement of 'The Big Music' contains details of an essay by John MacKay Callum Sutherland, 'Innovations to the Piobaireachd', that refers to a tune being more than just a theme but is also about the particular deployment of that theme.

new. Fresh life out of old. That's what she is, the little one. What they'll need to understand, when he's gone from them entire and the baby too, hidden away in their secret place and they're not getting her back. Not ever. For they'll all come to understand it one day, that she's like the line of the notes set in front of everything, the pattern of what follows all because of her . . .

And how beautiful it is.

Though he doesn't know yet how it will be, how she'll come out of the ground and turn into the deer that leaps off the edge of the hill and takes a crown upon her head . . .*

Though he can't see or hear yet the space between the notes and how she'll leap into that space, gathering up in her crown all the variations of the tune . . . Some sense of it has begun. Been with him for a while, it seems, before the morning and the day, before his father and his son, before the laying down of the ground upon which he still stands, the beginning was there, of the music's plan. The knowledge that's in her, the little one. And they'll understand at last, all of them, what he needed to do. To make a new music from the stubborn'ness of old, find the fresh sequence he will be playing soon, soon, when he gets her to the hut, to be alone with her there. The crying done by then. The sky itself gone away and replace it only with music.

---

* The crown here refers to the Crunluath movement of 'The Big Music' — crunluath meaning 'crown', and the important concluding 'narrative' section of piobaireachd music that is then followed by the show of technique that is the A Mach.

insert/John Callum

Of course he shouldn't be surprised by time by now, and he isn't, not
really.

Even before he stopped taking the pills there was a growing sense of
having left daily life for a different kind of world where the days and
nights and months were all the same. Moving around from room to room,
from breakfast to lunch and to tea with no awareness of his presence anywhere he stayed, going as easy from one dark place to another as though
he were a shadow or a kind of ghost.

Certainly that is what it has been like for him long enough, well before
these papers were being gathered. Time become unmarked that way, days
lived in with no dates, no words to record them. There's one week in summer that's like a week in the spring, and that in turn's fast gone back into
winter again or to the autumn. And all the weeks are like the week before,
and the month to follow. The past is there, one man's history written down
and lived in, maybe, but with nothing to say for it that he can make sense
of. No one to listen. He's there in his chair or in his bed, taking only into
himself his story with its memories that may have made him happy once or
sad. Of his weeping one day, or his breaking on another into song.

Will all be in the tune.*

---

* Appendix 7 indicates those sections of 'The Big Music' that refer to John Callum's
family; history; business interests. Throughout the book we come to see how John

It's what Sutherlands know, anyhow, time. The way time goes. As so many of the families who live around here know it, how, in the end, you keep in silence all the information you once carried, how, in the end, things don't change. And maybe it seems to this one man that he's gone through youth to strength to age in no more than a splinter of life, in just a fraction of hours played out beneath the sky, but in this too his life is no different to the others before him. Time keeps the people who live here still that way, it holds. So they may have been cleared off their farms and crofts, some of those families long ago, or people left, or said they would never return, even so they were staying, too, somehow, all of them, kept deep in to old time, old ways. So they may have lived in Nova Scotia or New Zealand or somewhere far away, on the other side of the world, yet they remained here amongst the hills. In their thoughts, their memories, 'Nothing changes' they might say. 'I don't mind.' All their lives gone into the same silence of the sky.

No wonder, then, the place seems lonely. Or that old Johnnie has that kind of quiet that's deep in, darkness born of isolation and become quite starkly lodged in him by now as one specific illness of the mind. For a doctor may say that it's as though it's because he's been allowed to carry on in a certain way, doing what he wants, following the lead of his own thoughts for so long in his life, without listening to others, without taking into account their needs, that he's given himself a kind of depression, mental heaviness and instability come from living in a world that may as well have no other people in it at all. And a generation or so ago there would have been no pills, no doctors. It would have been called just loneliness then, just loneliness his condition and that word for keeping himself close to himself: a 'canniness' – for going out to seek the company of others that way. Like his father before him, who kept his own counsel – no matter how many pupils or pipers or musicians he saw, no matter how many people came to the House for lessons or instruction or recitals. So did the son have that same kind of spirit. A holding on to himself. A holding in.

Sutherland may have vowed never to return to the place where he'd been born ('I'll not be back!', p. 14) but did come to live out the end of his life at The Grey House after all.

Perhaps it had always been that way. The Sutherlands always a family who kept themselves from others, even from the old days* when the door was open to strangers and those who wanted to hear music or take instruction. They were set back then from those who came to them. Maybe that's why now, with his father's Winter Classes long over, and the recitals and competitions that used to take place at the House all finished and done and even his own friends don't come back here any more, too much time has gone by ... John Callum MacKay doesn't really hear the silence.

It's what comes of living in this part of the Highands – so they might have said in the old days, too. That silence is what comes from staying in this particular place with its unchanging hills and grasses. That the landscape itself will make for a man that kind of narrow holding – and all the music in the world, all the concerts and the playing, won't take away the feeling in the mind of being isolated and wanting it, to be in this beautiful lonely place, as John's father had wanted it. And his father before him. And his father's father. And to be used to it, too, the sense of nothing else exists. So it is a sort of madness is what John has, maybe, and he's been diagnosed for it, finally now, towards the end of his life, and been given tablets to help it a little, the amnesia and the confusion, and tablets too for to regulate the beat of his wild, undependable heart. Because although he may have called out into the air as he drove away 'I'll not be back!' and gone miles and years from the hills and his father's music – his father's 'Damn music!', what he used to say for a long time when anyone asked him about it, in the midst of parties or a busy London street – still the silence of being alone would always be with him like a return, like part of the tune his father played.

So he'll play his own 'Lament for Himself' – is what he knows about himself by now, this one John Callum MacKay, when this story begins – *I don't mind* – that it's always been this way. Pills. Quietness. Nothing counting for anything. Only hills. Only sky. The past is there but it's like an empty cloth spread out with small things set against it, and all he can do now is try and hold on to the small things, the details and remember them,

---

* The Taorluath and Crunluath movements give details of the Sutherland family's history.

see them, turn them into little notes and embellishments that maybe later he can use. There are certain small things he knows, for example, that already he has seen, that come into his mind as phrases, little sequences of notes. There's the sound of his mother's singing, for example, or the tap of his feet as he sits as a boy on a low stone wall, banging the backs of his shoes on the slate. These the kinds of small things that could be useful in the tune. There's the Grey House behind him with some parts that are known to him, others not. The table in the dining room, that is known. Or the whisky bottle and the glass water jug. Or here another room where they've moved him, next to the little sitting room by the hall's bright light, and the bed is made up for him. And here again, from the dark room, he sees quite clearly, under the eaves at the top of the house, another room that is long and low that is also his room, used to be, long ago, and in it he can see . . .

A ball.

A wooden ship.

A little toy dog.

. . . As if he could touch them. Though he never goes into that room now. He could pick them up. The ship with its pale blue funnel and the red and white ball. Because he was a child, once, in that room. He was a boy schooled by his mother there, down one end where there's a desk and a board with chalks and he kept books on a shelf by the desk and he did his chanter practice on the chair that sat in the corner. See the room? He's in the room. There's the sound of the room.

Could be in the tune.

That he had 'My Room' on a piece of paper once, and stuck upon the door. That could have its own particular note, a run of notes. Of course it could. Something lovely to play, for he loved that room, and later, much later he went with Margaret there . . .

But it's nowhere near where they've put him now.

For where they've put him now is in this other little room down the hall from the old Music Room* where his father took lessons with pupils,

* The Music Room, or the Study, as it was also called in John Sutherland's father's day, is also the little sitting room at The Grey House.

where the men used to tune up or practised their chanters or sorted their reeds. And it's dark here. In this old part of the House where his father's pipers would always be. There's nothing in here. It's just dark. Whereas in that other room at the top of the House where he first learned from books and talked and played with his mother . . . The notes are everywhere around it.

It's because the room was his mother's room and from the beginning . . . That there would be little runs of phrases and embellishments that would want to gather there in the Schoolroom at the top of the House where she could teach him to read and write and tell him stories and hold him on her knee. And she would have gone in there to sit, after her son had been sent away to school she would have sat at his little desk, thinking of him, thinking of how quickly the time has passed since he was born, then he was gone.

And I wonder . . .

Putting this together now, inserting this paper . . .*

Did she get used to it? His mother? The sending away of her little boy, the saying goodbye before either of them were ready? Getting used to the particular kind of silence that follows the leaving of children, the road that stands open at the gate to take the children away? For it is another kind of loneliness, this other inevitable kind of silence that carries with it no sense of choice. As minute by minute, one thought after another, the children take themselves apart from us and all the contents of their conversations, all their many words, only preparation for that single word: goodbye.

They write a letter home maybe, but then the letters rarely come. Less talking then . . . And less . . . Less . . . So in the end you may as well come to think of the wind, the grass as your children. The garden, all the little flowers. May as well make silence your daughter or your son.

---

* Note the use of first person in this segment of the text; also refer to pp. 8 and 25 in the Urlar, as examples of a certain tone, style of voice emerging in the narrative. Also, opening section of Taorluath movement.

narrative/2

The people at the House and what they thought of him

Iain

It's all just more work for them. Is how he sees it. For his wife. His daughter. They just work for him as they always have, from back in the early days. Just more work, more cleaning, more meals. More sheets to strip and replace on the beds, more tidying away to do after the big parties at night with the pipes going until dawn, and the glasses cluttered through the sitting room and in the hall, and the door left open sometimes into the morning from where they'd been out drinking or pissing in the grass, for all Iain knows, taking their pipes out there and playing like idiots, God knows, to the moon.

He hates it, this kind of work. For Margaret, Helen. The clearing up. The sorting out. He always has, and now, with him back here to stay — and all right there aren't the parties any more, and there haven't been for a long time, even so — the old boy's so off with the fairies he can't sit to anything but needs help with it all, with this or with that. And it's Margaret who has to go running. Running after him and sometimes they're together alone, she'll be drawing back the covers of his bed or something like it, far too near him in a room.

It's too much.

And it's been going on too long.

And look at him out there on the hill today. Like a child. A child that's wet himself and is crying.

Like a little boy.

And Iain hadn't known what to do, say.

Though he hates the work of him, the way that other seems to draw to himself all thought and care . . .

Yet he found himself, Iain did, out there out on the hill with him – and for the first time – what?

Felt . . .

Well, he'd gone over to him, anyway. Where he was shivering. Got a blanket on him. Got him home again.

~

Margaret

(from transcript)*

I've never minded his little spells. You get old, that's what happens and we should all be prepared for it and hope we're treated with some patience when the time comes. Certainly we've gone here long enough in the same way, with things not changing and, yes, it's been hard, sometimes, and there were days when he'd be gone for hours and I'd be worried about him, I wouldn't know where he was, but I've never minded John, never.

When he took the child, though. That shows at last how it's different from before. That he's gone that far. It makes everything different from how it was, no more pretending we can let time hang and drift. For it shows that he has well passed by now any kind of sense, those kinds of refinements in his mind, I mean, that he could do such a thing. And it's been like that for a while, I suppose, but I didn't want to see it, but now I do. That his mind must be fully gone.

---

* As described before, these transcripts are excerpts from a wealth of recorded and written material kept as part of the archive of The Grey House and are available for perusal and use. Further details of domestic life can be found in Appendix 8/i as well as in the List of Additional Materials, and in later sections of 'The Big Music'.

And I've got Sarah on the phone. After I called her today, to let her know there's been this change in him. And I'm guessing she wants him back down there so she can keep an eye on things with him. But I won't tell her everything about what took place here today. Just let it hold a few more days even. I want to tell her instead: let Callum come. Send Callum. Ask him if he'll come up and see his father. Let his father see him, it's what his father needs. I'll call her myself and ask her: can Callum come?

~

Helen

(part transcript)

What's that poem that she loves? That home's the place where, when you need to go there, they take you in?*

It's how she feels here.

'And now, ' she says, 'I have a daughter to look after. I have her to keep me. To hold me – for she, more than anyone, makes this place my home. In having her here with me. Reliving my mother's life that way. Returning to have her here as though it were my right.'

So, yes, it is the poem that she loves. For though some might say she could have married her baby's father, or could have chosen not to have a child at all, instead she made the decisions that would bring her back here, to the House where she herself grew up and came of age – because she knew that she could return here, that she'd be safe. And now that she is here . . . It's as though that choice has become a responsibility: to make The Grey House her home again, reclaim her old room and lay out papers there upon a desk, turn on the lamp, start writing.

---

* This is from a poem by Robert Frost, and describes Helen MacKay's interest in American poetry (that in her journal she refers to as 'real-voice poetry', a phrase lifted from her PhD thesis), from Whitman through Dickinson to the New York School. Appendix 8/ii: 'Helen's notes and reading' shows her interest in particular poets and novelists, as well as general understanding of and research into various schools of literary modernism.

In this way make somewhere for her daughter to grow up in where she might feel she could also belong, say: I came from here. This is where I was born. So she can grow up as Helen did, so give her the same wild places and the air and in time this very room where Helen sits now with the window open into the night. It is how Helen can make something for her daughter that is strong, to give her somewhere she can step out from, into the world. That she may go to the ends of the earth and know always who she is because she belongs to that one place, and that place was her beginning.

That when she needs to go back there, that same place would take her in.

~

Margaret

Helen's young. That's all. Don't mind her large ideas, then. And her quiet-ness you could take for fierce anger, that sense of her independence and opinions and her clear sense of a way – but no. She doesn't have that certain kind of ire. She's herself. And I know why she keeps to that room of hers, reading and writing, the window open to the seasons the way she has it open. Even in winter I've seen the casement wide open to the air and the cold inside the room like glass.

She's young, still. That's the all of it. And, as I say, I know why she stays in the room. The window open in the way of her imagining she might be leaving, as I know she does, imagining leaving all the time. Although I think it's here she'll stay.

~

Iain

Anyway, it's not like he needs to feel sorry for the old fool. He can go to hell and no way back. After what he did this morning, taking a child away from her mother . . .

There's nothing about him that is fit.

And it's been going too long, with his mind poor, and getting weaker, and that means even more work to do for Margaret and for them all.

Helping him.

And never once a word of thanks.

Just like through the old days. The 'Bring the Land Rover down' days, the 'Get the dogs ready for the morning' and the 'We'll be needing the rods' days. The 'Tidy up the place a bit after, the bottles and so on, at the riverbank . . .'

Never once a word.

Of thanks.

And not today either. Out there. After getting him in. There was no thanks for that either – and the state he was in. The fool. Acting like –

'Iain, I'm back!'

But no. Not like that, like before. Not 'fool' like that. Today . . .

Was different.

Crying and alone out there today on the hill. Wet through to his trousers and not able to stand.

That was not like he used to be.

'Iain, I'm back!'

Because look at him, Iain thinks. Lying through in that little room in the dark. He's not back anywhere, the old boy.

He's not back and he's not going.

Anywhere.

~

Margaret

And Helen? Yes, I can understand her kind of dreaming. I've been like it myself. Parts of me still feels what it is to be that girl who wanted much, much more than home could give. To go in amongst the hills or across the flat cliff paddocks or to be taking a boat around the top of the firth in a little schooner, deep into the cold of the North Sea . . . I imagined these voyages, saw myself on them. Taking the train south or way across to the west. Visiting Edinburgh, maybe, Glasgow. All the cities. Going away as I did to the university for that year in Aberdeen.

Little came of it all, I know. Those dreams of mine, when I was a girl, or thoughts or plans. In the end it was only a ride on the bus, sixty miles away. That's how far I went away.

Still, one might say my restlessness has come out in Helen.

If it didn't come out in what went on between me and John Sutherland, you could say it's come out in my daughter. All my restlessness, in the end, all her travelling and her shifting my idea of what it was to change.

Because when I think of it, the way it was for me when I went to John those nights back then, when I was younger, the way I went up to the room we shared at the top of the House and waited for him there . . . Some nights when he had his friends in, too, and he'd be late, but still I'd wait for him . . . All those times. Or I would go to him where he sat, in the evening or at the table after dinner. I would put my hand to the back of his neck, to the soft dent at the base of his skull and he leant back into me then . . . All those times. Those small, small times . . . It was a yearning, a moving in me, kind of restlessness, maybe, that wanted to be near him and the small times with him could be enough. To have me inclining towards him, that I needed his leaning back. For all during those years I had a good husband who loved me, and we looked after each other, Iain and I have always looked after each other.

My Iain Cowie.

My shy, shy man.

What restlessness must have been in me to take me away from you? To wait in another man's bedroom that he'd made for me under the eaves, at the top of the stair?

~

Iain

And, yes, he put a blanket across the old boy's shoulders today, because anyone would have done it.

Like he'd hope someone might do that for him, when the time comes and he's alone and doesn't know who he is or where he's going.

Even though he could have brought him down.

Just as easy, if he'd wanted to, he thinks. He could have.

As he cleans his gun.

Because who is old John by now, anyway, that Iain couldn't bring him down if he wanted to – but just some old man with money, half dead. And so he has enough to pay for a housekeeper, a hired gun. Let him feel what that gun could do.

He would have felt it this morning, sure enough, if Iain had seen fit to use it.

For let Iain show him, the hired gun. Let them be together just once and there to be an excuse for Iain to take him on . . .

Has always been like a sort of prayer for him.

Just once.

Let him have the excuse. For him to show the old boy then what real power's like. Not money. Or a voice that calls and commands.

But a stone or a rock or a gun.

Because it's like a clench for Iain, of the fist, in his heart, the way that voice calls for him. With his ease, his damn music that he thinks makes him a Highland gentleman – it doesn't make him a gentleman, the way he is with Margaret doesn't make him a gentleman.

'Tidy up here, will you? After we've finished here?'

Though he may have been born in this House, John Callum MacKay, and his father before him. Though he might be the son of a family who made of this part of the land something that could be owned . . .

He despises that, too, Iain does. That one family could shear off from the ways things have always happened here and gain some portion for itself. He's read enough, he knows the stories of what went on around here – though his own family are not from around here – he knows enough, Iain does.* And he knows all old John Callum's family ever did was charge tenancy for the time the animals could be on the hill, like a tacksman might charge other men, or a factor. Like a thief.

---

* Iain is referring here to the notorious Highland Clearances, and the way the Sutherland family stayed clear of the evictions and relocation that took place at that time. There are further details of their position in the Taorluath and Crunluath sections of 'The Big Music'; also Appendices 1–3, and parts of 4–9 may be of interest here.

So all of it . . . Despise.

Because his reading and knowing tell him, Iain: no real Highlander would ever do that, think that way about the land. As money and business. That the land could be seen as no more than a path from one place to another – how that's all wrong. And just for the fact that some ancestor or other had a few more sheep than others, more than one or two, but charged out the land to his neighbours for theirs so it might stop his own bit of scratching at the earth. So it's other men's work's made him rich.

Another man doing his work.

And times have changed. And people learn, and they watch. And when something happens like what happened here today . . . Just as well Iain has his own life, that he doesn't feel he must be owing to anyone.

He has his own gun.

And shouldering it this morning as he did, stepping out the door. Down the brae in the Argocat and off up the hill the other side of the river, the dogs all about him – to get him, like a hunt.

That felt real enough. That was real – not the other, false Highlander who took himself away.

Because once you've gone you don't get to come back.

Do you, dogs?

Is what he's always thought, what he thought this morning while he was going up there.

When it was like a hunt.

Hunting down a criminal off a hill.

And that he could have finished him off this morning, too, easy, with a bullet or a stone.

Could have. Course he could have.

But . . .

Once he was away up there on the tops and had caught what he was after . . .

To see the poor old fool pissed himself through to his trousers and not able to stand . . .

He didn't do that.

And yes, he put a blanket around him.

Put a blanket about the false shoulders.

Though anyone would have done it.

And, yes, he lifted him, the body of a criminal, the body of a man who had lived the way he had, treated people the way he had, who would behave towards Margaret the way he behaved . . . Still he lifted him. Laid him into the seat of the Argo, laid him there.

But so he might hope another would also lift him. Lift Iain.

If he was wet through and alone and shivering. And had not a wife to go back to in the House, or a young woman who's like a daughter to him and he's looked after her all these years.

So he might hope then he would also be lifted.

And he was light, the other man was. Like a child, lighter even. Like a leaf.

And –

'Come on now, John' Iain had said. 'We're here to take you home.'

~

Margaret

So, through all those years with him . . .

Who could say I didn't love John then?

When I was a young woman and when I first met him I was only a girl.

Who could say I wouldn't love him?

The way we came together, that first time – though . . .

He'll never know, nor Iain.

Only Helen.

Because only Helen has the story in her, of how John Sutherland and I came to be together and what happened then.

insert/John Callum

For sure, there was not much else for her, Johnnie's mother, by the time her little boy was sent away. Her husband was long lost to her by then, deep into his practice and composition and would barely have known the difference between whether the child was there or gone. He'd be in his room alone and rehearsing and practising or else he'd have his students staying with them at the House, or other musicians and composers, and they'd be together, all the men, and John's mother would see them at the dinner table only.*

'A fine day, Elizabeth?'

'Oh, yes, a fine day.'

So there was her loneliness, the heart of it, in his mother, the way she learned to gather it up, making herself be surrounded by it as though she were used to it, silence after silence. And as for her son, well. Few boys of that generation would ever remember much, would they? And sure Johnnie can't, of ever feeling that he had such a great craving for that man who

---

* By now there have been a number of references to the piping school (known formally as the 'Winter Classes') that took place, along with various recitals and competitions at The Grey House under the direction of Callum Sutherland, the father of John MacKay of 'The Big Music'. The theme of this School continues within the structure of this book – as part of its history and positioning within the culture of piobaireachd – and in the Crunluath movement, in particular. There is also related information contained within Appendices 4–9 and in the List of Additional Materials.

was his father. Wouldn't remember, for example, missing him or wanting him home. When Callum Sutherland was in London, say, and this just after the War, or in Edinburgh or somewhere else and always for music. When his father was away, or even when he was just at home but off in a room somewhere playing, the room where he sat with his piper friends or his pupils . . . All that time John Callum can't remember being after his father's companionship or attention at all. He was used to it, not wanting it. Like his mother made herself be used to it. No expectation there to have the man's time or his tenderness, much less again the thought that he might give his love.

I don't mind.

Like he didn't have a father.

I don't mind.

Like he never had.

So no surprise now, why should it be, that he's come to seem as though he's the same man himself, could be, as his own father. Put to the same instrument his father was put to, set up from the beginning to have his own long hours away from anyone else he might care for.

His father someone he remembers just in bits, in little pieces.*

Only his mother comes back to him entire. Her hand on his head. Her taking of the chanter** from his lips, to set it to one side: 'That's enough now. That's enough for today.' And those times when his father would ask him into his room to have him play for him, the tough cast of his father's jacket, the tweed cuff as he reached in to straighten the pipes in the boy's arms. Was there a smile then? A word or two spoken?

A word with a tune?

All this is way back in Johnnie's past now and hard to remember. Not much left, of the memories, not much besides. Of those times. His father, and his cuff. Maybe a word was spoken, a phrase that comes back to him: 'Do it again!' For the section of the music he'd been playing but the notes

---

* These memories survive as fragments only in 'The Big Music' but later sections of the book cast some light on the character of John's father, by way of various transcripts and related papers.

** The parts of the bagpipe are illustrated and listed in Appendix 13.

were all bad. That whole line wrong, his father said, all bad and the fingerings were smeared – so: ' Play it again! Do it again!'

'And again!'

'Again!'

So many times. The notes were all bad.

So there's nothing left. Nothing. Only –

'Who are you, Johnnie?'

He asks in the dark.

'That you would remember your own father so?'*

---

* These snatches of phrases are inserted here to show continuity with the ongoing
project of describing how 'Lament for Himself' has been composed. The phrases appear
in the patterning of notes at the beginning of the Urlar, in their repetition and pacing.
The fourth movement of 'The Big Music', the Crunluath A Mach, also contains details
of how these fragmentary style notes contribute to the whole.

Urlar/final fragment

Green/grey: the shape of the hills against the grey sky. The final part of the first section before they bring him back off the hill, wrap him up, inject him, bring him home.

SECOND MOVEMENT:
TAORLUATH

two/first paper*

Certain roads you get to a part of them, turn a corner, say, come over some kind of a hill, and you feel . . . No going back now. The road there to take you and all you can imagine is the place that lies ahead and who's there, who's waiting.

Callum Sutherland, he'll be like me enough that way. A man in his car now, coming along that exact same piece of road I'm writing about, and it's early morning, a grey light and soft and cold, but look at the place, darling, all around you. You can't help but see it, feel your heart clench like a little fist behind the bones of your chest as you sit forward slightly in the seat of your car with the land falling away like blankets on either side.

Beallach Nam Drumochta.

The Pass.

It's a part of the journey they talk about a lot here. About the length of it, time taken. The road north altogether, when you get up this far, is something they'll always ask after but this stretch of road in particular —

'Did you make it over all right?' Iain will ask it, or my mother. Someone in the pub at Rogart, in the midst of a high summer although there were winds, so asking 'Drumochta, how was it? You managed okay? In all this air?'

---

* Refer back to p. 8 and previous pp. 25 and 56 etc. of the Urlar for evidence of a first-person narrator involved in 'The Big Music' as though we have emerging an ongoing 'note' or particular tone in the tune. The reference to Iain Cowie and 'my mother' suggests this 'sound' or voice in the music belongs to Helen MacKay.

They used to ask me, too, the same, and I became used to my own answers given. How there was no traffic on the road, or there was a bit, or a report in the paper about another accident on the long stretch coming back off down the hill, someone taking over on a bad corner, and though the road's improved still it's bad in places and dangerous and fast. But Callum would say nothing, would he? About any of those things? Nor the excitement for the journey, the way the light opens out and the size of the country unfolds itself before you. He wouldn't feel himself entitled. To speak about his sense of the place that way because what right does he have to claim that kind of attachment, the idea of coming back to somewhere that's so familiar, so known, when he's never lived here, wasn't born here? When this is where he's only ever come for his holidays is all.

Is what he'll think. What he'll believe.

And anyway, his reasons for coming up this time drawn out from necessity, not desire – the call that came through from his mother, the arrangements he had to make.

And he'd have had his wife asking, his family: Do you really need to go up there? Now? When who knows how long your father will go on, how he'll treat you when you get there? When maybe this is just a turn of his, something temporary, and he'll go back to the way he was and nothing much wrong with him in the first place that's not just to do with age and his stubborn will? For all this is his decision, it's not yours, Callum. Come from where your father's decided that he wants to live, at the other end of the country, and that that's where he's going to stay – but nothing to do with you, is it? What your father's decided? Who he thinks he is? It's not for you to be dealing with, is it? And Callum might be thinking that, too. For certainly his wife would be asking, and his sons. Does he really need to come all the way up this road to be here?

Yet even so . . .

To think of the son coming back up here to be with the father . . .

Though it's against his will, perhaps. Against his wife's desire to have him stay.

Still, it's hard not to see it as returning. Though it was his father used those words, *the return*, and Callum himself may never use those words. Even so there he is in my mind now, looking for the House in his windscreen, though he's miles away. And there's the excitement even so. In the getting up. The getting over. Of Drumochta,* and the rise of the road as the journey takes form beneath him, the distance and the time closing up any space between the last time I saw him and now. So it does mean something else, coming back, after all. That's more than duty. More than need. That's more than his mother's insistence on the phone that he's the only one can talk to his father and get through to him, stir up some kind of recognition in his mind. That's more than all those things. So that he's switched the headlights off five minutes or so ago to let himself have a good sense of it, the land, the pale colours. Up there on the tops, looking north.

And . . .

Callum.

Callum, Callum.

Of course you are entitled.

You're the son. You're the only one.

Look for us in the windscreen of your car and we're waiting for you.

~

The call came through yesterday while he was at work.

His mother, in that quick way of hers of talking. 'Your father' she would have said. 'They've told me at the House he's bad again. It's been that way a while it seems. But not taking the medication so now they're worried enough to let me know.'

There would have been a moment then. I can see it, imagine it quite clearly: when the phone rang; when Callum picked up. A moment when he would seem to be taken by surprise – still thinking about what he'd just been doing, plans for a project laid out on the white desk in front of him, his eyes still on the drawing he's just completed.

'Callum?'

---

* Appendices 1–3 give full details of the region, including information about the Drumochta Pass as part of the definition of the Highland region; Endpapers and the List of Additional Materials show maps of the North East region.

And someone else, maybe, speaking to him at the same time from another part of the office, and him nodding, holding up his fingers when he picks up: *two seconds*. Mouthing the words, then saying to his mother, 'Okay, I'm here.'

Because at that point, though the call had been half expected, his father not well, he knew that, and his mother concerned, still he hadn't been thinking about any of that just then, about his father, and I think he might have wanted to prevaricate, not quite take his eyes from the papers in front of him to listen to his mother, to answer her straight away. Not quite ready to take the weight of the content of the sentences she was passing over to him, down the line.

Now they're worried enough to let me know.

So he just said 'Okay' to her then. 'Okay.'

For there was a big commission, perhaps, come up at work, that's what the plans were on the table, a busy time after the long summer break and suddenly deadlines ahead of him, a building to be finished in the first stage same time next year. And there were to be meetings. And accountants, lawyers. I don't know. Reschedules to be drawn up, alterations made.

So 'Okay' he might have said, like trying to put it off, the moment when she would ask him what she was going to ask him to do. 'Okay.'

'These people' she would have said then. 'They tell me now what's been going on. That he's been out roaming on the hills, it turns out, is the latest. For weeks, apparently, this has been going on, and on his own. After all this time and they tell me now. These people. How can you get through to these people?'

And he might have laughed then.

'Mum –'

But she would have said, and insisting, no choice in it at all, 'I want you to go up there, Cal. I want you to. To bring him back and I'll take him for a while. If he won't stay in hospital at least I can make sure he gets back onto a proper care programme here. With the right attention, the right medication –'

And he would have replied then, a different tone in his voice, 'He's not going to want it.'

So it would have been his mother's turn to laugh, though not a real laugh. 'It doesn't matter what he wants.'

'But he'll not agree' Callum would have said. 'He'll not let himself —'

'Cal.'

'Be taken.'

Sarah wouldn't have heard. 'You'll have to go up there' she would have told him, the laugh of hers never a real laugh. 'As soon as you can, Callum. Get up to the House and bring him back here to me.'

And all this was — when? Yesterday? Only yesterday and yet already it feels like another phase of his life, that he was another man altogether who had stood there at his desk in his office with a cup of coffee in his hand, the plans laid out before him, when the phone rang and interrupted. And though in so many ways his mother's request was not unexpected — when he looks back on it now he's here, on this road, driving back up North to be with him again — still it was like he was someone barely connected to his father that moment, when his mother talked to him that way. As though his father was someone else entirely, with no mind or past or will that Callum had ever known. As though he were not someone who he'd grown up with, learned from. Who had emotions he was familiar with, the impatience and judgement and rage like his father has had rage all through his life and when Callum was a boy he had to suffer that rage, when he had to make the journey up north with his father for the summer and his father hated the driving to get there. As though, for those moments when Callum had stood with the phone in his hand and heard his mother talking, he was unconnected to any of those memories he might have had, unconnected to the idea of this journey, even, with the boy grown up, the father old, and he, the son, the one who was driving . . .

But all that's gone now, now he's here. Now that he's actually on the road, on his way. So it's the day his mother called him that's become the time that's unreal, that's not linked to this present, the feeling from yesterday already gone from his mind, of his distance from the past. All gone because now it seems like it was only minutes ago that he was last on the Pass, and as the incline of it increases, gradually, and now the day

is lifting . . . Everything else has slipped away. The day before. The night.
The wife in bed with him this morning in the dark, the two boys in
their room. The streetlights and the oily wet of the road where he lives,
pulling the car out of the drive . . . All of it gone by now . . . Left way
behind him, in another country, and it's all that's ahead of him now, not
the other, that is the real.

~

It's the light does it. How it takes you to another place, casts off, eclipses
all the skies you've seen before, all the places you have been. I've felt the
same way coming back up here, and approaching the Beallach Callum
looks out and it's as though the entire sky of the world is open, poured
out, let loose down upon the hills. Like there was never such a thing as
darkness here, like there could be no darkness, only this bare, clear air.
There are the clean open flats of the moors, pale grey and dun and
heather streaked with dark and peat, and blackish watery burns some
places coming down cut with broken stones, rocks, and all of it, the sweet
land, available to him somehow, that sense of reaching out to it like you
might take it, all of it, be able to gather it into yourself and make it yours,
a universe of endless land and sky and distance and pick out the mountains for your stars.

But it's the road keeps you from disappearing. The grey of it, and thin,
with no place much for passing. You have to concentrate on that, don't
you, think about that, the present moment of your driving, or you'll run
into trouble, no doubt about it. That's what they say up here, remember?
When they talk about the journey. And since childhood, for Callum, that
memory's been in him, through all the years of the road being difficult to
manage in certain stretches, and it holds him to common sense, concentrating on that, being reminded, as I wrote before, of coming along here
with his father, and lagging behind caravans or estates hitching trailers,
maybe, or boats, and his father's frustration, then. His rage.

Christ, get a move on, man!

His hands gripping the wheel.

Christ!

With those eyes of his trained on distance. For first: Drumochta. Then Bonar Bridge. Dornoch. All the places he was wanting to get past, to get through, to get there, get there. And terrifying, that cry of his: *Christ!* Like the man would himself put a sword through Christ's side, Callum used to think, as a boy, he could see it, that image. His father! Christ! Like any second they could die! Like they could crash into the back of something! Drive off the road! His father's profile as he sat beside him in the car, seeing his father out the side of his eye, not daring to say a word, not wanting to breathe even . . . For fear of what his father might do.

'Christ!' Callum says himself now, but he's smiling too. For the atmosphere of his father, the memory of him is like he's in the car with him. All those things about him coming back to Callum, rising up in the car around him like the recordings of those piobaireachds he used to play as they drove north, the sound of them filling up all the space between them and no room for anything else.

'Christ, again!'

And where was his mother then? She was never in the car there with them. It was always only ever him making the journey with his father, enduring that silence of his, or the frightening cries. Having the full sense of him, that man, and his tunes playing top volume off the cassette recorder, no doubt, flying within him all the time – Callum could see the patterns of them played out by his father's fingers on the wheel. That music of his father's and wanting out, is how it felt, sitting there beside him. Like the music itself wanted out, into the hills and the water, the rush of notes seeming to be pushing his father onwards, along with the car getting faster and faster, and pulling him along, great pieces of sound, the music, in his mind unfurling like there may as well be someone coming down off the hills now with a set of pipes to call him in.

How different, for sure, Callum thinks, from how it used to be. And how for a long time by now it's been different. For it wouldn't be for nothing that they'd called his mother from the House to ask for help. So there can be no doubt his father's close to the end, by now, and he must be failing . . . But still Callum can smile a bit, for all that. Thinking of his father not as now but as then. The Christs! The thinking of the past and the sound of it, all green, grey/green, the great swathes of it, like his father tuning up into that first 'A' to match the drone and just beginning. A whole life stretched out in front of you with that sound and his father in the midst of it. Like getting into the tuning practice is what it's like, the notes of the bass and the treble right there, in place and perfectly in tune – and for Callum there's the strength of that thought, nothing about age in it or death, only the tune, being perfectly in tune, and though it's going to take a couple more hours to get up to the House from here, and much easier than back in the old days when the roads weren't as good, the particular emotion that comes direct out of thinking about his father is fixed ready in Callum and holding him, keeping him steady – 'A' to 'A' like a clearly tuned pipe to its drone – while it also moves him on, the ground at his back, beneath his wheels, it's moving him on.

For here he is approaching the summit and just because the roads may be better than before when he was a boy and faster with the new bridges and the curves around the bends straightened, still. The view in the wind-screen's the same. And out to the sides, it's all familiar. 'A' to 'A', indeed. It could as well be that nothing's changed, and he's the same scrawny, scared'y kid coming up through Inverness and Ross, all the way up into the hills you had to go then, to the bridge and over before you could come back wide again and down onto the coast. The whole journey right back with him and travelling with him now. And how he used to get sick on it always, remember? That bit of the road there, and on the long rounding part of the ascent that's behind him now. He still has the memory of the churn-ing in his stomach, all the way from here to where they turned inland at Golspie, the sick taste in your mouth, but at least you were nearly there.

His father stopping for a whisky then. The hotel bar at The Royal, and –

Not much more in it now.

Is what his father would always say. And he'd go inside then, to the bar, and Callum used to sit out on the grass with a bottle of lemonade, maybe, something to take up the time, otherwise just sitting, through the long summer's afternoon, into evening, and his father happier, Callum could hear it, through the open window of the bar, in his voice. He'd be talking by then, not about money or business or what you read in the papers but in his real voice. There were snatches of it earlier, in the car. 'Aye' instead of 'Yes'. Little pieces of Gaelic, maybe. But it was only when he got up here, with people that he knew in The Royal, back in the part of the country where he'd been born, like an animal off the cold hills back where he belonged,* that you could hear the difference, Callum could. In his voice, the sound of him. In his 'Aye'.

No wonder his father had returned here at the end.

~

The day is fully in by now, the grey rain heft of the morning's drive sliced down the centre, like a fish opened clean out of the water and the red of the sun and gold coming through it with Callum at the Pass and over it. And something starting for him here. For Callum. Like a story beginning, not the first part, for that's already been, that part of a piobaireachd set down as ground, but this, another fresh opening broken into – Callum coming into the story now. It's a particular set of notes commencing, the Leumluath it's often made as,** a new way of describing the theme,

---

* In later movements of 'The Big Music' we learn how John Callum MacKay returned to playing his father's instrument, eventually beginning to compose music himself, after his father's death. One of his early compositions, 'The Return', was always supposed to be based on his return to Sutherland after the years away – although notes and details that appear later in 'The Big Music' suggest that the title of that piobaireachd is ambiguous, that 'The Return' may also indicate his return to Margaret MacKay, whom he'd met at The Grey House some years prior to Callum Sutherland's death. Indeed his notes show that the alternative title he gave that piobaireachd is 'Margaret's Song'. The List of Additional Materials shows that piobaireachd as a handwritten manuscript with that second – previously unknown – title. A full list of the compositions of JMS, as he always signed himself, is available in archive, and details of music composed, generally, at The Grey House appear in Appendix 9/ii.

** The Leumluath is a variation that is often included within the second movement or the Taorluath of a piobaireachd and carries the meaning 'leap' (of music) – traditionally the 'Stag's Leap' – to denote the way the notes take a risk on the theme. One of the notebooks of JMS shows him writing about the 'Stag's Leap' as a metaphor for creativity. In general, the Taorluath movement plays hazardously around and about the notes of the theme, barely touching it sometimes as it weaves its own pattern around its shape. So we are left with the strong impression of the theme even so, in the middle of the patterning a variation upon it that's a reaching out, a lengthening, the way Callum's drive north is bringing him in.

For certain roads . . .

You get to a part of them and you feel . . .

There's no going back. For Callum, that's it, that theme's established* – how far along he is, this road here become the only road and the season, the autumn by now, the only season. The further north he goes, the colder it is. And the light, the big fish laid out glistening and new . . . A sense of something torn open to show the day in it. That every minute it seems to enlarge around the car, the road, the man. So he reaches the summit, passes it, and the light is still lifting, it lifts –

That feeling . . .

Darling.

Of coming back to us now.

---

of the music of this variation, even though we have not heard it play, as such. A risky and exciting movement that brings the piobaireachd on and develops its maturity and complexity. Appendix 11 describes the general structure of a piobaireachd, its various movements, etc.

* Appendix 10A: 'The Piobaireachd "Lament for Himself"' gives details of John MacKay's composition, including the original MS of the Urlar. Later, in the List of Additional Materials, we see how this was 'completed' by an anonymous composer to give readers of 'The Big Music' a sense of the full piobaireachd. In that 'finished' version we see how the Taorluath comprises embellishments that play around the various notes and their meanings that were established in the Urlar, e.g. John MacKay's theme, the Lullaby, and, as we will see, the significance of the 'F' note as the note of Love, that also figures throughout 'The Big Music' as a note of return.

insert/John Callum

What happened there? This morning, was it?
　　When was that?
　　What happened?
　　When he could hear the dogs barking and it's woken him —
　　What was that?
　　There was the early start.
　　That was the first thing. The day.
　　Yes.
　　There was that.
　　The first 'A' — to sound, the tuning.
　　And the light, remember? The paleness of the light and of the sky and being out on the hill . . .
　　But then — what? After the light? The other notes to follow? When his father was there, and Callum was there and he heard how they came in, in the singling and the doubling of the tune. *
　　What happened then?
　　After the Lullaby, and the hill?
　　With the dogs still barking? When it's not day now. It's dark now, in this small room — and it's not his own room . . .
　　This small room.

_____

* Refers to the 'dithis' variation on the Urlar on p. 46 of 'The Big Music'.

He knows that, at least. How he's always in the small room now. And how it's dark. How there's a lamp on out in the hall and he can see it from here, from his bed, the light of it, but where he is he can't see where he is lying. And they used to call this the Butler's Room, didn't they? In the old days? Though they never had a butler so why call it that? Some joke of his father's, but his father never told a joke. He never heard him tell a joke.

Yet here he is and he's in the Butler's Room, all right. In the dark. And the dogs are barking so someone's come in. It'll be Callum. For, listen! That's Callum's dog there, barking louder than the rest –

Let me out!

She'll be jumping up at the wire, to get to Callum, against the side of her pen.

Let me out!

So that's Callum come home.

And –

How have you been keeping?

Callum will say to him, will he not?

'Oh, fine' he says.

'This and that. I was up at the back loch, in the green pool. The trout were jumping.' He hears his voice.

'Callum.'

He hears himself saying the boy's name.

'And fine, you know' he's saying. 'The Argo, I've had it all over the place. Right up behind Mhorvaig one day, I've been all over. I've been out for hours, every day, for hours. Keeping an eye on things, the animals, the weather.'

'And fine.'

He says.

'Yes, fine, thanks.'

Talking to Callum now. Giving him the news. Callum replying –

Dad.

Though when did he ever do that? Talk to his son that way? This and that? And why isn't Callum here now? If he's talking to him? Why doesn't Callum come to see him now?

'Eh?'

Dad?

If he's here? If he's come home? Why not let his dog out, who's barking for him and come in here now, with the Labrador, to see him? He could come and sit here on the end of the bed.

Dad?

Though when did he ever do that?

Sit on his bed that way?

And have the dog at his feet?

'Eh?'

When did he let the boy ever come in? Though he could do it now, Callum.

'Just come in.'

Or does Callum not know about his father lying in the dark? Lying here and waiting? His father. Whose father? Callum's? His own father?

Yes, him.

That other Callum. The 'A' note – because the 'A' is always the tune's note, the Piper's note.

Because his father was always called Callum, too.*

So it must be him, his father.

The 'A', the octave note.

But Johnnie is Callum's father, too.

So the boy . . .

Should just come in?

No, that's all wrong because his father was up on the hill with him this morning. Remember? He was in the theme, and the singling, and the doubling. He has it written down already. And Callum was there, too. They were all three of them together. The father and the son, there before him on the path this morning, and they were walking together and he was thinking about the lessons, with all the 'A' notes and perfectly,

---

* All first-born sons in the Sutherland family were christened John, however John MacKay's father was born Roderick and his name changed to John following the death of his elder brother – though he always went by the name Callum, also a strong Sutherland family name. Details of family history and genealogy appear in Appendix 6/ii; iv.

perfectly in tune. Thinking about being with his father and his mother away somewhere else in the House, sitting quietly somewhere . . . In the little Schoolroom at the top of the House, maybe, she was there. Remember? With the striped ball? The toy ship? Only he wasn't with her, was he? Johnnie? In that place? Where the lovely toys were? With his mother? He was away somewhere else again and with his father, it was his father shouting and the – 'Play it again!' The having to play it all over again, that little bit of the tune, for he had it wrong, that bit, the notes were wrong. His father saying to him to – 'Play it again!' And the two of them there in his father's study, the Music Room it was called, and he was just a boy, he was just a boy . . .

'Again!'

For the notes were wrong. They were all wrong.

So – 'No! Play it again! And again!'

That Callum.

The father.

His hand with a cuff, the green of it, the rough tweed.

'Again!'

His father shouted.

'Again!'

He must play it again!

Though he's not a boy now.

His father dead for forty years. His mother thirty.

And his son is not here, his Callum.

He never let him come in.

He's alone in the House.

He's alone here.

In the dark.

first variation/The Grey House: an account

The foundations of the building, which in turn extend to form the central part of the house which is now the main sitting room and the little study annexe off to the side – these date from the mid-1700s. That's when John Roderick MacKay or 'First John' Sutherland, of the parish of Rogart, the great-great-great-great-grandfather of this present Callum, six generations before he was born, formally put up a place on this flat part of the land, near the end of the strath between the two hills – Mhorvaig and Luath.* This area takes more shelter than the surrounding landscape, lying as it does also in the lee of Ben Rhuar and so is fronted away from the worst of the winter winds. The place before then was no more than a sheiling, a bit of a byre for some sheep and an enclosure where a shepherd might stay.

    This was in the days of the great cattle drives over from Rogart all the way through the rest of Sutherland, passing through the strath here at Ben Mhorvaig and down into Easter Ross and onto the Black Isle for the Autumn Markets.**

---

* Appendices 1–3 contain all information on the North East region pertaining to 'The Big Music' and relevant maps etc. can be found at the back of the book and in Appendices 1 and 2.
** In particular, Appendix 3/iv depicts a version of landholding in the region that differs from the usual post-Clearances narrative; see too family records etc. contained in Appendices 4–9.

In these days there were few places for men and beasts to shelter. There were byres such as the one mentioned above along the route, but for the most part the shepherds and drovers would manage by knowing certain crofters as they made their way south and staying with various families as they moved their herds across the hills and down onto the flat lands below, where there might be some grazing. If there were enemies, old feuds, some marriage that had gone sour or a marriage that should have never happened at all . . . Well, there'd be no shelter for that man. He must make do, then, at the base of a tree, or in some kind of little dug-out into the side of a hill, some place the deer might have used for shelter in heavy snows, or taking refuge in a little wood, maybe, such as that group of rowans that are down by the Black Water near this House of which I'm writing.

Anyhow, enough to say that as the years passed old John's son, Roderick Mor, he was called, John MacKay Sutherland's grandfather's grandfather,* seemed to have been a great tacksman on the Sutherland Estate, back in the time when to be fair and reasonable and sound at that kind of work, which might be unfavourable in a great many places in the Highlands, could go fairly to a man's advantage. For in that period of employment he earned certain privileges to work a piece of land which was not seen to be of any use to the estate as it was way up high on the hill, and half of it in scree, but which in turn he was able to clear somewhat of the rock and to drain the boggy south side and could extend it then to form a kind of 'corridor' that sat between one side of the county to another and which would much later become the main route from the east south, not only for the black cattle but also for the sheep. So he had the foresight then to see land not only as a piece in itself but as a part of a bigger pattern, something that could be seen as a particular section of the entire region, connecting it, one part to another and not just of someone else's portion. As though it were a small estate, though not like that, not so grand – but nevertheless a part of the country that would be his own.** Roderick Sutherland could

---

* Appendix 6/ii, iii and iv have details of the history of The Grey House and the Sutherland family who lived there.
** Other examples of similar types of independent ownership can be found in various histories of the Highlands; also Appendix 5/i and iv direct the reader as to how life was

see that. And he had the wit, too, and foresight, you could say, to build on the small base of stone and flattened land that had always been there as a dwelling place, and to mark up the sides of its walls into more of a croft house, a longhouse, than a mere byre. This way, he could offer those passing through something like proper accommodation, a place to sleep, to shelter, and in time he arranged this in such a manner so as to be like some form of hostelry, taking a kind of a tithe from the shepherds who passed through and stopped there in the form of those animals they couldn't keep on the move south so that over time this meant he could build up a flock of sheep more than the one or two he'd always managed to keep for himself. And he was able to manage it, too, that those same shepherds, who'd paid him in tithes of a newborn lamb or a ewe injured or old or in other ways animals not good anyway for the journey, could take in turn his own beasts to market on his account, and sell them there for him – so he could spend his time in something like leisure then, in the summer months, later. Only it was music that was his leisure, and some might say that art of any kind will give you no leisure at all, only a kind of endless restlessness and yearning. To find and make more and more time for it. To make it better, clearer. To create the space for its devotion and study and practice. And certainly this was how the music developed at the House and became strong and was refined – because of the way it was worked into the day and the life and the routine there. That art might become part of work, was how it started, part of the life of the Grey Longhouse, as it was called then, and in time to become the work itself – to be an end in itself. But not like any other work that people from around there knew, for this same end held within it its own beginnings, with always more to discover, more ways in which by attending to it one might learn and grow. So the Sutherland family described the music that was their art. By then they were able to afford to set aside dedicated time for playing, composing, to be autonomous that way – and there is evidence, from fragments of tunes that survive from this period, and indications of a rudimentary kind of piping school that would be built on and developed to the full over the

---

lived at The Grey House over this period.

succeeding generations* – the playing and its development, its processes, connected only to itself. Needing nothing else for its completion or beginning. Only its own first few notes to start it and then it was real.

Anyhow, be that as it may, the point here is the beginning of an enterprise that came to be known, by the time of Roderick's son, John Roderick Callum (known as John 'Elder'), across the Highlands as 'Callum's Rest'** – the comforting walls of a house on the flat of a bare hill, at a time when a man may need it most. And it became something that the Lairg shepherds would talk about as they came over, getting nearer to that place: how much they were looking forward to the warmth of the fire there, the bowl of soup prepared by John's wife, Anna Alexandra,*** and the music that would be heard while the sheep too might have some shelter in the byre out of those winds.

Now all this marks a different kind of climate, you might say, to that which raged and made a thin kind of air with snow in it around so many other parts of the Highlands. For Roderick Sutherland, and by then his son John, with their own sheep and cattle which, by this time, had increased greatly in number, could challenge in the markets for better prices for animals they themselves had raised and tended and so were not like those beasts that had just been collected and driven by shepherds who were working in bondage for the estate. All this put the Sutherlands in a better position than most, this enterprise of their family strengthening their resolve to build on it further, increasing the value of the land on the tops by burning off the heather there and turning it to some reasonable

---

* The sensibility of this early 'school' reached its apotheosis in the 1950s when John MacKay's father, still known to this day as the great 'Modernist' piper of the twentieth century, established the famous 'Winter Classes' that were held as part of the Piping School formally set up by his father, John Callum MacKay, at The Grey House.

** Appendix 2/ii carries details of local place names; and Appendices 1 and 2, also Endpapers, show relevant maps.

*** Appendix 6/i–iv give details of family names and genealogy; also Appendices 4/ii and iii give details of the construction of the House. The List of Additional Materials contains information relating to the domestic archive of The Grey House including recipes etc. Appendix 5/ii refers to the role of women, rooms of the House and their use, along with domestic notes, etc.

grazing, taking what they had and managing to make something more of it even so. And that's not to give the impression here that any resented the tithe that had been taken in the past, in exchange for shelter, for the opposite was the case. Agreement had been made and understood amongst the men themselves, at the beginning, and in time, as John Roderick developed these arrangements further, the way 'Through Callum's' became known, so it was established that the big estates of the district would also pay a reasonable fee for the improvement of the route for the good it did both their animals and the men they had working for them, that would in turn favour their own fortunes. So too should I mention that, in part, there was good feeling for this enterprise because of the music that this area of Sutherland was known for, so the men who passed through the district viewed the family Sutherland as friends, as people who, through hard work, had made something of their lives and yet were as they were themselves, with frugal ways and making of little education as much as they could, and with none of the glitter of the landed classes that had the big houses tucked away into the hills for their pleasure. Indeed, it was the music more than anything else set them apart – as old John Roderick had been known as a great piper in his boyhood and his son had continued that tradition, and so had his son, too, John 'Elder', known as 'Callum', who was taught, it is said, by the last MacCrimmon* and was a composer whose work was known at the time by Angus MacKay of Raasay and is written of in accounts of that time.** And in the same way, as the century

---

* The Crunluath movement of 'The Big Music' gives details of the MacCrimmon family and their role as musicians and composers of great piobaireachd from the 1500s onwards. There are details of the various generations of MacCrimmon pipers and their famous piping school of Skye, listing Iain MacCrimmon as the last member of that family, who died in 1822. It is believed that John Sutherland may, as a young man, have taken some instruction from him, around the turn of the nineteenth century; references in letters and journals of that time attest to 'much learning and knowledge' that was 'passed on by the great M'; 'M played the Lament for me on the chanter, and sang it to me as he went'; 'Skye is a place wet and grey but full of music'; also the Bibliography lists certain books that include information on the MacCrimmons and their legend.

** See Bibliography/Music: Piobaireachd/primary – MacKay, *A Collection of Ancient Piobaireachd*.

progressed, and the generations continued, many felt, by the time of John Callum MacKay, that the Sutherlands had been a family that had used its wit and cleverness to put back into the way of life up in that part of the hills something of the goodness of the land and its ways that, over the time of the Clearances, had, for many, been lost.*

The music of course played its large part there. Giving life and a colour, a sense of the past and its traditions to the present way of doing things, making occupations that were otherwise quite simple – some may say menial and poor – to have dignity in their own right, laid down as they could be upon a grand ground.** For a man tired, living outdoors with animals, to be able to stop at this part of the world and hear the piobaireachd that he's heard his grandfather talk about or sing, hear again a tune that comes right back from the grand times of the MacCrimmons,*** to hear again the complexity and the depth of that music that reached back through centuries yet had relevance to him now . . . It lent structure to his world but softness too. After a hard day of work and great physical labour and exertion the music gave easing place, that rest.

So, in this way, life continued in this part of Sutherland, through the 1800s and into the turn of the new century when John MacKay's father, Roderick Callum, was born. By now the House had itself well settled as a place where people could come and hear a tune, and where they could send their boys for some tuition and to learn canntaireachd and the true

---

* The terrible history of the Clearances, a time that has been described as a version of ethnic cleansing when families throughout certain Highland areas were forcibly removed from their homes and repatriated, has been extensively recorded and researched. Details for further reading are available in the Bibliography; also see Appendix 2/i and ii in this book.

** The Third Movement of 'The Big Music' has sections that describe how The Grey House of the Sutherland family developed, over time, into a great centre for piping. Appendix 5, relating to domestic life, also gives more details of its day-to-day activities as a place that was both a home and a school; and the List of Additional Materials shows various relevant documents.

*** The Crunluath movement of 'The Big Music' contains more information about the MacCrimmon family of hereditary pipers; also Appendices 4, 12 and 13 give an introduction to and history of piobaireachd that relate to its earliest compositions and are relevant here.

phrasing and the marking up of the tunes so as to be able to play them thoroughly and well. Everyone then would talk back to the great days of Skye and the MacCrimmons' School of Piping on that island, all would take a dram, have stories of their own then to follow – about that incredible family of musicians, and about their tunes and what they knew of the origins of those tunes, or how they remembered various people playing then a certain way – and they would make a toast or two to the assembled company, that here they were in Sutherland, three hundred years later, and setting up a School of their own, you might say, where the pipes were played and compositions made in the proper style of the old laments and salutes.

Johnnie's father, then, this John Callum, known, as his grandfather had been before him, as Callum, 'Himself',* grew up with these men and boys around him, some of whom were near his own age, who might come to stay for a part of the winter when there was little to do on their own crofts and holdings up in Caithness or down by the sea, with the weather too brutal to take out the herring boats that time of year.** So they would gather at the House through parts of those winter months, boys and their fathers, old men who had fathers who as boys had known old John 'Elder' when he was an old man, who may have learned some of the old tunes from him that they could get them down on paper to remember.*** And these the tunes their sons were now playing in the annexe of the House, away from the kitchen and the rooms for sleeping, in a room that became

---

* Earlier pages of 'The Big Music' have described how John MacKay's father was given the name John after his elder brother's death, but always was known as Callum, the name of his grandson, whom he never met. The Crunluath movement also tells more about the musical history of John MacKay Sutherland, the subject of 'Lament for Himself', by way of giving information about his father's teaching methods and famous 'Winter Classes' that he himself emulated by way of his summer parties and invitations to pipers to come to The Grey House and play and give instruction there.
** Appendices 1–3 give the history of the North East Highland district and describes its rural economy and industries.
*** This refers to the generation of John Callum MacKay (1835–1911), who first encouraged the writing down of tunes as a way of teaching them, in addition to the traditional canntaireachd sung method; also Appendix 9/iii and the Crunluath and A Mach sections are relevant here, as are Appendix 5/iii and certain documents in the List of Additional Materials.

known by them all as the 'Study', also 'the Big Music Room' – and you can imagine the feeling it must have given those who gathered there, people who worked outdoors in all conditions, who had little in the way of material goods, who may have crofts of their own but paid hard for them, or were indentured to the factors of the estates that were managed . . . To come into this House that was like a free house, a free-held building and not part of any estate but sitting there on the hill in its corridor of land and no man could take it . . . And to have something of a room called a 'Study', a 'Music Room' – you can think about that. What it did to the minds of people who came there. That there was a room for the playing of 'The Big Music' . . . In a house that was established for teaching and learning . . . How it enlarged the spaces in the visitors' minds. Sent them home again in the early spring with a sense of their own place in the world, with dignity and pride and a largeness come out of the music itself, that there was more to life than work and feeling poor and powerless. That you had this other thing in you, as part of who you were, that held you up.

So John's father grew up, following the lessons of his father before him, to become a great teacher himself and known, not just through the Highlands but down south in Edinburgh and further, in London even, where by now the Society for Piobaireachd* had been established and 'Young Callum', as he was known to the old pipers of his father's day, 'Callum Og', some of them called him, with a laugh but in deference to the MacCrimmons' famous son,** was invited over and over to come down there and play and to talk and to give his own private lessons to those in the south who might not otherwise, apart from having the manuscripts of the old music to hand, have a chance to hear it played in the right way, with the right phrasing and nuance.

---

* Appendix 13/i gives the history of piping music and in 12/x, with particular reference to the work of Archibald Campbell and the Piobaireachd Society.
** Callum would have been nicknamed 'Og' perhaps as a way of differentiating him from his father, John Callum, who had also been a teacher and known for his music school. In this way it is also a friendly reference to one of the MacCrimmon sons who was similarly differentiated from his father by the addition of the suffix 'Og', meaning 'younger' in Gaelic. See Glossary and Bibliography for further details.

Therefore the House became well known throughout Britain at that time by pipers, and was referred to, though unofficially, as 'The Highland School for Piping'.* And we may consider here the significance of such a 'School' in that part of the country then. For this was the time before the First World War and the area was still held back, you might say, by an old economy, and by the stripping of the population through the work of the Clearances – with many still alive to remember how that was, to be turned out of a home, a place where you had given birth to the babies and nursed the old – and all this to be argued over, of course, and this not the place for it here, but to say just that there are many too who also believe that time of our history was a natural thing in so far as it was brutal, as natural things often are, who will say that the land could not support the kinds of numbers were living there, and badly living, many, on bits of food and only barely managing to survive in dark places in Caithness and in the Sutherland Hills. And others will say it was the fashion for the grand houses and their sports that caused such disruption – that there are no economics in it at all and nothing natural in it or fair – with the land to be kept apart from the many just for the summer shooting or the salmon for the few . . .

But as all these arguments go on, here is this House standing, and people coming to the House, and the man who lives in it and his wife known all over the country and respected for what they are doing here, what they have done. Making more of simple talk or the songs that may have been sung in blackhouses at night, through ceilidhs or for weddings, creating more than just a kind of entertainment that would simply exchange information in the traditions of spoken word. Because now you have a formal culture: music written down, performed in Edinburgh and in London, competitions established all through the Highlands and through Scotland to support and encourage technique, the art, the excellence of the music.**

---

* Appendix 9 describes The Grey House as a Piping School, its history; details.
** There is information on the history of the teaching of the bagpipe and piobaireachd, of Skye and the MacCrimmons and later music schools, traditional and contemporary, throughout the narrative of 'The Big Music' – particularly in its Crunluath movement, and in certain of its Appendices, particularly Appendix 11 onwards.

And at the heart of all of these activities, by the mid-twentieth century, is John MacKay's father, Roderick John Callum, 'Himself', son of John Callum, and before him John 'Elder', son of Roderick Mor, son of 'First John' Sutherland.

Piper. Teacher. Composer. This was the man who was Johnnie's father. Who stood over him as the boy played. The one who shouted at him that word 'Again!' That man.

two/second paper

They knew at the House that Callum would be on his way. Sarah had phoned and spoken to Helen first and then to Margaret and said that she'd talked to Callum yesterday afternoon and that he'd leave London as soon as he could. This after Margaret had already called her, after the long morning out on the hill, finding the old man up there having got all that way with the baby in his arms, but Iain faster in the end – and he was havering by then, old Johnnie, out in the rain and thinking his father was with him, and that Callum was there . . . But Iain had had the injection ready and they were able to give him that, get the baby safely in her mother's arms and dry and fed, old Sutherland slumped like a body into the seat of the Argocat, so it took no time at all to get him back to the House and into bed and the doctor was called, though what would he do, or say – there'd be nothing.

In his dreams all that day the old man was still talking to his father. It would be the afternoon but he was well away from them by then and thinking he was with his son and with his father as though they were both right there in the room with him, laughing with them both at times so you may have thought they were just there at his bed. Just as up on the tops this morning you'd have thought the same thing, that they were standing there beside him – his father and his son – you'd have believed from the way he turned back on the path to talk with them both that they were present, not just ideas or hopes in his mind.

In the end that's what made Margaret want to phone them in London
and tell them, tell Sarah that Johnnie had had a turn, out there on the hill.
Not tell her what he'd done, of course, with the baby — that would just
bring the police in, or Sarah would find a way for locking him up in that
hospital of hers for good — but just to let her know that help was needed
now, that they could no longer manage on their own. And that he'd been
calling for Callum, Johnnie had, that he was lying in his bed now and asking for his son.

So there in turn Sarah had got hold of Callum, she'd called him at
work where he was trying to finish a project he'd got started, a big project,
Sarah said, and he'd been going over the final drawings for it when she'd
called. So he would have been busy thinking about that, she said, and not
about his father at all but about the plans before him and perhaps thinking about his wife's birthday, too, for it was Anna's birthday that next day
and he might have been thinking about a dinner or doing something to
celebrate in the evening ahead . . .

But all that changed when the call from his mother came through.

'I need you to go up there' she'd said. 'I need you to leave straight away.'

Which is why Callum had done what he did. Missing his wife's birthday and just getting in the car. Not bothering with organising a flight
because that wouldn't have been much quicker in the end, he worked out,
by the time you allowed for the schedules and getting out to the airport
from work and then the hiring of a car. It would be easier simply to get
up in London and be gone.

'See you soon' he'd whispered to Anna in the dark before leaving, and
kissed her, going through to his sons' bedroom to kiss them, too, on the
tops of their heads. 'I'll be back in a few days.' He'd had a couple of hours'
sleep, no more, the night before, but was wide awake, alert, ready to be
on his way. The feeling in him then that what he was doing was the right
thing, he would say later, getting up like that and leaving, and that long
before the coming dawn and later on the road when the knowledge in
him had fully risen that here's the right place to be, coming up here to be
with his father. That none of the rest, the sleeping wife or children, the
business plans, none of it matters as much as getting to the House. The

seconds counting off, the distance closing. That nothing is as important as that. His father's life.

~

For all that, though, he takes his time arriving. Having stopped off, finding himself waiting, hanging back, at the service station where he lingers for petrol, water. For all the sense of urgency before him and at his back, still he found himself there near Clashmore and stopping at a services again. Checking the tyres. Buying some food, fruit, sandwiches, a coffee that he drinks right there in the forecourt, leaning up against the side of his car, reading over the headlines in the papers that are bound up outside, looking at advertisements for chocolate and lottery tickets and cigarettes. Taking time, more time. Then after that, driving some more he stops again, switches off the engine again, at the side of the road, twice, just before the turnoff, trying to call the House on the mobile, on the clear open bit of the road there, but of course there's no reception, and then again, later at the pub in Rogart, going into the bar but nobody he knows or recognises, still . . . He found himself anyhow taking a seat at the bar, buying a beer, and waiting some more.

So that finally when he gets up the road and turns off into the farm track it's late afternoon and the light's near gone. Here's the sky that's been all around him from dawn to long morning and silver grey, clouded as it was back over the Moray Firth with a kind of a sun in it beneath the cloud, like an underbelly and soft, but since then, leaving Rogart, all that's been getting darker, and darker still, so all he sees as he drives the long narrow track to the House is the peaty bank cut in deep either side, reflected back in the car's headlights as black welts in the heathery dark grey land.

Then he comes around the final corner and there it is, lights on in the side lodge but the House itself, its peaked gables in darkness, just a silhouette against the last of the colour, when he turns off the car's lights, of the sky.

The End of the Road.

A good name for a house, Callum thinks. A good name. Ailte vhor Alech. The End of the Road. A good name for a place that has nothing more ahead of it, and now that he's here in the growing dark, no sense of anything behind him either. Better than The Grey House, 'the End of the Road'. And better in English, too, than the Gaelic that makes it sound less lonely than it is. Just say 'End of the Road' instead.* When the track he's been driving on has disappeared into shadows and all around is the sense of building night, the hulk of the hills, the sweep of distance contained within the quantities of the night time . . . The Grey House. The end of the road, all right.

Margaret's at the door in the time it's taken to turn up into the drive-way.

'We thought it would be today you'd come' she says to him as she approaches.

Nothing about her changed as far as Callum can see, though it's been a good ten years.

'Your mother said, when we spoke to her . . .'

'Margaret' he says.

'Hello, Callum.'

'How are you?'

There she is. Still the same stature, the same calm. He takes her hand, gives her the customary kiss upon the cheek and the dogs in the kennels up behind the generator have started barking. It's the strange car, their sense of an arrival, that's set them off.

'You'll see a difference in him' Margaret says, straight away. 'We've had the doctor in but —' She pauses. The dogs' barking increases. They're wanting to find out who it is, who's there. 'I know I don't see it in the same way' she is saying, 'when he's here all the time, as he has been, and these last few years . . . But even so. Just today, after yesterday. I've noticed him quickly going down, going right down. We've all noticed it. Quiet!' she calls to the dogs then — as though she's only just become aware of them —

---

* All references to the Sutherland family home, in the Appendices and List of Additional Materials, and throughout 'The Big Music', refer to 'The Grey House', that name being a version of the building in its earliest form as a traditional eighteenth-century grey longhouse. NB: There is a piobaireachd 'The End of the Road' by JMS that may be in Callum's mind at this point.

for their barking sounds desperate. 'Quiet!' With Callum standing there, the strange car — it's as though the dogs can sense him and know that it's him, that it's Callum, even though they're not his dogs and the kennels are turned the other way from the House where he is standing, still the sound of their barking makes it seem as though they all this minute want out, to fling themselves out of their enclosures and rush out to meet him, whirl all about him, barking, to greet him. *Hello! It's me! It's me! You're home!*

Margaret is still talking. 'You'll notice' she is saying, 'that in his mind — he's wandering now. Imagining. Seeing things. The doctor says it's to be expected.'

They've started walking towards the House and the sound of barking is even more frantic. *It's me! It's me!* Callum feels as though he can barely hear Margaret's voice over it. There's the sound, too, of some of the larger dogs thrashing themselves up against the wire meshing of their pens, he can hear that too, through their barking and Margaret's voice. *It's me! Let me out! Let me come and say hello! Please!* As though it's his return they've been waiting for all this time, that it's Callum they've been waiting for, all this time they've been waiting.

'He's not the same as he was' Margaret is saying. 'And yesterday . . .'

Yet really there is only the one old retriever who would remember him. Callum stops, as though just now he's recognised that one particular bark. A pale yellow Labrador who he used to take out on the hills when she was just a young dog, in the same way that he'd taken her mother and her mother's sister. So this last dog of his now is the one whose bark is louder than the rest — or no, not louder, more insistent: *Let me out!* she's crying. *Let me come to you!* Just the one dog, then, but making all the dogs bark louder as though they too remember him, as though they're all of them not Margaret and Iain's dogs but that they're his dogs, Callum's dogs, and he's home to take them out again.

'Where did you find him —' he starts to say, but Margaret's pulling him inside against the cold, and this noise, the sound of the animals at their enclosure.

It's me!

Please!

It's —

Then she closes the door behind him.

'He'd not just gone for a walk, you see' she says then. And suddenly it's very quiet. 'He was far away, Callum, high up in the hills.' She waits a couple of seconds. 'For the best part of the morning' she says. 'He must have taken himself off at dawn, Iain thinks it must have been, for he'd gone a fair distance before he got to him. And the weather had turned, you can feel it now, winter's on its way. And worse. For he had with him . . .' She goes before him, opening the kitchen door that leads from her little hallway. 'Well' she says, 'you'll find out soon enough, I suppose. Helen —' She holds the door open for him, looks at him.

'What?'

'We couldn't tell your mother that part, though. She'd worry. And Helen —'

'What about Helen?'

But by now they're inside the kitchen and it's bright, and strange all at once, to be inside and in the warm. Callum feels faint, suddenly, with it — the lights on everywhere and hearing Helen's name. *What about Helen? What was it that Margaret just said about Helen?*

'Here we are' Margaret is saying, to him, and, he realises, to Iain, where Iain is sitting at the table, with the guns and a bottle of whisky and a tumbler set before him. He looks up at Callum, nods.

'Callum.'

'Iain.'

And there's a pause then, like there's always a pause. As though the time between when he last saw Iain was nothing, as though the drive up here was no distance at all, as though it makes no difference at all actually whether Callum was here or not. As though nothing makes any difference.

Yet —

Helen.

There was her name.

What about Helen?

Twice Margaret saying her name and nearly something but not saying it.

Helen.

Helen.

Like Callum would say her name a hundred times over and still be wanting to say it:

Helen.

Helen.

Helen.

Helen.

But instead he says, 'How are you, Iain?'

It's what he does, of course. No matter what happens, what has gone before, what might come after. Even now, with circumstances so changed, and him being here for his father and the way his father is and something happened, something taken place and twice Margaret not finishing the sentence that she started with Helen in it . . . Still it's what he does, what he always does when he comes here, nods, 'How are you, Iain?', then shakes his hand. As if any of that might mean anything to Iain, too. As if any greeting he might give would ever change the way things are between him and that man. It's the same now as it's always been, whether yesterday, or ten years ago, or when he was a teenager or when he was a boy.

'You're well?' he'll ask Iain. 'Things have been going okay?'

'Okay enough' Iain says. He unscrews the head of the barrel, looks down it, takes up the cloth again. 'You'll know from your mother Helen's had a baby now.'

Iain turns away then, gets up from the table, lets the words settle.

'Just this past month she's back from the hospital' he says.

Callum looks at him. At Iain's back. 'No, I didn't –' he says, starts to answer but he can't speak. He just stands there. It's as though he's waiting, only he's not waiting.

Iain turns around and picks up something on the table.

Then Callum says 'No, I didn't know. Margaret?'

But Margaret's busy at the bench.

'Congratulations, then' Callum says

'Aye, well . . .' Iain looks briefly at him, just for a second, then sits down again, continues with his work.

'She's a little one, all right.'

It seems to have gone very still in the room, like there's no air, nothing to say, no way of saying it, but then Margaret starts talking to him, about Helen, about the child. She's at the kettle, still doing something at the bench but telling Callum now how old the child is, and her name.

'Katherine. Her name is Katherine' Margaret is saying. 'Katherine Anna.'

And Callum can take none of it in. Anna? That's his wife's name, isn't it? Anna? So he does hear that. He takes that in.

'And she *is* a Katherine, too' Margaret is saying. 'Dark-haired but fair. My mother was a Katherine. She was Mary Katherine.'

But Callum's not taking any of it in.

Only:

Helen's had a baby now.

Helen.

So . . . Katherine.

And Anna . . .

They're somewhere else, it seems. Along with everyone else, Margaret and Iain and his father . . .

When he's supposed to be here for his father, arriving here for his father – not this, to hear this. To be hearing this, but not hearing . . . Is not why he's come. It's supposed to be for his father is why he's come, he's here for him, not anyone else. It's his father who is waiting for him . . . Waiting for him to go through to him, to say hello . . .

'She's beautiful, of course' Margaret is saying. 'And Helen is enjoying her. After she'd finished helping here last summer, she went back to Glasgow, but she came home again. To have the baby. To stay. She's here for good now, she says.'

'But –'

Helen.

Still Callum can't speak.

'She says it's for good, anyhow' Margaret is saying. 'She says she doesn't want to leave again.'

Helen.

'I –'

He starts again, stops. Because that's the only part he's really heard.

Helen. That Helen's here with them. That she's somewhere in the House.

'You'll see her later, in a bit' Margaret is saying. 'When she's settled the baby down, she'll come in and say hello.'

Slowly, slowly, Callum lets a few seconds pass, watching Iain with the guns, letting himself breathe in, breathe out, while Margaret is still talking — about his father now, how they've moved him, some weeks ago, from his own room to the little bedroom off the hallway downstairs. That he can't sit up at all, these last couple of days. After what went on. That resting is all he can manage now, and for a while has been so very drawn, and tired and frail.

'Helen noticed the change in him' Margaret is saying, 'after being away, she could see how he'd aged.'

And slowly, slowly with each second it comes back to Callum what he must do, how he must be. How, despite everything, he must manage to behave as he always does when he's arrived here. Stand, for a time, certain words exchanged. Iain will offer him a dram, he'll say thanks but later maybe, and then in the past Margaret would have taken him through to the main house, to the sitting room, the 'Music Room' they always called it, where his father would be waiting.

Which is what he must do. Go to his father now, to see him. What he will do.

But not just yet. For a few seconds more he must just stand here, wait. Talk a little. Nod his head, perhaps. Yes, he might say. Or, No. But not go through to see his father yet. Not just yet.

'So you got here at last' is what his father always used to say when he arrived here.

Even so, not yet.

'Took your time, didn't you?'

Because everything is changed now.

You'll know from your mother Helen's had a baby.

And no, he didn't know. And neither is his father through there in the small sitting room, where he always used to be when Margaret took him through, sitting in the big armchair with a whisky in his hand, those pipes of his resting at his feet.

Because everything is different, everything changed.

And he can't stand here any longer. Callum needs to sit down. Take the dram when it's offered. Needs to sit, wait. With somewhere in the House, Helen. And somewhere else, but not the little sitting room, his father.

And so he does, sit, and when Iain asks him, nods, yes, and Margaret puts a glass on the table.

'Your health.'

For he needs to let some time pass here before he moves towards what will happen next. When he sees Helen. When he sees his father lying in a bed.

insert/John Callum

But his father has been dead for forty years! And his mother thirty! So what good now remembering all that before, clear out of the past?

What good any of it coming back to him – the House, and the way his father was, and his mother? For it's been his whole adult life since they've been gone.

His mother. His father.

And he was a boy who grew up, and there was a child of his own then, a wife of his own – and now she's away from him, too, back in London and a voice on the telephone's who she is.

A whole life gone by.

With marriage in it, a business.

And money that was made and lost, and affairs of this place to manage, this House where he is now, in this small room within these stone walls, and outside all around him the wide hills.

I don't mind . . .

And he's still here. In the dark. He's all alone – and how long, lying here? Feels like a lifetime, yet – what? Two days? Yesterday? When he went off and all for the tune, to make the tune, find the end for the tune.

'I'll not be back!'

Remember?

Not ever to come back! To his father and his father's damn music! Yet here he is. And remembering. Even when it's no good remembering.

When it's all of it gone into dark and lost. When everything he might have had, he let it go.

And there was a lovely note.

The clear, long 'F' note and he can hear her in it . . .

In the note that's there in the Lullaby . . .

But did he get her fully in the tune? Was that note enough?

When she was lovely and he needed her?

The long, lovely note?

For he can't know now whether he has her there, truly, in the tune. Though the 'F' is there, he has heard the 'F', along with other notes – listen! He can hear them. He can remember them all. And the little Lullaby – it's safe. The main part, the theme. That's set down and in notes, the written manuscript up at the hut, put down in pencil first, and then in manuscript inked in.

So safe, safe. That part in black ink. And the 'F', he knows he's heard it, set into the ground that's laid out and protected on his desk by the window up there in the hills, laid out on the papers where he's to finish the whole, when he writes the whole piobaireachd out with the end and the new beginning.* But whether that clear note will be enough for her? To be able to sound? When he makes the Taorluath, will it be enough? The 'F'? For her, that she can be in the tune, be able to sound? The note of 'F' he's already heard enough for Margaret and to hold it? He sings the phrase now, that he knows, aloud . . .** And beautiful, the 'F' to 'G' – with

---

* The Crunluath A Mach movement is the final completion of a piobaireachd and in 'The Big Music' (e.g. three/first paper, pp. 183, 184, 185 etc.) we see examples of John MacKay's notes and thoughts about the composition of his piobaireachd, its beginnings laid down and intimations of how it may end. Appendix 10/ii may also be of interest here, giving further details of how 'Lament for Himself' is constructed.

** For those who read music it may be possible to sing through the lovely phrase of the second line – indeed, the whole piobaireachd can be sung or played using the manuscript that appears in the List of Additional Materials. One must bear in mind, however, when playing or singing from this manuscript, the slightly different tuning of a chanter that gives the bagpipe scale a subtle shifted octave to the one we are used to – one, experts say, that is more attuned to an ancient Greek pipe, the type that was played to classical audiences by

the child coming out into the theme. For remember that part? When it came to him? Of the little one? Is why he needed her in his arms before, her cry like a beginning, let out clear and strong into the open air. Is how it should be. 'F' to 'G'. Not gone into darkness then but high clean notes with tiny, tiny doublings to keep the tune going, on and for ever . . . Like that. Hear them? All the lovely notes? So, yes. It's there, the tune. The dark not got in. Only 'F' to 'G' with a lullaby and he'll get back to the hut where he wanted to take her and in time to finish it.

'F' to 'G', 'F' to 'A'

'F' to 'G', 'A' to 'A' . . .

And he will. Get back there. The place like his mind, the little secret place, set in amongst the hills and no one knows about it, no one can find him there. With all the papers and his manuscripts about him and he can stay there, he can never come back — and maybe he'll find out there whether the notes he has already are enough? Whether the tune has enough? If he can just get there, stay there. To that place he built for himself all those years ago, a place that's for himself, for his own music — and not his father's music. Only there will he be able to hear, if he has all the notes written down. He can see the manuscript lying on the desk by the window that looks out onto the loch — he can see it from where he's lying. And listen! He can hear the notes again that are already put down. From the hills to the secret hut, the ending and the beginning. And his mother there, it's all written down, and his father seated before him and the chanter practice going slow, over and over, playing the same bit of the tune until he got it right.

Again!

So the first movement is done by now, and the second arriving, something unexpected come out of it, clear out of the Taorluath that's coming to him now.* There's the new set of notes' variations — alongside the past

---

way of preparing them for one of the great tragedies of Aeschylus or Sophocles.

* Refers to this section of 'The Big Music' that is starting to take shape here. Also Appendices 10/i and 11 describe the movements of a piobaireachd and how the traditional structure relates to 'Lament for Himself'.

that sounds like the old: the ancient 'A' of the drone and a fall from the high gracenotes to the theme, a different finish for the third line, just slightly different,* containing all the thought and the patterning of the movement that will follow. For it will follow.

All notes he might play for his father.

'Can you hear them, Daddy? Can you?'

Though his father has been dead for —

what?

— and his mother —

. . . Yet it's not thirty years! Can't be! Nor forty!

For that part he heard just then, with his father in the study, wanting for him to play those notes, over and over, and his mother somewhere upstairs and he can hear her, too, in the music, walking through the rooms of the House . . . This part is as clear in the tune just as surely as the baby's cry. Both his parents there. Just as fully sounded as the Lullaby, this part as fine as the earlier notes, and strong. Not dead at all but rising up to him, in that change of the sequence in the third line, in the second half of the third line — is where the idea came from. That third bar of the third line. Just changed enough to make everything set to change.

From the 'G' to 'B' to 'E'

'G' to 'A' with the 'D'

'F' to 'G', 'E' to 'A'

And they say that, don't they? About the Taorluath? He's said it often enough himself. That it's a movement that can rise up at you that way, unexpected, a Leumluath, a 'Stag's Leap' it might be,** it's been called. From

---

* The slight alteration to the notes in line two to create the phrase for line three contains the 'leap' that will bring about the change of orientation in the second movement of his piobaireachd — the different sound that allows for the story of his parents and his past in the tune of 'The Big Music' and, significantly, will describe, in the Taorluath movement, Callum's arrival to the House.

** The Leumluath, or 'Stag's Leap', that moment of risk or change in the music, is contained within the Taorluath movement here.

the ground that's been set beneath, rising up out of nothing it seems or it jumps clear into nothing. The 'Stag's Leap' there in his own mind. Taking all the notes he's written and leaping clear off the edge of the hill –

into nothing.

Making everything change.

That he can hear it now, the holding down in that third bar as a sort of gathering, of his father, his mother, the repetitions of the 'G' . . .*

All the notes . . .

Even in the dark room . . .

Is proof of how strong it is – the leap.

A sound full of something you didn't know was going to be there before.

Out of nothing risen up – and over.

'And you didn't think it was there before, Johnnie, but it was there.'

~

So he can rest now.

He can.

'Calm yourself, man.'

He must have everything he needs here.

Everyone is around him. The past, the future.

And maybe sleeping now.

So he thinks about that, for a bit. Just sleeping. Just letting his mind settle with it, with everything he knows is in the tune, and the lovely gap and not having to worry because they're all here, all the people he needs, and he'll get back to the hut for the papers, he'll find his way up there again. He'll walk up there on his own some morning soon and they'll be there, the papers with the marks on them laid out by the window in the sun.

And Margaret is here, too, he's seen her lovely face at the door.

'Come in.'

Though he's still waiting for the sound of her and he could never manage without that sound and so he'll keep waiting . . .

---

* 'G' is the note of Gathering on the chanter scale. The Last Appendix carries the full chart of the chanter's scale.

Even so there's nothing else to do right now but sleep.

He'd just said to her, 'Come in.'

And she did come. She would, always.

'Shhh . . .' she would whisper to him. And soft, in that soft way of hers.
'Shhh . . .'

Though he isn't a child. And not a lover. Still she comforts him with
her presence, with the way she comes in.

And he's never told her, has he? What she means to him? He's never
used those words, not been truthful that way, or brave. With his whole
life gone by. With marriage, and a wife and a child of his own and he can
hear Callum's dogs. Hearing them through his sleep, maybe. With the
others all about him and his mother upstairs and Margaret at the door.
And here's Callum as well for he can hear Callum's dogs.

So –

'Where are you, boy?'

But it's only Margaret saying 'Shhh . . .' at the door. For she's the one,
Margaret. Who always brought Callum in.

'He'll be here soon' she's saying. 'Callum will be.'

Though he's never once told her . . . When –

'Callum?' he says. 'Where are you, boy?'

– Margaret was the one used to bring him in.

And all of this is unexpected. Being here in the gap, feeling the empty
space about him. When he was out on the hill with Callum this morning,
wasn't it this morning? So he should be here by now, his boy. Or was it
before, he saw him? Another morning, that he was with his father? The
three of them were together then and with the dogs and he can still hear
the dogs.

So, again –

'Where are you, Callum?'

Because everyone else is here. Margaret is here but Callum's not come
in. It's not as though Johnnie can see him.

'Are you there?'

He can't see him, he can't.

'Callum?'

It may as well be all his adult life the boy's been gone.

Just as his mother's been gone. And his father.

I'll not be back!

Though he was the one who's been gone! He was! It was him, calling out on the road that day, I'll not be back! And, now, all the time he's lost . . .

While lying here . . .

All the time . . .

Gone. Just the sound of the dogs far away, his own boy far away, and then the 'Play it again!' of his father when he, Johnnie . . . He is the father, too.

He is the father.

And the son.

Those notes he heard before, his theme with the singling, the doubling . . . They're variations of that time when the father was a son and the notes the same now as the notes for then – for the same 'Again!' he heard before and the crack of the electric flex his father used to punish him, the crack of it against his fingers as he tried to play the tune properly, and against the back of his legs.

'Again!'

And he never said that to Callum, did he? The 'Again'?

But he said other things, maybe. He did. Or he didn't bother saying anything to him at all.

And where has that come from, that thought just now, like the other? Rising up at him out of the same place where the stag leapt from, the past coming out to him after all this time? Of himself a father and his son a boy. Of himself a boy and the smart of that clear knowledge at the burn and cry of his skin, the blood that came and the ugly mark that his father didn't care for him at all? Hated him even? And is that why his mother was never there to see? Why she took herself off to the Schoolroom then? To the room at the top of the House, under the eaves? So she couldn't see him crying? For he's crying now. In the dark with the light on in the hall and yet still darkness where he is, and Callum is not coming, though the light is on and the dogs are barking, though Callum's dog is out there barking to welcome Callum home.

second variation/The Grey House: family history

(Roderick) John Callum (b.1887 – d.1968) and John Callum MacKay (b. 1923 – d. within these pages): some facts; history

They gave his father a proper funeral in the end. The flag on the coffin. Twelve pipers at the graveside down in Brora. His father inside, in the space cut into the earth, in the box. There were three hundred people, more, must have been, in the tiny cemetery and outside its walls the cars were parked up all the way down the road. His mother was greeted and kissed by every single person who came that day, every student his father had ever taught, every farmer he'd ever known, every official or representative he'd ever had dealings with. There were men from the museum at Fort George where they kept his father's medals and his kilt, the music he'd composed in France,* for the assault into Ravenna, where his father had taken the lead. There were people from the War Institute in London, where they had the original manuscript of his father's three Battle Strathspeys in a glass case, and there was the current commissioner, too, from the battalion where he'd been Chief Piper all those years ago, and there was the present Head of Piping who still taught those same tunes that his father had first taught to the new recruits every year. So his mother stood by the

---

* See Urlar of 'The Big Music', p. 67; also Appendix 9/ii and the List of Additional Materials.

graveside and back at the House as every one of them came up to her to pay their respects.

'Elizabeth.'

'I am sorry, Elizabeth.'

To take her hand, to kiss her cheek.

Every one.

'I'm sorry.'

They were all there.

And so John Callum may have gone away all those years ago, got away from his father and his music . . .*

So he'd said 'I'll not be back!' to his mother, to his father, driven down the grey road, leaving behind him the flex of the cord and those same tunes that were playing in the grey air that day . . .

So, too, was he also there. For his father's funeral. For the music that played. And after that, well. Started the returning.

~

It may be necessary now to establish the kind of man John Callum was through those years that he was away, that he would leave his family in the way he did — 'I'll not be back!' — and nothing but judgement for the place with its endless isolation and its music that went on and on with his father's schools and compositions and his playing and his relentless teaching but in the midst of all that never speaking, not really, or reaching out in thought or deed . . .

For certainly he was no more than a boy when he said goodbye to his parents and made that vow of exile — not intending ever to return — yet, as the years went on, so he would also remember the place, too, as though some part of him was left behind there, you might say, and some day he would have to go back and retrieve it. After all, what kind of life must it have been for him? That he'd made for himself so far away from where

---

* Appendix 12/iii gives details of the different styles of piobaireachd music; additional information about compositions of the Sutherland family can be found in the List of Additional Materials.

he'd been born? What kind of habits had he established, what did he
do? That his was a very different kind of life, to be so far away from the
House and country he'd grown up in, is certain. Who was he at all, what
kind of man could he have been? This before he started coming home
again, first to attend to his mother, to manage the affairs of the place for
her, but then spending weeks here, to bring his son for the summers, and
then longer, weeks turned into months, and then finally coming home for
good? We need to know, don't we, who he was, who he became, before
these papers begin? To establish his time away as being equally real as the
pages before now have also established him. For it was as real, was it not?
The life that was spent apart from this House? These hills?

Real as the life already written?

God knows he'd had to get away from his father! He'd had to! So we
know from that, from the 'I'll not be back!', that he was that kind of man.
Someone who could leave his own father, strong enough to leave, and certain.
And because of that it was no wonder, then, after breaking with his family
and taking himself as far away as possible, that he'd get himself sorted out so
quickly somewhere else, first in Edinburgh, then in London – with his own
business, his own concerns. No wonder, too, you could say, the kind of time
it was for him then because – look! At the young man he was! His father's
son all right. From his father's family. With that same kind of determination
of a Sutherland to have a venture succeed, to make the practical side of it
successful. Only different from them in that he would make his success far
away from the place where they came from. Far, far away.

So he settled, first in the New Town, this was straight after university
in Aberdeen, where he didn't graduate but left to take a single room in
Edinburgh and he had a phone there and a desk. That was the start for
him – there with his phone and his desk. He obtained work with one of
the merchant investment companies and found that he had a way with
talking to them abroad, in Singapore and in Hong Kong, and that he
could decide easily, it came to him easily, where the money should go, how
it should be invested. Whether to place in this stock, or this new kind
of bond, that he knew about this sort of security for the different kinds
of goods they were exporting then, out of the East, that he knew about

insuring against those risks – all this came naturally to him, this kind of thinking. And he was a young man, remember, at this time. A very young man – for he never went back to the university, he'd left it for his single room – but then, before you know it, he's in a larger place, a flat of his own and then a house and soon that was not enough for him either, and indeed nor was that city large enough for this young man, for his plans. So he came further south, he was twenty-four, and it was in London that he really established himself. That was when it all came together for him, as a businessman, you might say, as a city man – not a country man, not a man for music or for land but a man for banks and investments – with the rush of a great metropolis about him, with the sly business sense of all those at his back and at his elbow who knew about investments and dealing, and opportunities, anyone with a head and appetite for risk . . . These people were his friends. And did it matter that he'd never finished at the university, those years ago? Did it matter that he had no family who might support him? Did it matter? It did not.

He was out, he was having the life, he was making the plans and the decisions. He was everywhere, he was in the back streets, he was in the boardrooms, in grand offices with great desks and windows that looked out upon all the buildings in the world. And all of the people he knew? They were from that world, they came out from those buildings, they went into them again, arriving, leaving by the front door – and they were living the life with him, oh, weren't they, they were out and there was whisky, and God, the women! You could get anything you wanted in that place! It was thick with it, money, London. Vivid with the excitement of being young and not thinking about a thing except where you might go, who you might go home with, where you might find yourself at the end of the day, when night fell.

And so, for a long time, John Callum lived like that. In long nights. Long days. With no tiredness at all but just fresh thinking, new directions, more ideas. He changed his clothes, the way he spoke. As though the past had been a separate thing. Those voices of the past, the sounds. His father's tunes. The Schoolroom and his mother's touch. That sting of the cord even. It was as though all of it had never been near him. That he was someone else again, who might never have had his mother's lovely sharp and flowery scent right there at her neck when he puts his arms around her and she lifts him up. That there'd been no memory of that or the scratch of the old man's jacket, there at his sleeve, and the flavour of his tobacco that the boy could seem to taste in the air. These things were put away from him and he would not let them in. He would not. For years, in London. Not talking of them, thinking of them. So they could sit up there together on their own, he thought, his father and his mother, by the fire, not speaking. So his father could tutor all the children in Scotland, have all the pupils he wanted come from the ends of the earth, and all his piping friends to see him but still John Callum MacKay Sutherland would not take his own son to meet him, he was decided. If ever he had a son. He would also keep him away. And he would not think of his father or his mother or the place where he'd come from and the music from there. Not ever. 'I'll not be back!', remember? Was how he thought then. When he was a young man. When he was so young and strong and sure.

And yet . . .

The past was waiting. Like the tunes that played that day they lowered the casket of his father into the ground. It was in the air he breathed, in the ground he stood on, bedded in. Though John had work to do and a different life, and experiences to create for himself, new memories to make, to keep. Though for all that time he was away and not thinking of that other life and nothing to do with that life, so he thought, with his mother, with his father. Or his father's father and that place of theirs that had always been there, in that part of the hills . . . Nothing. Yet. It was always there, within him, dug in. The place in the ground, the Urlar, for his own box.

While the nothing went on, the years gone on, from Edinburgh to London, and letters written, maybe, sometimes the letters would arrive from his mother and he would write, yes, sometimes he would write back to her* but, even so, he continued to think 'I'll not be back!' He was on his

---

* The List of Additional Materials includes details of letters kept, like those of the young John Callum and his mother after he was sent away to school. These are part of the domestic archive collated by Elizabeth Clare Nichol Sutherland and Margaret MacKay and are available as part of an ongoing project to raise awareness of the

own. He had his own friends. He was with his own friends. It was his own world he'd made for himself, after all, and he'd say it again and again: That he was not the same, was he? As his father? The hero? The 'Play it again'? He was not? And he would not labour under that same tutelage, would he? Johnnie? Not wrap himself in the banner his father wore?

Is how he continued to stay away.* Continued to grow and change. For just as it had been Edinburgh at first that he'd set himself up in, but then it was London and surely when he got there, to the centre of things, then he would never want to turn back . . . So he continued to stay apart from everything that had been familiar once. By now he had his own company set up off the back of contacts he had up north, a bigger operation altogether, with greater risks but better, altogether better, and the people he'd met through his dealings in the Scottish capital – well, he'd traded them for the future he was making for himself in the south, for the family of his own he would have someday and the money he would make! The money! Christ! He'd stay apart from the past for that, all right, for the banks and for the contacts. Because the money! Christ! If you had half a brain and a way with investments, for seeing opportunities, and all around in that place there were opportunities . . . Then of course you'd never leave, why would you? He'd never leave.

And so there were things he needed to accomplish and he did accomplish them. And eventually he was married, he did have a son of his own, and his business was growing and so his son would one day inherit that business . . . He was moving into that phase of life that was even more demanding than before, with more to do, that time when his boy was born, during those early years when he was small, more than ever to plan and organise and think about, and he sold his house, he bought a bigger house . . .

---

significance of domestic life as a subject for literature; see Appendix 5 and 'The Big Music', later movements.

* We know that John Sutherland did return to The Grey House once during this period of his life, when he was still in his twenties, and shortly after he'd moved to London – to see his mother, who was unwell. Important details of this visit are present in the Crunluath movement of 'The Big Music', in particular pp. 219, 220, and later pp. 274, 364.

But his father died, suddenly, in the midst of everything. When he was not thinking about that, about any of it – but then. All at once. He was a man on his own. With his own son. A son with his father gone.

And so he travelled all the way up to Brora to attend the funeral. And he saw his mother. She was there to greet him, at the church, at the side of the grave.

'John.'

And at once, it was back. Or rose up at him, rather, and all around him, the past that had always been there, waiting.

His mother's scent, the same flowery scent as when he'd been a little boy.

And him putting his arms around her, not for her to hold him like she used to when he was a child but now for his arms to encircle her and she was like a stalk, like a little branch, but something of the blossom about her still.

'John' she'd said, and he'd held her. 'John.'

While even then, he thought, this wasn't returning. How could it be?

With the child grown into a man.

The mother to a twig.

The old man gone.

With everything he'd done, and been so long away? When he was so marked himself by distance, and so changed? How could this be, he thought, returning?

Yet the music was playing, his mother was there at the grave. And that was the beginning. Coming back for his father's funeral, to help his mother first, then to have the summer with her, and then it was the following year and he found his old chanter then, in the Schoolroom, his old set of pipes, and he took them up and tuned them. The 'A' to the 'A' and perfectly they sounded. Then after that it wasn't long – two summers, more, three summers – until his mother died but enough to form a habit and by then it was habit. To come back to the House where he'd been born, where his father had been born. To want to stay.*

---

* The story of John and Margaret starts the first summer Margaret spends at The Grey House and comes into the tune of the Crunluath movement, later in 'The Big Music';

Is how the years continued, for John Callum MacKay. A Sutherland from Sutherland after all, and nothing surprising then, in the habit of being here, put back again into place after all the time away. And back again, too, the old habits. Of silence. Of music. Of expecting and getting what you might need. Of keeping all your secrets close. It wasn't long until it seemed to John that the time he'd been away hadn't changed him at all, not really – only that what he'd come back to had always been in him and was just waiting for him to let it out again. More and more, as time went on, that's how it felt. That though he'd thought he'd once been someone else and had done those other things – had his work, his life, with marriage in it, had a son – any idea of being that other person was now as thin and disappearing as a dream. And, just as before, when he'd been a young man, he'd not been able to honour his past, find the words to factor its content and meaning, so now, as the habit of being home again continued with him, did he find himself counting everything that might have been dear to him once, the things he'd bought and the deals he struck, as nothing.

The substance of his whole life . . .

Just parts, bits.

Nothing.

So that though he was staying longer each time at The Grey House, after a while bringing his son with him, the boy whom he'd christened after all and even before his father's death, as Callum . . . Still, nothing was how he felt about his boy. When the boy was – what? Eight years old? Nine years old? And they'd drive up together and stay the whole summer . . .

And his wife phoning, Sarah. On those old telephone lines you couldn't hear, phoning long distance to check her son was all right –

'John?'

All through those summers, checking up on him, asking 'Is he okay? Is Callum okay? Has he something to do? Are you keeping him warm?',

---

see also earlier sections of the Urlar and the ambiguity surrounding the title of the JMS piobaireachd 'The Return'.

John listening to her voice down the static of the line . . . Still all of it was just parts, bits. 'John, can you hear me?' Nothing. Whether she called or didn't call. Whether his son was cold or not cold. Whether it was raining or whether it was fine. The nothing so taken hold in him – and Callum twelve by now, thirteen – that nothing would let John Sutherland realise that maybe if he'd not been so interested before in all those other things, the getting away, the business and the bank accounts and the houses . . . He might have been able to make sense of his life before now. Maybe. Learn that something had always been wrong for him, deep in. That he'd had a wife who would be phoning him the way she did, but who'd never wanted to come back here with him, not ever.

'John?'

Only phoning.

'Are you there, John?'

So of course it's been a while since the marriage was as good as over, may as well have been, and his wife . . . Well. A voice on the telephone is who she still is.

'Can you hear me at all?'

Though the line is better now. With her calling him once a week for the past year or so since he came up here to live for good and he can always hear her.

'Are you keeping well?' she'll say. 'Are you doing what the doctor tells you?'

In that smooth English voice of hers.

'John?'

'Are you listening to me?'

'Can you hear me?'

'John?'

'John?'

'John?'

Is what becomes of nothing.

'Are you there?'

For give it away, your past, and what do you have but only talk, only words, all the sentences . . . Gone clear into air. There's no tune, for how can there be, from nothing? No sounds. No string of bright notes that would make up a theme. For of all the certainties in the world, all the houses and the marriages and the children, without the past there's only nothing — so never let it go.

Margaret had always known that best.

And somewhere, within his sleeping . . . John Sutherland knows it, too.

That what he's left for himself is nothing.

Just parts and bits . . . Pieces . . .

Nothing.

When, with Margaret, he could have allowed himself the all.

~

And they did give the old boy a proper funeral in Brora, at the end there, didn't they? The army? Wrap his box in the flag? With the medals, for his time in France. For the work he'd put in to the music school through the Highlands, for his work with education and the children who would come to learn to play, and the bands that he tutored, the competitions that he judged. And though none of it was Johnnie's life, was it? None of it? Though his marriage over, his life in London done . . .

Though —

'I'll not be back!' he had said.

So he did come back.

His father's tunes all around him in the song he himself would now play.*

---

* This song, of course, is his own 'Lament' — a song made of nothing, only of 'Himself' — that slowly allows other elements in. The Crunluath A Mach movement of 'The Big Music' describes some of John's thoughts and ideas for the content of the piobaireachd and his sense of it being part of an ongoing story of the Sutherland family; also see the earlier Urlar of this book and later movements.

two/third paper*

Callum has to go through now, and see his father. It's where the day has been taking him, to the moment when he will walk into the darkened room, see his father's body lying out there in the bed, asleep.

And for him, what that feeling is like . . . I wonder, Callum. A father's son who's driven all through the day to get here, a man who has no belief in what he's doing, no understanding about himself, who he is, where he might be going, the direction he wants to take. Who is acting out of duty here – that his mother has asked him to come and get his father, to bring him away – left the others in the kitchen and come through to the little sitting room, to be standing by his father's chair. And yet it is not as simple as simple duty either. To be standing as he is, unable to settle. Facing the north window looking out into the darkness and I should go in and draw the curtains but instead there's his face reflected by the lamplight, in the dark glass.

For duty, I know, may be no more than duty but still duty can be all. Here, where we live, duty is like return, is fixed, it's known. It's part of who we are, inevitable. And so there was his mother phoning him the

---

* As will become clear, this paper takes in fully the first-person voice we have heard from before in 'The Big Music', that will become an increasing presence in the pages of the story as it develops. It wasn't difficult for me to see, when I was editing these papers, that this was intended – that the 'I' should come to have an increasing role, and it helped me greatly in the arrangement of the text.

way she did, asking him to come up and check on his father, see how he is so that he can take him away, put him in some hospital or other, some hospice or home . . . But that was just the start of Callum's journey. For of course she would think, wouldn't she, his mother, that old Johnnie should not be here with us, that the man who is her husband should not be in such a place of terrible and dangerous isolation, she can't imagine it. Yet Callum understands. Why his father is here, why he must stay. And he knows how duty turns to will and will into desire. Now that he's here, after his long day, so now there's nowhere else he wants to be but here. Because look about him in this warm room, and beyond it, through the glass. Every part of the world where he is now, he knows. He stands at the window registering that fact, of every part, seeing through the dark. The straggly tree on the hill line, that tree stripped of leaves and bent over by a wind, one tree, he can see, he knows. The strike of black water down there on the moor, broken up with sharp boulders, and he used to sit on those rocks, years ago, looking up at the hills, at Mhorvaig, with Helen.

And Helen.

'Christ!'

That scene in the kitchen just now!

With the news that she's here!

All that come in on him the way it did and — Christ! again, making him feel like his father, but he needs a drink, goes over to the sideboard and pours himself a whisky. For he may be here for duty, of course he is, for his father, and not those other memories — not that tree, that water, that hill and the two of them together — but how do you keep them apart? That memory, the green face of the hill and climbing higher and higher to get to the top, always wanting to go further, higher, with a new set of hills falling away to the west — how keep that separate from everything else? The light and the sun and the cold coming in across the tops so you could feel by the time summer had got to its end that he'd have to go back to London, and he'd have to say goodbye to Helen then . . . How be here just for his father, to tend to him, think only of him, when there's all that other as well? Him and Helen and a new set of hills, the two of them together on their own and the past coming raging in?

Best to have no old stories from way back, just try not to remember them. That's what he must think, taking a sip of the whisky, another sip. Keep them silenced, those thoughts of what they used to do, he and Helen, the two of them sitting there on the black rocks and all the broad hills spread out before them to the sky . . .

Just forget. Forgetting is best. He'll try and get reception in a bit, call Anna and the boys, remind himself what he's here for: to see his father, nothing else. His father who is through there in the room off the hallway, waiting for him. Is what he'll say to his wife and sons. How he's here for duty, remember? For his father. To be standing here at his father's chair, just as he used to when he was a boy, when he would come through here to wish his father goodnight –

'Goodnight, Daddy.'

'Goodnight.'

And yes.

For there's always that.

The *Goodnight, Daddy*.

The way Margaret used to bring him in here all those years ago, taking him by the hand to come in and wish his father goodnight. And sure there's nothing of Helen in that. So he can think about that, remember that. What his father was like. Tell that to Anna and the boys. How it was to be a boy himself and coming in here to see his father in the evening. What that was like. Or later, when he was a young man, arriving like he did tonight after a long drive north and his father sitting here in this same chair, waiting for him, a tumbler of whisky in his hand and tapping out a tune against it, where the glass rested on the arm of his chair.

'Hello, Daddy.'

Because that was just him and his father then.

No thoughts of Helen there.

The way his father would take one sip from his glass, then another, before replying.

'You took your time, though.'

So certainly, yes, there was always that. To remember, to keep hold of here. To tell his wife. His sons. The way his father was. The way he is. That one memory on its own should keep all the other thoughts away.

'My father . . .' he could say.

As though he's speaking now to Anna, or to the boys: *My father.*

'There's nothing about him that is easy.'

For what was it like all those years when he came through here to wish his father goodnight? Nothing like thinking of Helen, anyway, that's for sure. No room there for any other thought or idea. Only ever: *My father.* It was the way his father was. Wherever he was. In the chair, in the car, when they were driving up here. That terrifying profile, his hands clenched on the wheel. Whenever he was with his father his father's presence took up all the space, he seemed to dominate the air around him.

My father.

Sitting beside him in the car.

Coming in here, as a boy, as a young man, to stand and wait at his father's chair.

So, yes. Just think about that.

Callum.

Remember that.

The *My father* . . .

A man, Callum says to himself now, *who could never come close.*

And this, after all, is his father's House. It's not Callum's house. So there's that, too. To remind himself of, tell his family, his wife and his sons. How none of this – him being here, seeing the rocks through the glass, the high hills – how none of it should be to do with Callum any-way, because this is his father's home, his father's House. Callum is only visiting, remember? He's passing through. Following the call from his mother to come up here and get his father away. And any minute he'll go in now to the little bedroom off the hall where the man who used to sit in the chair is now lying . . . And – *Goodnight, Daddy* indeed. For that will be intimate enough. Going in to see him there, to stand right next to him, kiss him on the forehead . . .

Callum takes a sip of his whisky. Takes another sip.

God knows none of this will be easy.

No more than it was easy all those years ago, when he was a boy and he had no choice then but to have to come through to his father in the evening – so in the same way there's no choice now but for it to be Callum who must be the one to go in there and this time try and get his father to leave, come away with him to London as his mother thinks is best.

And tell Anna that, too. Tell the boys. That it's only him here. Who has to do that. There's no one else.

You've got to be the one to do it, Callum.

Because his mother would never do anything.

By now it may as well be as though his mother's never even been married to his father.

You've got to be the one.

So, yes, it's only Callum here.

A man who could never come close.

Leaving his family so early this morning and driving through the dawn, coming up all through the hours of daylight to that bleak and lovely road, the cut peat into the earth and the crumbled drying heather . . .

You took your time, though.

Arriving . . .

And don't think I'm coming with you either.

Is where this is leading, Callum knows. To the dark room and what his father will say.

~

Callum moves to the window again, restless, then back to the sideboard. It's that word again, inevitable. That run of duty into will and to desire. All of it wrapped around him now, holding him, keeping him – because he knows of course that his father won't be going anywhere and his own presence here makes no difference to that fact. But that doesn't mean he now wishes he hadn't come here either. Because now he's here he sees so clearly how the end of his father's life belongs here, of course it does, met with him in the place where Callum has arrived, the place where his father started out from. It's like his father's music, Callum thinks, is the way it feels – the 'A' note always wanting to keep the tune, to hold the other notes against the line of the drone below. So there's no choice about where the tune will go, only the inevitability of its eventual return. And it's a lovely sound, how could it not be, with a High 'A' to pitch the harmonic off the base note and the fine wide octave in between – though there's no straying from it, there can't be, from that lovely 'A'. The beginning of all the music is there.

And it occurs to Callum then: where does his father keep all the stuff for his music, anyhow? All his books and the papers and the manuscripts? There's no place for any of it here he can see, in this room, though his father's always called it the 'Music Room' and he used to do all his practice here. And it can't be upstairs, all those papers and notes, when it's clear he's not been up in his own bedroom for some time, since they've moved him down here.

So where are the papers? On a table, they used to be, laid out . . .

Where is that table?

Where –?

And then, something.

An image.

A memory, though he was not to have any of those memories and he was to call home, remember, he was to phone Anna and the boys . . .

But –

something.

About what he'd heard today. And after his mother's telling him, he'd remembered, too . . . Something. About his father.

Margaret saying that they found him up on the top of Ben Mhorvaig and trying to get over on the west side . . . And he'd thought about it yesterday as well, when his mother called . . . Started to . . .

But now the memory is complete. With seeing that part of the hill just now when he looked through the glass – to the black rocks and the river and in the distance Ben Mhorvaig – the memory . . . Of papers on a table . . . Another table . . .

And himself and Helen.

Helen.

That memory.

And no good now, trying to suppress it. No good trying to think about his father, or the way his father is.

No good saying again to himself the words *My father.*

No good. Because the memory is here. Of how they had got up to the top of that hill, he and Helen . . . An old, old memory that he hadn't allowed . . .

Of a private place.

That they had used. He and Helen.

Helen.

'Yes.'

When they'd got to the top and gone over.

'I do remember' he says.

Because he'd seen all his father's papers that day, hadn't he, when he'd been there to that place with her, with Helen, as she'd drawn him to her and . . .

Helen.

Helen.

Helen.

All his father's music was there. In files. In boxes. On a big table by the window . . .

Pages piled up, and books and notebooks and manuscript papers all covered with notes, with writing . . .

All the music there that day. Long ago when he'd seen it. When he'd been there in secret with Helen, to his father's secret place. With all his father's music around them there – and not thinking about it since, remembering her, the sensation of her . . .

Helen.

But it comes back to him now.

That it's where the music is. And where his father was taking himself to today, when they found him . . . It was to that place. To that same place. But with a child – why a child?

With Helen's child.

~

He's restless now, all right.

He could be doing without any of this. He needs another drink. He pours himself a large measure, takes a sip from his glass. He could be doing without any of these thoughts now pressing in. Of touch and taste and scent and the past, his past, not his father's past. He could be doing without all of it. Thoughts about himself, his own memories and a girl he used to know when he was a boy, she was just a girl, although she behaved towards him as though she had known him all her life . . . Still she was just a girl, even though –

Helen.

Helen.

She's all through him now, in his mind and body. When he's supposed to be in with his father. Thinking about him, being with him right now and he should have gone through there by now, to see his father. As he takes another sip from his glass, and another. And he must go through to him, he must. Not stand about here, thinking about himself, remembering. Listen to the dogs! Even the dogs know it! That going through to his father is his duty here. He can still hear them barking now like they were when he arrived. Just before, when he'd excused himself from the kitchen, gone back out to the car for his bags, Iain behind him to help him –

'Don't bother, Iain. I can get them.'

– though Iain was there already, grabbing the cases, the two of them, and 'Be quiet!' Iain had shouted at them, the dogs had seemed to be reminding him then, what Callum is here for, for his father, his duty, for they were still at it now in their kennels, in the same way their barking had started up when he'd arrived. As though reminding him. That he should be through there with his father now. That that's what he's come for. Their barking his welcome – to be with his father, at the end of his father's life – their barking his return.

But Helen is here, too.

In the midst of the dogs' cries. As much as any other memory of his father's life, she's here, as are the black rocks and the hills and the secret place. And so are all the parts connected . . .

Helen and Callum in the notes of the tune with his father's music all around them.

All of it connected.

The 'A' to the 'A'.

And so he'll go in to see his father because there's no undoing of the tune that holds them all together, though his father will be like a corpse already, Callum knows, lying in the dark room. He's been given something to help him sleep, Margaret said, before. When he'd been thinking he'd seen all kinds of people out on the hill with him this morning, his own father, he was talking about his mother. Thinking he himself was his father, then, and that he'd seen Callum, too. Whoever he thought he was, he was calling out, Margaret said, from the room, and calling out for him, for Callum, ever since they'd brought him down off the tops and laid him out through there.

And it is like a tune, all the parts of it intricately made to be together, and familiar to Callum, all of it somehow familiar . . .

Though he's never been in that little room before, has he? Callum?

Just as he's never been here at the House this time of year before — when it's so dark now, and so cold.

As he turns from the window, turns.

And there on the sideboard by the whisky is a recording of one of his father's tunes. He picks up the recording.

And terrifying, yes. To be back in this country of his father's now, at the time of his father's leaving it. To be in a place of such emptiness and bitter beauty, bitter cold. There's the endless light but also the dark this time of year, like a cloak to cover them all until the spring will come again as it will come but how long to wait . . .

And here's the recording in Callum's hand, written on the case, from fifty years ago:

*Ceol Mor/23.**

---

* The piobaireachd known by all as 'The Return' but that also goes by a second, secret name that has been referred to earlier in 'The Big Music'; see pp. 120, 121. In his musical archive JMS left all compositions listed by number; the names were held separately. Appendix 6/v has details under 'Family records of music kept, compositions'.

So that everything – Callum is aware of it now – is here where it needs to be. This House alone in the landscape, and his place in it, lit rooms in the dark. Beyond the thick glass of the window, the fires, lamps in small rooms, the entire hillside falls down around him, all the air, the storms, all the riverfalls, coming in off the lochs, the straths, down from all the high streams . . .

And looking back through the dark through the window, from out in the open land, there's his father's chair, the pipes lying like an animal at his feet silent for now but any minute he'll pick them up in his arms, his father will knock the bag into place beneath his arm, straighten the drones which start up that second, tuning them – the first 'A' – then a better – higher – 'A' to 'A' .

This.

And this.

And this.

Callum turns on the CD – turns the volume right up – and his father begins to play.

insert/John Callum Sutherland

No wonder he got to London after Edinburgh so fast!

'No wonder!'

There's his own voice saying the words!

'Johnnie!' he calls out – or is that his father? Calling for him?

'Johnnie!'

Or is it his own voice he can hear?

It's all dark here, in the room – only it must be his father talking. Or his grandfather. His grandfather or his own voice he can hear – or could be any one of them, all of them in this together – and it is no wonder either! That he got himself fixed up there, in that big city! Away from his father and the flex and with his own business, too, and nothing to do with the old man by then, nothing at all! So he would put himself apart! From that old man and from his land and his music and all his concerns! So he would get out of bed on it, so he would! Just get up right now and take him on, his father. Like on the hill before, this morning, and he'd had a few words with him then, after all the time they'd been apart, they'd met and they'd spoken – and he'll say a few more words with his father now, too, if his father's here in the room. For it was a good thing, it was, that he did it! Went away! A man would do it! Set himself apart from his father, well apart, so he can make his own way in life! He feels it still – the setting of himself away from this place and from the past. So let him stay up there, he'd thought back then. His father. Let him. With his mother.

Let the pair of them sit up there if that's what they want, what they want to do.

'I'll not be back to crouch at their fireside, listen to the silence all around!'

'I'll not be back!'

Is what he used to say — to friends, to people he once knew. And he can hear now that they are his own words he is listening to in the dark. 'I'll not be back!' they say. As though the words themselves are company, and talking back to him as though they are familiar as those people who were out on the hill with him this morning, his father, his son — and someone else. The boy who was himself once. He's here, too. That boy who remembers the touch of his mother's cheek, the scent at her neck. The rough tweed of his father's cuff and the crack of the flex at the back of his leg, the smart of that clear knowledge at the burn and cry of his skin, the blood that came and the ugly mark that his father didn't care for him at all. Hated him even. That is him, too, who is lying here. The same boy. And they put a needle in him today, to keep him quiet, and they took him away with them, sure enough. Off the hill. Away from all the light and the air . . .

But he came back.

Remember?

That day at the funeral when everyone was there?

He came back then, to stay. And everyone his father had ever known was there that day — though who were they? All those people? He didn't know them. Like a whole life come up to take his mother by the hand and every one of them a stranger. With the piobaireachd being played by a soldier — 'MacKay's Lament', and it was one of his father's favourite tunes — a grey tune in the grey air. Thin and high and lovely through the upper register on a day that had cold in it then too, winter, and he'd come home then, hadn't he? With the tune? To lie here, himself the stranger.

Is how his thoughts are running now. Fast and low.

So it's his own life, not his father's life, that's come to nothing. So the pills are flushed away and the food is not taken. None of it matters. For the thoughts are running low and fast and lovely. Up before dawn this morning and away from them all like a hare on the hills, away from the dogs, gone, and not his scent left even to guide them.

Is in his mind now.

To have left them all and be away.

Up at dawn and to the Little Hut, he'll get there. Out on the hills and far from them all to the secret place and the child with him – to stay there with him for the rest of it, for the tune to be done. New life coming out of old. Green shoots for the grouse to feed on after the heather's been burned way back to soil.

And they won't find him then, old Johnnie. Won't find the old grey hare for he's gone.

narrative/3

The people at the House and what they thought of him

<u>Helen</u>

And I don't know who Callum is. Or where he belongs. His father no longer there in the little sitting room where he used to wait. After a time, I suppose, he stopped waiting — for his son to return home. And it's been a while, anyhow, since he's been able to sit up for any length of time in that chair of his. Though right up until yesterday he asked to have the recordings of certain tunes played at night so he could hear them from his bedroom. As though he were still in the little sitting room, perhaps, on his own and with a dram. Listening to the same recordings or playing himself, like he used to, all the tunes he'd composed over the years. The Music Room they used to call it, in the old days.

Even so, though it's quiet now, my mother will go through to light the fire there. Each evening, early, she'll crouch at the grate and put the match to the clean arrangement of twigs and paper I set for her in the morning. I've watched her, still kneeling while the flame catches, flares up and starts through the paper and the peats, staying close, making certain the fire is good. Then she returns to the kitchen, heats through soup, rolls, puts the water on to boil for tea. It's her routine, part of who she is. What she does keeping faith with a certain order, is how I think of it. Her present embodying all that is in her past.

When I come down from my bedroom – for Katherine is settled now and sleeping – to take the things through, the tray with the tea on it, the soup and the bread, my mother is away upstairs and Callum is standing at the chair where his father used to sit. There's music playing, he's turned the stereo on, something of his father's though the notes are too bright on the recording and not as sweet and soft in the embellishments as when he used to play the tune himself in this same room. The volume is up high enough for Callum not to notice me open the door, but not so loud that I can't still hear the dogs, intermittently now, but they've been at it ever since he arrived, poor beasts.

I set the tray down on the small table by the window and Callum sees me.

There is nothing, at this second, we can do, either of us, or say.

~

Iain

He could have gone out to the kennels at least – but he's not done that. Though the noise won't let up until they've satisfied themselves they've seen him, got the smell of him.

But he never went.

'Be quiet!'

So I was the one yelling at them. When I'd taken his damn bag from him and you'd have thought then he might have turned back – there's one old retriever there who he'd still remember if he bothered himself at all. But he just walked on ahead into the House empty-handed.

Like his father before him.

You could say that.

No thought for anyone else.

And –

'Be quiet!' I'd shouted at the dogs – but animals. They know. And you can't always will them. No amount of what I said or did was going to stop them wanting out and into the House if they could, and all over him, knowing something was different here, someone come back only they've not been able to get the scent from his hand to know if he belongs here, if he'll stay.

~

Helen

Callum says, after a few beats, 'Helen.'

The tray is there. The soup. The tea.

He is facing me so I can see how he's changed.

'Helen' he says again — and then, like someone's just told him to, turns away to put the music down.

'I heard about the baby' he says then. 'From your mother.'

He's been drinking. He fiddles with the volume control, turning it up, right up and then down, then up again, too loud.

'And my father' he says. 'Margaret told me about that, too. What he did. About yesterday and taking —' Suddenly it's quiet. He's turned the switch off completely.

He straightens up to face me.

'She's fine now' I say. I look fully at him, into his eyes. I can see everything there.

'She's okay' I say. 'She's sleeping.'

And I want to fall against him.

Fall.

Like I always wanted to fall. Like Katherine Anna should be his daughter. Like I should be his wife.

Fall, Helen.

Fall.

Fall.

~

Margaret

He looked awful when he got in. Frightened, is how I'd put it. His face — like that. Like a knife. And tired, of course he'd be tired, after that long

drive, coming all that way — but something more than tiredness in him.
Reminded me straight away of how he used to be when he was young,
getting up here at the beginning of the summer, the way he used to arrive
with John, the two of them together, the tall father and his son, getting
out of the car.

That was long enough ago.

Long enough.

But he was up early this morning of course, Callum, and that may be
part of it, why he looked the way he did — it was three o'clock or thereabouts, he said, when he left London. So it would have been like driving
through the middle of the night for most of it. And that might explain
something of his appearance — the feeling showing in his face of being
shocked out of time, kind of. Leaving his wife and finding himself back
here with us, his father in the condition that he's in.

And I had to tell him, and straight away. What his father had done.

And Iain also told him that Helen had come home, that she'd had a
child.

So there's also that.

As well as everything else.

And it's a lot. For him to be taking in.

His father. And Helen. Helen's child . . .

Not his child.

A lot to find out about so soon in and of course it would show on his
face, poor man. Poor boy. Always the look on his face when he arrived, all
those years ago, of shock and fear and not knowing where to put himself,
what to do, who to be.

Callum.

It's all right, son. Come here to me.

~

Helen

'A baby' he's saying. And I can see the whisky bottle on the sideboard
behind him yet even with the drinking it's as though there's light around

him. Here in this room, as I see him, after so much time away from us . . .
So it takes time for me, just then, to hear what he's saying, to take him in
as I do, everything about him, with the light collecting all around him,
holding him, so it does take time . . .

But it takes time for him, too.

Callum.

There so close I could reach out and touch him, my hand at the side
of his face. The light holding us both like a press, taking away all the air
between us. Then he says my name again – 'Helen' – and in one movement
comes towards me and at that moment my baby starts up to cry.

'You should go to your father' I say.

Though he doesn't seem to hear me, his face clouded by tiredness and the
whisky, and he's looking at me as though I might have said something different, as I might have, with the light all about him, about us, I might have
. . . But my daughter is there, needing me, and his father is waiting and . . .

'He's been asking after you' I say –

And that breaks it. My words. Katherine crying upstairs. Whatever it
was, holding us before, the press of light, and time and timelessness. He
seems to stumble.

'I know what happened' he says, but he seems confused now. By me.
By his father. By the idea, maybe, of the two of us together – two names,
two people side by side in his mind. 'I know what my father did' he says.
'Margaret told me – your baby –'

Your baby.

Those words in his mouth.

He looks away.

And for a minute, though she's crying now and I must go to her, I want
to stay. Tell him everything, tell it all. For it's true, she is my daughter,
Callum – and nothing to do with you – my child who was picked up
from her basket yesterday morning when she was sleeping and taken off
to the hills . . .

Your baby.

My child, who I thought, yesterday morning, I might never see again.

My baby.

My child.

My daughter.

And nothing to do with you at all.

But not as simple as that either. And part of me wants to explain that to him, to Callum ...

Your baby.

About the way she was taken — because otherwise how could he ever understand? About why his father would steal my daughter away as he did, to have her with him up there in the hills? Because if I don't tell him, none of it makes any sense to him — why would it? And part of me wants to tell him now, everything, the story of us together, how his father is wrought in with us here, so twisted into the makings of this place, to me and Margaret and my child, our lives here and Iain, too ... That nothing's as simple as: *Your baby.*

Though, God knows, I wasn't happy that John took her off the way he did. God knows that it was a terrible thing, to take a baby away like that, a terrible thing and it's right that Callum would be horrified by his father when he heard about it, and ashamed ... But if I could just explain to Callum, too. How his father's carrying away of my daughter, *my* daughter, and my mother's daughter's daughter ...

If I could just explain:

'It's not as simple as you might think.'

Not as simple — as though his taking her were a crime or confusion or bad intent — when:

I want to say to him:

'*Your baby*, my Katherine Anna ...

'She's your father's granddaughter, too.'

And from the moment she was born all she's heard is the sound of the pipes playing on our father's recordings, Callum. Our father. So she knows them like you and I know them, all the notes, all the semibreves and embellishments of that strange mismatched scale of his. Our father. You know how he sounds, Callum — and for her, too, he is also familiar. Her hands forming little fists up at the side of her head as she slept those first days but still hearing that particular music of our father through her dreams ...

If I could say all of these things, but of course I don't say them.

So that Callum will never know, any more than his father will know ... That none of this could ever be as simple as: *Your baby.* That although, yes, it was unknown to me that my daughter would be taken by an old man, and so early in the morning that he could get far, far away ... And, yes, terrible for me to be blank and powerless with the fear of what might happen, then, what he might do ... Yet it's also not strange that my daughter would be so taken.

'When it was her grandfather who took her, Callum', if I could say that. 'My father. Your father. So she's part of him, my Katherine Anna. That's why he wanted her out on the hills, now he's old and dying and can hear only silence in the air. That's why he wanted to keep her with him, to hold her in his arms.'

But I can't say any of it. I have to go to my baby now. And he knows nothing, Callum. Nothing. He doesn't live here. He wasn't here yesterday when it happened, when his father stole my child away. He hasn't seen his father, not for ten years, more. He doesn't know him, the reasons for what he did, why he might have done it. Though he may go on talking about it, saying now, 'I don't know what I can do to make up for my father, Helen. If only I'd been here. I could have stopped it. Could have stopped him. I could have helped you.'

Callum.

And starting to be distraught now, like he used to get upset when we were children, worrying about something, something to do with his father, what he should be doing, what he's not doing. Something wrong.

'It's okay' I say to him. Quietly, gently.

I have to go.

'Shhh ...' I say, 'There's no need ...' for I'm calming him down. 'Shhh ...' – like I used to when we were young. *You don't have to say anything, Callum. You don't have to do anything at all.*

Because there's nothing he can do. As there was nothing he could do then, either, when he was a boy – to feel better about his father. He doesn't know him. He was never there to know. So just leave it at that, Callum. Let him go. Forget about your father. We can take care of him here. We've taken care of him for a long time. Just go in and say goodnight like you have to.

I must go. My daughter is crying. All I can do is go to her – so I've turned to leave but Callum says then, 'Tell your father I won't be needing him tomorrow.'

And for a second I stop.

'I saw him before' he says, 'with the guns, he was cleaning the guns but tell him –'

He means Iain.

Though for a second I had thought –

Your father. My father.

Then I say, 'I don't think –' I start to reply, but . . .

What are you saying, Callum?

That you would talk to me like this?

Who are you trying to be? Who are you?

That you would act this way?

'I don't think that he's expecting it' I say. 'Iain. To take you out, I mean. He's not expecting to do that. With your father so ill.'

And I look at him again, the poor man. He's drunk. That's all. The whisky bottle is there on the sideboard half done. He doesn't know what he's saying. Doing. He's drunk and he's scared.

'But yes' I say. 'I will tell him.'

Because I must go to my baby now, before my mother gets there before me. To pick her up in my arms, feel the pang of milk coming, unbuttoning my shirt for her as I go up the stairs.

And poor Callum . . .

He doesn't know. Anything. Can't say.

He's let everything be gone. Let himself down before me, be lost, be scared. Weak and with no father, as though he's never had a father.

Callum.

For who were you trying to be just then?

That you would talk to me that way?

'Goodnight' I say.

Yet, as I turn, finally, to leave the room – the piece of light is still there. Left from before with the two of us together. From this man who's come to us from where he was, come back up the long road that's behind him and I don't know what will happen with us now. For I can't talk to Callum about any of it, what happened yesterday, why it happened, what we're going to do. That his father has stopped taking the medicine, doesn't sleep, not really, any more. That for weeks before now he's been going off on his own, for hours sometimes – and we don't know what he's been thinking, how to help him. We can't help him, not really, not at all.

I can't say.

None of it would make sense to him now. It's too much, and it's also not enough.

So I say nothing. I leave the room.

Yet still I sense the broken piece of light behind me as I go down the hall. It's there at my back as I hear Callum call out, 'Please tell your mother, Helen, I need her! To talk about what we're going to do here! What I should do! Please, tell your mother –'

Even in those words, drunk words, half meaning and undone, light.

As he slumps back into his father's chair. Slumped down, eyes closed, with his father on his way by now, way up into the far hills, he's already there, and staying. There where the music is and he'll not be back, Callum.

Come up over the top of the hill and to the other side.

insert/Callum

It's late now, outside the night drawn into itself with darkness, and this man, this Callum Innes Sutherland who's driven north today, a man who is acting out of duty here, or so he thinks, so he'll believe . . .

Who is he, really?

For he hasn't gone through there, has he, to say goodnight? Just as frightened of his father as he ever was.

With number 23 playing in the room.*

Just as frightened.

The sound of his father is all around him by now, and loud, coming in on him, holding him down. And with the sound of his father's pacing in the music, too, the tread of his footsteps heavy, beating out the rhythm beneath the notes . . .

'The Return'

And where do you go with that? How to proceed? How enter into the man's bedroom at all when there's nothing but the sound of him here and the thought of him and the memory of him. The sound and the pacing and the notes of him and the beat of his tread . . .

Though his father, Margaret said before, is light as a leaf.

A leaf. That's how she put it, such a light, pretty way of talking about

---

* To remind the reader: the tune playing in the Music Room is called 'The Return' but, as noted on p. 132, also carries the secret title 'Margaret's Song'. This appears in full in manuscript at the back of 'The Big Music'.

something that could take Callum's breath from him. For when there's 'The Return' or 'Retreat from the Hills' or 'The North Ascent' or 'On Going into Battle at Lochinver' or 'The March to the Western Side' or 'Tune for Murray, Son of John Murray' or 'The Birds' or 'The Capture of the MacKays'... Or... Or... Or... Any of them... Any of the tunes ... Numbers 23 or 15 or 7 or 2 ... All the CDs and cassettes lined up in their places in the cupboard below the sideboard, each with its title, its number, each carrying in its depths the sound of his father, of his heavy tread... To say that what's imprisoned in the dark room through there is light as a leaf, as light and delicate and frail ... Still he is his father! He's Callum's father! And this – Callum may indicate around the room, the firelight, the black panes of glass, and the huge expanse of the emptiness beyond – this ... 'Home', he might say ...

Is his father's House.

With his number 23 and his music everywhere in it.*

And it's his father in that bed through there now, not a little thing – not a light and delicate thing, a leaf, Margaret – it's his *father*, and God knows how he could have made it out to the hill yesterday for there's nothing to him, Margaret says, just nothing ...

But listen to the sound he makes! John Callum MacKay! Even the night is listening, pressed in at the glass.

To the Ceol Mor. The Big Music.

To all of it, its ground and mountain and hill and its stepping off the edge into air.

Its variations and embellishments and lovely, dazzling crown. **

---

* Details of the compositions of JMS and the Sutherland family appear in Appendices 6/v and 9/ii and iii, relating to the musical history of The Grey House, and in the List of Additional Materials. The full handwritten MS by JMS of 'The Return' or 'Margaret's Song' can also be seen at the back of 'The Big Music'.

** This and the previous sentence describe the three to four movements that comprise a standard piobaireachd: the first laying out the 'ground' or principal musical idea, often also with a dithis, a singling and doubling on that theme; the second a movement away from the central theme into something more complex, that often carries within it a variation known as the 'Stag's Leap' – a leap into the unknown, where great risk is taken with the central musical idea; the third as a grand embellishment of the first

It's here. Listen! As Callum stands, drinking his father's whisky from a glass that's his father's glass, and hearing the Urlar and Taorluath and the Crunluath and the Crunluath A Mach.*

A tune imagined for somewhere much larger than this room can contain. All playing in this one small room.

So that, yes, his father may not be here with him but so he is also here. With his music, his CD case open and his dark writing, No. 23, inked on the paper flap. With the sideboard and the shelf where his father keeps the recordings of all his other tunes, the cases with his father's marks, his hand, his signature, the numbers marked from No. 1 to No. 30, with No. 4 and 17 and 27 and 11. Recordings of all the piobaireachds he has ever made, the strathspeys and the marches and the songs and the laments. All of this . . . And this . . . And this . . .

All music that plays back to . . .

The secret place.

Where the tunes were written.

That hidden, secret place.**

And not you, Callum thinks, of his mother, of his wife, of his sons, of his father, or Margaret or Iain, *or you or you . . . Not one of you know.*

His father doesn't even know.

That he and Helen went there, that they found it, his father's secret place where the tunes came from, and that they went in.

---

two movements, where a great deal of musical information about the original theme is given; and the final A Mach movement, a reflexive display of embellishments and variations wherein the music itself seems to describe its own making, the prowess of the musicianship and the musician, in a final show before the piobaireachd returns to play the notes of the ground or theme again.

* The movements as above, according to their original Gaelic descriptions.

** The secret place refers, of course, to the small building known as the Little Hut, built by John Callum in the years after his father's death to be a retreat in the hills where he could be on his own to compose and think and write, and be free, perhaps, from his father's still-living musical influence. Creative material and fragments from that place are on display in the Crunluath A Mach movement of 'The Big Music' and details are also contained in the List of Additional Materials at the back of this book.

two/fourth paper

It was always Margaret used to take Callum through. He would be too scared to go in on his own, first too young and then later, when he was a man, too aware of the absences between his visits, those long months passed into ugly gaps of time that made it difficult to return then and so he felt ashamed and, as though he were still the little boy, afraid.

Yet there were reasons for his staying away. His father telling him increasingly not to bother coming up, so why would he? Arrive just to stand and wait? With his father there in his chair, gone deeper and deeper into himself and not caring about anyone else. Sipping at his whisky and not even answering for a time his son's *Hello, Daddy*. His *How are you?* Not answering that question even.

Back then Margaret was the one who had always taken care of things between himself and his father. Just as she was the one, long ago, used to bring Callum into this room where he is now, holding him by the hand: 'Best come and say goodnight to your father.'

All the time, back then, it was Margaret taking care. Callum would be through in the kitchen with her and Helen for his breakfast and his tea, a sandwich in his pocket and then off with Helen for the whole day, away at the hills or the river. Margaret looking out for him as well as looking after his father — because, always, she's been looking after him and hadn't it always been that way?

Margaret.

His father would say her name and the air around him went soft.

Just – *Margaret.*

Just so.

For she did everything for his father. Everything. And maybe that was why
it was easier, later, when Helen was gone and Callum himself finished at
university and working and away . . . To stay away. Knowing Margaret was
there. For, after all, what need to come back when his father had Margaret
and her family in the House, when Margaret herself had been part of the
House for so long and knew everything about it, how best to take care
of his father over the years, what best to do? And, anyway, Callum always
thought – with the old man not speaking, not caring whether anyone
came to see him, any member of his family, his wife, or his son – what
reason would there ever have been anyway for him to make the journey
back here? So that, over the years, the visits became fewer, and more years
passed between them, and by the time Callum was married, had a family
of his own, sons of his own . . . How often did he come here then? Not
often. Ten years ago the last time. Maybe more.

So, Margaret.

Just –

'*Margaret* . . .'

Is what his father used to say.

'Just so.'

She's the one who's made it possible for him to stay away.

And by now – well, he's used to it, Callum is. With his father the way
he is, the life he'd chosen for himself a quiet life and alone . . . So Callum
is used to not having to come here. Until just now, and his mother's phone
call – because really, what's the need? Really, why bother? When –

Don't bother.

Is all his father ever said to him. When he was a young man and newly
arrived at the House after a long drive, or a boy coming to wish his father
goodnight and always Margaret would take him through –

Took your time, didn't you?

So, really, why would he bother? Come all the way up here? When –

Don't know why you bothered

– is all his father ever used to say.

But there was Margaret then. She was always here. And she would help him, take him through to his father – and she would stay on in the sitting room with them, she'd ask Callum questions, she'd talk to him and his father both. 'How was the journey?' 'Tell your father how well you're doing at school.' 'At university, how is it there?' 'Have they given you a pay rise yet?' 'How's the business?' 'How is your wife?' 'How are your boys?' All –

Margaret.

Back then. All –

Margaret.

Margaret.

Margaret.

As the air would soften around his father then, as he looked at her.

As she stood there with them both, by his father's chair.

Margaret, his father's eyes said to her and everything could be soft.

Margaret.

Margaret.

Margaret.

But she can't take Callum into the dark bedroom to see his father now.

~

The soup is untouched, and the roll, and tea, where Helen left it. He's had too much to drink and should take something to eat but his mouth is ashen and his stomach turns at the thought of food, at the sight of it, there on the tray.

The light in the hall casts a dim glow down the little passageway off the sitting room, down the east side of the House where his father sleeps these days, no longer in his own room upstairs but down here where he can be looked after, in that little single room with its single bed. It's the place where, Callum knows, they've all been brought – all his grandfathers, his father's father, and his father before him. All the long line of Sutherland men. All the Roderick Johns. The John Callums. All brought down in

their time to the bedroom on the ground floor, the first bedroom,* where
they can be looked after and then laid out in. The narrow room where
they come to die.

Callum has had a fair bit to drink but he's steady on his feet, and he
must go in there, to that same room. After all these years away and now
he must see his father, with Margaret not here to guide him, he must, and
be strong, go in there. He will be strong. So he pushes wide open the door
of the sitting room and goes down the hall to where his father is, and
the room is dark where he is but the moment he steps inside it the voice
comes from the bed –

'Daddy?'

His father's voice.

'Daddy?'

His father calling for his own father.

Christ.

Who's been dead for – what? Thirty years? Forty years?

Calling out, 'Is that you?'

'No.'

Callum steps towards the bed. 'No, Dad' he says. 'It's Callum here.'

There's a pause then, a minute, half a minute, a mark of time. Callum's
eyes adjust to the darkness, and he can see . . . The bed, a form outlined
upon it.

'Callum?'

'Aye.'

---

* The room referred to here cannot literally be dated back to the early eighteenth
century, when records show The Grey House as 'Grey Longhouse' or 'Langhouse' – a
traditional three-roomed building attached to a byre. At that time there wouldn't have
been a single bedroom such as the one described here, but only a separate, larger room
that would have accommodated many members of the family. However, that first house
comprises the foundations of the present Grey House, and so the bedroom where John
Sutherland lies now does date back to his great-great-grandfather's day, when plans
of the House show a separate bedroom next to what was the kitchen. Plans, some of
which are quite idiosyncratic in parts, are included as additional material at the back of
the book, and show the building and extension of The Grey House over the years, and
indicate these original rooms and their use.

'Callum?'

And –

Where did that come from, just then? That *Aye*?

Yet 'Aye' he says again, when his father asks him for the third time, 'Callum?'

So it's started.

Aye.

The being home.

The being here.

It's started and it's finishing here.

All at once Callum is exhausted. He sits down on a chair in the corner of the room. He could sleep now. Right here. Close his eyes. As though all the day has just come down upon him, on his shoulders, on his head . . . So all he wants to do is close his eyes.

'My Callum?' his father says. 'Or are you someone else's boy?'

'No, Daddy' he replies. 'It's me.'

And what was that Margaret said before?

Light as a leaf.

So how? Is all Callum can think, right this second. How? Now his eyes have adjusted fully to the dark and he can see fully the frailty of the figure lying here. That's calling out for his father like a little boy . . . How could . . . That? Get up onto any hill? Get out of bed even? How do anything when what is here before him is just a shape, the outline of a man, beneath the bedclothes? When what is left is no more than a voice, a shallow breathing in the dark? How could that . . . Even be his father? Yet it is.

They've given him something . . .

Margaret had said that the doctor had been.

To help him sleep.

And, yes, Callum thinks now: Just sleep. Is the best thing. For his father. For him. Is what he wants to do, sleep. Here . . . In this room . . .

Let the dark come down heavy on his own head and sleep, sleep.

And just as he does, feels himself pulled right down into the centre of unconsciousness where his father and all his father's fathers are waiting . . . There's movement from the bed, a rumple of sheets, the figure trying to right itself, to heave itself up – and in that second Callum is awake, is up and over to the bed. He lays his hand on a thin restless arm, his hand enormous upon it, and there's a sigh then, and the figure lets itself fall back upon the mattress.

For a space, an intake of breath, nothing happens. Then Callum hears his father's breath starts coming again, shallow but even. In. And out. And in. Out. Like a dry strip of paper let out of an old machine, one breath, another breath. In. And out. Tick. Tock. Goes the machine. Then a word. One word. Two words. More words:

First, 'Callum.'

First, his name.

Then –

'The dogs.'

Two words. Then –

'Were barking.'

Tick, tock.

'Before . . .' say the words. First one, then another. 'When we . . .' they say, 'were out . . . today.' And on the hill . . .' they say. Printing, breathing. In, and out. Upon the page.

'Callum.'

And there's a gap then. His father shifting in the bed. As though the last of the words that have come out from out of the dark have gone back into it again, printed back into silence.

So it is still again.

And only the breathing . . .

The quiet . . .

Is left. The figure on the bed who is his father but who is also barely anyone at all.

Callum takes his seat like before in the corner of the room. He's wide awake now. He won't be sleeping. All he can think, like before, is . . . How could that . . . Whisper? That . . . Figure, beneath the sheets . . . Take itself . . . Anywhere? Do . . . Anything? Though his mother had said when she called that his father had been missing, and Margaret told him that it was all yesterday morning his father had been gone, away up over the hill, and with a baby in his arms, and singing to himself Iain had said when they came upon him, and calling out . . . How could that . . . Story? That Margaret told . . . How could it have happened at all? When what is here in the bed is no more than a shape in the bed, no more than an outline of a sheet on the bed . . . ?

But, despite his thoughts, there's a shift now in the room and his father has turned his face towards him in the dark and he's speaking to him again, and stronger now than before, sounding like himself again, nearly, only quieter, saying, 'I knew when I saw you today on the hill, Callum. I knew then that you'd come home for good.' Then he says 'Come here,' and he pats the sheet beside him. 'Don't sit way over there on your own' he says. 'Come here to the bed and sit with me. For when the dogs found you on the hill you were so thin. Callum, you were forlorn. Come over here, boy, and sit with your father now.'

Callum can't speak. This could never happen. First the dark and the strangeness of the dark and now – and now to have to go over there to the bed and sit with his father in that close way. To be with him, close. No thoughts can even attach themselves to that idea, no words, no phrases. Even so, going over to the bed is what he does all the same, like sleepwalking, in a waking dream. He goes over to the bed and sits down on it beside where his father is lying. Though it could never happen, he sits beside his father's body. He covers his father's hand with his hand, though he would never do that either, touch his father's hand. Still he does, he sits there. He holds his father's hand while his father speaks.

'I knew of course it was you they'd found' he is saying. 'Always missing you, since you'd been gone. That was them barking, they were after you before. But of course you would come home to them. To give them a good run. And to be with your grandfather, too, of course. Out in the hills. I know. I said to my daddy that of course my son would come home.' He shifts again in the bed, sighs. 'Though he wouldn't believe me' he says, and his voice is quite regular by now, as though this dream Callum is having is a conversation anyone might have, one man to another, father to a son. 'He wouldn't, Callum' his father is saying. 'He was always stubborn, my father. They played the pipes for him at the end and they gave him a flag, did you know? That they gave him a flag to wear? But he wouldn't have worn it. He wouldn't have dressed himself that way. It was a suit he always wore, my father, even in the House. The suit had a hard cuff.'

He makes a swift gesture then, brings his hand up from the bed as though to strike his own face – and for a second, as his father had loosed his hold, Callum's own hand grazed the side of his father's face. For a second he'd felt the dry rub of stubble on his skin.

'It was a harsh cuff' his father says. 'And he had his hand there, like this –'

And now with his hand he does fully strike his own face.

'Here –' he says, and hits himself again. 'When I played I'd angered him, you see. And the cuff . . . It had an edge.'

He goes to strike himself a third time – but Callum stays his hand, and his father turns his face to the wall, a cry coming out of him that's like a child's cry. 'I was bad to play that way! For I had no right!'

And he is weeping now, Callum can hear. A kind of dry, silent weeping. He has a fist brought up to his mouth, a bony little fist that used to be such a hand, the hand on the steering-wheel driving north, remember? Remember that huge hand? No, he can't. Callum can't remember. He can suddenly not remember any of it any more. The room's dark, has taken it all into itself. All those days when he feared the size of that hand, could not look his father in the eye. All the – Christs! You took your time! All those days – because where are they now? In this dark? Where is he? The man who said those words? Banged his hand on the wheel? Shouted? Christ? He's not here in this little room, not in this bed.

'I angered him.'

Not in the dry sobs, the tiny cries.

'I played badly and there was a cuff and there was a flex.'*

Not here in the face against the wall.

'And I had the cuff at you, Callum. The cuff was at your own soft

---

* Earlier sections of 'The Big Music' describe the notes for this and other instances of intense emotion that cannot be fully expressed as a falling back, a withholding of the theme in the embellishments that are set around it, that will be released back into the tune in the display of technique and bravura that is the Crunluath A Mach.

cheek. When you were just a boy, you were just a boy . . .'

'No, Dad.' Callum leans over from the chair and lays his hand again on the arm of the figure who is lying there. This figure he doesn't know, who is his father. 'You never taught me the pipes, Daddy' he says. 'That wasn't me. I've never practised for you. Getting the notes right . . . That was you. It's you who plays. Your father who taught you. I have never —'

'Shhh . . .'

His father closes his eyes.

'Don't trouble yourself' he says, he's drifting back into sleep.

His breathing slowing again, settling . . .*

'You'll know by now . . .' he says. 'I'm not going anywhere . . . And can you hear that?' he says, but it's a whisper, his voice already gone far away by now, and sounding far away.

'How quiet it is?' he says.

Callum places his hand upon his father's little head.

'The dogs were barking before' his father whispers, 'but they've stopped now that Callum's come home.'

---

* This regular, even breathing is a feature of the opening bars of the Urlar of 'The Big Music', the notes patterning the resigned inhalation and exhalation of a single man, lying in the dark and awaiting, at the end of his life, his death.

insert/John Callum MacKay

Him answering his wife even now, after all these years, as 'Aye' not 'Yes' because he knew how she hated it, and he wanted her, it suited him, to have her hate him.

'Aye, taking the pills like the doctor says' he tells her, just to keep her quiet. 'Oh, aye' so he'll tell her that he's been swallowing them. Like an old boy off the hill's how he makes out with her now, to annoy her, like he's never lived anywhere but here.

What's your name again, missis?

He could say to her that!

Hah!

And it would make her wild.

What's your name again then, my dear?

As if he wants to be a stranger! That's how he could behave! As though to have never been married to her! That he wasn't even with her in London, as her husband, all through that time. That Callum was not the baby they took home from the hospital that day – in London, too. And don't think he's going back there either. With Callum. He's staying right here.

So he can say all he likes, *Aye.*

What's your name again, missis?

Do I know your face?

Because I'm just an old boy from the hills. And never been anywhere else but here.

Hard to think now that he ever was.

And to think that his own boy was born in London. London! There were the Houses of Parliament, in the hospital window there they were, and he had the baby in his arms, looking across the river, the Thames. His son!

With the silence of him, the boy, remember that? The silence of the baby in his arms? Like the silence of the baby in his arms this morning. And he must get that in, too. That silence. The way you get the gaps between the notes and the harmonics coming off them like an emptiness there, in the tune.* He'll need all that for the music. The silence and the emptiness when it had all been so beautiful then.

So put that in. Write that in.

That gap – the emptiness and gap and nothing to follow.

The pipes so perfectly tuned the silence can come in.**

And listen . . .

Hear it?

How the note of Love can only follow the note of Sorrow?*** He can hear that, too. It was there in the Lullaby and continues now all through the tune . . .

The sorrow in the air. The crying. For thinking about what he's lost – the baby in his arms all those years ago.

'F' to 'G', then 'F' to 'A',

but then 'F' to 'G', again.

And *Shhhh* . . . he had whispered to the child on the hill. For quietening her, to comfort her. But he had never comforted his son, who he'd also carried. Perhaps he could have, but he never did.

'F' to 'G'.

---

* There is no 'space' as such between phrases or groups of notes in bagpipe music, as the drone keeps up a steady tone beneath throughout the playing of the music. However, harmonics that occur in a perfectly tuned instrument create this effect – of 'gaps' in the music that sound like silence.

** In contemporary times, the piper Donald MacPherson is considered to be one of the best piobaireachd players in the world due to the sound he gets from his instrument – the result of perfectly tuned and matched pipes.

*** The High 'G' is the note of Sorrow on the piper's scale; the 'F', as we know, the note of Love.

Only everywhere he turns to listen, all he hears is sorrow now.

So . . .

Go back, MacKay.

To 'A'.

And 'A' again.

Go back. Go back.

It's your own note, after all, what you've always started with.*

So go back to that, then Johnnie – before the crying and the weather. There was always that and perfectly in tune. To start with and to finish with. So it might help you now. Because you don't need much more than that, do you? You've always thought that way. The 'A'. The importance of the 'A'. Who is there who would deny it? The need for the note to match the drone below?**

So . . .

Go back.

Back you go.

And let yourself be held for ever by your own held 'A'.

'Lament for Himself', all right. Just let that be enough for now. The sound of old MacKay just sleeping, just breathing, and all of it, all of it . . . Just . . . Himself.*** Because he has the theme completely in his head by

---

* Various sections of 'The Big Music' hint at the ambivalence that surrounds this note – for John Sutherland, in general, but also in the way the note figures in 'Lament for Himself'. Yes, we have read already that 'A' is the base note, from which the pipes are tuned, the first full note of the octave, therefore known as the Piper's own note, following the Low 'G'. But High 'A' is also the 'reached for' note and, as we will come to see, represents Margaret throughout the piobaireachd as well as John himself. In this way, some might say, John and Margaret can come together in 'The Big Music'.

** This describes the octave of the scale – the matching of the High and Low 'A' to the bass drone of the pipes. A detailed drawing of the bagpipes, showing its various pipes and drones etc., is found in Appendix 13/ii, along with related information.

*** 'Lament for Himself', as we know from the Urlar of 'The Big Music', opens with the repeating sequence 'B' to 'E', 'A' to 'A' / 'B' to 'E', 'A' to 'A' etc. that has about it the regular sound of inhalation, exhalation, as though breathing. Refer back to pp. 3, 4, 12 for a reminder of this.

now* and written down, and all of it to sound. Come together in his head out of the silence, the morning light and air, when he'd thought he was going to get away . . .

So –

'Aye.'

He'll say.

And 'Aye' again, to all of them, to make them mad.

For they don't know what's in his head.

And 'Aye' to Sarah most of all. For he'll not be taken.

'I'll not be back!'

When it's years gone by, all the empty time and marriage in it, and a son. And Callum a man now, did he hear that once? With children of his own – did he hear that, too? Was that in the doubling there, back there on the hill?**

'Aye.'

Or is it himself he's talking about?

For he himself did have a little boy.

And was he kind to him? If he never comforted him: *Shhh?* Was he kind? In all those years, that time with marriage in it, when his son was growing to be a boy . . . Was he kind? To his own boy? Can he say, 'Aye'? To that? That he was kind?

For suddenly he was grown up, Callum, and away.

To Edinburgh, was it? To London?

I'll not be back!

He said that – didn't he? But he did come back. They came here together in the summer . . . He and Callum came here . . .

'Aye.'

They did.

Goodnight, Daddy.

Yet he's not seen the boy. Not for all these years. Not since that time,

---

* The preceding Urlar indicates this.

** Refers to the singling and doubling of the Urlar back on p. 46 of 'The Big Music', when John Sutherland thought he was meeting his son – and also his father – out on the hill; the three generations come together in his mind in the way they never did in life.

long past, when they used to drive north and he left his wife behind him.

'And don't think I'm going back with you either!'

Is what he says.

This – 'A'.

Out loud in the dark.

'Lament for Himself'

Because he's not leaving. He's not going anywhere.

This endless, endless 'A'.

third variation/family history:* recent

All his life he's not belonged here. Is the fact of it. Not born here, Callum.
So not like his father, returning. Or his grandfather, or his grandfather's
father, here from the beginning. He was never going to be real that way.
Sarah said from the moment she got married pretty much that she'd have
as little to do with the place up north as she could, so Callum was never
brought here as a baby, an infant, as a young boy, he never came here. At
that time his father was so involved in his business that he had no reason
to return to the House. Thinking, no doubt, that it was a long way from
London – and his parents. So what need had he to see them? What were
they doing anyway, up there, all that time? Just sitting? For sure Callum's
father had no cause to take his newborn son to see them – is what Sarah
told Callum later. And he'd always believed his mother, Callum had,
when she described her husband's life that way. That, during that time his
father had the business to think about – not sentiment, emotion. All of
his interests then gone into making London a success – so what reason
to go all that way up north to an empty bit of land? What would be the
point in doing that? Callum's mother would have said.

  She'd been up there the once, that was all. Just after the registry office,
she'd told him. His father getting them the sleeper up to Inverness, then

---

* Some notes on the House, including additional information on the building, its
history and construction is available in Appendix 4.

taking a hire car and driving up that long deserted road: 'So I could be presented!' Sarah said. 'Presented! To those people!' *Those people.* His mother always used that phrase. When she was talking about Margaret or Iain or her husband's parents. About any of them, all of them: 'Those people!' So, she'd said, she'd been up to the House once. Had a cup of tea, the new bride had taken a cup of tea and with it a dram, but then she and Callum's father had driven back down the road again and away. Putting behind her her new husband's parents. And the man and the woman they had living there to help them with the place. And their daughter. *Those people.* Though all of them had been there at the door to wave them off. They'd never see Sarah again.

Is how the years went on.

So that it was only after old Callum's death that Callum's father started coming back up north again. At first to see his mother, to take up the place that had been left. The seat at the table. The plate, the knife and fork laid out.

'There's your supper, John,' his mother saying.

But then more and more . . .

Returning.

With less and less time spent between returning.

Arriving here finally, to stay.

And with enough suits hanging in the wardrobe that he can put them on someday. If he needs a jacket, a pair of trousers . . . His father's clothes will fit.

And Callum can remember those clothes.

How there were enough jackets, shirts in the wardrobe belonging to his grandfather, his great-grandfather, and that his father kept them. Margaret told him, one of those summers when he was a boy, how there were enough suits in the wardrobe 'that John says they'll put him in one of them the day he dies'. That day, she'd said, he'll be dressed all right. In his father's suit, or his father's father's . . . She had touched the top of Callum's head as she spoke. Three generations and they look enough the same.

But not Callum. He thinks: Three generations not the same as four and he's never belonged, like his father belongs . . . To the jackets backed up in the wardrobe, to the narrow bed that's left to all the men here in the end.* He wasn't born here, Callum, is the difference, is what he always told himself. 'And you don't resemble any of those people in the slightest' is what Sarah used to say. *Those people.* By then she was including her own husband in the phrase. She'd be phoning, his mother would, when Callum was up here in the summer, spending more and more time as his father stayed on each year. 'You're not like them at all' she would say. Phoning every day to check the child was all right: Had he enough warm clothes? Enough things to do? Was he eating properly? Were they taking care of him? Those people? Even though he was only visiting, not staying on, and it was his father by then who'd become set in the place – and this long after Callum's grandmother was no longer there to lay his knife and fork on the table, draw out his chair. Still Callum's mother called about her son all the time as though, Callum thinks now, she had reason to fear for him that he might also stay. When it was always so clear to him that it was his father's home and it wasn't Callum's, it would never be, he wasn't born here. Still Sarah would be calling as though she might lose him, too, to The Grey House, in the way she'd lost her husband by then. 'Is that woman still working there?', saying. 'What's her name, anyhow? Margaret?'

So the years pass, and his father is finally here for good, returned to the place where he was born and not ever to leave it. And Callum may remember the touch of Margaret's hand upon his head but still he's never been anything more than the visitor here. While the House is still the same House where he came to as a boy, where he's come to as a man. But not his House. Though it goes back on his father's side for generations and though he's spent long summers here, a long time . . . It's not his House. He's never belonged here.

~

To clarify: Where they've brought Callum's father, where they're keeping him, looking after him now . . . It's the oldest part of the House – dating

---

* The List of Additional Materials contains floor plans of The Grey House; also Appendix 5/i and ii give domestic history and further details.

back to the original building established back in Callum's grandfather's father's day. The little sitting room where Callum was earlier, where his father used to play and where he kept recordings of his music that Callum was looking at just before, they used to call that — rather grandly one might say — the 'Music Room' in the old days.* That's where all the men would sit together, Callum's great-grandfather, then his grandfather, then his own father and his piping friends, a gathering of hard-backed chairs that are still kept, in various rooms: there's Roy Gunn's chair and there's Iain McKay's chair and Donald Bain's . . . All these names of well-known musicians of the time, and the men would talk about *piobaireachd* then, on those nights when they came together, and how it *might be played*, how it *should be played*, and how they themselves might *attempt* it.** Talking, taking a whisky now and then, before getting up, one after the other, to pick up his pipes and start them. Hitting the bag for the low drone with the first steady blow, taking some time there, in the room, to adjust the tuning, and then, once they were going, all the pipes in tune together like a rhyme, using the hall just beyond the door as the place where they could pace out the tune, going up and down, using the sitting room itself, the Music Room, to make the return. So they went, these evenings, for hours, some nights, until midnight and beyond, the slow tramp of their feet in time to the music's long breves. Up the hall, then back again. Up and down. Up and down. Urlar. Taorluath. Crunluath. Return, return, return. And that single room, the one just off the hall where they marched to, where Callum's father lies now — that would have been the original bedroom

---

*   This great sense of the past that was contained in this part of the House may have been what prompted John Sutherland to build his Little Hut away in the hills — so he could have somewhere else, disconnected from that history, that would allow him to compose and think outside it — Appendix 10B, referring to the Little Hut and the Crunluath A Mach movement, will be of interest to those who wish to explore this idea further. Note also: the next movement of 'The Big Music', the Crunluath, gives more details of the evenings described here, including accounts and personal recollections. Finally, information about the House is included in Appendices 4–9, along with details of the 'Winter Classes' — a more formal version of the kinds of evenings described here.
**   The stress, in italics, on certain words in this sentence might indicate music in itself, a rhythm, sense of phrasing — of pacing.

after all. From that first, early, part of the House. Long before the grand extension was made, with the long and lovely drawing room there, and the dining room, before the rooms upstairs were added on and furnished by Callum's grandfather and grandmother – that little single room would have been where Callum Sutherland's grandfather's grandfather used to sleep, at the end of one of his own long nights of return, return – pulling up the thin wool blankets. There was the same room, the same music: Urlar, Taorluath, Crunluath, return – sounding in his mind as an echo, just as it would sound to his son, and his son's son, and his son's son's son, as they all went to sleep.

So, yes, the room is inevitable. Is what needs to be clarified here. Inevitable that Callum's father would end up there. Like his father before him. His father's father. Despite the lovely rooms upstairs where large beds are and tall windows. Despite the wide halls that have been created, the landings. There is this part of the House. The earliest part where, when Callum was a boy, he remembers that you could not hear the telephone ringing for it was in Margaret and Iain's part of the House and only they could hear if Sarah were to ring now and ask whether Callum or his father are all right. That's how far away it is, then, this part of the House. From the rest of the House. His father's room.*

And look at the room. It's a fine enough room for a man at the end of his life. There's enough space in it for a single bed and a chair, and a small wardrobe that would take, what? Two suits? Three suits? The rest of his clothes are all upstairs and he doesn't need them. The room would be modest in all ways, with a window giving onto the rowan tree that grows at the back there, that waves its branches so heavy with orange berries that in the high winds in autumn you'd think the berries would scatter and tumble but Callum's father sees, in the daylight hours, as he lies here, how they hold fast to their tree.

And so he'd tried to stay away, Callum thinks, his father, as he himself

---

* As before, floor plans etc. of The Grey House, showing renovations and change of use, can be found in the List of Additional Materials at the back of 'The Big Music'. Here see Appendix 4/iii.

has been away . . . But look where his father came to in the end. Only to his own father's room. And Callum has been there before. For though his mother never knew, Margaret's told him, a long time ago when he was a boy and she'd taken him by the hand to this same room, to show him: *John says* . . . When she'd touched him lightly on the head, remember? As she'd described what has already been detailed in the pages here? That just as at the end of his life this was where his grandfather came to, and his father before him, so would Callum's father come to the same room one day. The box room.

With the three suits waiting in the wardrobe, he doesn't need any more, and she'll put him into one of them on the day he dies.

two/fifth paper

Now that Callum has seen his father, said hello, wished him goodnight
. . . Really, what is there left for him to do here?

Because of course his father is not going to leave this place. What was
Callum thinking? That he was just going to come back here — after all
this time away? And take his father off, just like that, to London? What
was he doing even letting his mother talk to him about it? *I want you to go
up there, Callum, and bring him home.* For what home? London? Home? That's
not his father's home. This is his father's home. Here. Where he is. Where
he has always been.

So there is nothing he can do here. Callum. To turn this situation,
change it. He'll have to call his mother tomorrow and tell her. Tell Anna
and the boys. That it's not as simple here as he'd thought, 'I'll have to stay
on, for a bit longer' say. 'Because the situation here, it's fixed, my father's
fixed.'

Just like Callum had thought —

I'm not going anywhere.

Those were the words. They're sounding in Callum's mind like his
father has just said them. So of course he won't be telling his father:
Come with me, Dad. I'm here to take you to London. Mum wants you
there. A hospital, doctors. She's got it all worked out. He was never going
to be able to influence his father in any way. Like before, in the little
bedroom, those words coming for him, out of the dark . . . That was

his father there, speaking, but the whole situation here is no longer just about one man, his father is part of something that's gone on longer than that ... His father, his father's father ... Because nothing is any longer as simple as: now. Now that his father is at the end. Now that the present has become the past, and all the pasts are collected into this one present Now. So what chance does he have, Callum, one son? Coming in so late in his father's life to say: Come away with me, Dad. Come to London, Mum's waiting. That's a joke, that's never going to happen. It was never going to happen.

He feels exhausted. He needs to go to bed. Tomorrow he'll make the call, tell Anna and his mother – what? That he will leave? Stay? Say he'll come back to London but later? Or stay on, but if so, how long will he have to stay? Days? Weeks? He can't imagine any of this. Can't think about it. Can't think any of it through. Realises, in the thickness of his tiredness and his whisky, that he doesn't even know what he's going to do this minute, this second, let alone tomorrow, anything else. Where is he even sleeping? Iain or Margaret – they've put his bag somewhere and he doesn't even know where that is. Everything changed since his father's been moved downstairs and not in his old room and everyone in bed now and asleep, so who can he ask: Where is my bag? Where am I staying? With his father no longer in his room and all of upstairs may be closed off, for all he knows, Margaret arranging things differently now, and Callum supposed to be somewhere else in the House, and not where he used to stay when he was a boy? He hasn't asked anything. So he doesn't know. Where his bags are. Where his bed is. He knows nothing here.

He's exhausted. That's the only thing he knows. The whisky he drank earlier has left an edge of grittiness in his eyes. He wants to go to sleep. He switches off the light in the sitting room. Just think about everything tomorrow, ask Margaret about everything tomorrow. He closes the door behind him and makes his way in the half-dark to the foot of the back stairs, starts up them to the landing – but the first floor looks shut up and dark. It's as though all the rooms are closed off, and his old room down the L-shaped end of the hall ... Sure enough when he gets to it the door is closed, stiff when he pushes it – and inside it's empty.

So he's not sleeping in there. He was right, Margaret has changed things — and instead the one light that's been left on at the top of the main stair is by his father's old room. He walks towards it, sees the door is open. Someone —

Margaret?

Has gone in there and placed his case by the bed, turned down the covers. Turned on a little lamp. Someone —

Helen?

Has been in here. In his father's old room and prepared it for him. Knowing he'll be coming here. Knowing he'll be tired. Imagining him . . . Pushing open the door . . . Seeing that it's light in here and it's warm . . . Seeing his case sitting there by the side of the bed.

And somehow . . .

To be seeing that now, the case placed there, by his father's bed with the covers turned back . . .

To see his jacket there, laid on his father's bed . . .

He needs to lie down.

To think that Helen's been here. To think that she knew.

That he'd end up here. That she had turned back the covers for him in that way . . .

Oh, Helen, Helen — but he wants to close his eyes . . .

He wants to leave this room, he must leave it. He doesn't belong here. Not in this room of his father's that Helen's been to before him, with his jacket and his case.

Please.

Helen.

If he prayed, he'd be praying now.

To think he's supposed to finish this day here. In his father's bed. In his father's old room. With Helen somewhere in the House. When he's supposed to be here for his father, and none of this about Helen, but about his father, and he's supposed to be here for his father, and he's had too much to drink and he's tired and he must leave this room, please, he must get out of this room . . .

But she's been here before him, Helen. She's turned down the bed.

And as he thinks those two sentences, he's sitting down on the bed and it yields to him, lets him in, in a way that's so comforting, so inviting of his rest . . . That in a second he knows . . . He'll be asleep. Despite Helen. Despite the soft light from the lamp she's left on for him, the low light and the heavy curtains drawn against the darkness and it's warm here and it's peaceful and he's so very, very tired . . .

Because he has the energy for nothing. No thought, no piece of a sentence, no desire or bit of hope. Because nothing's going to happen here. He may as well call his mother in the morning and tell her so . . . That there's nothing . . . Any of them . . . Can do . . . Only . . . Sleep.

He's so very tired. Starts taking off his clothes where he's sitting, his shirt, his shoes . . .

And really, what was he doing . . . Even thinking of doing . . . Coming here?

I'm not going anywhere.

He doesn't know. He never knew anything, Callum. He's always been the outsider here. Remember? And his father may have spoken to him, into the dark – but they're not in this together, him and his father. Those few weeks each summer, they count for nothing. A few years, that was all.

Coming here . . . Arriving for the first time and he was already, how old? Nine?

He unbuttons part of his shirt and pulls it over his head.

Yes, he was nine years old.

He's exhausted.

Nine years old when he first came here.

So tired he can't move. As he unbuckles his trousers, still sitting on the bed.

Nine years old.

Nothing like being born here.

Coming here for the first time when he was nine, nothing like. A few weeks in the summer, that was all. Arriving that first time, he was always someone who was just arriving.

Helen there with her mother at the door.

What are you doing here?

Remember?

What's your name? How old are you?

Her looking at him with those steady eyes of hers.

My name's Callum. I'm nine.

And him looking back at her, remember? But also not able to look.

Well, I live here, she'd said.

His eyes are closed by now. He's lying on the bed. He has to take his shoes off, his trousers . . .

I'm older than you but I'll be your friend if you want.

But for now, just lying . . .

I'll be your friend, if you want to. Do you want to?

Looking at him.

What?

When he was nine years old, then ten, then eleven . . .

Be friends?

When he has to take his shoes off, then his trousers . . .

Do you want to?

When he wasn't ever belonging.

What?

With the grandfather and grandmother he'd never met long dead . . .

Be friends?

And always he was just arriving . . .

Do you want to?

Always . . .

Yes.

He sits up, pushes off his shoes. His socks . . . His trousers, all his clothes . . .

Helen.

Please.

Help me here.

He gets into bed. Turns off the light. And from far away somewhere, somewhere else in the House altogether, as he falls into a deep sleep he hears a baby's cry.

~

Callum's eyes start open. In the middle of the dark after dreams – such dreams! Has he woken? There was a cut of a cord – a flex – the harsh sting of it across his skin and – a boy, was it him? Sitting at the chanter in a big armchair? And the chair's too big for him to sit in. His legs don't touch the floor.

'Play it again!' comes the voice out of the dream – and he is awake! Eyes staring into the dark.

'I can't!'

For it is completely dark here. He looks around and for a second can't remember where he is. Then it comes back.

That he's in his father's room. And it's cold here. He feels cold.

Part of him still in the dream – a man downstairs, sitting by the fire, but it's cold and he's crying, the little boy. Callum can feel the tears on his cheek. That the man would so hate him that he would whip him across the leg with the flex, shout, 'Do it again! Play it again!' Callum squeezes his eyes shut to stop the tears, but he can't stop them – 'I can't!' He's cold and he's crying.

Then, as he starts to waken, hearing his own voice 'I can't!' as he emerges from the dream, he is aware that someone is there, really there in the room with him, but not from the dream.

Someone.

'Are you okay?' she whispers.

He turns, and she is there, a shadow beside him, in the dark.

'It's me' she says.

Though he can barely see her.

His hand goes up, instinctively, to touch her face.

'I heard you shouting' she says.

'Helen?'

'You were having a bad dream.'

Then she takes his hand and puts it to her face. He can't see her. It's been . . . How long? Twenty years? Since she was last near him? Twenty years? Longer. It's been for ever.

'Helen?'

And he can't see her.

'Shhh . . .' She kisses his palm, the soft insides of his hand.

'Shhh . . .'

He can't see her.

Though she leans down to him, he can't. Still he can't see her.

'Helen –'

'Shhh . . .'

Though he still can't see her.

'Shhh . . .'

Still . . .

Can't . . .

Still . . .

'I'm here with you now' Helen says.

insert/John Callum

It's late. But the House is here. It's looking after him.

All through those years away, the false years, there's been this place, waiting.

And so he'd cast his eyes about the hills today, had he not? And claimed it all? The air, its sound? Only casting about him this fine day, the last of the summer in it, and the future in his arms . . . There was all the future then, as it's in his head now, the fine late summer air and the Lullaby he's made for the little one he's carrying – and you see? He does know how to carry a child.*

So – everything he needs, then, for the tune, completed.

Even with the clouds slipping so there was darkness in the sky and he needs a lullaby then to stop the rain, her crying . . .

Even so . . . Everything was there.

As he took up his father's life.

And the life of his father's father.

Gathered up and collected in the set of notes that are playing now.

And all of it . . .

---

* Refers to the Urlar of 'The Big Music' as before – to the Lullaby theme where we've noted the way one part of the music is developed into more complex patternings: see the insertion of an outside narrative voice, the child's mother and her lullaby on pp. 19, 20, and 21; see also the leitmotifs of carrying and being held that are played out in the story of John Sutherland and his own son in pp. 159 and 160 of this movement. The Index of 'The Big Music' may also be of interest here.

Perfectly . . . It's been perfectly done.

Where there'll be no fault or smirring of the tune,* the myriad of demi-semi-quavers of the third movement to mirror perfectly with their hundreds of embellishments the notes that precede it and the sequences all following in ready succession . . .

Of his father, his father before him.** One generation to the next, multiply articulated, line after line, in perfect fingerings . . .

On and on and on, one movement to the next. Over one hill, to another . . .

To there.

To, 'Hush, my darling.'

'Hush.'

And he should have married her.

He knows that now.

For what else is there but to hear the sound of the past coming up behind you as you walk towards the end?

Only love.

And, these past weeks, now . . . They may as well have been all his life.

When each day he rises . . .

And there's the coldness of the rooms but then Margaret makes them warm again.

There's the smell of fires, the burning peat in flames and sometimes wood, and cooking. Soup, maybe, and maybe bread.

A door opening somewhere, a far voice, a person calling out in the House. Iain it could be or Helen, or there's the clear infant cry of Helen's child.

---

* The Glossary describes 'smirring' as a general smudging; often it is used in the Highlands as a metaphor for a light rain. Here it refers to a smudging of the notes – as imperfectly played, the fingers sliding over the holes of the chanter to create a note that does not come out clean. Appendix 10 carries details on the 'Lament for Himself' and the MS itself shows these embellishments.

** There is the suggestion here that the JMS piobaireachd 'Lament for Himself' bears similarities with some of the piobaireachd written by earlier members of the Sutherland family. Similar musical relationships can be discovered in a close analysis of the MacCrimmon piobaireachds. The Bibliography/Music: Piobaireachd/secondary will be of interest to those readers who want to pursue this idea further.

Then the nights come in again to the blackness of the glass. And dreams come . . .

Like the 'Play it again!' or the crack of the flex. Like the sound of his own voice calling, out of the past, for his father to forgive him, 'I promise I'll try harder!', and crying for his mother to come back whole out of the dead earth and pick him up and hold him . . .

For people in this part of the country are lonely enough.

There are large intervals in the music.*

'I'll not be back!'

As though a theme all in breves** to begin with.

'I'll not!'

And the fingering, too, is spare.

So, yes . . . Lonely enough.***

But then there's the dithis and the doublings as the sons come in.

And their sons.

So the singling.

The doubling.

And gradually, slowly, each white page is marked up with the variations and the turns, over time the whole manuscript crowded with the notes, the phrases, the bars all connected. Drawn in right there in black ink upon the stave, or at the bottom, on separate bars, notes jostling and calling. Filling the white space with a crowd of music . . .

And yet all the while, as the theme busies itself and turns, plays and turns again, he sees himself fading, the player, this one man . . . His own

---

*   Intervals are the spaces between the notes – the Urlar of 'The Big Music' describes some of these. Also Appendix 10/i and ii explain why certain aspects of 'Lament for Himself' are quite particular, in musical terms. This Taorluath movement also describes similar spaces – as certain ideas that may have seemed at first far apart come to be related.

**   A breve is a long note, traditionally held for eight beats, and rarely used – though bagpipe timekeeping is different and holds to its own time signature. The Glossary carries some musical terms.

*** The opening bars of the Urlar articulate this sense of loneliness – there is a relentless quality to the repetition of the notes, as one can see on a final completed MS or listen to in full on the finished recording of 'Lament for Himself'.

notes getting softer, smaller, as he walks further and further towards the edge of the hill . . .

For what can you do to stop a thing once you've started? You don't stop it. Keep walking.

Only to discover you've found the place where you started.

Took your time to come back to us, didn't you?*

So just pull the blanket up, boy, right there to your chin, and listen, listen to it all around you:

The music that's always been there in his head finally getting to hear itself be played.

From childhood and manhood to age . . . All here, laying itself out like a map of all the places he knows and of his history and the people he has known, stranded together in this grass under his feet, spread out at his feet as he walks, further and further away . . .

His own life turning to wave goodbye as he disappears over the brow of the hill . . .

Then the crown, the last part, with Margaret's note. The note that's still to come in.**

So that finally, with the end, there can be the beginning again.***

---

*   Who speaks here, and about whom? Is it John MacKay himself, addressing Callum on one of his return journeys home? Or is it the narrative voice we have been hearing more and more throughout 'The Big Music' – Helen asking this question of Callum, then? Or is John's father or grandfather or any of the Sutherlands coming out of the past to speak to their boy? Or is it, as is most likely, all of these? Certainly that idea, of many individual themes coming together in a layering such as this, is in tune with the idea of the piobaireachd itself.

**   This refers to the Crunluath movement of 'The Big Music' that follows this Taorluath movement, Crunluath meaning 'crown', as we know, but carrying also in that definition of something that is glittering and beautifully complicated and royal the meaning, too, of resolution, the completion of an idea that until now, perhaps, has only been hinted at.

***   As can be seen in the relevant Appendices relating to structure of the piobaireachd (e.g. Appendices 11 and 12), the final lines of Ceol Mor always return to the original theme laid down in the Urlar. Appendix 10A/ii describes this, as does the structure itself of 'The Big Music'.

Taorluath/final fragment

The stag leaps/into vacancy . . . The pure air like a white page. Now that he's stopped taking the pills and at the House they won't know that he's been gone. With this being the end of the summer and his last chance to make a go of things, get back up onto the hill . . . Look! He's already there.

THIRD MOVEMENT:
CRUNLUATH

three/first paper

So then, the plan for John, the plan itself . . . It's written already – as the
central tune of this piece. You've heard it in the opening lines of the
Urlar, the theme of the piobaireachd that's the final thing he'll compose,
the 'Lament for Himself', with the first movement down, and the second*
gathering together in the leap of its variations a story that's his but not
his alone. Now it's the third part John Sutherland needs, to wrap around
himself by way of a finish, the crown.** For that is what it is, the third
part, the Crunluath, the crowning of the music that carries the ideas that
were there from the beginning, in the tune of the little one he took up
with him onto the hill, this morning it was, only this morning . . . But
a finish to that same story now that has a sense of its own performance
about it, the showing off of its makings as it is played, its construction
revealed, displayed in all its intricacy and colours and shape.

So, in a way, one might describe this 'Lament' – in its forms, in its
structure and central tune – as more dependent than most upon a theme
that can be taken far, far beyond the notes' initial calling. For as all great
piobaireachd are dependent upon the stability of their ground for their
variations, as they all need a musical line that, if you like, can bear the

---

* Earlier sections of 'The Big Music', the Urlar and Taorluath, have already described this.
** Appendix 10A/ii shows the original MS of 'Lament for Himself' and the Crunluath
movement here will describe the development and extension of many of the theme's
original ideas.

weight of its embellishments, in the same way the tune here depends for its conclusion upon the strength of a frail lullaby, a song that's turned into an elegy, a story, a journey and a journey's end.

All this has been through John Callum by now.

Each note, how it must follow.

Each breath, phrase.

The construction of the whole a patterning that builds to paragraphs, phrases, pages in his mind, sung to himself through the solitary hours, laid down, much of it already, in notes upon a stave and papers that will be gathered.*

And so the completion can be said to be in place for him by now, the notes themselves collecting all about them every accidental and roundel that will, in turn, upon the crown's completion, make a crown of a crown . . .** His 'Lament' with the future embedded in it, in her Lullaby, his own farewell, the sound he's created gone out into the world with him gone from it – for he'll be lost by the end of the tune, he'll not last this night. A doctor entering into his dark room would confirm it: Old Johnnie. Time to follow the rest of them by now, my boy. Your suit is laid out and waiting.

So, yes, then, a Lament, for the one who's leaving – but a Lament too for everything he's let slip away, the pride and the thoughts of himself as a big man, the big man and all that come to nothing. Those notes too will be worn into the tune. His failure as a father, a son, as a husband and lover – those flattened phrases too and those lines will sound out amongst the theme,*** his return, no matter how high the music can reach, always going back to his own note, the endless 'A'. The sound of someone who's not been able to remove himself from his own mind to see the

---

* The following movement of 'The Big Music', the Crunluath A Mach, gives details of these papers. Canntaireachd is the singing of piobaireachd to denote the notes of the scale, as well as phrasing, rhythm etc. John Sutherland would have thus been able to sing through to himself exactly the tune he has composed. The Glossary includes relevant Gaelic musical terms.

** The Last Appendix describes the effect of a finished piobaireachd upon the listener.

*** Appendix 12/ii gives details. Also note: the pentatonic scale of the bagpipe has a more 'flattened' sound owing to the slightly different scale of the chanter and the presence of an extra note in the octave – the Low 'G'.

ways and needs of others, for one minute, not for one minute.

'Lament for Himself', indeed.

For that is how it has always been.

Always . . . Just . . . Himself.

There it sounds now, as though to remind him:

'B' to 'E', 'A' to 'A'

'B' to 'E', 'A' to 'A'

'B' to 'D', 'G' to 'G'

'B' to 'D', 'G' to 'G'

'B' to 'E', 'A' to 'A'

'B' to 'E', 'A' to 'A'

Himself.

Who's never let anyone in.

Lying quietly in the dark.

That self all he is left with now.*

Earlier, as he lay in his room waiting for Callum to come in, that was what he was aware of, too. How all that was left of him was just that self, bits of parts that were his life once, perhaps, but now scattered, broken. So there's the part with a son who might come to him —

Hello, Dad . . .

— but the boy like a stranger to him.

*You took your time, though.***

---

* This has an almost literal meaning here: the self is indeed the fragment of the 'Lament' that remains — showing clearly this sequence of notes in the opening bars — but it also relates to the self that is depicted here, and in the earlier Taorluath movement, that is a man who is at the end of his life, and more frail than ever following the incident on the hill yesterday, when he suffered another stroke and was after that confined solely to bed. Finally there is a more figurative meaning as, despite his thoughts and music, John Sutherland has been unable to make reparations for earlier decisions. The 'self he is left with', then, is the man he's always been.

** This phrase — in longer and slightly different versions — appears on pp. 126 and 150 of the Taorluath. Its layering of meanings there is less on show in the episode here,

So there's that poor part.

And there's the part, too . . . That had . . . Not only a son, but a wife . . .

Marriage . . .

That part.

Who'd had a father and a mother once. A home.

I'll not be back!

That, too, all jumbled in with him here – in the pieces of a blanket, all these parts – of a man who could have so much but would put it all aside. That he could come to be so cut off, disconnected, that he would have someone who would care for him and be with him, who would consider him in all her thoughts and actions, who moves tirelessly, endlessly around him, in these rooms of the House – but has given her little, nothing . . . Then Lament for that, too. For a man who has barely lived in this world is what he is – not lived. Who has absented himself within his own privacy,* who has been frightened of love, who will say 'Who are you?' to a man or woman he's been close to at the time, had in his home or in his bed, still he'll be able to say 'Who are you?' as though he does not know that person's name.

Because they've all been in his dark room today.

Those who know him, the kind of man he is.

Of parts, of bits.

They've all been here. His son. His father. His mother. Reminding him. Showing him.

And Margaret. The woman who moves quietly around the rooms of the House. Who comes to him in the dark.

The music of her – her particular note – that is yet to come in, that says to him, 'I am here with you. Be at peace.'

---

where John speaks with derision to the young man who has driven up all the way from his university town to see him – and who his father has considered has arrived too late.
*   This privacy, this absolute cutting off of himself from the world, is represented by the secret place for composition John Sutherland built for himself up in the hills. Appendix 10B shows the relationship between the isolation of this place and the creative work made within it – details of the Little Hut and John's time there in writing his 'Lament' emerge fully in this movement of 'The Big Music'.

Yet what did he ever do for Margaret in return? What did he ever allow her? What gift did he give?

As he lies, grey thing, in the dark . . .

Though she's given him everything, everything — the child in his arms this morning Margaret's daughter's child — and he should have married her, for he loved her, he'd always loved her . . .

So . . . Margaret.

Going up the side of the green face of the hill with a child who's Margaret's child and he's carrying her, the notes of her, strung all about her like a beginning.

Therefore quietly, my darling — and listen!

To the 'F' to the 'G'.

To the sweetness in the Lullaby and soft.

For there'll be nothing but the silence soon.

first return/lullaby: innovations; composition; derivations

The singing of a lullaby is as old as singing itself and examples of this kind of music appear as instances of narrative in ancient texts such as the Old Testament of the Bible and in the Qur'an – with early known versions in English dating back to the fifth century and before.

The Highland tradition of folk singing encompasses many very lovely lullabies that are still sung to babies and small children, to send them to sleep on summer evenings when it is broad daylight outside and they think they should be wide awake with the sun. Or they have been composed to calm the same children into dreams and restful slumber in the depths of winter when the dark sky is screaming with storms and rage.

Soft songs, all of them.

Some curious and beautiful lullabies sing of the taking away of children, or the loss of them to faerie kingdoms, their changing of one body for another, a sudden vanishing and the child is replaced by a sprite or a monster who may look the same at first as Mammy's darling but who is in fact a dire cast of the one who has been spirited away.

Strange, then, that the music would still sound as sweet.

In 'The Big Music' John MacKay has a notion of just such a Lullaby to be inserted in his piobaireachd 'Lament for Himself' – a sweet tune, a small run of notes we heard first in the Urlar movement that stand in for the infant Katherine Anna MacKay whom he has kidnapped and taken out with him onto the hill.

Fragments of the song appear here as follows:

(first verse)
In the small room, a basket waits,
A basket empty for no baby is there.
The mother is gone, left the room for a moment
— and in that moment he's mounted the stair.

(chorus)
You took her away,
Young Katherine Anna,
Carried her off, tall Helen's child.
You took her away, a baby sleeping
In your old arms, took her into the wild.

(second verse)
An old man taken the baby away,
He's snatched her up in his arms for to see
Her life in his, to stay his dying
— but the child's not his, her mother is me.

As seen elsewhere in these papers, in certain related information and notes that contribute to overall themes in this narrative, it is speculated that some piobaireachd music has its basis in certain Highland songs and airs that may date back to the fifteenth century or earlier. It is perhaps the knowledge of this tradition that worked upon John Sutherland in his thinking about his own final composition — the Lullaby that he had in mind being one, perhaps, that was already known to him. Certainly, while no records of such a song were found amongst his papers, the second line of the Urlar of his 'Lament for Himself' clearly indicates the structure of a gentle tune that might be sung to a child. It has a haunting repeat that seems to hark back to something any of us may have heard, as children, when we were distressed and needing soothing or were wide awake and restless and should be going to sleep.

This tune — the single line of it gone into a repeat — would have been parsed and set to the words shown above. Helen MacKay may have uncovered something in John Sutherland's private notes that suggested this musical treatment, and, most likely, found the words straight out of the events that took place that terrible morning, when her daughter was taken from her. Certainly the theme of babies lost or without their mothers was a common enough one in folk song – and the image of the missing child as a subject for song would have suggested itself easily enough as a poetic idea to a mother who had herself experienced the loss (though temporarily) of a baby.

You took her away,
Young Katherine Anna . . .

So it would be a simple matter to set her own story down on the page.

In the small room, a basket waits,
A basket empty for no baby is there.
The mother is gone, left the room for a moment
– and in that moment he's mounted the stair.

Thereafter, in 'Lament for Himself' the Lullaby appears as a sort of leitmotif throughout the piobaireachd.

This is an unusual idea to have appearing in a piobaireachd another subject altogether (the principal subject, according to the definition of the music, being the life of Sutherland himself) but it is by no means exceptional, as the piper and composer R. J. C. Gunn notes:

Many piobaireachd have a sound to them that could be a very gentle, sweet song. This is not often commented upon in a discussion of piobaireachd – that is, the tender, even quiet aspect of many of the tunes. But certainly it is there. One feels many of the great Laments could be sung – this is the foundation of canntaireachd after all: the singing down of a tune, and often yes, a quiet and gentle singing. Remember, too, that one of the greatest piobaireachd ever written, the great 'Lament for the Children', is also a beautiful and very sad song. One hears the voice in it when it is well played.

Finally, the Lullaby being composed by John Sutherland is distinctive in the way the composer imagines it as also sounding out through the music as a kind of declaration. He wants the child to sleep, yes, while he carries her somewhat clumsily up the side of a hill, but he sees her also as a new theme in the tune – 'new life from old' as he thinks of it – and so she has her own set of notes to accompany her on this peculiar journey that he has kidnapped her for. In this way the Lullaby works as a way of carrying the tune forwards into the rest of the piobaireachd, so that its theme becomes layered with other themes and gains depth and resonance – see the way certain notes, the return to the top 'A' in particular, come to represent other ideas and people as the story develops:

He's snatched her up in his arms for to see
Her life in his . . .

Lullabies, after all, are rarely written for just a single child. Remember –*
　'He looks down into his arm. She's awake, the child is, giving him that fixed look but not judging, deep and thoughtful as though she's from another world, as well she has been for she's been with her mother . . .
'Hush.' He whispers quietly like he's seen her do, the baby's mother, pokes in one of the little cloths to keep her from the breeze. 'You know fine' he answers her, 'what I'm doing with you here.'
　For it's a Lullaby, is what it is. The smallest, gentlest song against the ground, against the broad and mindless hills like quietness set into the great layout of a tune.
　'Hush . . .'
　He can hear it in his own 'Hush' and in her soft way with him as she lies in his arms, just looking up at him, just looking . . . The whole little song of a Lullaby coming in, the few notes, like a breath of breeze against the land and him settling her in close to his side again as though that will quiet her but she's not crying.
　'And this is the only way . . .' says John Sutherland then, clear into the air
. . .
　'The only way . . . You do understand me. How I needed to have her with me this way for the tune.' The theme of it worked in by now to the very sound of the whole. Its few spare notes spun into the crown the tune wears.'

---

* The following passage, although it differs from that version slightly, is from pp. 5–6 of the Urlar.

three/first paper (cont.)

And for now he must stop. Listen!

He'll hear the whole thread of it about them both, any minute, as he stands here on the hill. The 'F' to the 'G' and the 'E' to the 'A' and what it means for him to be carrying this child, for him to be here. Wait for it now and – there! Can you hear it? The last thin notes and what they mean? The understanding of who she is? The child you're carrying, Johnnie? Listen. Quietly, carefully. Can you hear who she is?

For she's so spun into the theme by now, with her mother, her mother's mother . . . That surely he must know the tune is safe, that it's finished because it will go on. The ending has been fixed by the beginning. Turning on through the first movement to the second and into the third and beyond, the notes changing, spinning, spun round and around and increasing . . . And embellishing . . . And finishing . . . And . . .

Surely you can hear that, Johnnie? Out here in the wide air? How the 'A' of the drone that began everything is in tune so perfectly with the pure high note of her. So spun into the theme by now with her mother's mother that you must keep playing, so you can hear, surely you must hear . . .

So keep playing. On into the wide air. All of it taking shape like a new blanket to be cast down upon the ground, Margaret's child woven and wefted into it from the opening lines of the Urlar to everything that is to come, so wrapped, knit into all the theme notes like bits of bright colour that have been woven, placed into dull tweed. See those bits of flowers out there on the grass that edges the yellow sand of the little beach at the edge of the loch? Yes, well, she'll be all those bright colours. While your tune lays out the greens and greys and the peaty darks, she'll be points of buttercup and gentian and the yellow grains of fine, fine sand.

So: Hush.

Out here with all the hills around you.

Hush, no need for weeping.

As Iain brings you in and the baby is returned to the mother, taken back from an old man's arms.

As Iain says, 'Come away now, John. I have you.' As he picks John up and carries him.

'And he was light' he told me later, Iain. 'As a leaf, and I saw no need for him to fall.'

And so the tune has been installed and will take the piper on, to where he needs to go. The notes have been established. His son has been in to say goodnight. His father is up there on the hill and his mother has taken him into her embrace. And still the tune is playing on, completing. Playing even now but only just hearing it, in these last few moments, quieter and quieter as it fades further and further into distance . . .

Yet with one note left to come.

gracenotes/piobaireachd: its development and expression

The art of playing the bagpipe was for the performer to produce the music with an even tone without pauses.

The art of playing the bagpipe was to play beautifully and well, with great expression and technical expertise.

The art of playing the bagpipe was to play fully and with generosity of spirit — as though the pipes themselves had feeling.

While bagpipes were played throughout Europe prior to the 1700s, differences in the pipe music were defined more by the local customs and have led to some vast variations in both style and composition. So runs an article published by the Piobaireachd Society for general interest.* 'Even in Scotland,' the piece continues, 'pipers occupied well-defined positions as town pipers, performers for weddings, feasts and fairs. There was no recorded "master piper" nor were there any recorded pipe schools. Lowland pipers played songs and dance music, as was expected by their audiences, so no effort was made to produce great musical compositions.'

However, during this same time in the same area of Europe, separated only by mountains and glens, were pipers of a different calibre. These pipers were strongly influenced by their background of the Celtic legends and the wild nature that is the Highlands of Scotland. The Highland piper occupied a high and honoured position within the clan system. To

---

* Further details of the Piobaireachd Society are given in Appendix 12/x.

be a piper was sufficient; if he could play well then nothing else would be asked. Most of the early history and songs associated with this instrument that still exist come from this small area in the North of Scotland.

As the bagpipe slowly left centre-stage throughout Europe a new form of music was starting in the Highlands. For more than three hundred years one family was to dominate piping in Scotland. The MacCrimmons were responsible for developing Highland pipe music and so established piobaireachd as a highly sophisticated musical form.

The basic structure of piobaireachd consists of an air with variations on the theme. The ground is the basic theme and is normally played slowly and is often the most interesting part of the music, laying out, as it does, its overall sound and central tone or idea. Some grounds are made up of short repeat phrases while others are free-flowing, but most are based on the pentatonic scale. The ground is generally followed by variations that are always simple and increase in complexity – with each one more difficult to play than the previous.

In concluding variations the composer's ingenuity and the piper's capability are tested. The piobaireachd ends with a return to the slow and impressive ground and the whole tune can take up to twenty-five minutes. Currently the ground is played at the beginning and the end of a tune only. In the past, the ground was played at intervals in the tune, often played between doublings of variations and the subsequent singling of the next variation.* There is evidence of a variation of even greater complexity than the Crunluath, called the Barludh. According to Joseph MacDonald,** it consisted of eighteen gracenotes after the theme note and finished on High 'G'. Thankfully Patrick Og MacCrimmon phased this out as an unusual fancy.

Each piobaireachd tune has been composed for a certain reason and recent studies have broken the music down into the following types:

---

* This could be of particular significance to readers of 'The Big Music', as the ground of that composition is returned to in a number of different ways throughout the entire piece.
** See Bibliography/Music: Piobaireachd/secondary – MacDonald, *Compleat Theory of the Scots Highland Pipe*.

gatherings; marches; laments; salutes; and other titled tunes. The idea that
the individual notes of the chanter take on meaning has been proposed
several times* and is one that John MacKay Sutherland of The Grey
House followed, as shown in his many notes about various compositions
– both of his own and others. Certainly 'Lament for Himself' follows the
principle of using certain notes to 'play' in different contexts or phrases,
suggesting the idea of a narrative or musical poem that might underlie the
composition from the outset.

In the past, this idea, this 'story of notes' as I may call it, would have
been sung, first, to make itself known. That's because in the days before
written music piobaireachd was always composed and taught by singing it
through, single note by single note, in a system of taught music known as
canntaireachd. The use of certain syllables, or 'vocables' as they are called,
to express different notes allowed the pipers to train their pupils without
the aid of any scales or other scores. This verbal system was used to convey both the tune and the emotion of the music and, as all true pipers
and musicians agree, is far better than modern-day written notation for
passing on the details and spirit – the sense – of the music.

Finally, piobaireachd is not easy to define or sometimes to describe. It
has been called the voice of uproar and the music of real nature and rude
passion. Many Highlander-pipers believed that their instrument could
actually speak and that piobaireachd is an extension of the tales told by
bards and poets to remember the clan's history. Certainly it is the speciality
of Highland bagpipes to seem to reach back through time to a chthonic
musical source and draw from it something unworldly and 'other'. No
other instrument can produce the particular emotional response that the
pipes do when playing piobaireachd. I know that. As others present here
in the pages of this book have been similarly affected. To us it may be as
though this music was the first phrase that was written.

---

* Readers interested in this idea should consult the Index of 'The Big Music', to see
how this same system of generating further layers of meaning to an art form applies in
that work – so particular notes and phrases have a literary as well as a musical application.

embellishment/I: domestic detail: Margaret MacKay

The history of women in these places is always a quiet story, it's quietly told. The mothers tell it sometimes, in pieces, to their children as they're sitting on their beds at night, in the half-dark, after reading the children a story. They may begin another story then, in a kind of whisper, about their mothers, their grandmothers. Telling it in a way a man would never tell a son about his father because these stories of the women have too much tenderness in them – and by 'tenderness' I mean parts that are hurt, flayed back, exhibiting their sting and their mark.

So the women will tell children these soft and exposed parts.

'Your granny lost her parents in a fire when she was five.'

'Your uncle was always a coward, he drank too much because he was frightened of his life.'

'Your aunt never loved her husband.'

So it goes on, the mother to the children, all the soft secrets.

'I myself was afraid of my own father when I was a child.'

Or 'I never want to be alone.'

The history of women in these places is often a story where there's strength coming from them but no power. They marry, sometimes, to men who love them, whom they love, but this love might not sustain them – yet still they remain married, and the children comfort them. They work in the kitchen, keep animals, vegetables and gardens, sometimes they may do considerable amounts of hard labour on a farm, or if there's a shop they may work in the shop, or if, like Margaret, there's no money to be had from the family for business of any kind, no prospects for a husband, then you find what work you can in the villages thereabouts, in one of the big houses, maybe, in the season, cooking or cleaning or housemaiding to one of the big shooting parties come up from London.

Either way, the passions get told quietly to the children. Helen heard her mother's passion as a quiet thing, and there was something that she saw, also, when she was a child and she shouldn't have seen it, and this may have affected how she understood her mother, came to know her with a deep intimacy. It would have. Her knowing that, indeed, her mother, despite the quiet manner in which she went about all things, had this huge tugging heart that didn't whisper at all, but that cried out, that carried exultation.

For Margaret, the stories that she'd heard had come early from her own mother, who had no husband. So she had been brought up, Margaret had, and her brother, by a small and clever woman who had never been married, who'd had no intention of it. This was Mary Katherine, Margaret's mother, Mary Katherine MacKay as she was, Mary MacKay until her death. She had been with the man who'd attracted her when she was a girl, an older man who lived along the road, somewhat away from her own village, back in the glen behind Dunbeath; he was a married man, but they went together. She'd been just nineteen when she met him, she told Margaret in a story, and, in time, had two children by him but never wanted him to live with, never wanted, like the other girls in the village wanted . . . A man at your feet or at your door, wanting things and proposing them and telling you about what to do. Margaret's mother, she told her daughter, when Margaret was small, wanted only to be on her own.

And for her, she was lucky this way, in that she could afford to do as she wanted. Her parents were living and prosperous by the time she bore her first child, Margaret's brother George. The MacKays had had interests in the herring — they'd been one of the first families in Caithness to supply haulage and carts for all the fish and tackle coming off the boats, in the days when all had to be brought in from the harbour after the catch came in, and was laid out by the long low houses that were inland

and sheltered, where the fish could be dried in long batches, slung up in the rafters of those same houses, and also the tackle was mended there, and the boat's sails. This was all from the time written about in Neil Gunn's book *The Silver Darlings*, he wrote of it there:* how families like the MacKays were able to prosper from the fishing in new ways around the middle years of the nineteenth century, and in the early 1900s – and so the MacKays found themselves, by the time their daughter Mary Katherine was born, with land and animals and a good-sized house back in the strath and away from the wind by a little water, with flowers in the garden, even, and a dog for the fun of a dog and some cats and chickens and everything gentle that could be counted for as some wealth in those empty parts of the Highlands in those days. They counted as richness like butter, like mutton, like fat.

So Mary had enough at her back to be bringing a child of her own on her own into the world. She didn't need a husband to provide for her in the way other women might need a man – for those women had nothing, nothing, while for Mary, when the children came, her father had someone from the village build a house for her, along from her mother and father's house, where her mother could help her with the babies, where her father could be sure she wasn't so much left alone. He wanted to protect her, I suppose, this capable and strong and healthy young woman. To that extent a man facilitated her life – is what Mary told Margaret, later, in one of the stories about what it is to be a woman on your own – but in general it was because the family was sound and careful that Mary was able to grow up and do as she herself willed. Both Mary's father and her mother would not have wanted their daughter left isolated and showing her aloneness to the village – if you know what I mean by that expression: *showing her aloneness.* Not picking up attention in a way that was unwelcome. So the presence of a house of her own near her parents' house would protect her against that.

---

* Neil Gunn's *The Silver Darlings* also published by Faber and Faber is set in a Highland area not so far away from the setting of 'The Big Music', and very near to where Margaret MacKay was born and brought up.

Therefore nothing was straitened for her, this Mary. Is how she explained it to Margaret, when Margaret was old enough to understand. Everything was as she wanted – with this care from her parents – and so there were just riches, to look around her. The riches she had! A home, food, a little work at her mother's kitchen garden, with the children playing beside, and later, as they grew older, she might take a small position in the village on a Tuesday and a Thursday at the post office, weighing the letters and stamping out the pension books or the coupons for radio and later television. She'd been well schooled down at Latheron for all kinds of work like this, and her mother would take the children then, George and Margaret in their turn, would have them playing at her own house, sending them off to lessons, while their mother drew on her lipstick and went into the village for a job to do.

Is how the years passed, one to the next. This one woman's life running from season to season, with stories told every night and the children listening, the children were taking them in. This story and that. Who was well, who unhappy. The house that stood empty because it was haunted; the granny who killed herself, back in the time of the Uprisings, for love. The story of the twin brothers who never spoke a word but to each other in their own language and had power of second sight. All told to show the children how people lived, the choices that they made and what became of those choices. Stories told that may be stripped back, some of them, to bare detail that is so raw, so full of feeling, that no matter how many years have passed in the telling, the people in the stories still seem to show their pain: this one whose babies all died of typhus; this other who was called a witch and was made to live alone. Each small history of every one of these people tells the children who are listening something they need to consider, have in their own memory that they may think about the consequences – of personality, of action. To wonder: Could it be made different, that story? Would they themselves behave in another way? So the children can learn by hearing about the lost lives of others. So the mothers, in the stories, by revealing the wrecked and damaged parts, help the children understand how life – their own – might be made whole.

Is how Margaret, listening, grew up to understand. As she, too, passed on the telling of her mother to her daughter,* that Helen herself was made familiar with all these stories, these quietest of histories, narratives unwinding at home and in kitchens, bedrooms, those scenes and dramas and epics that might play out on a stage that no one can see.

'She was ahead of her time' Margaret would say, stroking her daughter's forehead as Helen lay in bed, for perhaps she had been sick from school that day or needing to get to sleep or needing again some kind of comfort, her mother's presence.

'Was she clever?' Helen asking. 'My granny? Did she read and talk about her reading? Tell me something about her cleverness and how she was strong, on her own when you and Uncle George were little children.'

'Oh, she was clever' her mother would say. 'Sometimes she would tell me: Be quiet, so I can think my own thoughts, be inside my own mind and be free there. She would have this look in her eye, as she spoke to me, fixed on a part of the wall, maybe, or out the window at the way the wind was pulling on the branch of a tree. As though I wasn't even in the room . . .' And Margaret herself would take on that same look then, as she described it. Fixed and distant. Deep in her own imagination and memories, and thinking – what? About the decisions she'd made in her own life? To leave her mother in the way she did and go out on her own into the world and stay there? How she never saw her own mother again? And so thinking, too, about her mother and her mother's will? That woman who became so set in her ways that she ceased even seeing the man who'd fathered her children because his thoughts could not keep up with hers? So she was considering all these things, then, Margaret? How she herself showed equal will that she would leave behind her own mother to go and live at the House of the man she wanted to be with and had never returned to visit Mary, not even before she died. How she had also left behind her brother, a man who had lived on at their mother's house after her death before selling up and emigrating to New Zealand and so she never heard from him then. So thinking all these thoughts, perhaps, Helen wondered.

---

* See Urlar movement, sections marked 'narrative': pp. 28–34.

How her mother and her grandmother could have come so far apart that they could cast each other off in the way they did. Mary's judging and deciding that her daughter's staying in a place for the sake of a man was not worth the inheritance she could gift her; Margaret's own stubbornness and pride preventing her from ever returning.

All this, Helen thought, and more, coursing through her mother's mind. All stories of the past and asking herself: Was it worth it? Was it right? Her daughter could read these questions of her mother by the look on her face as she stroked her daughter's forehead, telling brick by brick, stone by stone, the small events of family life that build to houses, monuments. Thinking about Mary's strength, perhaps, Margaret was, because she herself could not break free of the man she had been with, her first. Thinking, too, maybe, that though she could have been like her mother in one way, when, just like her, she had been a young girl when she had met someone she wanted, how, in the end, unlike her mother she was in finding in that same man someone who would be in her mind and stay there from the beginning and she would not want him ever to leave.

'Mum?'

A man she would have lived with, in that way, every day.

'Mum?'

Who she thought about, cared for.

'Mum?'

Though could she ever say 'loved'?

'Mum?'

Could she, ever?

'Mum?'

Though there, at the end of her thoughts – Helen's voice – was their child.

'Did you hear what I just said to you? Mum?'

Helen herself there as proof of love – still could she use that word?

Love?

'Mum?'

How could she? When he was married to Sarah all the time and living away and it was only his House she had, to look after, its rooms and kitchen and windows and hearth, the House the only part of him that was constant.

'Mum?'

Though he was tender with her, when they were together, and they'd find ways of being together and he said he loved her as he lay with her and put gently back in place the coil of hair from where it had come undone from behind her ear.

'Mum?'

For was it love? A swift time together that brought about a child? That caused her to leave her mother and live apart, staying on in the House this man might return to in the summer, for a few weeks each year? That, love? That took thought from her and feeling, still making that charge, after all these years? When love was care, thoughtfulness, kindness. As her marriage to Iain was, and his taking care of her and Helen, taking care of Helen from when she was small . . . That . . . Surely . . . Was love. But not the other, how could it be? The creeping up stairs to the room at the top of the House when her husband and her daughter were asleep, when Iain and Helen were asleep, her dressing gown gaping open as she ran from them, quietly so they would not hear . . . That . . . Not . . . Love . . .

Surely . . .

That –

My darling . . .

– though something lovely . . . Was not –

. . .

It could not be, could it? Though it was also . . .

Love.

gracenotes/piobaireachd, a music to be played outdoors, brought in

The house is a place of safety, shelter, warmth. It was that for Margaret MacKay when she first came there, as a young woman, and returned there, pregnant and unmarried, to work and have her child. For her husband Iain Cowie, too, a shy, awkward man who had never been at ease in the world and who'd found it hard to find employment, The Grey House from the beginning described these qualities of shelter to him exactly as it had to the travellers and shepherds who sheltered within its walls, stopping off there on their way west and south and finding in the stone small rooms of what was, in the beginning, a modest home, comfort, companionship and, though Iain himself had never cared for it, a music that was played and given as a gift to strangers.*

This music, the House had always been known for. Iain Cowie respected that, despite his lack of interest in the pipes – close as he was to old Callum Sutherland for whom he worked until that man's death. In his lifetime Callum Sutherland had developed The Grey House into an internationally known piping school through what became known as his 'Winter Classes'. It is true, as far back as records of the House show, that the Sutherlands' home was a place known for piping, and more especially, for piobaireachd – and from the beginning there were ceilidhs and recitals

---

* As we know, these details were all played out in the Taorluath movement of 'The Big Music'.

held, outside yes, when the weather was fair, according to tradition, but also, as was practice at the great house of Skye,* there was a history of playing piobaireachd indoors, within modest rooms.

This was unusual. The story of bagpipe music, generally, throughout the world, is that of an instrument that is played outdoors. Historical papers relating to the history of bagpipe music note how the end of the Middle Ages signalled a way of life that was more urban than rural – so that social life was now conducted indoors and no longer on the village green. Loudness, therefore, of a loud-sounding pipe that could be heard across the fields, was no longer a necessary quality of music; sweetness and delicacy were more highly prized. Chamber music and, in time, the modern orchestra and its pleasures were to follow the new social pattern-ings that emerged after the end of medieval times and the beginning of the early Renaissance. This new era was when our definition of all the aspects of what we now call Western music was laid down.

As Seumus MacNeill notes:** 'The bagpipe of course did not give up without a struggle.' In some countries the instrument was altered, to make it smaller and lighter-sounding, introducing certain new devices that might extend its range and so cope with the new array of musical instru-ments on offer. But demise was inevitable. Slowly, year by year, in every country except one, the bagpipe either disappeared completely or was left 'to the lonely hill-men or the occasional crank'.

The one country was Scotland – in particular, the Highlands of Scot-land . . . Which is why today when one thinks of bagpipes one thinks of Scotland. Not because that is where they came from – but because this is where they remain.

Why?

Seumus MacNeill gives us this reason: that the lifestyle of the Middle Ages continued in the Highlands of Scotland for much longer than in

---

* There are details in the Appendices and elsewhere in 'The Big Music' of the great family of hereditary pipers and composers that played for Dunvegan Castle on the island of Skye and established a piping school there early as the fifteenth century.
** See Bibliography/Music: Piobaireachd/secondary – MacNeill, *Piobaireachd: Classical Music of the Highland Bagpipe.*

the rest of Europe. Despite some interchange with the outside world, the way of doing things had not much altered in the subsequent years: houses were still shelters, and in general – which is what makes the Grey Long-house of the Sutherland family exceptional – not places of recreation and entertainment. Work and leisure both were carried out in the hills and glens. So in these circumstances the bagpipe could and did flourish – for no instrument can compete with it for a party outside at night, in the summer air, or during the day for a wedding march or a country dance across the grass. It was used to rally spirits when times were hard, keep the rowers in time as they battled foul waves on the Pentland Firth or across the Minch. The music carried the elderly to their graves and cried the arrival of a newborn baby. And in a sheltered strath between the hills of Mhorvaig and Luath, a family established a home that was not so much a place, as a world – somewhere that could hold both the beginnings and endings of a music that had always been composed to be played some-where much larger than one small room could ever contain.

insert/John Callum MacKay Sutherland of The Grey House

Though many papers and notes are filed and kept in archive as a record of
the life and compositions of the Sutherland family, and of John MacKay
Sutherland in particular, there is little in the way of personal information.
Journals and diaries that have been kept tend to give an inventory – of
lessons taught, provisions bought, visitors, trips, accounts etc. – that sum-
marises the activities of a family rather than giving an insight as to what
that family were like, how they expressed themselves, what they thought.

However, a number of letters have been held in the House (the significance of the correspondence between John Sutherland's father and
mother has been noted already), as well as certain fragments gathered
from the Little Hut,* that give us a more intimate portrait of those who
lived at The Grey House and show the workings of John MacKay's mind
as he brought together his composition 'Lament for Himself'.

He was afraid of his father, we know this, and he longed to escape that
man's musical and physical dominance.

He flourished, emotionally, under the influence of his mother but this
was not something that could be encouraged by the society of the time, in
particular the Highland society into which he was born that valued disci-
pline and restraint and a withholding of emotion as being key attributes
of manhood. So those aspects of himself, of feeling and sensitivity, that

---

* The Crunluath A Mach movement of 'The Big Music' shows some of these.

came back to him as he lay dying – in memories of the Schoolroom his mother had created for them both, the pictures on its walls and the toys he kept to play with there, and in memories of his mother herself, how she seemed to him when he was a young boy to be a source of gentleness and softness and fragrance – were never let out to express themselves, not fully, in his life.*

'I'll not be back!' he called out into the air as he drove down the road away from the House, a young man of only eighteen, on his way to university but not intending ever to revisit that place where his father lived. So he cut himself off from the past – and though he was made to travel up to the House when his mother seemed to be gravely ill, this some years later, when he was a man, and he met Margaret then, and again, after he was newly married, to introduce his mother to his bride . . . That was never going *home*. He barely spoke to his father on either of those visits, or the older man to him. It was only many years later, after his father's death, when he came back for the funeral to look after his mother and the affairs of the House, that 'well, started the returning'.**

The 'Lament' shows all of this, of course: the sadness that there is no note for John's father, Callum Sutherland, any more than there is for his son who goes by his grandfather's name. The singling and the doubling of John MacKay's own theme – for his father and son – is what we have instead. The same notes, one might say, that might speak for all three men together.

---

* This is why the detail, in this same movement of 'The Big Music', of the John who 'put gently back in place the coil of hair from where it had come undone from behind her ear' on p. 203, and others like it, are significant. It is an instance of tenderness that is largely absent in the life of one who has conducted himself almost entirely according to the principles of business and society rather than the human heart.

** The phrase comes from p. 75 of the Taorluath and previous pages, describing John's homecoming to The Grey House.

narrative/4

The people at the House and what they thought of him
(appears as dialogue/possible fragment of a play)

Helen:

All of today has gone into the past. Already the early morning, going up
to my room and seeing she was gone — it's like that happened in another
life, to another woman. The baby . . . She was some other woman's baby.

Yet the feeling of the leap into nothing, into vacancy — the jump of my
heart when I saw the empty basket — that's with me. I'll remember that.

I've never felt such absence like it.

Margaret:

But you were calm. You didn't cry out. Later — yes. But not at first. When
you saw that she was gone . . .

Helen:

Though anything, anything! Could have happened to her! And I myself
knew at that second of the empty basket that I could have done anything.
Killed. Gone mad. If I could have protected her.

And if John had kept her longer, Mother . . .

If he'd had her longer with him out on the hill . . .

Mother?

Margaret:

I know.

What would have become of her then, our little girl – although people say that babies are hardy and your daughter is hardy. Still he's an old man and he could have perished up there on the hill and that would have been the death of our Katherine Anna, then, would have been.

Could have been.

Helen:

But the day – it tided over, changed. Iain went out there . . .

Margaret:

He did. He was like lightning, he was gone.

Helen:

And he found her . . .

Margaret:

Iain brought her home.

Helen:

He did – and he gathered John up, I watched him, he gathered him up in his arms. So carefully, Mother, he was so gentle with him. He was so careful, and he laid him in the back of the Argo – and she was fine, our baby was safe. She was wet and cold and cross but she was safe, she was well. The hours that had seemed like hundreds of hours, the long, long morning since breakfast and the terror of realising she was gone . . . All those hours turned back into an ordinary day then, unbelievably, just an ordinary day, when I fed her, put her to bed . . .

Margaret:

And then I told you that Callum was on his way.

Helen:

Yes. Callum.

And what must it be like for him now? With his father the way he is? When it's been so long ago since he was last here? Poor Callum. That family of his so spoilt with their own dissatisfactions that they never see each other, look out for each other.

It's been that way with them as long as I can remember.

Margaret:

When he first started coming up here, he was perhaps eight or nine.

Helen:

I thought he was such a city boy.

Margaret:

And he was. But he was his father's boy, too, who was born here. And the two of you together. You showed him all over the hills. And he loved the dogs, he had dogs that he looked after while he was here. He was just a boy.

Helen:

And I loved being with him then.

Margaret:

You two were together all the time.

Helen:

All the time, those summers.

Margaret:

The two of you, I never saw you all day. You were together all the time. Then the years went on and the summers went past and he was starting at university. And you yourself had left to go to Glasgow by then. It became harder after that, didn't it? For him to keep up the visits here?

Helen:

And by then I had gone away.
    I could no longer help him, look after him.

Margaret:

So how old were you then, when you last saw each other?

Helen:

I was seventeen.
(aside:)
Going up there to his father's place . . .

Margaret:

You were still very young.

Helen:

I was seventeen.
(aside:)
And no one guessed. No one knew . . .

Margaret:

And you went away then.

Helen:

First Glasgow. Then Edinburgh. All those papers I wrote. All the time while I was away. In Glasgow, the exams and all the papers. Then Edinburgh, it was the same. I worked so hard, I was always working, writing. Then back to Glasgow again for my PhD . . . And all the time, all that writing on the pages. I missed you, Mother. I was away for years.

Margaret:

But now home again.

Helen:

Where I want to stay.

Margaret:

And all that time — in between then and now —

Helen:

Like nothing.
   (aside:)
   Because I know where that place is, where we used to go. And he knows, Callum. We could go back there now, we would both remember the way.
   (as before, to her mother:)
   Because for all the years in between . . . Callum and I . . . We get along fine, don't we?

Margaret:

You've always got along with him fine.

gracenotes/piobaireachd, the theme of the return, including a general account

Everything about the music of piobaireachd indicates a turning back to its origins – from the structure of the music and its return over and over to the ideas of its Urlar or first theme, to the anatomy of the pipes themselves that creates limitations in key and octave that must keep the variety of the notes to certain repetitions and rephrasings – and it is this turning back, while going forward with a tune, that, perhaps, lends the music its great melancholy and sense of feeling.

For to return, to return . . . This idea runs all the way through the pages and the lives of John MacKay Sutherland and those who knew him. Remember the lines in the opening section of the Taorluath: 'Certain roads, you get to a part of them, turn a corner, say, come over some kind of a hill, and you feel . . . No going back now. The road there to take you and all you can imagine is the place that lies ahead and who's there, who's waiting.' The tone of those words sounds exactly the inevitability of the pipes' own song that brings the piper home.

'To the make of a piper go seven years' wrote the novelist and short-story writer Neil Munro. 'Seven years of his own learning and seven generations before.'

So ... Return

Return

Return.

'Look for us in the windscreen of your car and we're waiting for you.'*

Now follows a 'General Account' of piobaireachd by Douglas MacDonald of Strathglass. He begins his remarks, too, with a reference to 'The Lost Piobaireachd', the short story by Neil Munro: *'To the make of a piper go seven years of his own learning and seven generations before. At the end of his seven years, one born to it will stand at the start of knowledge, and lending a fond ear to the drone, he may have parley with old folks of old affairs.'*
    Then he begins:

Piobaireachd is not the music of the pipe band (a nineteenth-century invention) nor is it the strathspeys and reels that folk dance to. These are known to pipers as Ceol Beag or little music. Piobaireachd (a Gaelic word literally meaning the playing of pipes) is called Ceol Mor, 'the great music' of the pipe that serious pipers revere as the height of their art.
    So what is it that goes into the making of this so-called 'great music'? Like the strathspey, this music is unique to the Highlands of Scotland. Generally tunes consist of a poetic urlar (a ground or theme), upon which several variations of varying tempi are constructed. These are embellished with a series of musical ornaments that become more complex as the tune progresses, culminating with the return to the urlar to complete the tune. The effect of these variations with an instrument that is harmonically balanced against its drones will provide an almost mesmerising effect. The piper uses subtle variations of note length to build poetic phrasing, expression and character into a piece to convey the story the original composer was trying to portray to the listener.
    These piobaireachd are repetitious gathering tunes that call the Clan, stately salutes about the heroes of battle, or notable gents and ladies, or a lament mourning those who deserve our respect or sometimes contempt. These tunes often date back hundreds of years to a time when the bard or piper held great esteem in the Gaelic community.

---

* This sentence appears in 'two/first paper' of the Taorluath movement of 'The Big Music' that refers to Callum Sutherland, John Callum MacKay's son who is driving home to The Grey House to see his father. We don't know whether or not Callum is to inherit the musical tradition of the six generations of Sutherlands before him that are contained within the book – but if he were to pick up the pipes and play he would be the seventh-generation piper to whom Neil Munro refers in his short story 'The Lost Piobaireachd'.

Legend says that the MacCrimmons were the greatest of the hereditary pipers, who had a college at Boreraig in Skye where pipers from all over Scotland were refined over a number of years and returned to their patrons. The origin of the music and the history of the MacCrimmons were lost in the mists of time. Our earliest knowledge stretches back to Findlay and Iain Odhar, sometime around the sixteenth century.

After Colloden in 1745, and the subsequent bans on many aspects of Gaelic life, which included the bagpipe, regarded by the English as an instrument of war on the assumption that no Scottish Clan had ever marched into battle without a piper, many of the old tunes were lost, or in fear of being lost. Piping, which was then to survive within the Scottish regiments now serving the British crown, began to change its character and piobaireachd was more commonly heard on the competition boards at many gatherings, being judged by the local laird or vicar. Those days have gone, and the judges are now piping experts, with the audience made up of piping purists and the general public usually regarding piobaireachd as an acquired taste, preferring to watch the caber-tossing or tug-o-war.

In the nineteenth century, tunes were, for the first time, being written to manuscript. This has certainly preserved many that would otherwise have been lost to us, but the criticism being that such music cannot be written. Piobaireachd is based on a rhythmic meter much like poetry, where the piper cuts or extends notes to mark phrases, the ends of lines, or even various notes of identical value throughout a line to create interest and the mood of a tune. This is not done at random, and there must be some historical source upon which the pipers base their particular setting. There are various schools of playing and they all have their own individual styles and settings. Some of the piper's own feelings and interpretation are no doubt always expressed in a tune, but variation from the existing settings is frowned upon.

Being an oral tradition, piobaireachd was taught using a canntaireachd. This was a method of verbalising the notes and embellishments in a tune and teaching it as a song. This method is still used today, with the manuscript used as a teaching aid. Rare is it to find a piper that has learnt piobaireachd with any success that has not had a proper teacher to refine his art using canntaireachd, even in this age of modern communication.

One of modern times' greatest exponents of piobaireachd was Pipe Major John MacDonald of Inverness. He wrote in 1949 that, 'A Piper should be a man of as wide a culture as possible, not only concerned about execution, but with strong and sympathetic understanding of nature's varied moods, translated by him into music.

'When a piper is at his best, and is being carried away by his tune, he sees a picture in his mind – at least that is how it is with me. When I am playing 'The Kiss of the King's Hand', I visualise Skye and Boreraig and the MacCrimmons. The tune 'Donald Doughall MacKay' brings to mind a picture of the old pipers, and how they played this tune. A piper in order to play his best must be oblivious to his surroundings – he must be carried away by the beauty and harmony of the tune he is playing.'

Piobaireachd with its length, intricacies, emotions and the need to have a well-set pipe is not the domain of the novice. To say one stands at the start of knowledge after seven years of learning is no exaggeration as this art encompasses a lifetime's study. The knowledge passed orally from our teachers cannot be underestimated and indeed I would say that any master's skill could not be honed in this art without adding the input of previous generations of pipers to his learning. I have heard piobaireachd referred to as self-indulgent music, as it may sometimes seem to the uninitiated. It is played only on a solo pipe, and the competent performer often seems to be drifting off to some faraway place, but be assured he is 'lending a fond ear to the drone' and expressing the thoughts of 'old folks and old affairs'.

embellishment/1a: domestic detail: Margaret MacKay

Margaret first left her mother's home in Caithness planning to return.

Is how that story started, the one about her mother striking out on her own. It's a known story – the going out into the world like a woman in a Highland fable or a ballad, or in a book by Neil Gunn,* say, and Helen asked to hear it many times, the tale of her mother's leaving, for in it she could come to read her own future, of going out, one day, to have adventures of her own but knowing she would also come home again.

'I wanted to see other parts of Scotland, down south or through the west' her mother might begin. Or 'Once upon a time . . .' And Helen would be sitting there, unmoving. Rigid with attention as she sat in a chair or at the table and not wanting to miss a single detail: of how her mother had planned on going away from the place where she'd been born to start university in Aberdeen; her taking up of a summer job in a house in Sutherland with a friend who would be nannying at a big lodge near Beauly. 'The two of us travelled up from Aberdeen in the train together, it was the start of June . . .' Ending with how Margaret had met Helen's father, how she had just been a young girl when it happened, that day when she first saw him and his eyes rested upon her, the moment when – according to Helen, the way she used to tell it when she was a child, as though it were in itself a story for a child – her mother had 'fallen in love'.

---

* The writing of Neil Gunn is referred to throughout 'The Big Music'.

She worked that first summer, Margaret did, for Elizabeth and Callum Sutherland, already quite elderly then, with no sign of any family nearby, just a local girl who came in and helped three times a week — and right at the beginning, when Margaret had only been at the House for a week or so, Elizabeth Sutherland came down with something they would have called 'women's trouble' then. Depression? Menopause? Something more than that, though, that ailed her, made her go deep, deep into herself and all of a sudden the doctor was in the room and telling her, telling Margaret, they would need to inform the son who lived away in London to come back to the House and see her, as he might be the only chance for her now.

So she was the one, Margaret, who telephoned London, to speak to him first.

She, in a way, the one who would bring John home.

For that was unexpected for him, we know.* That he would have to go back to the House at all . . . He had never intended it. This, to do with the family's estrangement and those details of his past that would come out later, that John would tell Margaret when they were alone together. About him and his father, the distance between them that had kept him far away, and how, but for this one telephone call from a woman he'd never met, telling him about his mother, what the doctor had said, he would never want to have to go back and see his father again.

Still, on this occasion he must return: 'You have no choice' was the way Margaret had put it, when she'd spoken to him on the phone. And when he arrived, there she was, the same unknown woman who had called him up unannounced in London . . . Come to meet him off the train, driving his father's car to take him back up the grey road to the House where he'd been born.

And so . . .

Margaret.

---

* Earlier sections of 'The Big Music' show this, in particular pp. 107 and 113 of the Taorluath movement that describe John Sutherland's feelings about his parents and background.

Right from the beginning, you could say, she was the one.

Is how the story goes. How Helen heard it from her mother when she was just a little girl. How it continued. How her mother was the reason that John Sutherland came home at all, that first time – for his father would have never called him. A high clear note is how you might describe her, Helen thinks. Like the upper 'A' of the scale calls the Piper's note in,* her sound arranges all the other sounds around it.

For she was the one, Helen knows, who placed her hand on John's arm to steady him, as she drove him home up the grey road when he'd never intended to be there, the one who comforted him with her presence that day, when he asked her about his mother: How long did she have? How was she now? This tall stranger beside him in the car, looking straight ahead at the road in front of her but who went to him that night, to his room, the strength of feeling such between them from the moment he first let his eyes rest upon her that there could be no avoiding it . . .

Margaret.

No wonder it's thoughts of Margaret coming in to the piobaireachd now, and high and fine.

Like 'Once upon a time'

With Helen listening to her mother, who is telling her daughter everything, everything.

A great love story beginning.

That Helen might learn for herself through words how the circumstances of her birth may not be so much like other stories she knew, those she had read about or heard, the relationship between two people not as fixed as it was in those stories, or as certain or as known – but that doesn't change the charge of it, its strength. Doesn't make it any less true or full or lovely. Doesn't make it less at all.

And old Mrs Sutherland recovered – of course Helen knew that, she could still remember the old lady from when she was small. The virus had turned out to be some freak illness that passed over quickly, and John

---

* This note – the High 'A' – though Helen thinks about it here – has nevertheless not yet sounded fully in 'The Big Music'. It is a note still to enter fully into the tune.

returned to London three days after he'd arrived, when it became clear his mother was perfectly well.

Only by then, Helen's mother and father had been together in the House and not apart for one minute and all night the night before John must leave Margaret the two of them had spent, until morning came, telling each other Goodbye.

'And afterwards?' Helen would ask, waiting for the next part of the story. 'What happened next?'

Well, it was a long summer for Margaret that year, she said, with plenty to do in the big House, to take care of the old couple, help Elizabeth get better again, 'and by the time I went back to see my mother, before starting into the second year at Aberdeen, I knew I was going to have a child.'

And when she told her mother that, Margaret said, her mother had held her in her arms.

'Just like you and me, Mum?' Helen asked. She was five years old, six years old.

'Just like you hold me in your arms?'

'Just like.'

'We'll be fine' Mary had said. 'You'll stay here and I'll take care of you, and the baby when she comes. Then, when you're ready, you can go back to university and finish what you've started. We'll get your books sent up, all the study you're missing out on now – we can work on that together.'

She had held her close.

'Your granny was strong' Margaret used to tell Helen. As instruction? Warning? 'A strong woman who loved me very much.'

'And yet?' Helen said, when she was older.

'And yet . . .' her mother replied.

For was it instruction, even so? That strength could carry in it also clear warning? That love could be too strong, judgemental, or nothing more than will?

For what turned from Margaret's mother's love? Would want to keep her captive within it?

Something.

And Margaret herself also contained it. The same force of opinion, singularity of purpose. So that when she found herself wanting to see the man again she had been with, to get back to the House, to wait and see if John might come back there ... It was no surprise, she knew, that her mother would change towards her, but still she herself could not change. Even though her mother asked her daughter, repeatedly, why? Why would she want to do such a thing? A man who had no interest in her, who'd gone away, why should she maintain any thought for him? If he had nothing to do with her life, her plans? If she couldn't see him — Why? When she might find someone else she could be with whenever she wanted, Mary said, as she herself had been with Margaret's father when she wanted — but why must she have to do this other thing, go there to a place where he might return, just stand and wait? Why that? When there were all her plans — her study in Aberdeen, her intentions to go on and teach, to inherit the land and house in Caithness and productively use it, along with her brother, to be independent. Why? She kept saying. Why? Change that now? Why? And all the time, by way of reply to her, Margaret kept her own will. In the midst of her mother's words. In her own silence. Only thinking about the baby's father. Keeping him close. Remembering over and over the way they had been together, his face and voice and body. That she might be with him again.

'I'll be fine, Mum' she said to her mother — but her mother wasn't listening.

Then what happened was this: a letter Margaret had sent to the House, enquiring after the situation there, Elizabeth's health, was forwarded on to John and a note came back — that his parents would very much like her to return, if she could manage it, to the House that next summer, and if she wanted, stay on. The virus may have passed but still his mother was no longer strong, John wrote, and could not manage the place in the way she used to. Another note was enclosed in the same envelope — Elizabeth writing to say she and old Mr Sutherland needed someone more permanent to help them with the housekeeping, for during the year and also for if their son might come home, if he might bring friends, or just come on his own to stay, the letter hoped, either way, would she consider it?

For that next summer?

It took no time at all for Margaret to respond. And when Helen was born, after a few weeks, she was able to tell her mother of her plans ...

To go and work for a while in this House ...

That the man she loved there may be returning and she would, this way, see him again ...

So would her mother help her, look after Helen until then? Until she was able to see him and they could be together again and decide what they were going to do ...

But that was the end.

When her mother, who'd been holding Helen while her daughter spoke, put the baby back in Margaret's arms.

Walked away into another room.

That the moment ...

When she gave everything up. Mary did. As Margaret had – is what she said.

'Everything!'

And for – what? Her mother blazed at her. Desire? Hope? Some idea, notion, that Margaret might have herself marrying this stranger she'd met for three days, only three days and yet here she is saying she'll return to him ...

That was when Margaret first heard, and from her own mother, that what she'd had with John Sutherland, the two of them together for those scant two nights ... Was not love.

With her mother looking at her the way she did.

Speaking to her in the way she did.

Another story beginning when Margaret left her mother's home for the second time and knew she would never see her mother again.

embellishment/1b: domestic detail: Margaret MacKay

Margaret told Helen, much later, when she was no longer a child, but the two women could talk to each other as women who might understand each other: how that day when she saw her mother's pitying look, saw that judgement on her face . . . Was the first time Margaret had to consider what she'd gone through the rest of her life considering: that what she had with Helen's father was not love.

It was a conversation between the two women that might go on for the rest of their lives.

For that idea – that someone who might so occupy your thoughts, who you hold close in your mind in detail and with care . . . Could be as nothing – was one the two women would return to think about again and again. Like in a story, one may return to a central idea that is never quite resolved, as in a fable or a myth there may seem to be an ending but the ending is not there. So here was a situation that didn't contain within it a simple solution that may count as conclusion to this piece:* a man, after all, who Margaret barely saw and yet had thoughts around him wrapped

---

* There is no formal conclusion, as such, to piobaireachd – the final movement may be demonstration of the overall structure, the 'making' of the piece, but the last bars of that movement mark a return to the Urlar that was played at the beginning of the whole piece. In this way the music has no 'end', the piper will simply determine at what point he is to conclude playing of the opening section, and will put down his pipes. Appendix II: 'General structure of the piobaireachd' describes this in more detail.

and with desire, and with care too, for she cared about this man, Helen's father. So why might not those feelings count as love? Just because she wasn't with him, wasn't married to him? Because he didn't claim her in the outside world? That certain actions and deeds would be necessary, to be in place and carried out, in order to call what was between them love?

These thoughts Margaret had first encountered in her mother's pitying face and could never let them go.

The 'Why?' and the disappointment in her eyes. The things she had said. Looking at her daughter, with pity and with judgement, before she turned and walked away.

Of course Margaret would think about these things, talk about them with her daughter. As the years went on, and she saw Helen's father again when he returned for his father's funeral and the two of them were together then but he left soon afterwards, to return the following summer, maybe, and the next and then the next and so on every year until just this last year but always, in the end, going away from her again . . . It wasn't as though she knew he was ever going to stay. Is why, over time, she came to consider that Iain's feelings for her, that were reserved for her alone – his tenderness towards her, his thoughtfulness for her and for her child – that this, by contrast, all added up to something that was real. For in Iain was the strength of habit, familiarity. The three of them, Iain and Margaret and Helen, sitting around the kitchen table every night all those years when Helen was small. Iain driving Helen down the end of the road to catch the school bus each day, Iain wallpapering her room when she was older, the paper with the stars . . . One by one these days built up to make a home.

And the other? By comparison? Barely there.

So, you see? Margaret might say to Helen. There was that to consider within the story that had been told: the absence of one beside the presence of another.

But then she could also say: What absence? Because as John started coming home more and more, the summers with him here getting longer, and she would go to him, Margaret would, in the night and they could be together then as though there had been no space between them.

Because that was real enough.

While all the time Iain was there, waiting.

And he was her husband. Never John.

Still, there she was, though Margaret kept it to herself, the thought, of what she was doing – and what was she doing, then? Margaret? When she had someone who loved her and looked out for her, who loved her daughter like she was his own daughter, who kept his eye on them both, to make sure they were all right, always all right . . . What was she doing? And with Iain the way he was, so shy and inward-looking it was hard for him to be with others – and Margaret knew that, she'd always known how Iain was – so what was she doing not looking out for him, during those times with another man? What was she doing, instead of looking out for her family, taking herself off in the night, up the stair?

So of course then she must stop it. Though it could have continued between them, and she wanted that, John wanted it – still they stopped it. Though John kept the bed up there, in the old Schoolroom and Margaret knew that it was there . . . Even so. Because it came to be that she couldn't bear it. To be with John that way. Couldn't. She couldn't bear it any more, to be with him the way she used to be with him, when all the time Iain was working in the House, paying attention to the things John would never even notice needed his care. So it was Iain coming in at John's back to tidy up after him, making sure that all the friends John had invited to the House would be provided for, that the guns were ready and the rods and the dogs . . . All of these things Iain thought about on John's behalf. That John might need. And working on the House and the buildings, keeping everything in order there and maintaining order, every autumn and spring there were repairs and leaks and painting and re-wiring – and all for John. All for another man – and he never noticed, John, did he? All the things that Iain did for him? All the ways in which Iain worked? John never noticed Iain at all.

'And he never asked me, either, about the past, about what went on there. He never asked about John. You must know: I would never have left Iain' Margaret told Helen, years later and Helen was asking her about the past, their family. 'Because Iain is my husband. And he has been a good husband and a good father. A good, good man. So, I would never leave him.'

'But you didn't have a child with Iain' Helen said.

Is why the feeling that Margaret had for Helen's father all those years ago, from the very first time when she'd gone to his room . . .

Had never gone away.

'Because it's part of you' said Helen, 'who you are.'

And it's true, Helen writes in her journal now: *That's the main part of my mother that I recognise, I know.* That quiet steady part of Margaret, that never stopped feeling the same way about someone she first met when she was only a girl, that had no regret about him or looking back or bitterness.

'For though,' Margaret said to Helen, 'after my year at Aberdeen, when Eileen and I went away for our working holiday, I left Caithness planning to return —'

'Your mother made it impossible for you' Helen says. 'To stay there. She didn't understand you, couldn't bear that you could be so different from her.'

'*You've described it exactly as it was.*' Helen writes in her journal now. '*For when I met your father*' Margaret said, '*that is when I may as well have said to my mother, goodbye.*'

Helen keeps writing. By now putting together more and more detail and understanding into her mother's story. More thought, more background imagining than was there before. Beginning: *Margaret first left her mother's home in Caithness planning to return* . . . And adding to that, extending it. *Despite everything that's in the past . . . Because Iain is my husband . . . Because of the 'Why?' . . . The look of disappointment in her mother's eyes . . .* Putting in extra sections to the story. Rewriting parts so they make more sense. Adding something about Iain, how it was that he never knew about Margaret and John and all because of his pride — and then taking that part out. Imagining other details like that, too. What her grandmother may have looked like — 'She looked a lot like you' Margaret used to say — and hearing in her mind the things that unknown woman may have thought about, opinions she may

have had. She could see the sequence of events, Helen could, by writing this way.* She could shape from them some kind of dramatic line, a
plot. How, when Margaret's mother died, the entire estate, her mother's
parents' house and the land with it, was given over to her brother George,
who sold up, emigrated to New Zealand leaving nothing behind, and
Margaret never saw her brother again. How Mary had never replied to any
of Margaret's letters, did not inform her even, through friends, of the illness that would be the cause of her death, when Helen was just four years
old. Helen could construct it all – these thoughts in sequence, the events
that followed, one after the other, creating a shape, a sound, a story of
her mother's life that could be read like a myth or parable or warning – a
mother's punishment of her daughter's will. That Mary had fashioned it
that everything that Margaret might have had, would stand to inherit and
be strengthened by, would become no more than a job down in Sutherland, working as housekeeper, an unskilled domestic. And all because of
a man who gave her her first attention as a woman, that made her decide
everything because of him, everything.

Is how Helen saw the story end: a terrible judgement that made Margaret's mother so fierce in not allowing her daughter to come back home
again, never see again the place where she was born, her friends, nor even
her brother, he was not going to be allowed to invite her. So all that part
of her life Margaret had had once was gone and the life she'd chosen for
herself, here at the House, what she was left with. *That she'd brought upon
herself*, as Mary would have it. That her daughter would have to say the
sentence throughout her life like penance: 'Because of my desire for a
man, I never saw my mother again.'

So Helen writes in her journal:

*When Margaret left her mother's home for the second time, she knew she would never
see her mother again.*

---

* The significance of this kind of writing becomes clear in a later section of this
movement of 'The Big Music'. It is when the earlier remarks and footnotes regarding
the provenance of some of the statements in the book are clarified in terms of how the
story has been uncovered and revealed.

But adds no moral to that sentence: *she knew she would never see her mother again*. Despite the fact that it was all for love, that kind of story. Despite the fashioning of a tale with a warning that's attached to it, a punishment, even so, there's no lesson here.

'For there was nothing else I would have done' Margaret said. 'The decision that I made – I wanted it that way. I still want it.'

To have never gone home again.

'That was my story' she told Helen.

While my own, writes Helen, in the same journal, by way of a reply,* *has been to return.*

---

* See the previous footnote regarding the provenance of these pages.

three/second paper

He hears the tune. Here in the Little Hut, where he always does his writing, where he's always heard the music when it's first coming, he's been hearing it – the first notes, a phrase, and he can hear it now.

He's at the table where he always sits to write when he's up here, the window before him and the water beyond and the main theme – the 'B' to 'E', 'A' to 'A', 'B' to 'E', 'A' to 'A' – he's starting to know it so well by now it's like breathing. More than following the passage of his thoughts, this is like something coming from deep inside him, forming itself out of the heart and ventricles and spleen and stomach and bowel – that 'B' to 'E' starting it, the return to the inevitability of the base 'A', and doubling the pulse there . . . It is like breathing. It's all of himself he can hear. At this rate, he thinks, he won't even have to be looking at the notes he's writing while he's writing them. He could just close his eyes and the marks would put themselves down on the page, his whole body simply taking in air and expelling it and the music will be there.

He reaches into the drawer of the desk where he keeps manuscript paper and the pens he likes, those kinds of thick, inky black felt-tips but with the little points Callum sent him once, a couple of them, and he's been using them ever since . . .

Callum.

Only where is the boy now? Only gone.

He arranges the lined paper in front of him and the pens. He thinks about having a whisky, just a small one, like he always does when he starts writing . . .

But he doesn't have long here.

And there's no time to think about any of that now, about when he last saw Callum – and not likely he'll be seeing him now, not this summer, or the next. Because it doesn't matter that no one knows about this place, he'll need to get back to the House while it's still light. While the days are still warm and fine get everything done with finishing the tune before the weather turns cold and more and more getting up here at all is taking a charge upon him he can't pay back.

So.

Callum.

And no doubt he should be in this tune, his son, but he's not heard him. Not a single note.

Only the other notes – of himself – they're called in all right. That theme of his that's put in now, deliberate, the repeat of it. Like his own breathing.

'B' to 'E', 'A' to 'A'

'B' to 'E', 'A' to 'A'

'B' to 'D', 'A' to 'A'

'B' to 'D', 'A' to 'A'

So he might, take a whisky. He might.

But . . .

No.

For it's all dependent on that, them not knowing and him getting the music finished while none of them think that he's been away for anything more than a walk and a bit of air. *

---

* As noted in earlier movements of 'The Big Music' and in relevant Appendices and the List of Additional Materials, the Little Hut was built by John MacKay Sutherland shortly after the death of his father. It was here that he started planning and writing his own compositions, and where the bulk of his creative manuscripts and notes were kept. In his younger days, he would have been able to spend a few hours there before anyone noticed he'd even been gone – being no more than a couple of hours' brisk walking from the House.

Because if they knew, if they had even the slightest inkling that he'd got himself way up into the hills and without the medication they're all so keen on . . . They'd have him back in the House and the doctor in and that would be him done for.

And there'd be no tune then. No Lament. Nothing written.

Just staying in the House and them putting him downstairs and feeding him the damn pills, one after the other, to keep him quiet.

second return/the Little Hut: location; significance; metaphor

To write about the significance of the Little Hut to the composition of 'The Big Music' one must first acknowledge the scale in which all bagpipe music is played, displaying itself most fully in piobaireachd as distinctive and 'other' and one of the greatest factors in contributing to the music's overall effect.

In a sense, we might say, the place of composition and the notes for it are intertwined: both cannot easily be described, both are hidden, somewhat, set apart and unknown – yet both allow, too, for the imagination to operate in a way that is untrammelled by the usual constraints of what we recognise as familiar culture.

By going somewhere that was unknown to others, that was hidden and secret, John Sutherland was able to take himself to a liminal, undefined space that allowed his creativity to flourish. Indeed, one could even claim that because of its distance from the House, its difficulty of access – especially for an old man who had suffered a series of strokes and a long-standing heart condition – the Little Hut represents a place of danger, a forbidden zone. Here, after all, is a site unmarked on the map, unknown, as far as John Sutherland is aware, to anyone else but himself. That in itself makes it a dangerous place to visit. If something were to happen to him or to the building, no one would know where to go for him, to save him.

Its very secrecy, then, makes the Little Hut a potent location for practical as well as creative purposes. The rules are different for this place – as though there are no rules. In the same way, the bagpipe scale is like no scale of music familiar to Western ears. To all of us who hear the diatonic scale as the 'norm', the notes for composition of Ceol Mor come from somewhere else; they too are other, somehow secret and mysterious.

Indeed, the sound of this scale has been described as disturbing and difficult to appreciate for those not raised on it. The intervals have been called 'uncanny', contributing to a music of 'barbarous power' that describes something quite shockingly different from 'any ordinary modern scale'.*

In his book on piobaireachd,** Seumus MacNeill writes about the scale in technical terms that define the breadth of the intervals between notes as being like those that would have occurred in the music of ancient Greece, where a particular interval on the scale, called a 'limma', was also present in the Phrygian scale of the music that was played before the great plays of Aeschylus and Sophocles and Euripedes. That too, the playing of that music, was a secret rite about which we know very little, except that it took place in a particular 'site' – an otherwise forbidden area that was the stage and its arena – in advance of the artwork that was to be performed, the performance of the tragedy, and that other elements were involved along with the playing of that music: the sacrifice of an animal, so blood, and wine.

These details fuse in the mind the idea that secret and imagination, site and place of composition, ritual and mystery in both classical and modernist aesthetics are inextricably linked – and that the history of 'The Big Music' and the Lament that it contains, play back to a much earlier story that is caught up with our understanding of what art is and our relationship to it – whether played in a diatonic or pentatonic scale.

---

* All quotes taken from Donnington, *The Instruments of Music* (see Bibliography/Music: General).
** Seumus MacNeill's book, *Piobaireachd: Classical Music of the Highland Bagpipe*, first presented as a series for BBC Radio Scotland in 1968, is commonly referenced by pipers and non-pipers alike as providing a thoroughly sound basis for an introduction to piobaireachd music. Certainly it is included in the Bibliography of 'The Big Music' and is fully and variously quoted in the Appendices and footnotes for this book.

MacNeill has this to say about the widely unknown set of notes available to the piper and his music:

People who are accustomed to think in terms of the just scale or the equal tempered scale find it very difficult to think in terms of any other scale, but it should be appreciated that all scales are based upon the same fundamental principle. And the test of whether a scale is musical or not is how well it satisfies the fundamental principle, not how close it is to some other scale. The notes of the pipe which sound peculiar to the non-piper are D and high G. The violinist for example will call the other notes A, B, C sharp, E, F sharp, A but has no name for the D or high G.

He goes on to help the general reader:

Because the pipe scale is not a variation of the diatonic scale* but is really an alternative way of solving the problem of dividing the octave into seven musical steps . . . there are no key signatures, because these have no relevance in pipe music. One might well wonder why the Highland piper arrived at such a unique scale for his instrument, and the answer might be just chance, because, musically, there is little to choose between the diatonic and the pipe scales. The diatonic however leads very easily to the equal tempered scale, which enables a fixed keyboard instrument, like the piano, to play music in many different keys. The pipe scale with its stubborn limmas could not readily give this same facility. It does however have a different advantage, and we have to go to piobaireachd to find what this advantage is, and the reason for the Highlander's adherence to the unique intervals.

'Unique intervals': the phrase alone, in this book 'The Big Music', carries the meaning of piobaireachd and the sound that is enabled by its composition. The Little Hut, that hidden space that exists beyond The Grey House, in a valley in a part of Ben Mhorvaig no one visits or knows, is itself an interval between notes, a curious reach, a space of sound. When John Sutherland went there to compose, especially in the last months and weeks of his life when he was working on the 'Lament for Himself', we understand how he was taking himself to a place that was not only secret and most private in order that he might have quiet and

---

* The diatonic scale reads thus: doh ray me fah soh lah ti doh; the pentatonic as: doh ray me soh lah doh.

thinking time. He was also allowing himself to enter into another aspect of his life, to disappear into a kind of gap – 'a unique interval' – between those notes that have empirical meaning in the world and thereby reference the significance of another scale altogether. That place is the gap between worlds inhabited by the artist rather than the individual. The usual rules no longer apply there.

three/second paper (cont.)

So he shouldn't have a thing to drink. With being up here and on his own and so much to do. And with hearing the tune inside him this way, the shape of it and the sense and the general lay of it, how the green-grey ground he walked over to get here will be the map for the whole, and the criss cross of the variations like red veins running over it, those roads and tracks the tune will travel. It would be a waste to squander it. The place. And his being alone here like he needs to be alone.

So not a drink at all.

With the secret room around him, and him in the centre with the paper and the pens.

He won't.

Though needing . . . Something. Even so – but what?

He has the pen, he has the paper on the table before him – and the opening is clear, the overall shape of the piobaireachd is clear to him, as he's registered already that's within him, part of him. But there's something else to come, some theme. Some extra set of notes, an idea for a tune that sits within the tune, a line of music that he hasn't thought of before but it should be there, set right into the Lament from the beginning and yet beyond him, somehow, apart. He can't hear what it is yet – but it's there.

And it will come to him in this place. Where the music always comes. Just the notes at first, would be enough to hear them – then think later how they might fit in, what they might mean. So what kind of notes, how might they appear? And maybe like a kind of song set in?

Can he hear that? Think about that?

The idea of a run of notes, a simple melody – and getting down the opening section to try and hear where it might come in, this other sequence . . .

And it won't be found in a drink at all. He won't get what he needs that way.

But . . .

Somehow. He'll have to find what it is. This tune within a tune that will exist beyond the music and will take it on, as into the future. That's it. The idea of it. As though the future of the tune, his future, can be taken up, carried, within the notes that are already there . . .

Like a child carried in his arms.

'F' to 'G', 'E' to 'A'

'F' to 'G', 'E' and 'E' . . .

There it is.

He can hear it now. As though singing to a child. So his child – then – Callum?

But no. It's not Callum.

This 'F' to 'G'.

This 'E' to 'A'.

Though Callum gave him the pens and he's using them now, it's not Callum.

He hasn't seen Callum for years.

Not for years and years.

His son.

That boy.

He has no note at all.

And yet these others . . .

'F' to 'G', 'E' to 'A'

'F' to 'G', 'E' and 'E' . . .

He can hear them and strong, and he starts writing now, and fast – and, yes, the sequence of another tune is emerging here from out of the main theme, the opening remarks of the piece, there is this other tune that seems to be set within it and just as the other was there within him like breathing so this part could be a song, all the notes already heard by him it seems – it's just a case of his hand moving fast enough across the paper to get them all down . . .

And in the end he might take a drink, though, he might.

For Callum . . .

Though he's not the theme that he needs . . .

Though you might think he would be – his own son, carrying his name after all – he's not, and maybe he should take a drink for that reason, for Callum, that he's his son and yet not the theme he needs here . . .

For where is Callum now but far away from the place where his father is seated.

So he couldn't hear him if he wanted to. He couldn't.

Callum.

He's too far away and his father can't hear him in the notes he needs to lay down.

gracenotes/piobaireachd, its style, meaning and effects

There is no doubt that, unless one has been raised around bagpipe music, and exposed to piobaireachd in particular, the sound can be foreign and strange – and in this way the complexity of Ceol Mor, as Seumus Mac-Neill writes, 'has at least one of the qualities of classical music – it does not usually make an immediate appeal to the listener'.

In part, this is to do with the sheer quality of its notes and tone, the sound of the scale and so on that has already been noted in various parts throughout 'The Big Music'. But it is also the sheer intricacy of the music's construction, the 'rules' it encompasses that, more often than not, are broken and altered, that makes piobaireachd more forbidding a musical genre than most. Unlike a simple melody played in dulcet tones, this is something that strikes up with volume and difficulty from the very first seconds of tuning.

In addition, there is a particular quality to the overall arc of the music that is heard before it is understood – much in the same way that T. S. Eliot has urged us to read a poem and hear it before (or if!) we attempt to break it down and understand it – and this arc may be a sound we stand under, look up at, feel shaped and surrounded by, a threatening concept, perhaps, to those who like their art packaged and delivered as a known sum of parts.

As Major-General Frank MacLean Richardson defined this most 'highly cultivated product',* the music we are addressing does not reach

* Richardson writes a personal and stirring Introduction to *Piobaireachd: Classical Music*

out to the listener in any populist kind of way whatsoever – though it may have as its basis the most human of situations such as the birth of a child, the death of someone who is now mourned, or to convey the great happiness at a meeting or gathering. Rather, it moves within its own terms and definitions, using its limitations, not the infinite array of ideas that might come from other sources, to create its endless variations and innovations. Nevertheless, despite all its technical and aesthetic aspects, the music is, more than anything, deeply human and empathetic in nature. In this way it is as direct and troubling and inspiring as someone singing low and relentless in the corner of a room or who stands right in front of the listener who must stay there listening until the musician has finished. There can be no looking away, no turning from the sound. Though, Richardson notes, an analysis of piobaireachd 'will perhaps appeal less to the non-piper than to the dedicated piobaireachd enthusiast . . . Even the latter,' he writes, 'may take comfort from my own admission that, much as I admire those who have profound musical knowledge of this sort, I have never found it to be essential to an understanding of piobaireachd. The great John MacDonald of Inverness certainly taught me to analyse a tune before attempting to play it, but it was always in terms of "lines of poetry" – one of his favourite expressions.'

It is according to this spirit of poetry that we may understand how the movements play out, one against the other – from the Urlar to its singling and doubling, to the Leumluath and Taorluath variations, to the third major musical idea of the piece, which is the Crunluath, where we are now. So, in general, we have a good understanding of the basic shape of a piobaireachd in this book, with its four movements similarly laid out according to the classical pattern and its meanings described and defined further in various footnotes and Appendices. Seumus MacNeill describes the result of such formal arrangement thus:

The effect on the listener of the leumluath and taorluath variations can be most impressive, especially if the performer is able to abstract the full

---

of the Highland Bagpipe by Seumus MacNeill, already noted. All quotations for this passage here are from those opening pages.

beauty of the singlings, and by careful change of tempo is able to convey in the doublings a sense of urgency without haste. The crunluath movements however are quite different in their impact. All the gracenotes in a row, rippling cleanly and evenly from the fingers, produce by themselves an effect which is independent of the tune. The trick for the expert piper is to be sure that the melody is not completely obscured by this display of finger dexterity, and to keep the crunluath variations from degenerating into pure pyrotechnics. A player whose technical skill is not of the first rank will make the gracenotes longer than they should be. As a result he has to shorten the theme notes (unless he is to drag the variation badly). Short theme notes mean less emphasis on the melody.

During the crunluath movement it becomes clear that the climax is being reached. With the start of the crunluath doubling the piper usually stands still (up until then he has been pacing slowly backward and forward) and in his playing of the movement he shows, without appearing to hurry unduly, that this is the limit and this is the end of his performance. One more variation can be played after the crunluath doubling. This is called the crunluath a mach. A mach means 'out' and this is intended to be a description of what the piper is doing.

The listener might well feel when the end of the a mach is reached, since nothing more can be done, the piobaireachd is finished. This is not so for there is no end to the Celtic symphony. The piper does not stop but goes on to play the ground once again, thus maintaining the similarity with the other Celtic arts — the serpent with its tail in its mouth, the never-ending line, the symbol of infinity. To appreciate piobaireachd properly we should now hear the sound fade slowly into the distance, until we are left only with the everyday noises around us.

three/second paper (cont.)

Callum was in London, it's true, during this part of the tune while his
father is getting the notes down for a new composition and using those
pens Callum had sent him in the post two or three years ago. It's that
time of his father's last few weeks of feeling strong, this paper – with
the weather still fair enough that an old man could get up onto the hill
and away to work properly on something he's been thinking about for
some time, concentrating on a piece that's taken shape more or less as
a whole in his mind, though he has no sense yet of how the parts will
come together in the end – and Callum is far enough from his father,
right now, far enough. It will be weeks yet before the telephone call
from his mother asking him to come up here, it's still only early August,
and Callum has a deadline on a project – the same one he'll be involved
with when Sarah contacts him – and he's hard at it, all through the boys'
holidays which is why Anna has taken them off to France to stay with
a friend, though they'll be home soon and he's glad about that for he's
been missing them. So, yes, it's weeks, well over a month, nearly two
months, before the rest of the story that's already been playing here will
sound out as music because it won't be until late September that his
mother will get the message from the House that his father's not well.
And that they're worried about him, something serious enough, Sarah
will say, for those people to be telling her about John then, finally giving

her some news – which is why she is telephoning Callum now.*

'Your father' she had said, straight off. Remember?** 'They've told me
at the House he's bad again. It's been that way a while, it seems.' Callum
was in the office, the same project from the summer still there on his desk.
'They've called to say he's had a bad turn' his mother had said, that quick
way of hers, of talking. 'They lost him today, they couldn't find him at all.
He'd taken himself off someplace. He's done it before, apparently, just
gone off on his own, on a walk somewhere, out the back, or down by the
river those people seem to love so much . . . '

Those people.

As she always calls them – Margaret, the housekeeper up at the House,
and her husband Iain, who are both looking after his father now that he's
gone up there to live permanently, though Sarah still won't call them by
name.

'Those people' she'd said. This time, they'd told her, John wasn't to be
found in any of those places.

He'll have gone to the hut,*** Callum had thought then, straight away.

~

---

* See earlier sections of this book, p. 18 of the Urlar and pp. 75–77 of the Taorluath
movements, to retain chronological time here.

** This was in the Taorluath movement of 'The Big Music' and p. 76 gives details of the
telephone call that echoes through that section into this.

*** One cannot overestimate the significance of John Sutherland's place of composition in
'The Big Music'. A bothan, or bothy or shelter, which is how the Little Hut is introduced
at the beginning of 'The Big Music' on p. 23, is defined as a small dwelling, a place of
refuge, rough-built and unobtrusive, yet a place of great importance to one who has been
out in all weathers and needs cover, or, as in this case, utter silence and solitude. More
often than not there are no markings for these secret dwelling places on any map and
they are very easily disguised against a Highland landscape – therefore near impossible
to find. John Sutherland's Little Hut, as it's known in this book, would have been built
from an earlier dwelling place that had been previously used by a shepherd or by one of
his forebears who may have come here in the same way he does, so as to be quiet and
alone. The original walls are stone-built, and he has replaced the window and refitted a
corrugated iron roof, lining out the interior etc., carrying out all works himself, over time,
and bringing his materials to it, piece by piece, and his papers and journals and books.

And he was right about that! Johnnie would have been pleased to know it. Because although, yes, it's weeks before the boy has that singular thought about his father, about where his father is, he knew about him even so – for here he is now, just where Callum believes he would be! Not in the dark room, where they've moved him to – but out here, in all the air and it's daylight here, beautiful sun across the water out on the loch, the sand on the beach ... He could be lying out in this weather it's so lovely!

For it's August and the days are fine and high. And he has the last of his strength all about him to write down this tune that he's been working on, that has come to him as a kind of a gift. So this is the last big time for John Sutherland, John Callum MacKay, and so a piobaireachd of course it has to be, a Lament in the style he's written before but in a way of writing, too, that's never been done before, to a subject so known, so intimate that it's not about someone else or for someone else, but it's his own life he's writing.

And listen! To the sound of the tune.

With so much of it down already ...

The opening lines, in this fine weather ...

And the second melody set within the theme ...

Then the variations ... How the embellishments might come in ...

The pen covering this page of manuscript and another and another.

So the Urlar.

So the Taorluath with its leap, its Leumluath change.

So the notes, all the notes ...

To coming around him by now, in this section, the Crunluath, the crown.*

John drums the fingerings against the edge of his table to remind himself, to remember. Hears in his mind the long draw of the theme that begins like breathing. The draw of his breath ...

---

* The structure of the piobaireachd has been covered already in footnotes and previous movements of 'The Big Music', as well as in certain Appendices; to note here is John Sutherland's awareness, at an earlier part of the narrative structure that has been established well in advance of the Urlar, of the overall shape of his composition. This does not include, however, key themes that have emerged and are still emerging in this same composition – his notes encompass planning, and a certain musical idea only, at this point of his writing.

'Lament for Himself' he might call it.

For that is what has been collecting here. In the papers and manuscripts ... For weeks, now. All through the summer making notes, outlining his thoughts for the content, his themes. Getting up here to his special place, where his music is, to work on the shape of the piece, the overall idea. To hear where it's going, where it's taking him ...

And getting everything in, he thinks, everything. The leaps, the change,* the variations and the shift that will come from the first movement, and the returning, too, while working on the changes, to build up the ground. So then the Taorluath and the Crunluath can come after. And the A Mach** to follow, the showing in the notes how the whole composition has been made ...

Before the Urlar returns and the music fades away into silence.

So don't stop writing, Johnnie, don't stop. Don't take a dram. Get the shape laid down across the pages and then the embellishments can be worked through as they should – they'll show through as detail and as fine, fine study. Then the main theme can be left to complete itself, worked through in a company of phrases as the ending is marked and the notes of the Urlar come back into the tune again.

'B' to 'E', 'A' to 'A'

'B' to 'E', 'A' to 'A'

'B' to 'D', 'G' to 'G'

'B' to 'D', 'G' to 'G'

---

*   As has been noted, after the laying out of the ground, a piobaireachd may take a kind of risk – some have described this as a 'leap' as in a 'Stag's Leap' – whereby the music takes off into a new direction that has not necessarily been formally prepared for in the earlier theme. This is one way the Taorluath movement can express itself as distinct from the preceding movement – a leap away from it. Invariably, the piobaireachd will come to show how this risk ('the stag leaps/into vacancy', to quote 'The Big Music') actually links to the overall themes and Urlar after all – but nevertheless provides depth and texture to the tune's original ideas by taking such a development.

**   The final part of the piobaireachd, the Crunluath A Mach, is, in many respects, reflexive – showing how the whole piece has been put together and made. The Last Appendix serves as a reminder of the way the overall composition is structured; also the Crunluath A Mach movement of 'The Big Music' displays content of the whole in this way.

Get everything down then so as to reach them, those last few notes. The ending that sounds the beginning. The opening lines played one more time before the piper moves off across the top of the hill and disappears over the other side.

The little black felt-tip pens he needs — to write everything down.

~

Callum never said out loud to anyone — not to his mother when she called, or to Margaret when she met him at the door, when he arrived and she told him about his father — that he suspected where his father had been trying to get to that day.

Though he had already thought it — *He'll have gone to the secret place.* There was too much going on, in those first few moments of him getting back to the House to even remember that that's what he'd thought. There was his arrival in the cold, after the long day's driving, the dogs barking in their enclosure, Margaret there, and Iain — and then his heart had dropped to the pit of his belly when he heard Helen had had a child, did he know?

No, he didn't know.

But everything seemed to be coming together then. Though in a way he couldn't figure. Still, everything.

Helen.

The Little Hut.

His father.

And he himself, his father's son, being back here again after all this time away.

All of it was coming together and making him feel sick, something lurched within him — for he could understand, though he didn't know why, it made perfect sense to him, that his father would be taking Helen's child with him, up there, to that place. Even though there's no reason at all he can think of why his father would do such a thing, steal a baby away, put her in such danger, head off with her that way into the hills . . . Still, his taking her could make sense to Callum even so. So from the minute Margaret told him . . . That she was there in the House, Helen . . . That there was a baby . . .

Did he know?

No, he didn't know.

All the parts were coming together, in a pattern, nevertheless.

So that, for a second, Callum thought he was going to fall to the floor.

~

Up until then, who can tell? Perhaps, he might have managed things. Perhaps. Managed as any visitor might have done, to be detached but thoughtful. He could have been involved in the situation here but only to the extent that a visitor may be involved. So – polite, he would have been then. Kind. Enquiring.

How are you, Margaret? saying.

Iain?

As though he were a visitor here.

You're well? You're keeping well?

As though he might be here again after all this time, to be seeing his father in the House where his father used to bring him when he was a child – but staying outside the intimacy of the place, his role to be a guest here, quiet and simple.

But from that second he heard that Helen was in the House, upstairs in one of the rooms and with a baby to care for, her baby . . . He could no longer think he might pretend.

'No, I –'

Even when pretending was the way he'd always managed things in the past, with Anna, or the boys. With any of his friends, even. Whenever he was talking about his father, pretending. Making it seem as though his father and this place where he lived had nothing to do with him, nothing. His own life and marriage demanding enough, he might say, without the strangeness of all that went on with his father choosing to stay way up there in the North of Scotland, 'the back of beyond' – how he always described it at the dinner parties in London. 'Crouched by some fireside', he used to say, to the people at the dinner parties, to his wife. To describe where his father had taken himself off to. 'Put it this way' he used to say to them all, 'I'll not be going back to see him!'

But that . . . Talk.

It was no longer possible to be like that now.

With knowing Helen was there, somewhere in the House. And when Margaret told him what his father had done, with taking Helen's child . . .

He couldn't imagine ever opening his mouth to act that way ever again.

~

Lying in bed with Helen now, in the deep, deep dark, back here again with her after all this time away . . . That's what he thinks – that he could barely believe who that man was who could act that way, talk as though this place meant nothing to him, nothing. Say, 'I'll not be going back!'

Because who is that other man now? He's gone from Callum entirely and who he is is who he turns to face now in the dark, part of himself, she's part of him . . .

Helen.

And how could he be anyone else. When she's here.

Helen.

When she's right here beside him now.

All . . .

Helen.

Helen.

Helen.

Though he knows, Callum, that at some point the other man will return, that he'll go back to where he lives, open his mouth there and speak, right now he can't think who he is, that other lost man, what he's composed of, what his dreams are, or his hopes, his fears – when all he can feel is Helen's body lying alongside his as she sleeps. Part of himself with him here, and close.

So, 'Helen' he whispers now to the dark, and to himself.

All, 'Helen' now.

So there can be nothing of that other, nothing left of him at all, but only Helen here with him, only Helen in the dark.

~

In the old days – and this has been mentioned* – what Callum always noticed, when he was a boy, was the way his father was when they were driving up north and he would revert to some old Highland way of speaking, a different rhythm in his voice, different words he'd be using, these smatterings of bits of Gaelic and expressions. It was as though he became a different man. In those days Callum used to make the journey regularly with his father – all this has been written about already – for his mother, as we know, would never go, and sometimes Callum would wonder about that, not really a thought so much as a slight question, why those two people ever married. Maybe it was because his father had been smart enough when he'd been a young man and full of plans and ideas and successful enough in Edinburgh and London by the time he met his wife that, he used to say, Sarah thought he was not such a bad result for a family that had come off some cold hill! Because really, what could the two of them have ever had in common? With his father, as the years went on, going on to talk about himself more and more as though he'd just got down off that same hill, just a Highland crofter after all, but with the fancy hand-made suits and the building with his name on it – what a joke. But there! he'd say. It's what you might expect of a Sutherland from Sutherland. And Callum as a boy would look at his father when they finally arrived up at the House, after that long drive . . . After hearing the change in his father's voice as they got nearer, seeing his impatience to get up the road . . . And he would see then how he belonged here. But so he would also see, as they arrived, his father in the suit and the brand-new car, the look in Iain's eyes as he shook his father's hand. 'Oh, aye, I'm sophisticated enough now' his father would say, to Iain, with the big smile, and Iain would seem more silent than ever in his reply to him: 'Sophisticated, eh?'

~

---

* pp. 80, 81 and 158 give various examples of the way John MacKay reverts to certain patterns of speech that are distinctly Highland in structure and sound. The use of the word 'for' throughout the pages of 'The Big Music' is an example of the way these same speech patterns may also permeate the overall text of the book.

Callum has always had these memories, they were with him in the car as he was driving up here today, and now that he's here, in his father's old room, with Helen lying beside him, they are piled up in the bed all around him. Thoughts, reminders, fragments from the past. Arriving with his father and the way his father was.

Iain's nod, just, when his father spoke to him –

'Can you get the car down to the station, tomorrow, Iain? Some friends will be coming on the train in the afternoon.'

'Can you have the guns cleaned and ready, Iain?'

'And the rods.'

Then his father walking away, leaving Iain behind him.

And yes, all of it in the past, and a long time ago, but here, too, with him and present. His father. And Iain. And Margaret . . .

Margaret.

Callum has that thought, too, as he lies here in the dark with Margaret's daughter . . .

Because by then, in his memory, when he came back to the House with his father, Margaret was there somewhere in the House but later his father would come and find her.

And Margaret.

And his father.

Callum knows about the two of them together. He's seen his father, as a boy he's seen . . . The way his father is when Margaret walks into the room. He knows . . . As a man he's always known it, about Margaret and his father, yet now, as he lies here with Margaret's daughter, he thinks about how he knows this about the two of them as though there was something else to know . . .

But he doesn't know.

Though everything is come together, here, all of a piece. Though he is back in this House, back with Helen again . . .

Still, he'll never know.

For, 'What's the baby's name?' he'd managed to ask Helen. They'd woken, briefly in the night, turned to each other again. It was still dark. It would be a while yet before dawn. 'Margaret told me' he'd said, 'but I forgot.'

'Her name is Katherine' Helen had replied. 'Katherine Anna. And she looks just like my mother.'

'Like you, then' he'd replied, and he wanted to kiss her again, be fully awake with her together again in the dark so that it would never get light, could never be light, that there was no such thing as day and that they might stay together always.

'She has the same face shape as my mother' said Helen, 'the same eyes.'

'Like you,' Callum said, smoothing her hair back from her forehead, 'All you . . .'

And Helen could have added, but Callum would never know for she didn't say a word:

And you.

~

So Callum may have remembered the past, and going right back, sometimes, deep into the past, but there he is and he doesn't know, any more than his father knows, of the way the music is coming together, the layers and the notes of it, wrought all in. Though it's coming together, there, on the page. And . . . Clever, he thinks. John Callum thinks now. As he lays down the next set of notes upon the stave. So, clever. The way he's made all this on his own, the little building here with its window and its glass, the table with the notes spread out, his music and his books . . .

And with the sun out there on the water! The sheer blue of the sky!

But can he get that part in somehow? That element that's missing, that he needs, like strength in the sun that all will be fine for him, that it will be as though he can live for ever?

He doesn't know.

Because in the end, like his son, he has no idea. And as Callum will never know, so he will never know . . . How the piece of music that he's writing comes to shape itself, how it fits. How the mother and her daughter who's his daughter, how the baby he will take from her basket is his daughter's child . . . How they'll come together in his arms, all caught up together, the theme of his and the melody within it and the embellishments to follow . . . He doesn't know. Any more than he knows, as he sits here working at the table in the Little Hut up in the hills, that in a few short weeks his son will be on his way to see him. And by that time he'll be in bed and he'll be dying – but there, Margaret's in to tell him and the dogs are barking the same:

That Callum has come home.

And, 'Margaret?' he'll say to her, looking for her, there in the dark.

'I'm here' she says. 'I've never gone away.'

So for now he picks up one of Callum's pens and draws in the clef, prepares the manuscript for the small piece of music to be set within the theme. The stave is open and waiting. And it occurs to him as he puts down the first marks on the page that it doesn't matter that he can't hear at this moment how exactly the notes will play out across the tune, because that will come to him when he has Margaret's grandchild in his arms. He looks across at the divan where he sleeps when he comes here. They'll lie together on it, he'll think, later, when the season has turned and he's up on the hilltops and he's windbeaten and cold and confused. He'll bring her here with him to the secret place and the music will be complete.

gracenotes:/piobaireachd, its genealogy, its fathers and sons

Preceding pages of 'The Big Music' have referred to a story of fathers
and sons, that, in turn, reference certain Appendices relating to that great
dynasty of pipers and composers, the MacCrimmon family, who, for suc-
cessive generations and to the present day, have dominated the sound and
character of piobaireachd music. This has been to highlight the theme
of hereditary musicianship that plays through the various movements of
this book – to bring about in the narrative a kind of echoing from one
generation to another, down through the years to the present situation of
a father who has been long estranged from his son, in the same way that
he himself was cut off from his own father – deliberately, and by design.

Yet, as we have seen, though there is the disjunction between the three
generations of men – between John Callum MacKay Sutherland and his
son Callum in the same way that there was between John Callum MacKay
and his father before him – so this rupture to the line of sons, this space
between the story can be closed up, somewhat, by the singling and doubling of John Callum's theme in 'Lament for Himself'.

In this sense, the space in the text might be seen to be closed by the
music. Certainly, while he is composing the Lament in the Little Hut,
though there is no thought of a theme or a set of notes for Callum –
and, indeed, the absence of his son is felt, in separate moments by the
composer – nevertheless the story of Callum, once introduced in the
Taorluath movement, comes to play stronger and stronger throughout

'The Big Music', both as counterpoint and reinstatement of John Callum MacKay's own set of notes, the 'B' to 'E', 'A' to 'A' sequence in particular.

This kind of layering, as we have already seen, is a distinct feature of piobaireachd and may be described as well in the table overleaf – itself a sort of 'under-composition' of 'The Big Music' – providing as it does a clear sense of the doubling and singling of the various generations over the years. See how the names themselves seem to sound as notes that are repeated and echo throughout the tune, one placed upon the other as though transparently, as though one man may be them all:

Sutherland Pipers at The Grey House

Note: seven generations are shown, although at the time of writing it is unclear as to whether Callum Sutherland will take up the instrument his father has bequeathed to him

John Roderick MacKay of 'Grey Longhouse' ('First John')
b.1736 – d.1793

Roderick John, a tacksman ('Roderick Mor')
b.1776 – d.1823

John 'Elder' Roderick Callum
b.1800 – d.1871

John Callum MacKay ('Old John')
b.1835 – d.1911

(Roderick) John Callum ('Himself' – the great twentieth-century
'Modernist' piper; known as Callum)
b.1887 – d.1968

John Callum MacKay
b.1923 – d. within these pages

Callum Innes MacKay – his son

embellishment/2: domestic and social history: Elizabeth Clare
Nichol

John Callum MacKay Sutherland: born 3 February 1923*

When Elizabeth Clare Nichol became a mother she found her life returned to her. Brought to a lonely place, far inside the hills of the north-
east Highlands, she'd been a town girl, a girl who had loved the shops and
the dancing in Perth, the lovely fabrics and stuffs there you could have
made up into any kind of dress you wanted, and they had the lace there,
too, for trimming, and all kinds of beads and seed pearls . . . She had
been that kind of girl. She had her hair cut short and went to the dances
in the town hall most Saturdays, and there were tea places, too, with
large mirrors set behind the tables, where she and her girlfriends could
catch glimpses of themselves in the glass, and there were thick white china
plates and cakes with jam and cream, and here was this young woman
with all her girlfriends about her, sitting there, all of them with their hair
cut short and shingled and their dresses to the knee and they put lipstick
on and powder, using the big mirrors to see their reflections . . . Like so
many bright daisies in a vase. This is how Elizabeth's life had been, before
marriage. With this kind of brightness about her, the light of the mirror

---

* Appendix 5: 'The Grey House' gives details of domestic life and the List of Additional
Materials indicates relevant information that is available in archive.

and the shine of the glass. All to lose for the empty hills of Sutherland and for a man she realised, after the wedding ceremony in her parish church in Crieff when she'd had to travel far north with him by motor car and train, was a silent kind of man, and frightening, she discovered, after their first night together in the bed. She understood then, when she was with him alone that way for the first time, that all the sweet words he may have had for her as they'd whiled away the hours in the dance halls of Perthshire, and in her mother's pretty sitting room, all the letters* he'd passed her the next day, after their short, fierce entwinings at the dance when the jazz and the tea music had stopped playing and he'd driven her home to her parents' safe villa on the dark streets of Crieff . . . Realised then, after the marriage, after the bed, that all those physical moments before had been as nothing compared to the way he really wanted her. For he wanted to have her. To keep and to be inside her, all the way in and have her silent there. To make of her a kind of possession, to create something between them that might be as implacable as the hills around them, the *I don't mind* of those empty hills, that would be as lonely as the land and the house he'd brought her to, that she'd had no idea of, its isolation and its quiet and high uncaring sky . . . She realised when it was too late to realise. For by then she was arrived. He was sleeping beside her. Then his eyes would open and she knew then he was wide awake.

~

But the baby! Who could have prepared her for this?

The birth of him one thing, dreadful, with the nurse coming too early

---

*   Extraordinary letters survived in a great mass of papers that looked at first to be nothing more than household bills. These were written in a fine hand, and went on for some pages, passionately declaring love, a desire to be together, 'to press my lips upon you', and rendered in miniature handwriting, the most tightly fit script you could imagine. Every line is straight, every character perfectly formed and crowding frantically to the very edges of the vellum – no doubt the product of Callum Sutherland's composition work: he was used to writing notes of music on hand-produced manuscript paper. Scores of these compositions are on view at the National Piping Museum, where the same miniature hand as in the writing of these letters mentioned here can be detected in the notation.

to the House and being angry with Elizabeth it had seemed, for not producing the child in the right kind of time, in the right way, and then being brutal with her in the birth so the baby would start, so she had to make a little cut – that one thing. And then the pain becoming so bad and the laudanum drops they kept giving her having no effect and the baby was stuck there part-way so the nurse cut freely again, and cut, to make him come out. All this, the horror of this, seeing the little knife, feeling the blood, and the great weight of the thing that was to be her own child then pushing himself out of her, trying to get out from the place where his father put himself each night . . .

~

But then! There he was, amidst the blood! Dainty boy, tiny living scrap of a thing and all she wanted was to hold him, have him right there with her, hold him close, hold him. While they took their time, it seemed, to give him to her, the fierce nurse and the maid who'd been doing so much work for her, helping her in the house, to get her in and out of bed when she'd been too heavy to move, now boiling water and giving Elizabeth the kind of cloths for between her legs and then to wrap around the baby . . . And no one told her – as they finally gave him to her and she looked into her son's unblinking eyes, his crumpled face red from the washing they'd given him to remove the smell of her from him when all she'd wanted was to cry out, oh give him to me now! – what it would be like to want someone so close, have him there with her so close. Him! Her own child, her son. She'd thought to herself, wildly, in those opening seconds after he'd been born and they were washing him and trussing him up to make him presentable to her: *Just give him to me now. I could lick him clean.*

To Elizabeth Clare Sutherland (nee Nichol) and John Callum Sutherland: a son.

John Callum MacKay Sutherland: born 3 February 1923.

Elizabeth's little boy.

first variation/the House and land: recent history

There have always been the affairs of the place to manage. That's in the life, too, as we have read already – the keeping of this House, the management of land a working operation always and with Iain there in place to organise the physical side of things, to take over, in time, the practical day-to-day running of what was a successful business as well as a family home, a House that could pay for its upkeep and the livelihood of those who worked and lived here – and Callum Sutherland had been able to be confident that, after his death, the House and land could continue to have the associations with this part of the country that they had always had: to be open and isolated, a place for music and weather and high, lonely hills.

It was a few years after Margaret and her daughter had come to live here, then, that Iain was employed by the Sutherlands to come and work at The Grey House. By then the old man and his wife were quite frail – though Elizabeth went on to live for several more years after her husband's death and continued to enjoy the things she had come to appreciate about living in this part of the country, its large and changing skies, the tenderness of the brief summers. Year by year she'd found herself further and further away from the Perthshire villages and towns where she'd grown up so that though it had taken all her adult life, the House was now her home. It was where her son had been born. These rooms the rooms he had grown up in, her little boy, where she had fed him and talked with him and cared for him. There were to be no more children. That was maybe something

in the Sutherland line – for they were never a family who had produced
a great number of sons and daughters, and through the years, going back
all the way to when the records were kept, there were never many sons and
many who died. Certainly Elizabeth was aware of it. The pattern of the
men not to father many sons. John himself would grow up to marry but
have only the one boy, and late in life – like so many of his grandfathers
before him – and as Elizabeth came to see and understand more and more
how the music might take the men away, so too she came to understand
how that might give a concentration to a woman of the things a woman
might need. For to have her own time . . . To be able to keep her own
counsel, think her own thoughts . . . These qualities were as much a part
of the world she'd become used to as its House and hills. In this way was
the girl she had been once left far, far behind. Here, after all, was where
she had come to be a mother to a son – and so of course she would always
want to stay, where John had been. Any day he might come home again.

Margaret coming to live in the House could only deepen this way of
thinking for Elizabeth. It was Margaret, after all, who had called her son
to come back here that first time when she'd been so ill, and then, after
Callum's death, when he started coming every summer and for longer and
longer, it might have seemed to Elizabeth as though the young woman
had been a kind of lovely charm. Besides, Elizabeth loved having the
presence of another woman and her child in the House, loved the sense
of them both there – another mother to hear calling out for her child to
come to tea, have a bath, go to bed, another child's laughter and shouting
and talking lifting out of the hallways and rooms. It was like an echo of
her own life come back to her, having Margaret and her daughter here.
All through the years there was Margaret restoring order and with a sense
of life and vigour, giving her back her rooms light and warm and aired
as though they may give nothing but pleasure. And, as time went on, she
was letting Margaret more and more be in charge of the arrangements in
this way, all the domestic responsibilities of the House given over to her
care – when there were guests or not – so that by the end she was doing
not just the cooking and cleaning but organising everything to do with
the House's upkeep and Elizabeth just managing a little in the garden,

sometimes, or tidying up a set of drawers here and there, to see if there was anything in them she might clear away. But for the most part lovely Margaret had taken over for her, was taking care, and so Elizabeth could just sit in her little armchair in the old Schoolroom . . . She could sit up there for hours if she wanted to and dream. All the time knowing that this other woman was somewhere below her in the House, preparing the supper in the kitchen or making up the fire, singing to her daughter who ran around the place with the same light footsteps John used to have, when he was that age, Elizabeth remembered, her little boy. Margaret like time given back to her that way, all time.

Thus was the House and land organised, increasingly, with the old couple giving up more and more of the feeling of ownership, of right and with Iain looking after everything from the leasing of the land to dealing with the Forestry Commission and the council and the plans for the road end. Callum Sutherland loved Iain. He loved his quietness, his sense of duty. He loved the way, when they might be doing something together, Iain would feel no need to have to talk at all and yet they could both get on with the job and complete it. Sometimes, towards the end of Callum's life, Iain might just come into the Music Room at night and help the old man from his chair to bed, and not a single word would need to be spoken but Callum could feel the strength of the young man's arm.

Is how, over the years, things were for them, the Sutherlands, with Margaret and Iain in place to take over all the duties that they could no longer manage. As if they had always been there, Callum and Elizabeth thought, Iain and Margaret and Helen like a family to them, that was what it was, having a husband, a wife and a child at home here. Their voices, movement around the House and grounds, giving them a feeling of life, a story they could be involved with, something ongoing.

And so it went for Margaret and Iain, too, it seemed, in the same way – that Iain could oversee the stock and the water, those parts of the job he loved, getting around the hills to shepherd the lambs in season, keeping the river tidy so guests could take a few fish out of it if they wanted to . . . Is how he always wanted to work, Iain. To be outside and on his own, he'd always liked things that way – and it's how his job was organised when he first came to work here, under old Mr Sutherland then, and he enjoyed it, working for the older man, the sense of freedom and ease he had with being left to get on with things in his own way, to organise the affairs of the place according to what he, Iain, thought best. They were good days, for Iain. They were good times.

Sometimes Iain would tell himself that, when he was on his own, up on the hill, or sitting at the kitchen table with a whisky. How they were good times. And how it was like a perfectly formed story for him, it was, that when he'd come for his interview, there was Margaret already here, doing what she had always done since she'd come to work here as a young girl. It was as though she had been waiting for him – is how Iain liked to think of it. As though she might have just opened the door to expect to see him there. She was housekeeping then, back in those early days, for the various guests who still came for the winter piobaireachd classes or any-one who was staying who had simply come here to play and to listen. She was organising the bookings and the schedule of each party's visit, just as Elizabeth Sutherland used to do when she was younger, Margaret catering for the dinners in the evenings, and, twice a year, the competitions and festival of piobaireachd and canntaireachd* that Callum Sutherland had established as a regular event in the House. Details of these are to follow, in the doubling of this section, with background information and some stories of how the House was during this period, earlier than Margaret's time now, this is – when people from the radio came up from Edinburgh and Glasgow, sometimes, to record the nights that went on there, with recitals and so on and the kinds of music that were played. By the time Margaret arrived at the House this part of its life was starting to dimin-ish, though still active enough and with plenty for her to do, but still nothing like on the scale it used to be when these events were established

---

* Appendix 9/iii gives some information on the musical history of The Grey House and the various classes and recitals that took place there. The doubling section contained within this variation also contains similar details, as does a later section of the third paper of the Crunluath movement. In addition, see Transcript 1, a BBC interview, in the List of Additional Materials for an individual recollection of music at The Grey House; and certain issues of *The New Piping Times*, 1934–58, also contain relevant details.

and competitors were coming from as far away as America, New Zealand and Canada. That was how it had been, for a long time. Old Mr Sutherland used to tell Iain. Back in the day. 'And I can manage a bit of it now' he used to tell Iain, 'because of your strength, young man.' Remember that: *young man.* Is how Callum Sutherland often addressed Iain. Iain remembers the feeling that address gave him, spoken with kindness and respect. He holds to himself the knowledge that he and the old man shared, that when the latter declined and became too frail to sit up for long, he was still able to offer some music sessions to young pipers – because of having the support of Iain and his family. The pupils could still arrive here at The Grey House and stay, and go on to win prizes at the Northern Meeting and at Oban and Braemar because Iain and Margaret had made sure that everything was secure here. That Callum, you see, could live as he always had here, with Iain to help. That he would lose no pride.

When he finally died then, with Iain and Margaret well settled, even with her son not around, Elizabeth knew the House could still run smoothly. And by now it was a big enough house, remember. The extensions Callum had put on in the early years of their marriage – building onto the south side of the back elevation the big dining room and the drawing room – had seen plenty of use, plenty. It gave the House a great feeling of depth and security, having the extra wing put onto it in this way so there could be more bedrooms upstairs, more space there as well. Not since the middle of the nineteenth century, when what had been an ordinary dwelling was given substantial additions in the Victorian style, was the character of the original House so changed by these developments. The building work through the 1930s proclaimed a home that was, if not grand, certainly most handsome in the Highland style, with a substantial façade and rooms that led graciously from the main hall through to the back where it opened up.*

So Callum Sutherland may have died, then, in the same room where

---

* Appendix 4 and the List of Additional Materials give a history of the various periods of The Grey House in terms of its architectural development; plans and details of room use etc. are available in archive and are also described in the Taorluath movement of 'The Big Music', pp. 87–96 and 165–7.

his father had died but the House itself was a different kind of house by the time his son would inherit it. And so there was always plenty for Margaret and Iain to do, to keep everything running and well organised – for a house of that size, with that kind of spread of land to it, needed to be so organised and practically set out – though now came a period of change, after the old man's death, and certainly the times for the Music Room seemed to be in the past by then, and the festivals and competitions and the School. Still, the livestock were bred and sold every year, the forestry people continued their arrangements with the renting of some part of the land and the felling of certain areas of trees. So, too, the river could still be rented out, at certain times of the year, with Iain getting something there, from the summer fishing and the odd bit of stalking in the autumn that was paid for, handsomely, by some of the big international companies. It was a business, after all, being here in this part of the world. That's what Callum Sutherland had always said to Iain – and that was why, because they were all so organised here, with Iain and Margaret working for him and Mrs Sutherland, he had always been able to rely on that business being safe. 'Because of you' he had always said to Iain. 'Young man. This place is in your hands.' It was why, because of Iain, John Sutherland could continue to keep on the House as he did. Though he lived far away, he could bring friends up here with him, if he wanted, from London, and there'd be parties . . . It was all because of his father, and what his father had established with Iain. *Young man.* The fishing, and some shooting. The big dinners in the lovely dining room that went on into the night.

But the calls for Iain then, on Iain's time, were different calls, commands – with the son arriving fresh out of the car in his London suit. It was as though he was energised by his father's death. As though he could come back now to fully claim the place he'd left so far behind and talk to Iain any way he wanted.

'Bring the car down to the end of the road this afternoon, will you, Iain?'

Talking back at him over his shoulder as he walked away.

'Have the guns ready for us tomorrow.'

'There are a few people coming up on the train would like to get a salmon if they can. So bear that in mind, won't you, Iain? You can fit that in?'

As though, Iain came to think, he were someone different about the place from who he had always been, no longer someone who had once been in charge. It was as though he'd become someone to be talked to that way, treated that way. And he came to feel it as something physical in his stomach, Iain did, to have to have the other man here with his big smile and his fancy suit. To have him physically present in the House, walking on the hills. A man not that much older than himself — but look at him, the way he was, and the way he was with Margaret . . .

And then, over time, spending more and more of the summers here. Coming back to the House, returning.

As the years went on.

Coming back more often, staying longer.

Even though, by then, there were fewer parties. Less fishing, shoot- ing. Fewer days out on the water, or up on the hills, and the guests no longer coming in the same numbers and then one year there were no guests at all. It was then, when John Sutherland was here on his own one year, that Iain had to acknowledge that whatever it was between him and Margaret . . . That he'd known was always there . . . That thing he'd seen between them, between John Sutherland and his wife, when that other had returned home for his father's funeral . . . The way he was with Margaret then and the look that passed between the two of them . . . Had never gone away. The kind of man Sutherland was, Iain saw then, and it made him feel sick, Iain, sick deep, deep in.

doubling on first variation/the House and land: recent history

'The Winter School at The Grey House' started as a series of lessons that took place at the House in the latter part of the nineteenth century – when certain tunes written by members of the Sutherland family were taught by way of parsing the principles of piobaireachd before going on to study the more well-known and established set of pieces composed by the MacCrimmons and others.

These tunes became exercises in the way certain Latin texts became rubrics for Classics study in some traditional schools in the last century – for it was believed by John Callum MacKay ('Old John'), who introduced the practice of 'play through close study', that the discussion of certain passages and the 'deconstruction' of various lines and embellishments would lend knowledge and expertise when it came to tackling the Big Music of Skye.

As it developed over the years, and John's son Roderick who became known by his third name, as Callum, took leadership over the classes, the 'Winter School' became more formalised: that is, it became a series of workshops and tutorials that ran in a timetabled fashion from October to December at The Grey House every year, offering billeted accommodation to a range of pupils – from schoolboys who were studying the pipes as part of their musical education for examination purposes, to those who had an interest in and facility for bagpipe-playing – either professionally (as enrolled in the Piping School of the British Army) or as

amateurs with a love for the instrument and its music. The classes ran for
two- to three-week sessions at a time – usually culminating with a recital
that was open to the public and visited by local aficionados from as far
away as Wick and Tongue, and, on occasion, Inverness.

The reputation of the School increased dramatically from 1927
onwards, and by the 1950s was world-famous – bringing pipers and pupils
from as far away as America and Canada and New Zealand. Various radio
programmes and, later, a television documentary record the texture and
content of these classes. They show interviews with past pupils and Callum Sutherland 'Himself' is heard playing sections of his own tunes and
those exercises created by his father, as well as older tunes composed by
his forebears, from John Roderick MacKay onwards.

An interview and transcript of the interview with a past pupil of one of
the Winter School classes is available in archive and the transcript reproduced in later pages of the Crunluath movement of 'The Big Music'. This
gives a sense of the atmosphere of The Grey House at this time when it
was at the high point, one may say, of its musical history.

When Iain Cowie came to work here, in the mid-1960s, the great
period of musical instruction and endeavour was on the wane. Classes at
the House were taught sporadically and then, as old Callum Sutherland
became weaker and more infirm, eventually ceased altogether.

Nevertheless, both Iain Cowie and his wife Margaret MacKay have
fond memories of being employed by the Sutherlands at a time when
their home was an international centre for Highland music – it was listed
that way on certain maps. Though Iain is a man for the hills and the
outdoors, he appreciated the way old Mr Sutherland conducted himself,
back in the days when so many knew of him and wanted to come here and
meet him. In all that time, Iain thought, it was strange that that man's own
son would not want to come and see his father at all. But then Iain met
him, John Sutherland, the son, when he came back for his father's funeral.
And nothing like his father, Iain thought, when he saw who he was, the
kind of man he was. The kind of man he was with Margaret, looking at
her, talking privately with her . . .

When he thought that Iain could not see.

second variation/the House and land: recent history, John
Sutherland

So it's been written of the others: Iain, what it was like for him to be here.
And Margaret, how her life was lived. And John Sutherland, with his father dead. We have seen how it was for him, coming back here again, like
a window opening and he could escape out of it into the endless hills.
Because although, at first, yes, it was just to come back for the funeral was
all he'd intended, by the following summer even that had changed and
later that same year he was here with a party, and then the next. Coming
home at first to see his mother, but coming back again. And with each
visit spending longer. At first arriving with friends, it's true, as though
he didn't want to be alone, but then, gradually, over time he'd be arriving
earlier and earlier in the year so he would end up by having most of the
summer here — Callum's school holidays became the length of time he
would stay, all of August he was up here, the best part of July.

And by then, we know, he'd found himself wanting the time alone,
needing it. Not thinking for a moment of the other family who lived
here, though he saw Margaret, of course, he would always want to feel
her nearby, somewhere close to him in the House. But more and more,
generally for him, the thinking when he was here was — why bother with
anyone else? Those people from London he used to invite? Those things
he used to do? Because by now he'd got out his chanter again, that he'd left
behind here with his father all those years ago. He'd found it amongst his

father's things and all his old exercises, his music. Though he'd said he'd
never be back for all of that. Never! Remember? That he'd had enough
of his father and his father's damn music? Even so. Just as in London,
those long years away he had always been able to hear the ghost of the
old tunes, and not just in dreams, but driving somewhere, in the middle of the day. Or coming out from a building in the City, out onto the
street, he'd hear the thread of some part of the old music then, one of
his father's tunes, or something he himself used to play . . . So he found
the manuscripts in time that gave him the notes for those tunes, that he
now needed – you could say it was just a matter of time. Looking out the
sheets of handwritten music, and the folios of printed tunes. All there
in the bookshelves above his father's desk in the Music Room. First one
tune, something easy to start with. 'Flowers of the Forest', say. 'Return
from Boreraig'. Then other tunes, more difficult, more interesting. He'd
read through the music, sing it. There were some later compositions of
his father's also, that he'd never heard before . . . He played them. Those
tunes as well, and more tunes . . . He went through everything in his
father's Music Room until he'd arrived at a place in his mind where he'd
think: What need to see anyone else at all? Talk to anyone? When he
was going through that music, getting out his father's pipes and his old
practice chanter and playing his father's big music, the Big Music, again,
and playing it again and again. Why bother by then, you might say, about
anything else? What need for anyone? Any conversation, any thought for
another? When there was this, in his life, at the centre of it, music. There
need be nothing else. No friends. No wife. No child.

      Is how the years had passed for John Sutherland, a routine in place for
him by the time he reached middle age about how he might live – with
Elizabeth long gone and Callum's headstone down in Brora green with
lichen – so once again the Music Room became the focus of the House,
the sound of the pipes playing again like his own father had always wanted. And by then he had brought out all Callum Sutherland's music in one
body of work, all the manuscripts, all his books and notes – a process
that has been recorded in a special interview that was run in *The New Piping
Times*, that describes all the sense of the son coming upon the inheritance

of the father, the understanding for John Sutherland that the teaching he had received as a boy had been at a master's hand.* Thereafter he'd spent his time, increasingly, going through each of his father's papers, one by one, checking each version of notes in one tune by another, going on to read and play them in their variations and those passages his father had marked up with his own doublings and embellishments. He was working in his own particular fashion, intent and serious but nevertheless in pencil – to keep vivid and present his own father's work that way and not overscore it – making copies off the original Angus MacKay editions** that his father had inherited from his father, putting in the accidentals in a miniature stave and key signature, right above the manuscripted notes. John couldn't believe the detail of the work when he went through it. How the pages of the original nineteenth-century folio his father had worked from*** were thin and yellowed and threatened to come away from the spine, and yet still his father had kept the book in such beautiful condition that he had sewed certain pages in with silk thread, or had Elizabeth do it, so to read through it when he came upon it years later . . . The music looked lovely still, could be secure in its original condition, and so these books were lovely things to hold.

---

* *The New Piping Times* ran a cover feature that comprised an interview with and essay by John MacKay Sutherland on the subject of the musical archive that was kept at The Grey House and his realisation of its depth and wealth of material. Sutherland's essay begins 'No son realises early enough the debt he owes his father – and the son of a musician, who himself is someone who is trying to be a musician, knows this to his cost, too late in his life. So it was for me when I uncovered the manuscripts and writings of my late father, Callum Sutherland of Rogart – known to many as perhaps the greatest modern interpreter of the ancient piobaireachd we all love, and certainly one of its most intelligent and serious champions.'

** The List of Additional Materials shows a reproduction of the original Angus MacKay piobaireachd edition of 1838, 'Lament for the Children'.

*** It is significant that Callum MacKay owned an original edition of the above, as these are rare, and for the most part held in public collections and libraries such as the National Museum of Scotland, etc. The editions held by the Sutherland family were passed down from John 'Elder' Sutherland, who knew Iain MacCrimmon and, it is believed, also took instruction with Angus MacKay in the latter part of his life. The fact that the Sutherlands owned these editions at this time denotes their increasing prosperity.

The strength of his father, his will, the detail and personality that sounded through in all his possessions – perhaps these qualities were behind John's need to create for himself another place that would sit away from the House, and so be apart from the intricacies and influence of his father's scholarship and musicianship. Perhaps. It could have been that simple, individual need that took him up to the hills to find the certain crevice in the land which would be unseen unless you knew where to go, that was flat enough, with the ruin of an old bothy on it, to build for himself a little shelter and be alone there, collect his own papers and materials and keep them somewhere that would be nothing to do with his father's tiny detailed writing and his priceless books. It would be somewhere that could be his alone, a place he would make for himself, where John need not feel, to quote his own remark in the *Times* interview, that his musical inheritance had come to him 'to his cost'. And who knows how long it took? To find the site in that hidden valley beside the water? To take the materials up there he would need, piece by piece, and quietly build up for himself four walls, a roof? How long to fit out his shelter and carry up there a chair first, a desk? Piece by piece. Item by item. Tune by tune. Yet he did all of this. Because then the Little Hut, as he always called it, in his books and notes – 'TLH' is the mark at the bottom of so many of his papers* – became the way John Sutherland could create his own part of the world that might sit outside everything else that was in it. The Little Hut would be a place that would be his alone.**

All this to describe how John Sutherland came back, one might say, in these particular ways – to do with finding for himself the qualities of his father's music, the wealth of it kept there in the House – to embrace all the things he'd left behind him. Not arriving to wait for a crowd of London friends to follow, but setting up the Music Room to be used again as his father had used it, to sit alone in there and go through the

---

* 'TLH', standing for 'The Little Hut', is the mark at the bottom of many of the original papers discovered in that place, as described in the Crunluath A Mach section of 'The Big Music'.
** The relevance of this place of composition has already been noted in earlier sections of 'The Big Music'; further details are contained in the following movement.

various manuscripts and to be playing from them. While not wanting to repeat his father's habits, either – for he would never be like him, the great teacher and scholar, he could never be that disciplined or as pure. Rather, he came to find in the music certain passages that would start him thinking how he could develop his own sense of playing, an idea of a variation, say, presenting to him as the beginnings of a tune he might develop – and taking pleasure from this, a growing understanding of what his own music might sound like, what it would be.

So nothing like his father, then, he could still think! Nothing like!

Though he was in the Music Room all the same, and playing the same tunes according to his father's markings, and over and over. And how would his father ever have guessed that one day his son might do that, look so clearly at his work, be so close to it – the child who was never good enough, who felt the sting of the flex across his knuckles, across the back of his legs, the strike of the cuff against his face when he made as much as even one mistake.

Yet now here he was, playing in his father's room.

And so friends might have still been coming to the House, but only rarely and they were different friends, sons of his father's friends, some of them, so pipers, and from the college in Glasgow, in Edinburgh – because it was the music they'd be coming for now, like in the old days. His father's days. And there'd be parties, maybe, but parties because of the music they were playing. Up most of the night some nights, through to dawn those summers. John here like an owner of the place, as though he'd always been here, in time bringing his own son with him and with every year it seemed to him there were more reasons to stay. More to learn about, to think about. The old tunes, though. Only the old tunes in the House.

His own music – that was for the little place in the hills. The only place where he could think about the other music, that sound that started in his own head, and tried to complete there. In the Little Hut that was his, and his alone.

He thought.

When love went off or tenderness hardened into something no more than gesture – then, well, 'Aye'. He had this. His own composition. No one else could have it, this secret part of himself he owned in a place that was, like himself, shut away and utterly unknown. It was somewhere he could ignore who he'd become, the things he'd lied about and never done. A place where he had no wife or son or lover or anyone in the past that he might remember — but one person. Only Margaret. As though she was a music of her own, exisiting outside the whole, the markings and pattern-ings of his mind, her own note. As though there was something in that note that he needed and that he could hear through all the others, but had never been able to reach, a note he'd never let himself fully play . . .

Margaret.

Because what if he did play it? That note? What if he, just once, had played it? Just once and pure and true?

Though he'd written her a tune that would be her own tune and he called it 'The Return' and secretly to himself 'Margaret's Song' . . .*

He'd ended up with only Himself here. In the little shelter in the hills.

The place that he thought was his alone.

---

* This composition has been noted already, on pp. 128 and 132, and details given of the change of title.

gracenotes/piobaireachd: the Little Hut as a place of composition;
also the history of the House as a school

The Little Hut, as we have already seen, represents a separate musical
context for John MacKay Sutherland. The Music Room in The Grey
House is associated with the story of his musical genealogy – of his
father's work, and his father's before him, that in many respects goes all
the way back to the musical nights of the original Grey Longhouse of the
eighteenth century – but the Little Hut belongs to him alone.

It was for the very reason of his father – the heft and weight of his
memory and influence that was always present in the House – that it
became necessary for John to establish his own creative space. To quote
from the variation that has just preceded this passage and other papers
not used in that section: 'While not wanting to repeat his father's habits
. . . Though he was in the Music Room all the time and playing the same
tunes according to his father's markings over and over . . . Nevertheless
thinking about his own music by then, that he might do something that
felt he did not have to acknowledge his father, that might be his own
endeavour. Thinking how, if he was to make something new, something
that might come from himself, he would need to be away from his father,
from the memory of that man, the thoughts of what he would say, if he
was alive, about his son's own work, these compositions of his that were
new, nothing like Callum Sutherland's work at all.'

In part, the reason the Little Hut may have represented such freedom
for John MacKay was due to the fact that it was not related to the idea of a

musical school at all. Unlike his family home that had always been used this way, as a place of piobaireachd education and tuition, the Little Hut had no history, no credited past. To his mind, John Sutherland was the only person who knew about it, and in this sense it was more private to him, even, than the room at the top of the House where he and Margaret used to spend their nights together. That room, after all, had a history associated with it. His mother gave him lessons there when he was a child, and later, as is detailed in this same movement of 'The Big Music' and in relevant papers, it also, for a number of consecutive years, became a Schoolroom for local children.

The little cabin or 'bothy'* that John built for himself in the hills, though, was altogether different, with the atmosphere of classes, tuition and performance as far removed from the ethos of the building as could be.

As has been noted already in the Taorluath section of 'The Big Music', the Sutherland Family of The Grey House district were renowned since the early eighteenth century as musicians who had established a form of teaching that became well known, from that time on, throughout the district and beyond (latterly referred to as 'The Highland School of Piping') when local pipers were invited to stay at the Grey Longhouse, as it was then, for weeks at a time, through the Winter Solstice so they could play and perfect their playing under the tutelage of John Roderick Sutherland.

Over the years, with ensuing generations, these classes became formalised by the time of John Callum MacKay ('Old John') and were advertised, to an extent, throughout Scotland as The Grey House was extended. There were built lodgings and outhouses to accommodate pupils who would arrive in October through to January, to take advantage of the expertise of the generations of pipers that followed the time of the MacCrimmons – from 'Old John's classes through to what became officially known as 'The Grey House Winter Classes', conducted by the father of the John MacKay Sutherland whose story is featured in 'The Big Music'.

John MacKay himself had classes, of sorts, conducted by himself and other pipers whom he'd invited to the House – this, after he began return-

---

* The Index at the back of 'The Big Music' gives various listings for the Little Hut, as they also appear in the opening pages of the Urlar.

ing to Sutherland on a regular basis and some years after his mother's death, when his guests were no longer the usual band of friends from London but those he knew who were connected with the piping world, past pupils of his father and their sons, members of various societies and schools. The Taorluath section of 'The Big Music', in particular, describes how, when he left the House as a young man vowing to 'never return!', John Sutherland would have had no idea that not even half his life would pass before he went back and took up his father's place in this way. But take it up he did. In fact, in those intervening years, after his mother's death and before the onset of his own age and ill health, the atmosphere at The Grey House often seemed to resemble, almost entirely, those old days of the past. Though Iain Cowie would not have said so. By contrast, he remains faithful to the purist memory of Callum Sutherland as conducting his lessons in a very formal, concentrated manner. Though he is no piper himself, Iain would say that as far as he was concerned, the so-called 'classes' of John's were more social in aspect, less dignified. But this can all be argued either way, and Iain, as we have already seen, had a great deal of time, one might say love, for the older man and would always think the way in which Callum Sutherland did a thing was the best way. Nevertheless, it is on record, by various pupils and teachers who attended John Sutherland's own Winter Classes and who remembered the old days,* that when there was a party of invited musicians in, the House really did seem to belong to another age – with John tutoring the young men who would arrive for a week's playing and then conducting a series of performances on the Saturday evening accompanied by many a good dram. Those nights were festive indeed and most convivial.

---

* At present there is under consideration a proposal to revive the spirit of this 'School', the so-called 'Winter Classes'. Callum Sutherland is putting together a business plan whereby the administration and day-to-day organisation of The Grey House can be reconfigured as a limited company, owned by himself and those who have lived at The Grey House as long as he has known them – Margaret MacKay and her husband Iain, her daughter Helen – and to 'buy in' the expertise of an international roster of pipers to take classes and give recitals. Further details of these classes will be made available on a relevant website and by advertisement as soon as they are confirmed.

insert/John Callum MacKay Sutherland

So he could be alone there. It was why he wanted it. As somewhere to go
to, where he could be private. As though the House was not enough —
even though by the end the House was private enough. But he was ill by
the end, and tired. But even so — he managed it, didn't he? To get up there
to the private place?

He did. And nothing there ever interfered with his thinking. He could
write there. He could listen to the notes that made patterns on the page
before him. He could sit at the table and look out across the water. And
still nothing to interfere there, nothing. With no memory of a father or
anyone else — because this was his own secret place. A secret. Somewhere
he found out that there was much, much more in the music than he'd
thought when he started, that more of him lived there, within the music's
lines and phrases of that small shelter, than in all the places he had lived
elsewhere, in the world, in the world.

For the world . . .

That was outside and in here he was alone and true.

Back in the House, well . . . It was as it had always been. He may have
started off inviting his London friends, he'd invited those kinds of people
then, and there'd been fishing, sometimes in season they'd taken out the
guns . . . But, when he looks back, he can see how quickly those times
were over, how short and thin the days. Much better that he had differ-

ent people who were coming to the House after that, sons of his father's friends, some of them, so pipers, and some from the colleges, in Glasgow, in Edinburgh. Because it was all music they were coming for now, like in the old days, his father's days. And so there'd be parties, maybe, but parties because of the music. Up most of the night some nights. Through to dawn those summers. And John here like an owner of the place, surrounded by people like his father used to be. The teacher. The host. As though he'd always been here – 'Welcome!' 'Come in!'

As though . . .

But not quite.

For though there was more to learn about the music, always more . . . And pipers to arrive and pupils to teach, the tradition of the Sutherlands unbroken . . . It was always only ever the old tunes. Only the old tunes in the House.

His own music – the thing that started in his head – that was for the other place.

Where he was completely alone.

narrative/5

The people at the House and what they thought of him

Iain

She's like his own daughter. She is his daughter. He won't think about the other – what went on, about anything else. She's Margaret's child, that's all he needs to know.

Says: 'She's my girl.'

And today . . . With him on his last legs . . . And after all that business, up on the hill . . .

She showed what stuff she's made of. Having the son back here as well and she hasn't seen him since they were kids – and after everything she'd been through with the baby the day before, the way the old fool had her off with him and everyone thought she was lost . . .

'Well, she showed us all' Iain said to Margaret that night.

'My girl.'

And there's nothing he wouldn't do to help her if he could – just like her lovely mother.

For he cares for them both, he's the man at the ceremony who said, 'I do.'

So of course there is nothing he wouldn't do – even let them go as he's had to, God knows he's had to stand by while . . .

~

Though neither of them, not the father nor the son, deserve them . . .

Deserve Margaret.

Deserve Helen.

All he has to do is say their names.

~

Margaret

Helen was doing fine with her, who said you needed a husband anyway, with a baby? That's what Helen herself said: 'You taught me that, Mum.'

So, all through her pregnancy – saying to me, Iain, anyone else who asked her, pretty much the same thing: 'I'm fine.' She spoke of her independence – and she's always been a strong girl – would say that independence and strength, these qualities, were the most important in a parent. How she sounds like my own mother that way! Saying that she didn't need a partner. That she would be fine. That she would manage, absolutely, on her own.

I came to see it, too. Thought then and now: She'll be okay. I said to her, 'Well, I was on my own, too, when I was younger than you are and without my mother to help me.' And Helen told me that she had always had that image in her mind, from when she was a child, of a mother raising children alone, that it came from the stories I used to tell her when she was a little girl. So. Of course. It all adds up. That she would follow to a pattern somehow, from me, my own mother. And the thing is, in her case, like my mother did, she has a mother to help. Because I am always here. And our dear little Katherine. For Iain and me . . . She's a gift.

gracenotes/piobaireachd and lullaby; a husband's understanding

Fathers and mothers all over the world sing their babies to sleep with songs that have been composed especially to calm and soothe and mollify. These songs are well known and even someone like Iain Cowie – to whom no lullaby was ever sung – would be familiar with certain tunes, certain words. Iain has heard his wife Margaret sing to Helen those quiet songs that he could hum to himself when he's alone. Indeed, the pale lovely strain of something that Margaret used to sing to Helen when she was small . . . It's playing in his mind now and soothing him.

And Helen – the child he has always considered to be his own child . . . She sings to her own daughter in the same way. Sings the same old songs, folk songs you might call them. And some of these, too, Iain knows, though some of them are new.

Certainly a different kind of lullaby has been an important theme of this book. It was there in the second line of the Urlar and has emerged as a developing musical idea throughout the piobaireachd 'Lament for Himself'.

You took her away . . .

That song for someone else's granddaughter, maybe, but she's Iain's own child, the way he considers it. So –

You took her away . . .

But he brought her home again. Iain did. And the notes, though they have that drop, of the shock, of a child who has been taken . . . Even so the tune has been composed to quiet all the crying.

That, hush.

Hush.

The Lullaby whispers.

As Iain himself sits quietly now.

For in the end, after everything that has happened, a lullaby will soothe. It's a tune made for calmness, contemplation. Indeed, most musicians will acknowledge that the idea of a lullaby, a set of notes that are intended to bring a still centre to a composition, is at the heart of anything they play or sing or write. No matter how busy the tune may seem to be, how agitated at first, or quickening, so it has always been that the music itself will bring comfort, solace – and though John Sutherland's lullaby that is annotated so clearly in his 'Lament for Himself' is perhaps the first example of this sort of thinking being incorporated within the piobaireachd form, nevertheless at the heart of even the most stately Ceol Mor we hear a soft song.

The earliest printed collection of this kind of music appeared, with no reference at all as to how it may be included within a composition of bagpipe music, in an edition published by a John Forbes in 1662 in Aberdeen. The folio comprised twenty-five old Scottish airs and lullabies, and established at the time a genre of secular music that was disseminated in a range of pamphlets and editions throughout the eighteenth and nineteenth centuries, including *The Scots Musical Museum*, published in six volumes from 1787 to 1803 by James Johnson and Robert Burns, which also included new works by Burns. The *Select Scottish Airs* collected by George Thomson and published between 1799 and 1818 included contributions from Burns and Walter Scott.

From then it took several generations of pipers and Highland musicians to identify and highlight the links between the lyrics and tunes of these publications and certain compositions played on the Highland bagpipe. Most recently, following the related discussion around the piobaireachd 'Lament for Himself', Helen MacKay of Sutherland has brought attention to the connections between the two in a number of scholarly papers published by Edinburgh University Press entitled 'The Lullaby as a Feminist Metaphor in Highland Literature – from the Ballad to Neil Gunn', and has also written about the musical link between the great MacCrimmon piobaireachd 'Lament for the Children' and the tradition of song and lullaby that exisited at the time of its composition. Seumus MacNeill, in his book *Piobaireachd: Classical Music of the Highland Bagpipe*, also establishes the similarity between the sound of the pipes, when expertly played, and the human voice when it is used to sing a song with great emotional and psychological content. The connection between piobai-reachd and lyric, sound and poetry, is at its most marked in these passages of his book and come to bear upon the timbre and tone of 'The Big Music' itself as a genre that blends together words and music.

embellishment/2a: domestic and social history: Elizabeth Clare
Nichol

From that first second when the nurse let her have him to her, to hold, she
felt herself to be undone by the strength of feeling for him. Like holding
her breath and then forgetting how to let it go is how it seemed, as though
physically she was completely changed now that she had this infant in her
care. There was nothing else she could do but be a mother to him, feed
him, clean him, incline her whole body towards him, as though protecting
him from the weather. Think about an animal in the field with its young –
I could lick him clean . . .
– is how Elizabeth's instincts came alive for her, with her first and only
child in her arms. He was tucked right in beside her, his tiny wrapped
body so close against her that he remained part of her, is how she thought
of him, *attached*, a part of herself just as he'd been inside her before, when
her body had been his room and cradle and now here he was pulled out
of that dark place, maybe, and in the light to look at, but still belonging
to somewhere no one but him knew about or could see.
    And how she pored over him, Elizabeth, how she couldn't stop look-
ing into his face, his scowling brow as he slept, changing in seconds to
joy and fear and wonder. All the emotions of the world passing over
him like weather, then opening his eyes to regard her with a shocked
and steady stare. *Who are you?* His gaze seemed to say then. *Where have you
come from?* Lying there unmoving in a shocked and steady stillness. Or his
hands would come up at the side of his face – those tiny hands with their

miniature fingers clasping like a bird's claw, fingernails so miniature they were unimaginable, somehow, even as she took one of his fingers between her own and examined it for size . . . Unimaginable.

Is why she couldn't stop looking. As though looking might make him real. And to touch him, hold him . . . She never wanted to let him go. That first day, after she'd had him against her, the frail weight of him in his blankets . . . She couldn't imagine then how she could ever let him out of her sight. Though she must, she knew — would have to give him up to the nurse that day, and those that followed, and when she was fully recovered from the birth . . . She would have to give him up for longer. Finally, at the end of the day when the maid came for him, she must go back then to the room where her husband was waiting.

And to do that! To have to hand her son over! Leave the nursery where his things were, his tiny clothes and blankets and toys, his ball, his little wooden ship. To have to leave that beautiful place and go to another part of the House, to have to see her tiny boy be taken away by the capable maid who would simply come for him, sweep him up from the crib where he had lain beneath Elizabeth's gaze, his mother's gaze, to have him plucked out from his mother's arms and taken off in a bundle away from her . . .

To witness him gone from her like that, possessed by another, held in another woman's arms and not her own and knowing that she could not have him again until morning . . . And instead to have to go to her husband, to be with him . . .

All this seemed impossible to her.

When she couldn't even think of her husband, couldn't listen to what her husband was saying. Couldn't reply to him, turn to him when he came up against her when she had no baby with her, the way he wanted her to respond to him, listen to him. The way, later, in the night he expected more of her and more and more when he came at her, when all the time she was thinking of her own baby boy and his soft head, his sweet, sweet little body . . .

It was unbearable, actually.

To have to live in that other world, where her child was away from her. Unbearable, she might say, not to have him to bear.

And as time went on that feeling didn't go away. It stayed with her and strong. Of her husband like a rock that might tether her to the ground but this other light and delicate thing that would have her away, the wonder of him caught in her held breath. The feeling didn't alter in its strength as the years went on – and she wouldn't give it up either because she wanted to keep it in her, like a room kept ready for a guest and it would always be there and waiting.

So as John grew taller his mother still wanted to bend him to the shape of her arms. She wanted to have him on her knee for stories and for kisses, though by now he was four years old, five years old, and he was not a baby any more. She'd go into his bedroom and never want to say goodnight, stroking the hair back from his forehead as he talked to her about his day and all his fears, endlessly she would listen to him, looking deep into his face as she had done since the day he was born for all the love she would ever think about or need.

'My Little Bonnie Boy' she sang to him in the dark. 'My Little Darling Johnnie . . .'

He grew up, though, was taller, louder. She could no longer fit him in her arms. That had been a secret anyway, that she'd done that, had him for so long to hold on to and she knew that if her husband found out she had ever had the boy to her in that way he'd be in a rage against it. By then Callum Sutherland had started his son on the chanter and to make a man of him had him practise two hours a day from when he was six years old. Then he'd have him sent away to school, he told Elizabeth, to be with other boys and in a more disciplined environment was what he needed – but unbelievably his wife managed to hold out against him. It was that same instinct came out of her again, fierce! A quality of love that challenged even her husband then. That the child would not go, she said! That she would not let him! She would teach him herself, she told Callum: in the same way he was tutoring the boy music – well, then, so would she be his teacher here. There was a room unused at the top of the House, under the eaves, and it would make a Schoolroom, she said. She would teach John there, in that little room at the top of the House, and he would learn everything he needed from his mother in that place where his father never went and it was quiet there and gentle with his mother's ways all about him. Protecting him and caring for him and making him feel safe.

embellishment/2b: domestic history: the Schoolroom at the top of the House

Under the eaves, where the roof slants sharply from top to base and where the floorboards are smooth simple planks laid down from one end to the other, there is a long room with windows at each end where the gables of the House mark its particular shape against the sky.

This is the room known as the Schoolroom, dating back from the 1930s when Elizabeth Sutherland taught her son John there, creating a part of the House that he would associate as a place where just he and his mother would go – this when he was between the ages of seven and eleven, before he was sent away to finish his education in a more formal way and his mother had to let him go.

So it wasn't for long, then, that the room was used in this way, and after that, too, when Elizabeth for some years taught the local children here, but even so the Schoolroom it has always been called – by any who know the House, who come to visit. For though it has been a long, long time since a child was brought up to this room to sit at a little desk before the blackboard easel, take books from the low shelf beneath the window to copy from or read aloud . . . Still there are a few decorations in place that marked it as a special place for John, when he was a boy, that held gentle memories for him of time spent with his mother as she went through his lessons. There's an alphabet chart on the wall, a pinboard that has stuck on it his drawings and painted pictures. And there are a few toys that were always there, that John was allowed to play with when the sums and reading and writing were done – his bat, dusty, in boxes, his wooden ship and his ball.

The room never achieves much light, it must be said, because of its length, and the fact that the windows at each end are north- and south-facing so the sun that gets in there, through the high windows that them-selves are long but not large, is not direct but oblique and slanting.

Yet the room is lovely to sit in. Like a museum now, is how it feels, with everything still in place from childhood – the shelf with the books upon it, the armchair where his mother sat to read. There is still some chalk that sits ready at the ledge of the easel where John's mother would correct his spellings, have him write out times tables and sums. And there are, when you lift up the lid of the desk, paper books inside that have a boy's hand-writing across their pages, dated and signed and with coloured pictures as though the child has just finished the work and run out of the room.

So there are these things in this place, the desk and the easel and the toys, and then down at the other end of the room beneath the north window is a bed that was moved up here when the boy had grown up and was a man. The covers are still on this bed. The sheets beneath the blankets, the same sheets, the pillows are the pillows that have always been used here.

And strange to see. In this room for a boy, that was laid out for a boy with a boy's needs, a man's bed. Strange to touch it, sit upon it beneath the cold north light, this bed that was brought up here for a man and a woman to use, when they came to be together, for a few nights every year, but those years went on and on and they came here no longer.

Yet both stories are contained within the same room. The Schoolroom. The Bedroom. A room at the top of the House that has a boy's desk in it and his toys, and a man's large and open bed.

three/third paper

John MacKay Sutherland of the Parish of Rogart was the sixth generation of Sutherland pipers that are recorded in local histories and papers
as having a role in society as teachers of piobaireachd, as well as being
great musicians and composers of that same music. As early as the eighteenth century, as we know from the Taorluath section of 'The Big Music',
there were versions of a piobaireachd class that took place at the original longhouse that makes up the foundation of The Grey House as it
stands today. These were conducted by John Roderick MacKay Sutherland (1736–1793) and by subsequent generations as verified by the dating
of certain domestic records and the entry in his book by Angus MacKay
of Raasay, who refers to 'the piping of the Sutherland Family so showes
such mastery and fullenesse that it might teach any one who would heare
it how to playe';* but there is indication, too, that a more informal 'school'
of piping had been available to those living in the area of Sutherland
north-west of Brora long before then, with certain documents** referring
to 'one schoole that does give lessons in canntaireach, and has always done

---

* In one of his essays, MacKay refers to John Roderick Callum Sutherland (1800–1871)
in particular, but sets him in a context that reaches back to the early eighteenth century,
so taking in the previous two generations of the Sutherland family.
** The List of Additional Materials found at the back of 'The Big Music' gives examples
of original documents etc. that establish the musical prominence of the Sutherland
family from early times.

so; that is provided by one Sutherland, of the Grey Hill that is east of the river Blackewater . . . and accommodation also there'.

Thereafter, throughout the nineteenth and twentieth centuries, we have more detailed information available regarding the frequency and nature of the various classes and schools that took place in the Grey Longhouse, as it was initially, and afterwards, following the extension and additions to the side and rear of the building. Examples of these classes – dates and duration, details of numbers of pupils etc. can be seen in Appendix 5/iii at the back of this book. A Visitors' Book kept in archive also includes remarks made by, in the early first half of the twentieth century, George Gunn, John Williamson and, in the second half, Iain MacKay, Roy Gunn and Donald Bain when the Winter Classes of Callum Sutherland were at their height, and of international renown. Thereafter, following his death and an elapse of some years, John MacKay, his son, revived the tradition of The Grey House being a place for music and tuition – particularly in the winter months.

~

Perhaps the best way to convey the spirit and ethos of those classes that were held in The Grey House and conducted, most famously, by Callum John Sutherland – with a much spoken-of recital that was held outdoors on a certain date in February when it was deemed that the season was turned from winter to spring – would be to reproduce here in full the Foreword from a book on piobaireachd* that was published anonymously, first as a pamphlet in 1957 as a record of one of these classes and then later as part of the current project. In this piece the writer makes clear his enthusiasm for the tuition and the benefit gained from detailed, concentrated study that took place under one roof, for a consecutive number of days and weeks. The concert, too, held in the cold open air during the scant hours of daylight available in the winter and that was the culmination of such intensive training and learning, is described here with freshness and clarity:

---

* This is listed in the Bibliography, along with other relevant publications that refer to the Winter Classes and bagpipe schools in general, especially the MacCrimmons of Boreraig.

Most had gathered on the first Friday night to hear what we now are all calling 'The Sutherland lecture' when Callum Sutherland 'Himself' drew comparisons between Gaelic song and Piobaireachd. There can be few with as much knowledge in both spheres, and his words, and fine singing to accompany them, were enjoyed by all. Roy Gunn and Iain MacKay had the unenviable task of striking up and going straight into their Piobaireachd after this address – not a drone to be touched – and both rose to the challenge.

The classes started in earnest on the Saturday morning. 'Transmission of piobaireachd' could well have been the theme. In summary, there were talks about John MacKay of Raasay and John MacGregor from Perthshire. Both had key links to the MacCrimmons, and both were central to the onward spread of piobaireachd. There was a presentation by Callum Sutherland of a style of playing that is almost never heard now, but which was common fifty years ago and that his own father was a great exponent of, that shows how phrasing and a slight sharpening of the high A can create a style of playing that is dramatic and with a powerful effect upon the listener. A subsequent chanter class showed musical ideas being given to two young players, and in the last session two experienced pipers, both from the district, demonstrated the tunes that were to be rehearsed by all for the competition and recital in two weeks' time, in open air: 'Lament for the Earl of MacDonald', 'I Had a Kiss from the King's Hand' and 'MacKay's Lament'.

Details of this concert, and others like it, were kept in a special file comprising handwritten or typed sheets of paper with some notes recorded by Callum Sutherland in a form of shorthand collected together in one folder. No doubt there were many nights when John Sutherland would have gone through these papers, playing through the various manuscripts on his chanter and in the order of their representation those tunes that had been selected for the competitions of the past. He would have educated himself, to a large extent, after his years away, by using his father's papers as instruction and inspiration. For it must have been with a great sense of his inheritance when he came upon these, and other records like them. The papers would have kept him company, you might say, as he got older and sat alone all those nights in the Music Room of his father's House. The words of his father's frail notes become as conversations with him he himself might have had.

third return/composition: lullaby; the Little Hut; loneliness

'Piobaireachd music is difficult for the ordinary person to understand,'
began Archibald Campbell, editor and author of the *Kilberry Book of Ceol
Mor*, in a paper delivered to the Piobaireachd Society of London in 1952.
'It may never become really popular,' he went on to say, 'but there seems to
be a feeling nowadays that enough attention is not given to it, and lovers
of bagpipe music seem more disposed than they were, to take pleasure in
hearing a well-played piobaireachd on a well-tuned pipe.'

John Sutherland took note of these words, it seems. He must have
attended the meeting of the Society that night – despite having left The
Grey House and his father behind him and with no intention in the world
of picking up his own pipes again – for scribbled in a notebook that was
found in his Little Hut up in the hills is the following: 'spoke to AC afterwards about my father. Asked after him –' and then appears in a margin
the phrase 'agree entirely re. human voice', followed by something else at
the bottom of the page that has been scored out. The paper delivered by
Campbell appears in more detail in gracenotes that embellish the Crunluath movement of 'The Big Music' and will follow in due course. For now
it is enough to note the lonely tone of that opening remark of his that
appears in John's stained and worn jotter, the words copied onto his page:
Difficult music to understand.

'This difficulty must be recognised,' Campbell goes on, 'and in learning
piobaireachd what will matter most will not be the time spent on it on

a chanter but the hours spent turning it over in your mind note by note and thinking how you lengthen one note here and shorten another there, or quicken up a little in one variation, or slow down in another. Many of the piobaireachds which we play nowadays have words attached to them. Angus MacKay gives some in his book but it is not always easy to fit the words exactly to the notes of the piobaireachd ground. This fact seems to indicate that what we now know as a piobaireachd was at one time known in somewhat different form as a song.'

These remarks appear here because they seem to describe so aptly the various elements of the particular piobaireachd that is John Sutherland's 'Lament for Himself', containing within it those themes of song, abandonment and loneliness that are captured in the metaphors of the Lullaby and the stolen child, the open hills exposed to the weather and the secret sheltering place hidden within them, and the end of life and the inevitable hope for life's return, as imagined in the image of the newborn baby held in the arms of an old man who is dying.

These musical ideas that come together in the Lullaby Sutherland hears as the second line of his Urlar, music that has already been written down and is safe on the desk in the Little Hut up in the hills, could only have been brought together in a place he'd created himself to be as lonely and as far away from others as he was. The meaning of that Lullaby, along with themes of breathing, of remembering, of holding on, just, to the condition of living, that are also captured within the sound of his Lament, as well as notes of exultation, of hope, of defiance, only comes to be understood by him following, not during, his composition. As far as John Sutherland was concerned – and as we know by now in 'The Big Music' – his piobaireachd was left, in manuscript, unfinished.

three/third paper (cont.)

'The Big Music' has already given something of the history of John MacKay Sutherland, in terms of his business activities and musical endeavours – in relation to his taking leave of and then returning to The Grey House. There is, too, an understanding of how John MacKay came back to the music of his father after a period of time away, rejecting the pipes and all they stood for – principally isolation, misunderstanding, a lonely kind of wilfulness – and embraced those qualities fully. Even the way he came to establish his home to be a place of teaching, giving up aspects of a private life for a public one, making of his home a School . . . These indicate how close John Sutherland was to the family who had preceded him, his father, and his father before him and before him. For in all of these representations of music and of education and of art there is loneliness that sounds out as a kind of silence in all the activities, in the midst of the lessons and the recitals and the competitions. A loneliness that some might describe as a quality of mind that won't let anyone in, come close. A loneliness that may be described as a quality of heart that can't admit love.

Of course, in John MacKay's case, as with his son Callum Sutherland, recently returned to The Grey House himself, it is unknown whether or not it is the quality of the music itself – 'difficult to understand'* – that

---

* The third return that has just preceded this section opens with this very concept at the heart of Archibald Campbell's address to the London Piobaireachd Society in 1952.

contributes towards this state of mind or whether it was fixed in the men by birthright. Either way, there can be no doubt that a certain kind of individual emerges here, in these pages. He is present in the room's laughter and brightness, but also he is far away.

There is no doubt, from all records and accounts that are available to us, that the family home of the Sutherlands – whether in its earliest configuration as a simple longhouse or later, by John Sutherland's father's day, as a large establishment fully set up to accommodate twenty people at a time, with rooms for entertaining and dining, for recitals and competitions and so on – had always been used as a centre for music. Nothing lonely about that, one might say – to have a home that invites people in. And no doubt there was a great deal of enjoyment to be had, much entertainment along with the seriousness of study of musicianship – so how can one describe silence in the midst of all that, laughter and music and whisky, and the lamps lit and no sense ever that morning might come?

And yet . . .

There sits Callum Sutherland at the fireside, his wife silent beside him.

There sits his son, in his favourite chair.

And they are in the same room where, not that long ago, there were parties and conversation.

It's the same House, the same room.*

'One night we had nothing but conversation' reports one visitor, recounting an evening with Callum Sutherland and a group of well-known pipers, in a radio programme that was produced for the popular BBC series *PipeLines*. 'None of us played at all – but it was of instruction,

---

* All excerpts here are taken from the wealth of domestic material that is available to the general reader and that provides a sort of backstory to the book 'The Big Music' and that is collected in archive. This includes a sound archive that comprises original recordings and interviews as well as transcripts of those conversations, preserved as verbatim accounts that have been used here. There are also letters, private journals and cards that all relate to the use of The Grey House as a school and centre for piping over the years – in particular from the 1950s onwards. In addition, the List of Additional Materials contains some transcripts that may be of interest.

to our playing, to hear what was said, and interesting in its own right, and of course great fun.'

Another instalment of the same programme and we hear this: 'On a visit to Raasay last year Iain MacKay told us he stopped for a rest to look in the graveyard, where he was excited to find the grave of John MacKay of Raasay, father of Angus MacKay. The tombstone describes the contribution John MacKay made to the furtherance of piobaireachd. He took out paper and made a rubbing of the inscription and decided to gift it, then and there, to Johnnie Sutherland and we had to raise our glasses to that. But he went on to tell us, on a more serious note, that he believes that there's a connection between the Raasay MacKays and the MacKays of Gairloch. This is something his own grandfather used to talk about, and he's researching this now, at the College in Glasgow.'

'Then there was the fact of my discovery in the National Library of Scotland' says another contributor to the same programme. 'I found papers telling of the pipers of the Breadalbane Fencibles, with particular emphasis on John MacGregor. The Fencibles began recruiting in 1793 – and John wasn't too keen to join as he didn't have a bagpipe. Perhaps the incentive to him of having the regimental pipes to play, together with the promise of adding land to the family smallholding, was enough to persuade him. In any event he soon had his own pipes and took them straight to the Sutherland family of Rogart, to have them seasoned and treated. He went on to win the prize pipe at the Highland Society competition that year.'

A further programme introduced an American piper, Jim Brown, who had attended several years of the Winter Classes in succession, and considered himself something of a regular on these nights that would go 'well on into the small hours!' He talks of one evening when he remembered his Highland grandfather, a piper from Gairloch, saying that his father often said that the old pipers in Scotland all played almost in the same way except for preferential differences and he then finished with a quotation by Duke Ellington – 'If it sounds good, it is good.' 'They laughed at that, some of these guys that didn't know what jazz was, let alone the Duke! They'd been so deep in their chanter practice all their lives they had no idea what I was talking about! But of course seriousness was at the heart of my remark, too. Because that's my litmus test' he finishes by saying. 'If it sounds good – then no matter what you're adding and taking away in rhythm and phrasing, and so on – it is good. That and a perfectly – and I mean perfectly – tuned pipe, of course!'

Another transcript has John 'Bobby' Bain remembering a Big Night with Callum Sutherland presiding at The Grey House, in November 1968. It is the same Music Room where later John Sutherland would describe his father and his mother sitting in the evenings, in the line: 'I'll not come back to crouch at their cold fireside!' Yet how hard it is to imagine cold and quiet, that sort of solitary life, in the following piece. The interviewer is David Graham, a young piping student of the time who was compiling a programme of interviews with prominent bagpipers of that era, including Donald McFadyen and Donald MacLeod.

DG: You say you can remember some of those Big Nights they had at The Grey House back then?

BB: Oh, aye, they were grand nights then. Plenty of good music, and of course old Callum, for he was getting on by then, would be in charge so you knew it would be good from the outset. I remember there was one chap, had come over from Canada and he was staying at the House . . . Well. He'd never heard so many good pipers together in one place, in one room, I mean. He said to us all [puts on North American accent], 'You guys sure do know how to have a party.'

DG: But this was educational as well, these evenings were part of the School.

BB: Well, that's true, too – but some of us would just come in for the evening, you see, as a sort of recital. We'd play a simple tune for the young ones, something like – ah, you know – 'Flowers of the Forest' – and then we'd discuss it with them, the progressions and so on. Then they'd play it after us and we'd look at how they could improve themselves. So there was that – went on in the evenings, also. As well as all the drams!

DG: And there was one night in particular?

BB: Oh, in November . . . And the snow, well . . . None of us would be getting home in that weather. So Callum decided, well, he'll make it a bit of a session, you see. So we had a grand dinner in the evening – this was all arranged by Elizabeth, his wife, you know she was just marvellous at these things, just a marvellous hostess and generous . . . And so we had this very grand dinner, and then . . . The music starting after it. Callum played first, I remember that – for it set a tone. He played 'Lament for Donald MacKay'. And just . . . Perfect. I remember it so well. How he played that tune, and we all know it, of course, it's such a familiar tune, but it was just as though it had been written for that room, for the moment of it being played there. It was as though the tune had been made to be played right then, by him, I mean, on this particular occasion – oh, it was something. And the atmosphere in the room . . . There would have been about eight of us gathered . . . Well, you could barely speak afterwards. Is what it was like. As though a kind of a spell had been cast. And then, after that was played, the next one got up then, and played, and the next – we all got up – just like that – one after the other – but with barely a word spoken between us and we played . . . You know, various tunes, the big tunes, 'Lament for the Children' and so on, all the big tunes . . . We just played them through, all of us, like in a row, and no words between us. And do you know? Not a single wrong note? Misplaced note? Just the fingering, everything . . . Perfect. Perfect. And then the last one of us finished and it was like . . . Well, it was like a dam breaking then. All of us talking, we were roaring! For after the silence and the music, suddenly, there we were – back to earth again – and oh, the party started then! The whisky came out. That was a night. We finished when light broke. And of course, well, by the end, the whisky had taken over from the music by the end, there – but before, the night before . . . Well, nothing could take that away. The magic, you see, of that first tune, and the eight tunes that came after it, one after the other, coming out of the silence. It was something. All of us gathered together and quiet like that, I tell you. It was something, all right. I'll never forget it. That particular night.

And here is Roy Gunn remembering classes with Callum Sutherland, conducted in The Grey House over four consecutive winters, 1953–56, appearing in a later programme also compiled by David Graham.

RG: Well, he was just a great teacher, and that's all there is to it. He had a natural instinct, for what was right, how a tune should be approached. I remember I went to him – this was one of my first lessons with him, you understand – and I had a tune, oh I thought I could play this tune. It was 'Lament for the Viscount of Dundee'. And I got up, and I started to play and he sat there for a minute or two and then he just put up his hand. I stopped, of course, straight away – but he said as gently as anything: 'We'll just set that tune aside for the time being, Roy.' That was his way, you see. Not to say anything critical at this point. I was a young man, I suppose I was a bit nervous – those first lessons with him. But he was gentle. He had a nice way with him. That's not what his son said, of course. His son has another version altogether, and never took instruction from him. I understand he left home quite young. That was something we young fellows couldn't get over. That you might have a teacher like Callum Sutherland and he'd be your father as well. Because that would be something. That would really be something.

And Roy finishing with: 'That House of the Sutherlands, what an atmosphere it had. Full of people, and music – is how I remember it. A real piping school atmosphere to it that made us all think of those great schools of the past, and what it must have been like then.'

gracenotes/piobaireachd: the history of its teaching, the MacCrimmons

The history of schools of piping in the Highlands of Scotland begins with the famous 'Piping College' of the MacCrimmons, who were musicians, composers, teachers and pipers to the chiefs of Clan MacLeod for an unknown number of generations. The College, as we know by now, was established at Boreraig near the Clan MacLeod seat at Dunvegan on the Isle of Skye and was famous from at least the sixteenth century onwards – and probably earlier – as a centre at which young men could be taught and trained in the art of piobaireachd.

The College was like any university college of the time in that it provided billeting and provision as well as tuition, and pupils' period of residency went for a year or more before they were deemed fully educated in musicianship and could leave.

Records are provided from the seventeenth century on that give indication of the arrangements made for young men – much the same as we may read for those entering Glasgow or Oxford or any of the great universities of the time. See the following notes by way of example.

An order from John Campbell, Earl of Breadalbane to his chamberlain, Campbell of Barcaldine, reads: 'Give McIntyre ye pyper fforty pounds scots as his prentices with McCrooman till May nixt as also provyde him in what Cloths he needs and dispatch him immediately to the Isles.' The order seems to relate to a statement written by the mentioned Earl of Breadalbane on 22

April 1697 at Taymouth in Perthshire: 'Item paid to quantiliane McCraingie McLeans pyper for one complete year as prentyce fie for the Litle pyper before he was sent to McCrooman, the soume of £160' (modern translation: 'Item, paid to Conduiligh Mac Frangaich [Rankin], MacLean's piper, for one complete year, as apprentice fee for the Little Piper before he [the Little Piper] was sent to MacCrimmon, the sum of £160'). The MacCrimmon instructor that is referred to may well be Padraig Og.*

The College was closed and the teaching finished with the Proscription Acts of the eighteenth century – which also brought about the beginning of the end of the great MacCrimmon dynasty of musicianship. However, the idea of the place lives on in pipers' minds to the present day and, as various pages in 'The Big Music' indicate, provided the 'blueprint' for piping schools that were set up, at first secretly, throughout the Highlands, and then more openly, in the West, in particular, and in the North East where the classes of the Sutherland family had become well established, right up to the present day when certain schools of piping have national status – such as the Army School of Piping in Edinburgh and the National College of Piping in Glasgow.

Certainly, the sense of history that attends the teaching of piobaireachd in Scotland today is what gives it its special place in musical education. Here is the idea of a music school that was established before any known music schools were founded in the United Kingdom and it was a school run according to its own strict principles and beliefs. To the present day – whether piobaireachd is being taught in a one-on-one class or in a tutorial at a festival or in one of the many classes available throughout the world – the memory of the College at Boreraig, set amongst the rocks with the sound of the sea and the wheeling gulls overhead . . . And at its centre the teachers who represented the pinnacle of a musical tradition that was being passed down, from generation to generation . . . This is carried in the minds of all pipers everywhere, old and young.

---

* See MacNeill's *Piobaireachd: Classical Music of the Highland Bagpipe* for a full account of the MacCrimmon family legacy and relevant periodical titles in the Bibliography for further examples of the role of the School and its legacy in the period both before and after Proscription.

three/third paper (cont.)

The following information indicates John Callum MacKay's position in his father's family as only son, bearing his father's name, and his role as husband, father — as well as giving some details regarding his endeavours and education. It may be noted that there is also a section devoted to domestic life and the history of the Sutherland family in relevant Appendices at the back of this book — but for now, here is how the life stands at the time of 'The Big Music'. Here is John Callum MacKay Sutherland, of The Grey House, Brora region, Highlands of Scotland, presented, at the end of his life, by way of a history: the boy who left, the man who returned.

1923: Born to John and Elizabeth Sutherland of The Grey House, Mhorvaig, Sutherland. Mother: Elizabeth Clare Nichol; Father: John Callum Sutherland

1934–40: Sent to Inverness Boys' Academy, as a termly boarder

1941–43: Attended University of Edinburgh to read Law; left before attaining a degree

1943–45: Worked first as an assistant, then manager, at Baillie Ross Investments

1945–47: Began Ross Holdings, a business involved in export/import investment, and took this over as MacKay Investments in 1946 in Edinburgh

1948 onwards: Moved to London; established MacKay Investments as a City operation with offices in New York and the Far East; set up

Sutherland Holdings, a private equity firm, as a satellite operation during this time (note especially the latter company name)

1964: Married Sarah Lutyens of Barnes, London

There follows, as we read in 'The Big Music', the birth of Callum John
Sutherland, only child; the illness of his mother initiating a return to The
Grey House after an absence of more than twenty years; the death of his
father, after which he starts intermittent visits home to Sutherland, often
in the summer months.

Then the death of his mother, Elizabeth Clare Nichol.

Moves back to The Grey House following an informal separation from
his wife.

And from then to the present: see all movements of 'The Big Music'
for further information.

His musical development can also be represented in similar fashion:

1926–35: Taught chanter at home by his father, John Callum Sutherland;
    introduced to pipes and drones at about the age of ten

1934–40: Played in the Inverness Boys' Academy Pipe Band; performed at
    local concerts, events in the Inverness region

1941–43: Joined the Piobaireachd Club at the University of Edinburgh;
    subsequently revoked membership

1944 to the period recorded in 'The Big Music'; ceased playing the bag-
    pipes altogether

After first visit back to The Grey House: began practising the chanter
again, and then the pipes.*

From then to present: Played seriously as a competitor, teacher, com-
poser; awarded the following: Gold Medal at Inverness; the Clasp at
Inverness; the Donald MacLeod Memorial Cuaich; International Pipe
Music Award; the Piobaireachd Society Award; BBC Scotland Award for
Composition and Play; the Isle of Skye MacCrimmon Memorial Cuaich.

---

* NB: This is when he first met Margaret MacKay of Caithness.

gracenotes/piobaireachd: the history of its teaching, the
Sutherlands

As noted in the Taorluath and in this Crunluath movement of 'The Big
Music', the Sutherland Family of The Grey House District were renowned, since the early eighteenth century (and no doubt before then)
as musicians who had established a form of teaching that was referred to,
from early on, as the 'Winter Classes' and that took place, generally, from
October through to February.

John MacKay conducted classes that followed his forebears' and particularly his father's models of teaching – this, years after he'd begun
returning to the House as a mature man and had uncovered the wealth of
musical material his father had left behind there, by way of instruction.
In this manner, the spirit and ethos of the classes remained the same, in
the twentieth century, as they had been in the eighteenth, and before then,
with some of the exercises that were played dating right back to those
dark nights in the 1700s when Roderick Callum had first invited a group
of pipers to come and spend the winter months learning to perfect their
musicianship. The idea, from the very beginning, was to create a place
of learning, to attain by practice and emulation the perfection of their
art that pipers had known back in the days of Boreraig, back in those
great days. During those winter months certain tunes were composed by
the Sutherlands and created to develop technique and expertise, from the
singing of canntaireachd through to chanter-playing, as well as instruction

given pertaining to tuning of pipes to drones, and the modulation of the treble to the bass so as to give the most beautiful sound. These tunes and exercises are still played today.

So John Sutherland returned to the world of piping that he'd left behind him when he rejected his father and all he stood for. In fact, in those intervening years, after his mother's death and before the onset of his own age and ill health, the atmosphere at The Grey House quite often resembled that of his father's parties and so-called 'Big Nights' that in themselves harked back to an earlier era — the time when the cold hills rang with music and a low house set in against the hill might provide, for a time against the weather, all the consolations of art and beauty.

three/third paper (cont.)

Finally, there are the following family records that detail those sons of the Sutherland family who inherited both the holdings and musical tradition of the House that had been established as early as the mid-eighteenth century as a place for music and education. As is clear from the chart that appeared earlier in this movement, a variation of which is reproduced below, eldest sons were traditionally named John, though in some cases, following a death, a younger son inherited. The details of other siblings are not included here, though a full family tree is available as part of the completed archive. In some instances, younger brothers who were also talented pipers may have stayed on at the House to teach, but in most cases, certainly by the turn of the twentieth century, The Grey House was home to one piper only, with a single tradition that dominated the teaching and playing of music in that place. Underlined names suggest name in use.

John Roderick MacKay of 'Grey Longhouse' ('First John') 1736–1793: early scraps of tunes survive; see Appendix 5, List of Additional Materials, archive

Roderick John (a tacksman) 1776–1823: extant tunes and writings: Notes on Canntaireachd; 'The White Flower', 'A Tune for Mary Jean'; extended the holdings of the House; also known as Roderick Mor, a piping teacher

John 'Elder' Roderick Callum (possibly knew Iain MacCrimmon, the last of that great family of hereditary pipers, who died in 1822) 1800–1871; famous tunes: 'I Knew MacCrimmon', 'The White Flower, Again', 'The Long Night'. Bought the 'corridor' from Sutherland Estates; built The Grey House on existing foundations, incorporating a part of the original Grey Longhouse

John Callum MacKay ('Old John') 1835–1911: all tunes as above, but formally printed and bound with his own notes; also 'Lessons, Notes and Tunes for Lessons'; first formal lessons conducted in a 'Study' or 'Music Room' at The Grey House that had been extended and renovated; also known as John Mor, after his grandfather who had also been known for his teaching

(Roderick) John Callum ('Himself') 1887–1968: always known as Callum; the great twentieth-century 'Modernist' piper; most known piobaireachd 'Salute to the Hills'; also many tunes for the Sutherland Highlanders and Army School of Piping; responsible for establishing the 'Winter Classes' at The Grey House as a fixture on the international piping calendar; oversaw further renovations that the House could accommodate large parties

John Callum MacKay of this book, 1923–present: see the Taorluath section of 'The Big Music' for a list of tunes composed, including 'The Return' and the unfinished 'Lament for Himself'; secretly built what he called 'the Little Hut' in the hills in front of The Grey House for composition work and writing

Callum Innes MacKay, his son, introduced in 'The Big Music': at time of writing it is unknown whether he will return to The Grey House and take up piping there.

gracenotes/piobaireachd: style and manner

The oral transmission of piobaireachd survives as a living tradition through diverse lineages of teachers and pupils, traceable back to the earliest accounts of the form. Distinctive approaches to performance technique and interpretation developed through different styles of playing and instruction, with two of the most influential coming to be known as the Cameron style, which is more rounded, and the MacPherson style, which is more clipped.

The Sutherland style of playing was one that took its name from the great Highland piper Roderick John Callum Sutherland of Rogart, who, with his son Roderick John Callum and his son John, went on to perfect a series of piobaireachd musical themes that came to describe a certain manner of phrasing and tone that relied less on traditional ornamentation and more on the hold and stay of the notes. Recordings of some of the later of these compositions survive but in the form of tapes only, which are currently being converted to CD.

More recently, recordings by acclaimed practitioners such as Robert Reid, a leading proponent of the Cameron style, and Donald MacPherson offer exemplary documentation of these performance traditions. In all instances, the beauty and complexity of the music must rely in the end on a perfectly tuned instrument, where reed and bag, drone and pipe are in finest condition and in unified accordance, one element to another. It has been said that the best way to think about playing a tune – and therefore about the qualities of the instrument upon which the musician will be playing – is to imagine all at first as something that will be sung. To tune the voice, the mind to the music in hand – this was the way piobaireachd was taught in the beginning, when there were no written manuscripts, when the notes for the tunes had no representation upon the stave. Such is the power of music, of poetry, that it can be learned in this other, mysterious way – not so much read and understood as listened to and apprehended. It could well be that the traditional manner of learning piobaireachd by canntaireachd, by way of a range of sounds that were sung through, teacher to pupil, may contain instruction for our understanding of all of art's mysteries. Certainly there need be no direct correlation between correct understanding and the power of effect for high art to make its charge upon us.

Indeed, the writer Seumus MacNeill has observed, because of this very fact – of the primacy of the human voice as being our way in to piobaireachd – that it could well be 'that the more incorrectly a piobaireachd is written, the better it is to be played – because the learner is forced to seek assistance from a piper who knows more than he does and who has been taught himself in the traditional manner'.

Certainly, the idea of a music that sits behind the words, of entire lines and phrases that sound rather than represent . . . Is at the very heart of the project here in hand, from John Sutherland's 'Lament for Himself' right through 'The Big Music' in its entirety.

embellishment/3: domestic detail: Mary Katherine MacKay

And what was left for Mary then? Helen wondered about her, gave stories to her, for what had occurred there, in that woman's life, after she'd turned her own daughter away?

Of course those actions of hers, coming from her strength and independence, had brought a consequence upon her she could not have forseen, otherwise surely would not have allowed? That was Helen's realisation, years after her mother had first started telling her about her grandmother's life. How she came to understand that a desire for freedom itself, and independence, can cause a straitening, a limitation that shows itself as narrowness and lack of feeling . . . Is what would happen in time to Mary.

For, as Margaret said, the way her mother came to end her life was to be without both a daughter and a granddaughter – though surrounded still by her own perceived and wasted freedom. For to be a mother of a daughter without a daughter . . . What loneliness there, what cutting short. That by judging her daughter so hard for following the conditions of her heart she would lose her, that by punishing her because she would leave her to follow a man, so that Mary herself would never see her own daughter, meet her granddaughter . . . What possible freedom could there ever be to make up for that, ever? In casting Margaret from her the way she did, what effect? What result? Only sadness.*

---

* We have seen the way lullabies and the tradition of Highland folk song often carry a plangent tune and lyric content that denotes loss and longing as well as a desire to soothe

This sadness has been described already, of course, in an earlier embellishment,* and other papers describe how the music of piobaireachd and the remote Highland landscape itself promote feelings of loss and loneliness. The line 'People are lonely enough' comes to mind here, along with countless other phrases that describe emptiness and longing – there is Callum's return home to see his father, driving up the long road in the gathering dusk, there are the implacable hills, the empty skies. So Mary's sense of loss here could be seen as one aspect of a larger landscape. Certainly she is not alone in her stubborn refusal to let tenderness guide her actions. But the significance here of her will is the way it played out upon her daughter's life. How, because Mary herself had never allowed a man to direct her actions in the way that Margaret was so affected, she became narrow towards Margaret and unyielding – is what Helen came to learn from her story. That independence could lead to judgement then to loss. Indeed she has made notes about this: *How sometimes everything you want,* she has written, *only draws you closer and closer inwards, takes you away from the open air and puts you inside.*

Poor Mary.

By the time she died, it was as though she had never known Margaret, never given birth to a daughter, or held her. Had never known her at all.

So the consequences played out in that woman's life – a particular effect of a particular kind of love: *That's a story many women tell,* writes Helen on a paper, *though never Mary.*

---

and placate. The casting away and loss of children is certainly a most present theme in these songs that are often sung most sweetly by elderly women, years and years after the babies have grown up and left and gone away. See Helen MacKay's paper 'The Metaphor of Lullaby' in *Studies in the Maternal,* vol. 1, issue iv, University of London, 2009; also the Bibliography generally for further reading.

* pp. 28–34 and 61–2 in particular give some of the history of Margaret MacKay and John Sutherland, a love story that is unconventional in the manner so celebrated by some of the great ballads and piobaireachds of the early eighteenth century. Appendix 12 includes information on the pre-piobaireachd music of the harp, that has relevance here, and the List of Additional Materials shows Laments featured in the book, and especially note details pertaining to 'The Return' or 'Margaret's Song'.

Is why she writes it down and keeps it here instead. 'In books' she says, 'in papers.'*

The history of women in these places is always a quiet story, it's quietly told.

The story of her mother, her mother's mother.

All caught up in those domestic papers. Embellishments. Variations.

The history of women in these places . . .

Writing everything down that the children might learn from the history, as Helen herself might learn from her mother's story: what strength is. And love. To be strong like a Mary, but with an understanding, too, of that which is tentative and can be frail. Therefore to treasure love and return to it, going back and back again to that invisible thing, even when it has no currency in the world, when some may say it has given you nothing, so you go back to it, says Margaret's story in the end, return, to find the richness there.

---

* The later section of this Crunluath movement shows how Helen's papers come to be seen to be central to the project of 'The Big Music', and have been from the outset.

third variation/The Grey House: history of land ownership

It's not to give the impression that the land up in this part of Scotland, connected to this family and developed over the years away from the estate system of leasehold and rent, quite separate in its management from the rural systems established in the North East at the turn of the nineteenth century,* not to imply that any of this put the Sutherland family in a position that could be regarded as elevated, in the district. This was not the case. That old John 'Elder' challenged in market for better prices for his animals was not to make him grand in any way, or standing one better than his neighbours. Rather, he was able to charge more for his livestock and so challenge the market because the animals were those he himself had raised and looked after – so better by far than any a shepherd might mind for the laird he was working for, and better, too, than leasehold beasts, for these sheep and cattle were his own. So, in all, this would put him in a better position than most with his enterprises – and gave others in the district a kind of template to follow: that you could raise more for your own stock by bringing in the kinds of innovations and care that were being adopted on the big estates down on the Black Isle and in Nairn,**

---

* Appendix 1: 'History/Landscape of the North East Region'; Taorluath section of 'The Big Music'; Carter, *Farmlife in Northeast Scotland,* and other related titles in the Bibliography, may be of interest here.
** As note above; also 'Story of a Highland Estate' in Richards and Clough, *Cromartie: Highland Life.*

that it was all about paying attention, success, being responsible for the development of your own land and beasts and not just letting them lie, in the old ways, unchanged, just making do with getting by.

So his sheep were cross-bred to create his own breed — hardy and fat, and with wool that could be clipped twice in the year; the effort worth it for the yield. So in the same way he slowly sold off the black cattle and brought in the slower, heavier red cows that could be driven for greater distance without losing body weight. And one should not give the impression either, in this paper, that any of those working for him resented the additional labour that these innovations brought — for the recompense was there, in money or in livestock. And not to suggest either that any resented the tithe he took, this John Sutherland, known also as Callum, following in his father's habits, in taking a tithe instead of payment in exchange for the land sub-contracted — any more than any would have resented the tithe asked for the shelter provided by the House back in the old days, when it was a necessary stopping-off place for shepherds on the Lairg sheep or cattle run.*

For just as the shepherds of that earlier time would rather be paying a man they viewed as a friend in tithe, so as to reflect a fairness, a reciprocity, in payment and in receipt, so those in later generations who were given work on the land regarded the extra clipping, the time taken with the lambs or the greening of the pasture by the river, as necessary and developmental to their own success — it came to be that way — as helping them in time with their own ventures. In this John or Callum was a sort of mentor, you might call him, someone they could go to for advice and help and who would give them a start, too, if they needed it, more often than not out of their own tithe. In all this, then, so you could say, he was the kind of man as they themselves were, is how they regarded him, straightforward, you might say, and with simple education, and though he had the House and with land and hills and a river going through it all . . . He had none of the glitter and empty cast, as they saw it, of the landed

---

* As recalled in the first variation in the Taorluath, and earlier sections of this movement and developed further here.

classes with their big ostentations hidden away in the hills and there only for the autumn shooting, or for the salmon, just. This man, by contrast, the great-great-great-grandfather of this book's John Callum MacKay, lived here through the year, he stayed here: a man who had used his wit and cleverness, it was said, to take back some of the goodness of the land that in the course of time the Big Clearances may have lost.*

And it's written like that, 'Big Clearances' – though this is something to argue with, of course.** Whether we are to think of what happened in this part of Sutherland as a straightforward 'clearing' – a sweeping away, and all that the word hints at and implies, the adjective containing within it, as it were, the force of necessity. For there are many*** will say that this was a natural thing, in its frank brutality, a force of nature that occurred by human agency – for the land was never going to continue to support the kinds of numbers were breeding and living like wild things in some of the conditions present up there in the back hills and valleys of the darkest Caithness and Sutherland Hills.

Or, on the other hand, whether one is to agree with the many others who say that the very scale of the operation has weeping in it, the echo of which carries in the empty hills to this day. They will say, those who argue to this side, that it would have been far better to have left things alone there, that they themselves had family who would have liked to have been left alone, that it's no one's right ever to turn people away from their homes when they were living in a way they were used to and could even say were accepting of and fond – for they knew no other. They had their family there, they will say, who gave birth to their babies, and gathered around fires to talk, exchange information: these were communities – and who can have the right to break these up into pieces, make the people

---

* Appendix 3/ii: 'Land Use and the Clearances' gives further details of this period of Highland History; see also Bibliography and pp. 88–92 of 'The Big Music'.

** See Bibliography/History: Highland and Scottish – Richards, *Debating the Highland Clearances*.

*** See Bibliography, in particular Richards's *Debating the Highland Clearances*, and related papers in 'The Big Music' that describe how the Sutherland family, like many, resisted the changes that were elsewhere sweeping the Highlands.

go away?* Also, it will be argued, that it was in the very days before the Clearances, when families would have their couple of sheep and their cow, would have some milk and cheese and some wool and the women kept looms and wheels, that there was a civility, dignity, to life. That, in the way these remote and impoverished people put themselves together, clothed themselves, told all their stories and made their music, was a culture that was lost to the mills and factories and gin houses of the town, a way of life that would be hard to find again, put back together again.

So it will be said.

So it is said.

For in those stories . . .

In that music . . .

Is where an Urlar might start.

Where you might make for yourself a ground upon which to stand.

And from that beginning, the rest can come.

~

So what I am getting at here** – in the idea of the home as ground, as the starting place – is an image of a group of people with a certain 'sound' to them, you could say, a particular clustering of notes that comes through the tune as a recurring theme. And there's a certain appearance to them, also, these people – in their story and that sound – certain genes cast down from the time of the Viking invasion*** hundreds of years ago, from inter-relations with those Northern armies, and with something left too from the original people of this place that's fast and animal, with a quick-

---

* Appendix 3 may be of interest here; also literary history – novels, stories and poems of the Highlands pre- and post-Clearances – listed in the Bibliography.

** This idea is present in the individual embellishments as they appear in this movement as the domestic histories of various women connected to 'The Big Music' and, it is becoming increasingly clear as the Crunluath progresses, is a central theme that draws many of the papers and writings together. See also the footnotes on pp. 19 and 41 of the Urlar movement that, from early on in 'The Big Music', bring the reader's attention to the use and provenance of the first-person in terms of the writing's tone and influence.

*** John Roderick MacKay, 1736–1793, one of these; also Appendices 1–3A and 6/i relate to general characteristics of the region.

foot-ed'ness that made them excellent for the hills and for getting over a river at spate or dodging the exciseman when he came. So that when parts of the Highlands were cleared in a mass of clans and groupings . . . These certain families wrested out a living just so much longer.

You can say, then, for these families — for this man — the Clearances didn't happen in the way of others. Yes, much was lost, much swept away, but, in the sense that this particular man used his cleverness to avoid the fate his neighbours were commanded by, he was not affected by the large scope of the operation. He and his family were let alone. For by offering at that point in history — when all was falling away for so many, for those he must have known and loved — to run the sheep that were being brought in, that were part of the great change that was affecting so much in the region, and to offer to manage the flocks himself for an absent laird on a piece of land that that man had perceived to have no value . . .

Was the beginning of his own ground, for sure.

His advantage gained, his place upon the land made good.

Though there may be some cannot understand this. How good can come out of ill, when so many others are suffering. But the fact is that this man's foresight and strength of character, of decision, cleverness — that word again — will always keep a family safe. So when the great House of Sutherland carved up that part of the Highlands and placed builders at the coast and inland through Strath Naver for certain fishing and shooting pleasure, starting work on building the fine lodges and estate buildings and bridges that you can see to this day in various places through that landscape . . . They had taken no account of this particular strath where the foundations of The Grey House are lying now.* To that extent cleverness can be a hidden thing. For that little mark of stone you see from a great distance on the low side of the greyish-green hills — you could barely make it out as a place where a man may start to think about creating something more for himself. Yet that is where it had begun for

---

* The earlier Taorluath movement gives more details of the House and its history, as do those Appendices relating to The Grey House and certain documents listed in the List of Additional Materials at the back of this book.

him, this one man. That first Sutherland's own grandfather's croft was that stone, his history already there, an understanding of the land already established in that most inhospitable place. So there was a stone you might not think any more than a stone but it had been where a whole family had kept itself protected, where generations of their forebears had grown and flourished — that, this family understood, knew about and could work with, this particular part of the hills.

One could say then, he might have said, that all he was doing, John Roderick Callum Sutherland, was making good that mark. Going to the factor, fixing for himself that bold appointment — to suggest that the great Duke of Sutherland's men might be better off were they to let him manage this bit of unproductive hill. It was where the shepherds came through annually for the Lairg run, he would have told them, and where there could easily break out skirmishes and thefts of the Duke's livestock, and could develop even various ways against him and those that worked for him that could turn into a kind of vendetta, a civil war. That there could be raids against the estate lodgings, and into the neighbouring estates even, and so animals continually would be killed and taken — but that if John Roderick Callum might keep this thin strip of land that was no more than a path, really (and he might have used that expression, even, 'no more than a path'), between Lairg and Rogart, where it was so bleak and wasted away that nothing could come of it, but bleak and wasted enough that it could be the scene, too, of a kind of a civil war . . .

He could then keep the peace.

And this, he said to the factor, at no cost. No favour. For look at the land! What could you do with that sort of land! 'Bleak and wasted' were the words used in the paragraph above but he could have just as easily used them.

So then the factor had taken back his proposal to the estate and it had been agreed — that indeed this man Sutherland would be best to keep the strip for himself, that he could buy it even, in time, as he earned it, from the Sutherland Estates, that the local people might know that he was in a separate dwelling, amongst the great and the good, perched between the boundaries of their lands like a kind of peacekeeper and known to be respected. Not that he was a man whose loyalties could be bought. For now that he had this thin strip of his own between the estate hills he was an independent landowner himself, with similar interests at stake as to the very rich and powerful, but because he was one of the people, too, who were his friends, so he could control them. This is how the Sutherland factor could figure it, and his laird: that if scoundrels were to rise up on the drove they'd rise up against this one man and not themselves, not against the life they'd made for themselves, the style that had been created. If it came to blows, was the thinking in the estate office, the people would damage the Sutherland, the John Roderick Callum, and not destroy anything of the history and sense of privilege that all the big landowners in the Highlands were trying to establish at that time, giving some glitter and swish of the grand cities and grand ideas of Europe to these bleak hills.

So they thought they were using him. So he let them so think. This John Roderick Sutherland of Sutherland. So he let them continue to think.

For his Urlar was down, the foundations already established. Free land. The stones upon the foundations of his grandfather's croft now set in a square – the longhouse of his grandfather extended.* And month by month, year upon year, the first Callum, Sutherland of the parish of Rogart, built upon that square of stone.

---

* Earlier sections of 'The Big Music' describe the history of The Grey House from the mid-eighteenth century, and how it was first a traditional Highland longhouse or blackhouse.

doubling on third variation/The Grey House: history of land
ownership in the North East of Scotland

The Sutherland family would have originally been tenant farmers (later
called crofters) who were, over the years, able to purchase the small piece
of land they farmed, and in time, extend it — at first by lease, from the
Sutherland Estates tack, and then, through ownership.

This practice, of building up land piecemeal — through lease then purchase — is more common than many popular Highland histories would
have us believe. See in particular Sir John Sinclair's *General View of the
Agriculture of the Northern Counties* (Edinburgh, 1814); G. and P. Anderson,
'Guide to the Highlands and Islands — Agricultural Intelligence', Ross-
shire Quarterly Report (*Farmer's Magazine*, 1815); J. Barron's 'The Northern Highlands — Agricultural Intelligence', Ross-shire Quarterly Report
(*Farmer's Magazine*, 1820); and J. Anderson, 'Essay on the Present State of
the Highlands and Islands of Scotland' (Constable, 1816). More recently,
Eric Richards' and Monica Clough's *Cromartie: Highland Life 1650–1914*
(Aberdeen University Press, 1989) provides a comprehensive study on
land and social mobility in a neighbouring area, using, in particular, the
case study of the MacDonalds of Strathpeffer.

Crofting, a system of landholding unique to the Highlands and islands
of Scotland, need not be the cramped, post-Clearances condition of life
it is all too often portrayed as being but can offer an independence of
state and sense of flexibility and options that, according to writers and

historians such as Ian Carter were not available to the indentured factory worker or servant. Indeed, he writes, this so-called peasant class in fact enjoyed autonomy and a sense of control over their means and end not experienced by many of us today – see in particular his book *Farmlife in Northeast Scotland* for a detailed record of life as it was lived over the period from the mid-nineteenth to the early twentieth century.

As we may see, by following on from this story of an autonomous peasant class, with its own particular mores and values, crofting is still a system of landholding in use today that goes against and liberates certain social and class inhibitors. That's because a croft is not, as many people think, a house but instead a small agricultural landholding which is normally held in tenancy and which may or may not have buildings or a house associated with it and can then, in time, be bought. Much croft land today is now independently owned because the former tenants have bought that land. There is no control over changes in ownership of croft land, although there is a statutory obligation to advise the Crofters Commission, and every change in the tenancy of a croft is regulated by the Commission whose written consent is required for every proposed assignation.

Assignation is a term used in crofting to describe the permanent transfer of a tenancy from one person to another. In a normal year three to four hundred croft tenancies are assigned. In more than half of these the current crofter passes the croft to a member of their family and the majority of the remaining tenancies are transferred to people already known to the crofter.

This is only the beginning of a process that is often complicated and private, wrought with families' and communities' and the individual's interests. There is, therefore, something almost fictional about the whole idea. It is like no other version of land ownership – and the land itself is seen in a different way as a result of its processes and history.

fourth variation/The Grey House: history of land ownership

By the time of the late 1700s, then, the foundation that had borne no more than a little bothy sitting at the foot of the long hills and offering shelter, a grey mark on the hill, was a substantial dwelling place. And as the old century turned into the new it was built upon again, the longhouse that it had been was further extended. As a thin tune from a ceilidh* rising up into the air becomes many stranded with the voices that contribute towards it, and continuous, so did the House take on rooms and a central stair and develop qualities around the original building, as Callum's son John Callum added to the central portion, developed the original and made it more substantial, a dwelling place of many parts.

Thus was the House established enough by the mid-1800s that if you'd been a shepherd then, by the next generation, you'd not have stayed with the family as in the past** but in a separate part of the house now – for The Grey House, as it was now called, was large enough to have accommodation within it for those who would come and take lessons here in

---

* A ceilidh translates as a gathering or dance, a party in which everyone participates; see also Glossary; and sources in the Bibliography/Music: Highland. Various gracenotes throughout the Crunluath may also provide insight as to the way the music of the culture permeates and is permeated by the Highland sensibility – the earlier sections on the House as a place that is both public and private, both intensely social and lonely, may also be of relevance here.

** The earlier variation set out this arrangement.

the winter – and indeed John Callum, or 'Old John' as he became known, was the first to make within the house a 'Music Room' and to conduct formal lessons there. Indeed, though the House had a musical history in this respect, of a place for teaching and learning piobaireachd, it was only at this time that arrangements were made for what became known as a full School of Piping – though the same shepherds whose fathers and grandfathers used to arrive at the House every winter were there, too, for the music and companionship and shelter. Coming into the kitchen still for the broth* made by John's wife Elizabeth just as John Roderick's wife, Elizabeth Mary, used to make it for them three generations before.

And by now it was 1870, 1880 . . . The House had the date 1878 carved above the door when Callum's son had added on the handsome front to the original part of the building.

'You've done fair for yourself, and no rogue either – for you could have been so . . .' – this is marked down in a history paper referenced from the Golspie Library, dated 1882, and the subject of the paper 'John Callum Sutherland and Land Management'.** For by now these records don't just itemise the open facts of one man offering shelter the way he did when it was required, a family history there, in a son following the traditions and practice of his father and grandfather, and great-grandfather. But they also take into account the way the hard-won good fortune of the family was allowed to spread around those he knew – that the benefit of good husbandry, increased yields and income might come to be of advantage to the region in general.

In this, this branch of the Sutherlands bears something in common with certain families further north and along the east coast who benefited from the herring*** at a similar time of the country's history – a similar

---

* The nineteenth-century recipe refers to an earlier 'reciepie of Elizabeth Mary' and has been collected, along with various other domestic papers, as part of the archive that is referred to in the List of Additional Materials at the back of 'The Big Music'.

** The full archive that exists in association with 'The Big Music' includes many historical documents such as this one, also copies of key papers kept in local libraries, museums etc.

*** See Appendix 3: 'History of the Highland North East region'; also relevant sections

atmosphere of good fortune come out of a past of hardship. For the money was not simply kept but tithed again, we must come to understand, in the same way it had been used in the past. A tithe not so much a payment as investment, so as to put back into development that which would be of advantage to all – in roads, and shelters, byres and pens. It is a cost, then, that is levied but that comes back upon the community in good – not simply taken by one individual and thereby held. So here's the House increasing in its place upon the hill, and the standard of fare and lodging for the men also therefore increasing – but there is, too, the additional benefit that becomes economic. For by offering certain sheep to the shepherds to raise as their own, returning to them the same methods of husbandry as the Sutherlands themselves had earlier had the advantage of and thereby raising their rural prospects beyond subsistence to greater stability and prosperity, in turn the payments to The Grey House may also be increased. It was in just the same way as in the past the old Callum would keep back certain sheep that otherwise would have foundered on the run south, down to the North of England, and further, some of them, holding back one or two of the black cattle that were destined for the Midlands and London even. So, as in those days,* John Callum now would let some of his own animals go to a shepherd who would take an interest in increasing the wellbeing of his flock, or would hold back stock that was otherwise in poor condition, not fit for the run south with the others yet young enough, and then return these animals to the men when they passed back again, heading home – well-fed and cared for in that interim, some put to the tup, the lambs increased in number and in size. All telling of, as is shown in these papers, in the histories and letters kept in local libraries, in Golspie and elsewhere, a sense of enablement that was extended beyond the gables of the House, beyond the Sutherlands' own land and livestock.

Livelihood and prosperity extended well beyond those four square marks of stone upon the hill.

---

of the Urlar and Taorluath movements of 'The Big Music'.

* As was indicated in the earlier variation.

doubling on fourth variation/The Grey House: domestic history

The foundations of The Grey House were established as far back as the early eighteenth century or before, when a simple 'blackhouse' or 'longhouse', as these buildings were first called, was built on the original south-facing site and life would have been set out as a simple routine whereby domestic needs were answered by the peat fire burning in the grate and sleeping quarters arranged so as to accommodate a large family all occupying the same room.

Meals were straightforward, consisting mainly of oatmeal and dairy products – cheese and butter from the family's cow and a few sheep and goats – some simple greens provided by the kitchen garden, supplemented sometimes by meat when possible or when occasion demanded it.

Because the Sutherland family have always been musicians – even from before the time of 'The House' being known as a stop-over place for crofters and shepherds – there would have been a social aspect to the domestic arrangements of their home, even when it was little more than a couple of rooms attached to a byre. This arrangement would have seen space made available around the fire for the singing of canntaireachd and outdoors on the flat for the playing of pipes for ceilidhs or musical nights – this when the weather was fine – and for this reason, the original 'longhouse' would have been slightly larger than usual (as the original foundations show) and the area around it arranged in such a way as to accommodate a number of guests when they arrived for the music. Later, when the House was firmly established within the 'corridor' region of Sutherland, effectively connecting a pathway through the difficult terrain between Ben Mhorvaig and Luath, the House was given over more and more to visitors – who were accommodated for a night or more in an extra room built on at the far end of the House. The kitchen was now set up as a dining area that would take eight or more adults, and the fire and grate areas were made more of a feature of the room. Family records show three large kettles from this time as well as four iron dishes, or casseroles – all denoting a significant increase in domestic activity – and there are still exisiting two skillets from this period and an early remnant of a tablecloth, that has been worked with a beautiful tatted trim.

The next hundred years saw the significant extension of that original dwelling, and with it development of a way of life that had been established – but without the necessary modernisation. So now the House was a substantial domestic dwelling, extended up and out to form the overall structure and architectural shape of the House that exists today. Of the original, as has been already noted, only the present scullery and pantry areas remain of the walls and floor; the rest has been absorbed by the more handsome extensions made that provide an entrance area, dining and sitting rooms, upstairs bedrooms, and, of course, a kitchen that is now provided with a large Victorian range, a large and decorative dresser and sideboard, and those other pieces of furniture that denote increased prosperity.

As the House was also known to be a centre of piping through the Highlands and beyond, the sitting room – that became later known as the 'Music Room' (when the House was extended again, in the early part of the twentieth century to add a gracious drawing room and large formal dining room) – came to be used for informal concerts and tuition.

This informality was part of the spirit of the House and its mood and atmosphere – as the number of bedrooms attest to a rule of hospitality and welcome that prevailed all through these years. With the later extensions, more bathrooms were added and a separate 'bunkhouse' built out to the back of the main House to take in younger pupils for schooling over the summer months.

Family records and a Visitors' Book from 1923 to 1959 show that the musical teaching was a year-round concern – and, in particular, there is reference to what became wildly known as 'The Winter Classes'. All through the first half of the twentieth century there were classes conducted and concerts given – these drawing to a close only when old (Roderick) Callum Sutherland (1887–1968), 'Himself', the father of the current John Callum featured in 'The Big Music', became too infirm and, with his son not at home to support him and not being able to play any longer himself, was forced to terminate the lovely arrangements that had been in place in the House for generation upon generation. (Though, it has been noted previously, meetings of pipers at The Grey House did continue on a more ad hoc basis when John Callum returned for long periods over the summer months through subsequent years.)

Again, records show menus, whisky bought, the buying of canteens and plate – all denoting a time, from the late nineteenth century on, of what, for the region and the social status of the Sutherland family, counted as considerable largesse. Callum Sutherland's wife, Elizabeth Nichol, was herself a talented cook and household manager and extended the gardens that she'd inherited from her mother-in-law and her husband's family so the range of produce that the House could provide for its own kitchens was always varied and substantial. In this, it continued a tradition that had been set in place all those hundreds of years ago when the original 'Grey Longhouse' had been such a focus for meeting and music – and the bowls of broth that were served always a highlight of the evening's entertainments.

fifth variation/The Grey House: land ownership; domestic and musical history

See now how the House has girth and gables. See the six windows across the front – the corner with a window on either wall – and that can be a drawing room, if you like, the place where later Roderick's son Callum will have the presentations of piping, the grand meetings where players from all over Scotland are invited to perform. There's the original sitting room known as the 'Music Room' now, if you please, for that is the preferred room for friends to gather in and play, take instruction from each other, listen. In the meantime it's enough that Callum's father extends, onto the side of the House, those separate quarters where pupils can come and stay, guests be billeted and made comfortable for as long as they need to remain there, to teach and offer demonstrations. And it won't be many more years until there will be a great dining room, in this same Grey House, a long table set for twenty people some nights – can you imagine it? And yet one needs no imagination for there were those that at the time wrote about the use of the House in this way, in certain papers and journals,* as being similar to those famous accommodations in Skye as they may have been at a much earlier time when the MacCrimmon family

---

* Relevant publications include *The Piping Times* and *Piobaireachd in the North East* etc., all listed as sources of information in the List of Additional Materials at the back of 'The Big Music'.

of pipers created their College of Music there for the boys and young men of the Highland region, this back in the fifteenth century, and its foundations going back earlier than that. And you can think about civilisation then, the glint and polish of it, you can think on it well enough and take that information back to your great concert halls of Europe, to your maestros and conductors, take this back to the lords and ladies and princes and kings of London and Berlin and Vienna . . .

That there could have existed in that time, in that remote part of the world, before orchestras, before concert halls . . . Such a place. And would the ladies of that time, the fifteenth century, have had their dining rooms and quarters fitted in that kind, to accommodate the composition of music, to school the young in the playing of a fine and difficult tune? And would the colleges of Oxford and Cambridge have envisaged that, while their own rooms and gardens were just beginning to be established, there was, on a far promontory on the remote island of Skye, a College of Music for men and boys from all over Scotland? And you can see it, can you not, in your imagination? That School of the North West, and its kitchens and the warmth coming from the big fireplaces in the rooms where the musical education took place, and the composition and the practice, long rooms for treading out the beats? In other places than here this is written about in full and with great detail.* How there would be a large fireplace such as John Sutherland's father had built for his own dining room, in this century just past, and in the large kitchen where his wife, John's mother, like her mother-in-law before her, and Anna and Mary and Elizabeth before then, still makes the bowls of soup** but she has girls from the crofts around to help her by now, and has so caught up, with the leisure time available to her, in her reading and writing

---

* The Bibliography carries details of a number of books related to the history of piobaireachd teaching and the MacCrimmon legacy at Boreraig; Appendix 14: 'The Cultural History of the Bagpipes' may also be of interest.

** The recipe, referred to in the List of Additional Materials, is the same recipe as was used by the original John Sutherland's wife, Elizabeth Mary MacKay, in the late 1700s and is described in an eighteenth-century document featuring other items of domestic interest; also has been copied out in a separate book, with other recipes and kitchen notes, by Elizabeth Clare Nichol of Crieff.

that her husband has even made for her a Schoolroom under the eaves of the main building where she teaches her little son, her only child, and sometimes local children come for their lessons, they can play with young John afterwards, for she doesn't want him getting lonely, through the mornings, anyhow, they can come before their parents need them back up in the hills.

So you can understand the tithing is working well enough. And by the time of the death of 'Old John' in 1911 his son Callum has already started giving classes in the Music Room his father created and planning how these may be extended, adding to the House at the sides of the front elevation. He had carved for himself the date, 1930, above the newly widened entrance, following exactly in style and manner the stone carving upon the lintel above the door put in place by his father before him in 1878.

That lovely work done by the man from Tain who's making all the new extensions for Callum now, the Schoolroom as mentioned, the panelling on the Music Room wall – and what laird could stop him? What factor? Law? By now, who or what could have ever prevented this . . . House? For that same family that had allowed the original Sutherland to keep a thin corridor of land have now, in the same spirit and act of political will, let the Sutherlands increase that land further up the side of Ben Mhorvaig behind the House, selling it to them in return for the Sutherlands putting forest there and for managing a portion of their own land. So The Grey House of this account, of these papers and inserts and parts, has for itself all the view in its own glass – of a forest and hills all the way up Ben Mhorvaig and beyond, to the hidden lochs and burns overlooking the Sutherland flats . . .

The same House.

Ailte vhor Alech – the End of the Road.

The same House.

Nothing can prevent its place. It is written. A shelter for the people who live here: my family, the Sutherland family. Farmers, agriculturalists, landowners. Musicians.

Walk through with me, through these lovely rooms – and comfort is here and warmth and music. In a place so remote – the lit-up colour and detail of a whole world.

gracenotes/piobaireachd, from a paper delivered by Archibald Campbell to the London Piobaireachd Society, 1952

The difference between good and bad piobaireachd playing is the same as that between good and bad reading or writing. The good reader pays attention to his commas, his question marks, full stops and the meaning of the words he is reading. The bad reader drones out a whole page without pausing for stops, without altering his pace, and without raising or lowering his voice.

Yet another rule could be stated that the conventional variations are to be played so as to keep the original melody of the ground, in other words so as to bring out what are called the theme notes and not to make them subordinate to the variation notes. Sometimes the strong accent is on the variation notes, but the theme notes should not be clipped away to nothing.

On the other hand the final A of the Taorluath and the final E of the Crunluath are not to be dwelt on. The older pipers (that is to say counting from the revival of piping in 1700) used to stand for Taorluath and Crunluath doublings and to play these doublings considerably faster than the singlings. They also repeated the ground after the Taorluath doublings and after the Crunluath doubling. Thus the Crunluath singling was played about the same pace as the first variation singling.

Nowadays as a rule the ground is only played once and the tendency is to increase the pace gradually throughout the tune, playing a variation doubling only a little faster than the singling and playing the singling of the next variation about the same pace as a doubling. This may be well enough but it is a pity to forget the old way. The old way had more variety, sometimes we would have a variation in the middle of a lament played quite briskly and then the player would slow right down for the singling of the Taorluath.

My own criticism of present-day playing is that the ground and earlier variations are played too slow, and the singlings of the Taorluath and Crunluath played too fast. However, as I have said already no general rule can be laid down except perhaps this: The two extremes to be avoided are dragging and hurrying, and it should be remembered that a piobaireachd ground or variation can be played slowly without being dragged or played briskly, without being hurried.

In conclusion I am going back for a minute to the other forms of music. In connection with them it must be remembered false fingering is a horrible error and that never should a desire to get in all the gracenotes he can manage, slacken a piper's vigilance against playing false notes. Steadiness is more important than speed.

insert/John Callum MacKay Sutherland

For what can you do to stop a thing once you've started? You don't stop
it. The laying out of the ground, the setting forth of the beginning. The
music that's always been in his head getting to hear itself now he's coming
to the end.

It's like walking, over this hill, another hill.

And look at the sky, it's lovely here. And the sound of the tune is laid
out everywhere in the ground around him, beneath his feet . . . Like a map
of all the places he knows and he's been to, and of history and his own
life and the people in it, each part with its own particular sound, and he'll
find the notes for them, even . . .

For this one, that one . . .

He can name them all:

There first —

Callum Sutherland.

Elizabeth Sutherland.

He can name them.

His father. His mother.

There, Roderick John. He was Callum.

Name him. His father.

And Elizabeth. His mother.

Before she was a Sutherland — a Nichol. From Crieff.

So, too — Elizabeth Clare.

His own mother.

And himself?

Name himself?

The one who's lying here now? Himself?

Or was that his father?

Himself?

Or is he the son?

That Callum?

And –

Callum . . .

And others . . .

Because others are here. The people in the House and what must they think of him . . .

What must they think . . .

Iain.

And Helen.

And her daughter, Katherine Anna.

And her mother, Margaret MacKay.

Her mother, Margaret MacKay.

Her mother, Margaret MacKay.

narrative/6

The people at the House and what they thought of him

<u>Iain</u>

(transcript*)

And all of it true. About how it happened that morning. You wouldn't credit but it actually did take place the way it's been said. I'll always re-member the whole thing in detail, all through the time leading up to us realising he'd disappeared with our little girl.

It was a nice enough morning. I'd been out to see to the dogs. Margaret had the water on to boil. It was still early but she was thinking he'd want a cup of tea, he always did, and she would take it in – I had to know that, of course, that she'd go into his room first thing with the tea. But . . . As I said before, I've had to stand aside for him in the past, I can do that. Any-way, I don't mind having something myself at that hour, and Margaret and I always take breakfast together later. But the difference this morning – that none of us had any idea then that his room would be empty. That his bed would be made and tidy. That was a shock, all right. For he'd been weak,

---

* This section and those following are taken from a tape recording made of a conversation between Helen and Margaret; certain questions were asked of Iain and this transcript comprises his answers with relevant edits.

hadn't he, and ill so long we thought that anything could happen with him. The doctor had said as much.

That every breath could be his last breath.

And not that much older than me, either.

Old Johnnie.

But old enough.

And certainly in the past, he was old enough then.

But look at him.

I've been in there to see him. Lying in there in the dark.

No point in hating him now.

Margaret

(transcript*)

And the baby . . . All the time Helen and I were both thinking that she was up in her basket in Helen's room. Our Katherine Anna. Lying there asleep in her white blankets. How could either of us have had even the slightest idea . . .

Helen was in the sitting room. It was early, but it was lovely, the day, and she was up, we were all up. Iain had already been out with the dogs down to the river and Helen was through in the sitting room. I know she was thinking about Callum, that he was coming back to the House. I'd told her the night before that I'd telephoned Sarah and that she'd said he'd be here by the following evening . . .

So, yes. Callum would have been on her mind.

You should be here, thinking.

Because . . . Well, we all needed Callum here by now.

So, yes, thinking . . . That the father needs his son. But also about the years passed. Her and Callum together – all that time ago and Callum never coming back here. But now –

---

* Margaret's version of events as spoken as a monologue, privately, into a tape recorder and simply transferred to the page.

It's time, now, thinking.
You should come home.

Helen

(inserted written page)

And I would tell him that, too. Not straight away, but later, that it was right that he should be here with us. I would turn to him in the dark . . .

But not straight away. Later. Much later.

When we're together, on our own.

Everything come together then.

Margaret

(story/journal extract*)

Her eyes go into distance. Thinking about Callum, that he'll be here. She puts her hand to her face, to smooth her hair back from her face – in the way that, tonight, Callum will smooth her hair back so he can see her more clearly. She'll say to him then that it's good that he's come home to say goodbye and Callum replying 'When I came up here I thought it was to see my father but all the time it was you.'

She sits back on her haunches, away from the fireplace where she is cleaning it out, that she may look out the window, let her eyes be filled with hills and sky.

I don't mind.

It's all in the distance for her, you see. My lovely Helen. Of course everything is like that for her now. She minds fine, of course she does,

---

* pp. 73–4 and 82 of the Taorluath movement and sections of the Crunluath movement show in fragments, scraps of sentences, similar use of Margaret's original writings, notes for a story.

who Callum is and how they were together all those years ago for he's still there, with her, in her thoughts and reflections . . . But she's had a child now, there's a baby, and everything changes for a woman then.

I don't mind.

So let the sky take his place, she has a child to take care of. And the air, and the hills . . . She can see herself out in the open with Callum and running, she's running. A young girl and never knowing that one day there would be this other Helen in the world, the one who is a mother with a child.

So –

Callum.

I don't mind.

It's why it's going to be easier for her than for him. Easier, later, to go to him, come to be with him from out of the dark.

Unexpected, maybe, but not so unexpected – that they will take up from where they left off.

'You've come home' she will say to him then.

Iain

(inserted page)

By now is trying not to think. Sitting at the table like before, and with a whisky, and cleaning out a gun. And trying not to think. Trying to leave, by now, all that other thinking behind.

(transcript)

'Because people do what they do.'

(inserted paper)

And he may know all about what took place today, why the old man took the child, what you might say will continue, continue to take place

. . . Because of course he knows about Margaret and John, the history of the two of them. He's always known, that look that has always passed between them.

But —

What he picked up in his arms this afternoon, that was all that was left of him now. He was light, like a child in his arms. 'Like a leaf' he described it.

So why ever think about bringing that down? Something that was barely there? With the clip of the rifle, or a stone?

And yet both these thoughts were in his mind today . . .

He'll see him dead before Iain Cowie does another thing for old Johnnie.

But no point thinking like that now.

Because he's old, old John MacKay.

And it was Margaret who made the call, so Callum could come home here. Otherwise his own son never would have known . . . His own son . . .

How sick his father was. How near the end.

And he'll die soon and there may as well be nothing to him, just nothing. That's what he'd felt in his arms today, when he'd carried the old man over to the Argocat and laid him down, how there was nothing to him, just nothing — and what's that word, that word that had come to him then? Out there on the hill?

Pity?

Yes, pity.

That was the word.

Because everything that other may have had he let it go and now he himself is leaving.

While Iain . . . The one who carried. He is still here. With his wife, his daughter, his granddaughter. His family are all around him. Though he knows fine, what went on, what will continue . . . With Margaret and John and their daughter, Helen . . . He would never tell.

Because look at him, Iain: husband, father.

He — not the other — is that man.

Walk into the room where his family are now and feel them rise to meet him. Feel the way they gather around him, his own family, and keep him safe.

(transcript — as before)

'And just imagine' Iain says, here at the end. 'Having no one else to tell you but someone who is not your family — that your own husband is dying. And of course it would be Margaret. Who phoned the old cailleach* down in London, to tell her to call the boy. Margaret who told her that old Johnnie had stopped with the medicine and was going down fast, who had the grace, if you like, to let her know, let the wife know — for you'd never hear from that woman one end of the year to the other and how you could call someone a wife who doesn't look to the man she's married? Well, anyhow. Margaret had told the woman that her husband was failing fast and that she should tell Callum, that he might come.'

Helen

She told Sarah to tell Callum to leave straight away, as early as he could — for suddenly it seems: There's not that much time.

Margaret

For a father to see a son.
    For a son to see his father.

Helen

My mother puts tea in the pot.

Margaret

And Helen sits back, sitting on her heels. The fireplace swept out.

---

* Translates as 'old woman, witch': see Glossary for all Gaelic words and expressions used.

<u>Margaret and Helen, as though in unison</u>

And there's not that much time.

The two of us in different parts of the House but our minds turned to the same thing . . . The ticking of the clock, passing of the minutes and our place within each and every one of them. Neither of us thinking of the silence in the House while the baby sleeps. One putting the breakfast things on a tray; the other returning her gaze to the room, taking up the log basket and arranging in the swept-out place she has made the kindling and the peats.

Not much time.

No thought of our child, then, that minute, or the next.

No thought of our daughter, in these silent early minutes, late summer and all is quiet in the House.

Only . . .

The ticking of the clock.

The story nearly done.

About to go into the room and see that the baby is gone.

gracenotes/piobaireachd, a summary

In musical terms, piobaireachd is a theme with variations. The theme is usually a very simple melody, though few if any piobaireachd contain the theme only in its simplest form. For it is first stated in a slow movement called the ground or in Gaelic the Urlar and then has added to this subsequent movements including numerous added embellishments and connecting notes.

The subsequent variations can be of any number, usually starting in a quite straightforward manner and progressing through successively more complex movements before returning again to the ground. Variations on the Urlar usually include a siubhal ('passing' or 'traversing') or dithis ('two' or 'a pair') or both. The siubhal comprises theme notes each coupled with a single note of higher or lower pitch that usually precedes the theme note. The theme note is held and its paired single note cut. The timing given to the theme notes is of critical importance in displaying the virtuosity of the piper. If the theme and single note are repeated or played in pairs, it is referred to as a doubling, otherwise a siubhal singling. The dithis is similar. The theme note is accented and followed by a cut note of lower pitch, usually alternating, for example, between an 'A' and a 'G'. If the coupled pairs are played in a repeating pattern, it too is called a dithis doubling.

The other more complex embellishments are: Taorluath (often including a Leumluath, or 'leap'), Crunluath and Crunluath A Mach. In almost all piobaireachd in which these later movements are found, the variations are played first as a singling and then as a doubling and with a slightly increased tempo – and the piper will have to learn not to be hampered by thoughts of the difficulty of technique in order to let the music sound out in all its psychological and emotional intensity. Neither will you have your time dictated to you by the notes you have learned from the stave, but rather, in the moment of playing, will be governed by what you yourself have learned from hearing the music sung to you, as pure tune.

Piobaireachd, as has been said before, is difficult music to understand. This difficulty must be recognised and in learning piobaireachd what will matter most will not be the time spent on it on a chanter but the hours spent turning it over in your mind note by note and thinking how you lengthen one note here and shorten another there, or quicken up a little in one variation, or slow down in another.

In those thoughts your own interpretation of the music will arrive.

embellishment/3a: domestic detail: Mary's granddaughter, mother of Katherine Anna, author and editor of all papers preceding and following that together comprise 'The Big Music'

Helen's Monologue*

I knew this man once and he had so much. He belonged to a part of the world I love, in the far North of Scotland, though he did not live there. It was too remote for him, and he was the kind of man could not bear to be remote.

For this place is somewhere few people drive to or would visit. If you take the A9 up past Golspie, past Brora, and turn in two or three miles after that, you'll come in time to a fork in the road where in both directions it seems as though there's nowhere to go. There are no signposts here, no indications of place or distance. Yet follow the way going north and as you cross the river and head deeper into the hills you will come to another small turning that looks like a farm road . . .

I write this paper here, at the end of that road, from out of the very

---

* All the way through 'The Big Music' there has been the sense of a strengthening first-person narrative that was first brought to the attention of the reader back on pp. 19 and 20 etc. of the Urlar. Now, in this final section of the Crunluath movement, the author of the papers is made clear as John Sutherland's daughter, Helen, whose mother is Margaret MacKay and whose writing, that seemed to enter the text or 'story' at first in no more than a sentence or two, now declares itself to be the entire contents of this book.

place that has no marking on the map, no direction given that tells you how to arrive. I write in a room in a house that sits in the midst of all that emptiness. In a high bedroom at the top of the House that sits under the eaves, used to be a Schoolroom once. That is where my bed is. Where my desk is: over here by the north window.

This, too, is where my daughter sleeps.

My room, then – a room for a quiet kind of woman who doesn't fuss much, doesn't make too much sound as she's moving through the House. A quiet, simple room for a maid, for an uncomplicated serving woman. The role I have made for myself here is that of a kind of employee, on loan to another's life. So, yes, a servant, an employee, a maid. A person who moves quietly around a house.

But in one way, not quiet. Because though, as is my place, I may watch and listen, I also record the life here. I tell. And the telling can become a calling out, a proclamation. If one is not careful a telling can become a speech. A novel, even, like a kind of false show. Starting with a quiet sentence, maybe: 'I knew this man once and he had so much' – but be careful, careful where the telling may go.

So, then . . . I first knew this man, the one of whom I write (quietly, quietly, Helen) because my mother came to work here at this House for reasons that, in the end, I think will always remain surprising to her. She never thought, my mother, when she was a girl, brought up in sound comfort and educated well . . . That she would end up living her life to further someone else's means. Yet that was what did happen – following a man she loved, wanting to be near him, to be here for him should he ever choose to return – she became someone who was in waiting. Loss was at her back, her mother's judgement down upon her, causing her to have to leave the village where she'd been born and brought up. So, though she was trained the way she was, brought up by a mother to be independent and free-thinking and clear in her opinions and thoughts, she made the decision anyway to be a housekeeper here. She stayed, and she married. Though Iain is not my father.

And you could say I've known Callum all my life. For when I think through my childhood I can't think of him not being in it. He came here in the summers with his father.

Margaret looked after him. I looked after him.

His own mother was never here.

In the summers when he was here we were like a family – is how it seemed then, how it seems now, looking back on all this. Even though he and I became lovers when I was seventeen, and it was strong, that part of things between us, still, people would have said we could have been brother and sister, the way we knew each other, the way we were together, did things, looked at each other, laughed. We were the same height, had the same colour hair. What do you expect? That just because we were sleeping with each other we were going to pretend we weren't that close? That being together in the way we were was going to change that? How could it? The other was too strong, too deep in, the belonging to each other, having something between us that was like an old, old story and we were just in it, that was all, we'd been put in the story and could not be taken out.

A brother and sister together on a narrow bed.

And we fit.

Long bodies the same, feet twisted together, entwined at the root.

Same hair, same eyes.

I knew this man once and he had so much. A bed, in a father's hut, in the hills. In a secret place where no one could find us.

~

The story of a family, then, and its secrets, here.

I've recorded everything I know.

embellishment/3b: domestic detail: Mary's granddaughter, mother of Katherine Anna, Helen Margaret MacKay, author and editor of all papers preceding and following that together comprise 'The Big Music'

(notes made at the kitchen table on the evening of Callum's arrival)

All of yesterday has gone into the past.

Already the early morning, going up to my room and seeing she was gone . . . It's as though that happened in another life, to another woman. And the baby. She was some other woman's baby.

Yet the feeling of the leap – the jump of my heart when I saw the empty basket – that's with me. I'll remember that.

I've never felt such – vacancy – like it.

The leap.

The jump of my heart.

That – gap.

And anything, anything. Could have happened to her. And I would have done anything. Killed. Gone mad. If anything had happened to her, if I could have protected her.

For if John had kept her longer – had her longer with him out on the hill . . .

God knows what would have become of her then – although people say that babies are hardy and my daughter is hardy. Still, the old man could have perished and that would have been the death of my Katherine then.

But the day . . . It tided over, the weather improved. Iain went out there. He told us all what to do.

We went out there together and Iain found them, we brought them back in the Argocat and she was fine, my daughter, she was wet and hungry and cold but she was fine . . . My little girl, my little girl. She was fine. And the hours that had seemed like hundreds of hours miraculously turned back into an ordinary day, and I changed her, fed her, put her to bed.

And then my mother told me that she'd called them in London, and that Callum was on his way.

Callum.

I'm writing this now at the kitchen table and he's through there, in his father's sitting room. He's alone. He came up here alone – though he's married, he has sons. He's here like a single man.

And what must it be like for him now? To be going through to see his father, with his father the way he is? For when did he last see him? That family of his so spoilt with their own dissatisfactions that they never see each other, speak.

Something wrong with them that they don't look out for each other.

It's been that way for as long as I can remember.

Those visits, when he was a boy, coming up here with his father in the summer . . . His father never bothered with him then. No wonder that after a while, when he was older, when he was starting university . . . It became harder and harder for him to come here and see him.

And by then I myself had gone away.

I could no longer help him, look after him.

And so how old were we when we last saw each other? When we were with each other?

A long time.

And I myself have been away.

For a long time I suppose I thought I would never come back here again. For years: Glasgow, the university there, and then in Edinburgh, London . . . I stayed away. I went to America. New Zealand. I'd started my own research work by then, the idea for a paper, for a PhD. All the time my mother was writing to me, she was telling me about the House, the land. Writing to me about her life and her world, right here, in this one place, her whole world – and still I was thinking . . . That I had no need to return. For such a long time I thought that. And by then I had something half written, a proposal of sorts, and my mother and I were closely in touch, we were corresponding, we were talking on the phone. 'The Use of Personal Papers, Journals and Other Writings in the Creation of Modernist and Contemporary Fiction.' Back I came to Glasgow then, and I wrote my dissertation there, met someone, the father of my daughter, and then I let him go.

All those worlds, all those words.

But now – despite myself, all the things I may have said – I am home again.

Where I want to stay. Look after my mother. Help Iain.

Bring up my daughter here, with the hills around her.

In this House. My mother's House.

And Callum . . .

Though I've gone halfway around the world and back, though Callum has left us, and has children himself and a wife who loves him . . . Though we are no longer children, and the girl he used to play with is here now, at the table, and has not yet gone in to him . . .

I will go to him and take him in my arms.

Because we still know where the secret place is. We know how to get to it, that cutting in the hill you can't see unless you are upon it. Our secret.

We can find it again – for we always got along fine, Callum, didn't we? We always got along fine.

Callum stepping out of the car with his father, in his town shoes. And Iain, Margaret, both there to meet him.

'Run along with Helen, now' is the first thing my mother said. 'She'll tell you what to do. You're the same age, nearly. You'll both get along fine.'

three/third paper: reprise

At the House by now there's fierce concern. They know he's gone. Helen's just seen the baby has gone.

She came down from the bedroom, and saw Katherine was not with her mother at the table. Did not even have to ask when she saw her mother's face, when her mother saw her daughter's arms empty, in her hand only a piece of the baby's cloth. In a second all three of them were up and all over the House then, with John not in his bedroom and then outside and all around the grounds and out the back, Iain squinting up against the light to see towards the hill, Helen running screaming across the grass.

'No!'

Screaming into all the wide air that her baby is not there.

Earlier, much earlier when she thought her daughter was sleeping, she had been in the sitting room, brushing out the grate and setting a fresh fire. She'd been thinking how quiet it was, but then, this time of day was always quiet – before the old man was properly wakened, before they laid out his breakfast for him, made sure he took some of it, when the baby had had her first feed and was down and sleeping. So, yes, these hours here, between eight and nine in the morning . . . There would be a peace settling on the House, and so it would be quiet then, just before the day would properly begin.

And it was a fine morning. 'High' she would call it – these kinds of days like you get in midsummer, actually, as though the sky is far, far away from you and the sort of blue you feel you could never touch or connect to the day's passing because it's so far away it's endless, still it seems like it will stay with you for ever. Though it is autumn even so you'd never know it from a day like today and it began beautifully enough just before dawn with Helen lifting her warm baby daughter like a cake from her basket and setting her against her to feed.

How could a day start any lovelier? The sky out there through the window, the beginnings of the day cast down on the white sheets, the covers of the bed. The quiet and calm of the room about her. The baby in her arms. What more could there be in life than this, Helen could have been thinking, with the kind of complete wonder that the world is so simple that really, to give you everything, the world need only pass you a child.

Then . . . She'd gone downstairs. When her baby was asleep in her basket.

It was still very early. It was five o'clock, five thirty.

She went though to the little sitting room, the Music Room, as she did every day, she crouched down at the grate and started sweeping there.

And occasionally she looked up at the hills beyond the glass and her thoughts went there, drifting, straying . . .

Not knowing how much time passed, in that little room, the sense of light moving across the wall, across the far hills . . .

Then Margaret came in to tell her that breakfast was ready – and the next Margaret saw of her daughter, she knew by her face, by the piece of white cloth she held, that something was wrong. Katherine Anna had been taken.

insert/John Callum MacKay

So he puts down the notes for:

The child, Katherine Anna.

He has minutes left, seconds. Before the dark comes. Women's notes are the softest embellishments.* He might write that sentence down some-where, the difference between soft and hard notes on the scale.** And he must, so as to protect them, the special notes — and to keep the baby safe he'll surround her with her own particular song, an eight-note sequence that will be set inside the large theme . . . She's very beautiful. Even though nothing should be overdone, in music as complicated as this it should not be overdone or it takes away from the core of the theme . . . Even so. He needs to give this scrap of new life a shawl. So there it is, lovely: An 'F' to a 'G', An 'E' to an 'A' . . . And so on into the morning of his fine, high day.

By now he wants to get all of his journey in, get it all in the notes. The waking alone very early, when it was just light . . . The sound of the scale holding, returning to the 'A', even as he walked higher and higher onto the hill . . . And is also there the feeling, in bits of the theme already started, that something's wrong with him and that he knows it, too — even as he

---

* John Sutherland's papers and writings on piobaireachd and fragments of composition notes for 'Lament for Himself' can be seen in the Crunluath A Mach section of 'The Big Music'.

** The Last Appendix gives a chart of notes and their meanings; see also the Index of 'The Big Music'.

makes his way towards a familiar place, that there's something not right here, what he's doing is wrong, and taking a child away. Because he's not the kind of man to fall into madness, even with seeing his father just now, the way he did, out there on the hill, and seeing his boy, his own son out there with the dogs all around him and happy, happy they all were . . . Yet he did see them.

Though he doesn't live in that kind of world, where ghosts are, and hopes and dreams of people that you wish could come back to you . . . Though he's not that sort. Though he's just a man coming to the end of his life, that's all, and thinking: Has he done anything to be proud of? To take with him into the dark? Before he says goodbye to all this light, has he anything? And love? Has he love?

For Margaret . . .

That part, that last note yet to sound.

The high, high reach of her.

He has always kept that note back . . .

Who she was to him. Who she is. Who, always, she will be.

That high, high note that is also his own note, the Piper's note.

The High 'A'.

It has always been the 'A'.

And waiting, waiting all this time, all his life, to let himself hear it . . .

Yet only now . . .

In the last of the notes, stepped into place, in the dark room . . .

Margaret.

The light shifts across the glass window of the Little Hut, shifts across the flat and silvery blue surface of the loch.

And she's there.

Crunluath/final fragment

Late, late summer but so light still you'd never believe time was
in it – that there could be a beginning, an end to the day. Only
that the sky has always been this blue. With the notes turning
and spiralling into the air to make of themselves a crown.

FOURTH MOVEMENT:
CRUNLUATH A MACH

four/last paper

After his father's death, Callum and I went up to the Little Hut in the hills and found all the papers, John's music and manuscripts, his notes and the writing that he'd set down that was to act as a sort of prompt for him in the composing of his last uncompleted piobaireachd, the 'Lament for Himself' that he was working on in the last months of his life.

We went there alone, to our father's place.

As I just wrote, this was directly after John's death, the day after — before Callum's wife and sons arrived for the funeral in Brora, before the great complications of that ceremony that would bring Sarah back here, and all those people in London John had known when he'd had the business there, the relatives from his mother's family in Perthshire and sons and relatives of his father's friends who still had a connection to the House through music or the Winter Classes from all those years ago.

It took us a morning to walk up the hill and over. The season had turned — in just the last couple of days the autumn that had been with us, that seemed on some days still to have a touch of summer in it, that was gone — and it was cold and raining when we arrived. The loch was not visible through cloud.

Callum lit the wood-burning stove and we spent the day and the night there together. We saw everything that I then went on to use to make this collection of papers — the music and notes providing everything for the story that I would need. I took the materials away with me and, after

Callum and I had said goodbye to each other in our own way, and after he went back to London with his family, I set up a sort of study in the room at the top of the House, the place under the eaves that has always been known as the Schoolroom, and I started assembling the papers there.

So what follows here, in this final section, are simply examples of what I have had to work with; the actual manuscript of the 'Lament', the outline of it as written by John Sutherland, is separate, of course, including the beautiful leitmotif of the Lullaby, the section of music that was written for my daughter, that appears as the opening bars in the second line of the Urlar. It is unlikely that John himself fully understood, as he was composing it, how that part of the music would give the final shape to the overall theme – though some fragments of his notes found at the hut suggest that his mind was reaching in that direction, trying to find a metaphor that would give meaning and depth to his composition, that it would not simply be an account of his life but tell a larger story.

My hope is, however, that the words I have put down for his Ceol Mor, 'The Big Music', can go some way towards providing the lovely tune of his entire – so that though 'Lament for Himself' was never completed, the entire piobaireachd may sound through these pages.

In the end, it was only by going through and reading all the material that was there in the Little Hut that I came to understand what I did of the man who had composed it. And it was only by learning what I did of his life and history that I came to hear the part that he himself was never able to include.

That is the part my tiny daughter plays.

Asleep in her basket as I write this – the flower on the grass, as John himself wrote of her, when, unknown to him, he was describing her in his journal . . . And what was the other phrase of his? I found it there in one of his papers: 'new life come out of old' – something like that.

He put it better in the notes he used.

Examples of notes used
for inserts; papers; stories and embellishments

The material below is arranged in no particular order and gives a small sample only of the kinds of notes and writings that were found in the hut. In some sections, I have added a line or two myself to indicate as to how the material may have suggested itself to be used as part of a work of prose, as well as conveying how certain musical ideas may have been represented in sections of the manuscript.

To understand best how all these disparate elements were brought together and assembled to make some kind of whole, the reader of course has already the previous movements – the Urlar, the Taorluath, and Crunluath movements that precede this current section, the A Mach – that together comprise the entire piobaireachd.

To this end, everything you need for 'The Big Music' is contained within its pages.

However, it should also be noted that, as well as all that material discovered in the Little Hut, the entire contents of The Grey House library and additional personal and legal papers of John Callum Sutherland, the piper and composer, are currently being assembled as a permanent archive to be used by musicians and historians and those interested in the ongoing place of the Highland bagpipe in Western culture.*

---

* For more information on the progress of this project refer to pp. 453–5 at the back of this book. The Foreword at the beginning of 'The Big Music' and the section 'How to use the Appendices in this book' may also be useful to the reader interested in building up a wider picture of the world of The Grey House and the kind of landscape it occupies. These pages indicate how one may use the additional material that has been compiled – notes, scanned documents etc. – and fashion it into a kind of installation, bringing all these elements together, as it were, into one room. Indeed, this is how 'The

i

You've heard it already said: No wonder he got off to London so fast.*

This to continue that theme.

That it was no wonder, after university in Edinburgh, that he put more and more distance between himself and the old man. No wonder he became so intent, the son, upon fixing himself up in a business that was far away from the family home and its terrible quiet.

That place always more like a school, anyhow, than a home, his father still teaching there even when he was very old.**

[from – journal/notes for composition]
But you can't labour under that same tutelage, Johnnie!

Big Music', as a whole, presents itself to us as a space we might enter as we might enter a gallery or a concert or an exhibition. It is somewhere we may stay for a while, or perhaps leave and return to, experiencing it in different ways at different times, before we finally close the covers of the book, walk out the door.

* The line 'I'll not be back!' resounds through the pages of 'The Big Music', in all three movements – though comes to be more and more complex in its meaning as the theme of the inevitability of return set against the more short-term force of will comes to express itself in the life of John Callum MacKay. See in particular pp. 107; 115–19; 123; 134–6; 160–2; 207–8.

** The history of The Grey House as a centre for music has been fully established in the Crunluath movement, in particular, see pp. 256; 263–4; 267–9; 273; 275–8. The role of Callum Sutherland as a teacher in this school is also detailed throughout that movement, and in relevant Appendices 5, 6 and 9 we gain a thorough sense of the domestic space functioning also in a social and educational context. As we know, from certain remarks made by Iain Cowie, Callum Sutherland's so-called 'Winter Classes' had a particular charm that even someone like Iain, who himself had no knowledge or experience of piobaireachd playing, could appreciate – and they were able to carry on, these classes, right up until only two years before the time of the old man's death. 'Because of you' old Callum Sutherland had said to Iain. 'This place is in your hands.' This is not to say that there was not a downside to a boy's home being given over to a father's activities – and it is clear from 'The Big Music' that John Sutherland's sense of isolation was due not only to his own nature, and that of the lonely aspect of the district of Sutherland itself, but to the ambivalent role society played in his life. While he was in the midst of the life that he governed and seemed to enjoy, his father was also isolated and unable to extend himself to his family. In the same way, in the midst of all the music that was played in the House was a remote and fearful quiet – pp. 135; 178; 296 of the Crunluath describe this.

Can't wrap the same banner around your body as that which your own father wore!*

[from – notebook/various dated entries]
Anyway I wanted nothing to do with my father by then, or his way of doing business, the kind or extent of his concerns. I wanted nothing to do with lorries or tractors or transport and roads. To do with land and getting more land and buying off more land and putting roads through it, or dividing it into sections, and selling or renting it off, piece by piece.

Those small industrial estates of his, for light storage zones or for private use and micro-farming . . . I didn't want any part of Sutherland that way, or Sutherland and Caithness together, for that matter, those sheds and roads and buildings a kind of industry for my father, with his machines and vehicles, boiling bitumen and tar by the side of the road – I didn't want that for Sutherland, it wasn't what I wanted stayed in my mind when I thought about the place,** while I was away getting married, fathering a child. Only hills and skies all loaded with weather. And the black water and the snow on the tops and the deer paths for walking.

I'd come back for that.

Not the other, the father. Only come back when the old man has died.***

---

* Refers to pp. 114–5; 118; 120; 123 of the Taorluath movement of 'The Big Music', describing the funeral for Roderick John Callum, with particular reference to his military connections and role as a musician and composer for the Army: 'So they gave his father a proper funeral in the end.'

** In the same way that Johnnie doesn't associate Sutherland with these activities of his father, neither is the story of 'The Big Music' concerned with this aspect of Callum's life – concentrating instead, as it does, on his role as musician and teacher. However, it has been noted in various inserts, variations and additional material that the Sutherland family in general were always entrepreneurial in their business as well as musical activities, and John Sutherland's father was no exception. Throughout the history of The Grey House we see a programme of continual expansion and development in operation, from the increase of holdings of land and stock and development of related interests to the various extensions made to the House itself. The List of Additional Materials found at the back of this book may be of interest here, as will Appendices 4–9, which give details of the history of the House.

*** This is the period of 'The Return', that piobaireachd written by John Sutherland

[from — various scraps of paper/uncollated, all written in pencil]
Come back to the familiar place. The Ailte vhor Alech, the End of the
Road.*

And when did it begin with Margaret, anyway?

For ever.

---

following his re-orientation with his birthplace, after his father's death. Yet it could
also be said that this is a return that had actually begun many years earlier when he was
called to the House upon hearing of his mother's sudden and apparently grave illness.
That is when he first returned home, after many years away, and that is when he met
Margaret MacKay. Indeed, she was the one who first called him home. It is significant
that the secret name for this piece of music, found amongst John's personal papers after
his death, was 'Margaret's Song'. The manuscript for this can be found in the List of
Additional Materials at the back of the book.

*   The Urlar movement gives the first indication of the House and its position as Callum
drives up the lonely road towards it and reflects upon its name in Gaelic, meaning 'End
of the Road', when he turns the corner and sees it there in front of him, standing out
against the dusk. It is not known when this older name for the House was fully in use,
as throughout 'The Big Music' it is generally simply referred to as The Grey House or
the House, but it is possible that it goes back to the period of the late 1700s when the
House was a well-used stopping-off place for shepherds and cattle drovers. The road
then, as now, would have finished at the House and from there on travellers would have
made their way down the open strath towards the west where there are no paths or set
ways, though certain tracks were established over the years. The End of the Road at that
time would have represented a welcome respite from days of hard travelling, a place of
rest, shelter and music.

ii

Remember: following the Urlar, there's a sense of a leap, sometimes, in the music – this is also known as a 'Stag's Leap' – it's like a preparation for the second movement.

Yet how can I say this is when Margaret fully enters 'The Big Music' when it's as though she's always been there?

[from – handwritten score/notes made in the margin]
She's that note: there.*

   The key would be strong, but hitting back off the minor notes and plenty of interval between them for embellishment.

NB: additional thoughts: taken from journals, letters:**

He couldn't say exactly when, but it was early into his marriage that he knew he should have had his mind turned to his wife, to his baby son, but he couldn't so turn for he'd realised, soon after the wedding, that he'd done the

---

* There is some debate throughout 'The Big Music' as to the note that Margaret comes to 'own' in the sense that all notes of the bagpipe scale have certain attributions and meanings. 'F', as we know from relevant papers and Appendices, is the note of Love, so could seem to be the note taken up by Margaret in the piobaireachd – chiming with clear and lovely regularity through the second line of the Urlar in particular – see the manuscript in the relevant section of the Appendices. Yet this line of the 'Lament' is also the Lullaby theme – so the note also chimes with Katherine Anna, the infant John holds in his arms up on the hill and tries to comfort. Of course, that she – unbeknownst to the composer – is related to him, as surely as grandmother and granddaughter are related, adds texture to the note being used in this 'double' fashion. In addition, however, we see in the Crunluath movement that when Margaret's note finally sounds in the mind of John Sutherland it is his own note he hears – the High 'A' – known as the reached-for note, the Piper's own note – suggesting that the 'double' here refers to the great love story that is John and Margaret's relationship – a story that is somehow invisible to the world, the note of the beloved hidden, as it were, behind the protagonist. Either way, Margaret's note is finally revealed to be John's own – and there is a hint in the above score that the composer was aware of this, on some level, while creating his great 'Lament for Himself', even with the 'F' note claiming a prominent position in the theme.
** This line appears in Helen MacKay's handwriting, on separate paper, yet is included within these pages. Evidence of her beginning to organise some kind of narrative, perhaps? The tone of her comments suggests this.

wrong thing. Being south. Being married, being a father. All of it wrong.
It started then, I think, that habit of cutting himself off from things, from
people. Then he'd come home for his mother, remember? When they all
thought she was going to die and he came home then after so much time
away? He'd finally got in, from the long journey, overnight first to Edinburgh then the connecting train north and getting in to the station, late, late
afternoon, opening the carriage door . . . And Margaret was there.

[from – a tape recording/words spoken, then sounding a note, a sequence
of notes]*

Margaret.

Margaret.

Margaret.

Thinking of her now, and full, in these last warm days before the real
cold sets in.

[from – letter to self, typewritten]
They might phone you, your wife and son, asking after you, they might
– but you've stopped taking the tablets now or you'd never get this piece
written. It would never be done. There's the first movement down in
manuscript, but something missing from it even so.
      But don't say a word to anyone about it.
      What you're doing up here.
      Because it's what you wanted, isn't it?
      To be up here, in this private place, with all the past set down on the pages?

---

* We have seen the use of tape recordings and transcripts earlier in 'The Big Music' –
in particular in the section 'The people at the House and what they thought of him' in
the Crunluath movement. There are many recordings and notes generally held in The
Grey House archive – mostly on CD or digital recording devices, including Helen's
mobile phone – and these are in the process of being transferred to one central 'file'
and transcript. The recording referred to here, however, was found on an old cassette
recorder, featuring voice and chanter music. It is significant that the 'F' note is played
here, as we hear the name 'Margaret' sounding over and over again.

What you wanted, Johnnie?

To be completely alone?*

[from – tape recording/interrupted chanter playing of first movement, spoken words and handwritten notes (indicated here in italics) inserted in the chanter case]**

Is there anyone else?

This music needs something else.

Is there another theme here, that could come in?

Something to suggest lightness, possibility.

Here's a phrase that keeps coming back to me: new life out of old.

---

* Of course this refers to the significance of the Little Hut – as a hidden and secret place John Sutherland could go to and feel himself there to be in the complete state of physical isolation that he believed matched his psychological state. Yet, as we have seen throughout 'The Big Music', the theme of loneliness can also sound out in the most social passages of the book – when John is living in London, say, or hosting house parties – and in this he follows exactly the manner of behaviour and sensibility established by his father before him. Nevertheless, the hut was built to be a place apart from the House and its dichotomies of intimacy and separation, sociability and emptiness. The Little Hut exists apart from all this.

** As before, this is a cassette recording found at the Little Hut. We hear repeated phrases and some notes and sequences practised over and over – all taken from the line represented in manuscript at the back of 'The Big Music' and including the following sequences:

'F' to 'G'

'F' to 'A'

'F' to 'G'

'E' to 'E'

(the final opening bar of the second line that was used in the final composition)

As well as:

'F' to 'G'

'F' to 'G'

'F' to 'G'

'E' to 'E'

And:

'E' to 'G'

'E' to 'G'

'E' to 'G'

'E' to 'E'

(both unused)

iii

As he got older, his visits back to the House increased; he stayed longer
and longer until he moved back permanently. By then it had been a long
time since he and Margaret had been together in the room they had shared
at the top of the House. After his last stroke, Margaret and Iain moved
John to the little bedroom off the hall down by the room they used to
call the Music Room.* That was from the days when his father taught
in there, and the various musicians played and made their presentations
there. It was thought the pipers would have marched up and down the
hall right outside that little bedroom – and John would have that to think
about, maybe, as he lay there in his bed.

It must have seemed to him by then that everything about his life had
gone into the past. The manuscript shows the 'Lament' following more
and more a minor trajectory that, in the opening section especially, seems
barely able to lift itself above the drone of the 'A'.

As though there's nothing to give him pleasure any more.

The single High 'A', that relief . . . It's as if he's saving that for later.

[from – tape recording/interrupted chanter playing spoken words and
handwritten notes (in italics) inserted in the chanter case]
*For what use a tune when the wind turns cold or the rain might start? It's more a blanket I
need than a baby's cloth, though I have seen the baby and she is fair. Still it's more a covering
for a bed I need, for a grave.*

She's Margaret's daughter's child.

The idea of having her with me, in the tune.

---

* Also referred to as the little sitting room and the Study, the Music Room is favoured
for its intimacy and acoustic – allowing for both chanter and pipe playing, when the
door down to the hall can be left open and the piper can go up and down, from the
room down the hall and back. It was first established as an important focus in the House
by 'Old John' Sutherland, John MacKay's grandfather, who first gave lessons there and
called it the Music Room, even though at that point it would have had additional more
general use.

If at all possible, to get away up here, and finish it. Find the little theme that's missing here. Like a blanket, like a baby's cloth.*

[from – journal/undated entries]
Another day – working on the second and third movements; written notes but nothing laid down yet. Overcast but warm.

An easy walk this morning, and they don't know I'm here.

Raining.

Clear today, some cloud later.

---

* All the themes above are explored and developed fully in the various pages of the Urlar movement in particular. See especially the following passage taken from p. 5 onwards: 'For it's a tune for her, is what it is. The smallest, gentlest song against the broad and mindless hills. He can hear it in his own "Hush".'

iv

NB: idea for insert – John Callum:*

To break the silence following the second movement: The young man thinks it, says 'I'll not go!' . . . But he did go back, sure enough, for the funeral.

And his father was there, inside the box.

John had stood over him, before the men came up behind with the shovels and the earth.

'Ready then?' they'd asked him. The day was cold.

'Aye, ready . . .'

[from – journal, notes written in third person]
For weeks now. Months even. Hearing it but having to be silent. For the work of the damn pills, and Sarah calling from London every minute to check up, ask the others, How's he doing? Are you keeping an eye on things there?

But the tune. It's coming.

And where, you might ask, is Callum in all of this?** Asking Sarah but

---

* This, like other notes not attributed to JMS and often marked NB:, appears in the same computer font and on the same paper stock as many of the pages and inclusions provided by Helen MacKay that were also written by her. The project of organising these files and stories and accounts is, to an extent, ongoing, and only a selection of a large volume of material finally could be used for 'The Big Music'. The Foreword notes: 'The more I read into these pages, the more deeply involved I became in their provenance and meaning. Were the sections part of one journal? They appeared to be, a large portion of them – as the reader will come to see – with all of a journal's quality of the personal, of something direct and urgent that needs to be told. Yet other sections of the file were more like transcripts, or notes for stories, or finished stories, some of them . . .' and relates how the pages were placed in sequence, over time, to reflect the shape and structure of the piobaireachd the various pages were referring to throughout. The fragment shown above in this Crunluath A Mach movement of the music indicates something of the process of the pages' – and inevitably the book's – composition.
** It is significant to the structure and theme of 'The Big Music' that there is no sequence of notes, no single note even, that has come to represent John Sutherland's son Callum, named for his father who, though he was christened Roderick John, was always known as Callum. In this there is a kind of absence to the music that reflects, exactly, the relationship between father and son – and indeed, plays back to the relationship between

getting no answer there, down the line. For there's no note in the music for him, for Callum, though he should be there.

Callum.

But how to get him in? When he's his son and he belongs there?

How make a tune for someone, put him in, when you don't know him at all?

John Sutherland and his own father. The three generations do 'meet', however, in 'Lament for Himself' in the sense of the use of the singling and doubling variations of the Urlar theme both in the manuscript of the music and in John Sutherland's perceived meeting with both his father and his son up on the hill: 'He's stopped./ Waiting./ For it's Callum./ It is. It's Callum there./ And very close./ Up there with the dogs, for they're his dogs, they're Callum's dogs . . . / Callum./ 'How are you, boy?'/ And with him . . . Yes. It's his father too./ Come up with Callum, he must have, and now they're both here together, just over that hill./ His father./ His son . . . Enough to turn the theme.' The last phrase suggesting how the use of the dithis singling and doubling will 'lift' the music, open it out and set it in a broader context outwith the theme of 'Himself', prepare the composition for the Taorluath and Crunluath movements that will follow.

v

[from – paper/handwritten]

Only . . .

That note.

Yet to come in.

The High, High – 'A' – of her.

Again . . .

And . . .

Again.

vi

[from – journal/undated entries]

The quiet room at the top of the House where we used to go.

It was the room that was the Schoolroom, once. Of course I remember it, why even write it like that, as a sentence when a theme for it will be in the tune, on three notes?*

I have that down already – an idea for the later movements.

It was where my mother taught me, as well, when I was a boy, the Schoolroom.

Reading. Writing. Arithmetic.

And when we were done she would take me up in her arms.

---

* It is not entirely clear to what notes John is referring here. No doubt he intended to hide the theme of Margaret within 'Lament for I Iimself' as she was hidden in the earlier composition 'The Return' – however, as has been noted earlier, the use of the High 'A' and its role as a note of confirmation, of statement, in the 'Lament', as a note claimed by the piper himself that is also Margaret's note, suggests that she comes to have a fuller role in this composition than one may have initially expected. Certainly, this is played out in the structure of 'The Big Music' itself – in the way Helen MacKay has presented those papers that refer to her mother and her mother's life as being key to understanding the structure of John Sutherland's composition. Perhaps it was intended by John himself to have a section of the music that celebrated his coming together with Margaret – by creating a leitmotif to represent a part of the House he always associated with safety and love. It would have been a great thing if he had been able to fully express that in the manuscript – but as it stands, this must be a theme that the music moves around, as do the pages of 'The Big Music' move around this love story without ever alighting fully upon it. In the end we must be content with the idea that a certain sequence was in the composer's mind, even if he was not able to express it. Perhaps we may imagine the sequence as containing the Low and High 'A' and the 'F', as being three notes with great significance and therefore emerging in a range of ways throughout the composition, bringing together in different patternings the notes of love, lament and return.

vii

[from – paper/found stuck between the pages of an old appointment diary]

I should not be here.

~

endnote:*

That scrap of paper is on my own desk now, a little wisp of handwriting, pencil. It's like a beginning.

For what does the line mean, for this one man?

If I'd written such a thing you might say it's because I've travelled and I've been unsettled, that I've lived abroad and in other places where I've gone unremarked in towns and villages and parts of the countryside, and unknown, because I have not belonged there.

But John Sutherland of this House?

A Sutherland from Sutherland?

Perhaps it really is where the whole book begins.

The following is on a separate sheet of paper, handwritten in pencil – many sections scribbled out:

That by setting down the details of this one man's birth and life I might uncover something, a meaning of that phrase, *I should not be here*, that sits

---

* Various pages and documents sampled in this Crunluath A Mach show the intervention of Helen MacKay in this fashion as one who is piecing together a narrative from these various fragments – here, shown by a separate piece of her notepaper attached by paperclip to John Sutherland's diary, in other places using Post-It notes, additional computer-written documents stapled to the back of an original file, or inserting handwritten notes into a file that also contains John Sutherland's original material. In all instances it describes a highly original and intuitive approach to managing and responding to John Sutherland's work and life. Each of her insertions seems to suggest a question more than an idea for reaching a conclusion. Each is like an opening door. As she writes herself, 'Perhaps it [i.e. the scrap of paper that has been found] really is where the whole book begins.'

like a shadow behind those words . . . A 'Lament for Himself' after all. And so by getting the papers back from the Little Hut, finding his mother's birth certificate, his father's papers, legal documents that show the history of the House . . . All this was to find the shape of a life, its sound, its modulations. Here are the details of his company in London if I want them, of his wife's house's mortgage, notes for Callum's school fees though nothing for him later. A family's business and affairs stuffed into drawers in the desk and some files, too, that he had – that I myself was responsible for clearing out. My mother was not able to do it.

And so it began. In time, from my quiet room at the top of the House, from these broad facts, documents, from the manuscript itself . . . Lines start to open up, ideas. One paragraph builds to a page, the pages are collected:

One paper . . . And another . . .

A marriage document, a registry office in London, forms to sign for a new car, for a hand-made suit.

A note from a journal dated three weeks before he died – that was there in the Little Hut, on a desk by a window that overlooks the water:

The hills will be the ground, but not giving anything back to the tune as it develops. The colour of them – yes, and to give size and scale to the piece . . . But I need something else, I can't be alone up there on the tops with being so near the end. So something then, to . . . Keep me . . . In my arms. And safe . . . Something to carry . . .

That can also hold.

Keep me safe, now . . . And always safe.

Like a new theme, to come out of . . .

Where I was, once,
where I –

Crunluath A Mach/final fragment

The hills only come back the same: *I don't mind*, and all the flat moorland and the sky . . . As though the whole lovely space is calling back at him in the silence that is around him, to this man out here in the midst of it, in the midst of all these hills and all the air. That his presence means nothing, that he could walk for miles into these same hills, in bad weather or in fine, could fall down and not get up again, could go crying into the peat with music for his thoughts maybe, and ideas for a tune, but none of it according him a place here . . . Amongst the grasses and the water and the sky . . . Still it would come back to him the same, in the same silence, in the fineness of the air . . . *I don't mind, I don't mind, I don't mind.*

APPENDICES

How to use the Appendices in this book

As noted in the Foreword of 'The Big Music', additional material is provided for the reader by way of various appendices and lists of information that relate to various aspects of the story that is being told. This ranges from background notes and a general history of the area of Sutherland in northern Scotland, where John Callum MacKay and his family have lived for generations, to details of the House there and its Piping School as well as information about bagpipes and bagpipe playing generally and its place in this book and in music and in art.

It is by no means necessary to read all or any of this material, it is simply a way in, for those who want to go there, to the landscape and world of 'The Big Music' – to indicate the hills at your back or the view that stretches ahead. As the preceding book was a place in which, for a time, you have lived, so may these pages extend its boundaries.

Appendix 1: Notes on history/landscape of the North East region

i

Historical geography

In geographical terms, the Highland area refers to the north-west part of Scotland that crosses the mainland in a more or less straight line from Helensburgh to Stonehaven – with the flat coastal lands that occupy parts of the counties of Nairnshire, Morayshire, Banffshire and Aberdeenshire often excluded, as they do not share the distinctive geographical and cultural features of the rest of the Highlands. In Aberdeenshire, the boundary between the Highlands and the Lowlands is not well defined. There is a stone beside the A93 road near the village of Dinnet on Royal Deeside which states 'You are now in the Highlands', although there are areas of Highland character to the east of this point.

The north-east of Caithness, as well as Orkney and Shetland, is also often excluded from the 'Highland' definition for the same reason of appearance – although the Hebrides are not. None of these definitions are, however, emotionally based, that is, giving a meaning carrying its own particular truth that can be just as descriptive as geographical precision, and when one refers to the Highlands as part of conversation or in a book or in a song or when pointing the way to a part of the country that feels remote and lost and far away . . . One is referring to a Highland region that is not so-defined by any geographer's manual or map. To be high up, on a hill or mountain, surveying the whole empty sweep of the country below you – this is to be in the Highlands. As it is to be in a car or on foot upon a road that twists and turns and thins to the finest thread on an Ordnance Survey map that marks the topmost area of the British mainland . . . Then you are in the Highlands, too.

Another way the definition of the Highland area differs from the Lowland region is by language and tradition, as there are many Highland regions that have preserved Gaelic speech and customs centuries after Anglicisation. This has also led to a refining of that cultural distinction between Highlander and Lowlander that was first noted towards the end of the fourteenth century. Even so, there are many areas in the Highlands where Gaelic is not spoken but a great sense of regional difference prevails nevertheless, a sense of being Highland more to do with manner and way, a certain turn of phrase at times or a weighting and a rhythm in the speech and syntax. These kinds of sentences and attitudes, this sensibility, mean more in Highland terms than the actual language spoken.

Inverness is traditionally regarded as the capital of the Highlands, although less so in the Highland parts of Aberdeenshire, Angus, Perthshire and Stirlingshire, which look more to cities such as Aberdeen, Perth, Dundee and Stirling as their commercial centres. Nevertheless the phrase 'gateway to the Highlands' is often used in association with Inverness, and the roads that open out from that city take the traveller off and away, to the North, to the West, to the Islands, to the Pentland Sea.

Finally, to add to the complexity of the term 'Highland' and its meanings, the Highland Council area, created as one of the local government regions of Scotland, excludes a large area of the southern and eastern Highlands, and the Western Isles, but includes Caithness. Even so, 'Highlands' is sometimes used as a name for the council area, as in 'Highlands and Islands Fire and Rescue Service', and consists of the Highland Council area and the Island Council areas of Orkney, Shetland and the Western Isles. There is much talk as to the use and relevance of these terms and Highland Council signs at the Pass of Drumochter, between Glen Garry and Dalwhinnie, saying 'Welcome to the Highlands' are still regarded as controversial. Nevertheless, it's fair to say that whenever any of us say 'I'm off to the Highlands' we know what we mean. For though there will always be different definitions in different contexts throughout the region, the emotional resonance referred to earlier that sounds from the word 'Highland' will always strike a particular note.

ii

Geology

The Scottish Highlands are largely composed of ancient rocks from the Cambrian and Precambrian periods which were uplifted during the later Caledonian land shifts. Smaller formations of Lewisian gneiss in the north-west are up to 3,000 million years old and amongst the oldest found anywhere on earth. These foundations are interspersed with many igneous intrusions of a more recent age, the remnants of which have formed mountain massifs such as the Cairngorms and the Cuillins of Skye. A significant exception to the above are the fossil-bearing beds of Old Red Sandstone found principally along the Moray Firth coast and partially down the Highland Boundary Fault. The Jurassic beds found in isolated locations on Skye and Applecross reflect the complex underlying geology that describes when the entire region was covered by ice sheets during the Pleistocene ice ages. The complex geomorphology includes incised valleys and lochs carved by the action of mountain streams and ice, and a topography of irregularly distributed mountains whose summits have similar heights above sea-level, but whose bases depend upon the amount of denudation to which the plateau has been subjected in various places.

iii

The North East region

Map showing Highland region in relation to the rest of Scotland

Appendix 2: Local history and geography – Mhorvaig/Luath district

i

General information

The area in which 'The Big Music' takes place is in the central region of Sutherland,
north-west of the coastal villages of Golspie and Brora, and set inland somewhat
from the better-known Helmsdale and Naver and Halladale Straths. This is a remote region, not easily accessed by road, even to this day; nevertheless it is served
by a rail link that has a 'request' stop that is a forty-minute drive or so to The Grey
House.

**County of Sutherland
until circa 1890**

Geography

Area - Total	Ranked 5th 1,297,846 acres (5,252 km²)

The map here may be of interest, showing an earlier configuration of the county
that is described in 'The Big Music', its land
mass in relation to the rest of Scotland.

Today, Sutherland is within the Highland local government area, the regions of
which sit well outwith that represented here
and which in Gaelic is referred to according
to its traditional areas: Dùthaich 'Ic Aoidh
(NW), Asainte (Assynt) and Cataibh (East).
However, Cataibh can often be heard used as
referring to the area as a whole.

The county town, and only burgh of
the county, is Dornoch. Other settlements
include Bonar Bridge, Lairg, Brora, Dur-
ness, Embo, Tongue, Golspie, Helmsdale,
Lochinver, Scourie and Kinlochbervie. The
population of the county as at the most recent census was 13,466.

The name 'Sutherland' dates from the era of Norse rule and settlement over
much of the Highlands and Islands, which is why, though it contains some of the
northernmost land in the island of Great Britain, it was called *Suth-r-Land* ('southern
land') from the standpoint of Orkney and Caithness and those lands further north.

The north-west corner of the county, traditionally known as the Province of
Strathnaver, was not incorporated into Sutherland until 1601. This was the home of

the powerful and warlike Clan MacKay that had connections in those earlier times to the Sutherland family of 'The Big Music'. Even today this part of the county is known as MacKay Country, and, unlike other areas of Scotland where the names traditionally associated with the area have become diluted, there is still a preponderance of MacKays in the region and nearby, settling further east through marriage, into the interior of Sutherland.

As well as Caithness to the north and east, Sutherland has the North Sea (Moray Firth) coastline in the east, the historic county of Ross and Cromarty to the south, and the Atlantic coastline in the west and north. Like its southern neighbour, Wester Ross, the county has some of the most dramatic scenery in the whole of Europe, and for the purposes of this book it should be noted that the great hills of Mhorvaig and Luath have come to dominate the central strath, the so-called 'corridor' through which the sheep were driven in the early nineteenth century and so became the place where the Sutherland family of 'The Big Music' established themselves. The emptiness and sense of isolation in this part of Sutherland is acute – more so, even, than in the neighbouring straths of the North East – which no doubt is part of the reason, after a long period of habitation in the area by the same family, the land was initially let over to the first John Roderick MacKay of 'Grey Longhouse' as recorded in the Taorluath section of the book, and then subsequently claimed as his own by his son's son for the family to therefore inherit. Mhorvaig and Luath are the two hills that most dominate this area of the landscape, side by side as they are, set into the hills around them, to the left-hand side of the strath and what is now called The Grey House.

So this part of the world is remote enough. Despite being Scotland's fifth-largest historic county, it has a smaller population than a medium-size Lowland Scottish town even though it stretches from the Atlantic in the west, up to the Pentland Firth and across to the North Sea. As would be expected, much of the population is based in seaward towns, leaving large swathes of the inner portions of the land utterly uninhabited – or where there are small settlements they are quiet and during the day can scarcely be seen from a distance against the grey-green land and at night lit just enough to show themselves as pinpricks against the endless dark.

And those hills of Mhorvaig and Luath? It's where this book begins: with these hills and the other hills all around them, sitting as they do against the sky and not changing but for the shapes of clouds upon their sides or the runs of water that flood them in the spring melts or at times of heavy rain. 'The hills only come back the same', remember? The first line of this book. As it is also its conclusion.

Comprised of Torridonian sandstone underlain by Lewisian gneiss, the land mass is formed in such a way that the same hills can only be traversed with great difficulty by even the most able walkers and have portions of them still that remain unknown and hidden. This is why the 'Little Hut', as it is called in 'The Big Music', could remain unknown; it is why the local walkers' guide to this area of the Sutherland region notes: 'Such mountains as these are attractive for hill walking and scrambling, despite their location, for they have a unique structure with great scope for exploration. On the other hand, care is needed when bad weather occurs owing to their isolation and the risks of injury and the fact that so many portions of them seem hidden to the eye until one is upon them or has dropped right down into a formerly unseen crevice or small valley to find an unworn path there that one may never have known existed.'

Transport links in this region are poor: the A9 main east-coast road is challenging in parts and there are few inland roads, the east-coast Far North Line north–south single-track railway line only, and no airports. Much of the former county is poor relative to the rest of Scotland, with few job opportunities beyond government-funded employment and jobs made available on estates or private houses – such as The Grey House of this book that was established as a Piping School from 1835 onwards and took pupils who would board for a time while lessons took place. Later, as its lands were further developed, it would also have employed more keepers and agricultural assistants, in the way Iain Cowie was employed by old (Roderick) John Callum in the early 1960s.

Owing to its isolation from the rest of the country, Sutherland was reputedly the last haunt of the native wolf, the last survivor being shot in the eighteenth century. However, other wildlife has survived, including the golden eagle, sea eagle and pine marten amongst other species which are very rare in the rest of the country. There are pockets of the native Scots Pine, remnants of the original Caledonian Forest.

Sutherland became a local government county, with its own elected county council, in 1890, under the Local Government (Scotland) Act 1889. At that time, one town within the county, Dornoch, was already well established as an autonomous burgh with its own burgh council. Parish councils, covering rural areas of the county, were established in 1894. The parish councils were abolished in 1931 under the Local Government (Scotland) Act 1929 and the county council and the burgh council were abolished in 1975 under the Local Government (Scotland) Act 1973. The 1973 act also created a new two-tier system, with Sutherland as a district within the Highland region. After 1975 the boundary between the districts of Sutherland and Caithness were slightly redrawn yet retain the shape and spirit of the two counties. Even so, the exact boundaries remain, in the inland areas in particular, in question – their position and lines like the writing of the postal districts on the letters that are sent to and from there, blurred as though by a light Highland rain.

ii

Place names

Map showing relevant areas; incl. Mhorvaig; Brora

iii

Domestic life

Up until the mid-nineteenth century most houses in the far North East Region were traditional 'longhouses' – that is, a traditional crofthouse comprising two rooms and a middle 'chamber' with box beds in both. The byre and barn adjoined that structure, built in a line from it, all single-storey with a thatch roof. A peat fire burned continually for heat and to protect against damp, creating a coat of smoke inside the dwelling that gave rise to the term 'blackhouse' to describe a house of this nature.

A rowan tree was normally planted by the front door to keep away evil spirits – and the doorway and ceiling were low, the whole structure set modestly into the ground with a place for domestic animals set to the back and usually a stone wall running along the front of the property. Practical gardens were maintained, shelter provided by the prudent siting of the house according to the weather and prevailing conditions. For this reason it is rare to come across the remains of a longhouse that is exposed frontwards to the sea, or facing down the strath, or across the water from a hill. Long and low the dwelling places were kept – describing, perhaps, as much as tradition and practicality, a condition of mind and habit.

Yet, while many retained the shape of this house over the years, right up until the beginning of the last century, in fact, others – those who had created slightly larger windows for their homes in the first place, or more flourishing, varied gardens – developed the basic structure and extended it. Most often, this was done by creating a first floor that was set into a tiled roof with dormer windows – and many of the standard domestic dwellings of the region to this day still adopt and show this shape – with a porch added to the front and a side structure abutting, often built of wood, or, more recently, corrugated iron.

Life at home over this period – from the eighteenth century's longhouses to the Victorian era that favoured a more substantial, bourgeois presentation of the domestic space – was modest and quiet, with the kitchen featuring at the heart of the domestic world. As the social world altered from one of *ancien régime* to a replacement of deference, dependency and loyalty with the values of independence and commercial ambition, so, too, did life at home become more outward-looking and more communally and intellectually engaged.

Families remained large but were more likely to intermingle outside formal events such as ceilidhs and weddings. Visits, one neighbour to another, were made more of; family members expected to do their part entertaining strangers at the door. Where the quiet life of the dark longhouse promoted introspection and clannishness, the lighter, open-looking dwellings of the late nineteenth and early twentieth century celebrated fellowship and community. Children were being educated for longer, and expecting a wider range of employment and social possibilities than a simple return to the family croft. Discussion abounds regarding the self-educating nature of the population at this time for it is clear that over this period, following the deep conservatism of the past, the house had become somewhere that was no longer simply a place of shelter and where practicalities were met, but, rather, had become an emblem of domestic life that itself had transformed and could now represent intellectual rigour, fresh thought and self-improvement . . . Change.

Appendix 3: History of the Highland North East region, 1700–1850

i

General background

The Scottish Highlands have been culturally distinguishable from the Scottish Lowlands from the later Middle Ages into the modern period, when English replaced
Gaelic throughout most of the Lowlands and the way of life in the North showed
itself to be more set and resistant to agrarian change. Nowhere is this resistance
more apparent than in the North East region, where a way of life that was feudal
and conservative in character was eventually set upon by agricultural interests that
resulted in a redeployment of resources and settlements that came to be known as
the Clearances; when that same way of life was dramatically uprooted and its clan
system destroyed. Until then the area, like much of the Highlands of Scotland,
had remained unchanged since the Middle Ages and before – and indeed, there
were certain parts of the North East (in particular Caithness and certain areas of
Aberdeenshire and a small portion of Sutherland) that, because of the particular
sensibility of their people and a certain flexibility in terms of class definition and
the degree of manoeuvrability that could take place within established hierarchal
lines, managed to flourish and improve under conditions that were unlike any others
that had prevailed in Britain up to that time.

   The North East area has always been sparsely populated, with hills and mountains
dominating the region, yet for a long period before the nineteenth century was home
to a larger population that settled in the sheltered straths and bays and developed
strong bonds of community and tithe that went unchanged from one generation to
the next. During this period, though other parts of Scotland were being swept up in
the innovations brought about by the Enlightenment and Industrial Revolution, the
North East remained cut off and apart – with lairds and clan chiefs maintaining a
way of life that was connected to the communities who worked their land, allowing, in
many cases, discrete family groups' and individuals' economic and social ambitions to
be realised within the prevailing fixities of class and hierarchy. So the area has its own
rules, one could say, around this time. It's different from the rest of Scotland – from
both the Catholic West and the more 'enlightened' South – and for this reason, for its
loneliness, for its isolation, we see a certain independence of character emerging from
a particular geographical region. We can see, beneath the rush and tragedy of the story
of the Clearances that is to so dominate any narrative of the area, a sense, nevertheless,
of autonomy and individualism and stubborn'ness and power.

In general, the era of the Napoleonic Wars, 1790–1815, brought prosperity, optimism and economic growth to the Highlands as the economy continued to grow through wages paid by kelping, in fisheries and weaving, as well as large-scale infrastructure spending such as the Caledonian Canal project. Where land was improved, high prices could be fetched for cattle and the sheep that at that time were still being husbanded according to traditional methods, yet bought and sold as far away as Edinburgh and the South. This, before the great 'sheepwalks' that were established after the Clearances, when a flock of Highland ewes raised locally and driven to market in the West and South could bring wealth and security to the community. Service in the Army was also an option for young men who sent pay home and eventually retired there with their army pensions.

By the turn of the century, however, this relative prosperity showed itself to be waning, ending completely after 1815, by which time certain long-run factors had undermined the economic position of the poor tenant farmers or 'crofters', as they were called. The adoption by landowners of a market orientation that had started further south in Scotland in the century after 1750 was by now beginning to dissolve the traditional social and economic structure of the north-west Highlands and Hebrides Islands, change moving inevitably eastwards with greater efficiency and ruthlessness even to the region that had remained set apart from change for so long. When the Clearances came to Sutherland then, they came hard.

ii

Land use and the Clearances

What became known as the Clearances were considered by the landlords as necessary 'improvements'. As mentioned above, these 'improvements' had started throughout the rest of Scotland in the early part of the eighteenth century when clan chiefs engaged Lowland, or sometimes English, factors with expertise in more profitable sheep farming, and they 'encouraged', sometimes forcibly, the population to move off suitable land to other less hospitable areas in the county or, often, to the new colonies abroad.

The year 1792 came to be known as the 'Year of the Sheep' to Scottish Highlanders and was the beginning of a brutal repatriation that saw those who were accommodated in poor crofts or small farms in coastal areas where farming could not sustain the communities off their land and pressed into military service or forced aboard ships bound for Nova Scotia or marched to the cliffheads of Caithness to eke out a living amongst the seaweed and the rocks.

In 1807 Elizabeth Gordon, 19th Countess of Sutherland, was touring her inheritance with her husband Lord Stafford when she wrote that 'he is seized as much as I am with the rage of improvements, and we both turn our attention with the greatest of energy to turnips'. So change had finally come for this near forgotten part of the kingdom; so change would make its mark. As well as turning land over to sheep farming, Stafford planned to invest in creating a coal-pit, salt-pans, brick- and tileworks and herring fisheries, and that same year his agents began the evictions: ninety families were forced to leave their crops in the ground and move their cattle, sheep, furniture and timbers to the land they were offered twenty miles away on the coast, living in the open until they had built themselves new houses. Stafford's first commissioner, William Young, arrived in 1809, and soon engaged Patrick Sellar as his factor, who pressed ahead with the process while acquiring sheep-farming estates and establishing for himself the reputation of being one of the most vicious and self-serving administrators of the new regime. Elsewhere, the flamboyant Alexander Ranaldson MacDonell of Glengarry portrayed himself as the last genuine specimen of the true Highland chief while his tenants were subjected to a process of relentless eviction.

See the account below, by Donald MacLeod, a Sutherland crofter, who wrote first-hand of the events he witnessed at that time:

The consternation and confusion were extreme. Little or no time was given for the removal of persons or property; the people striving to remove the sick and the helpless before the fire should reach them; next, struggling to save the most valuable of their effects. The cries of the women and children, the roaring of the affrighted cattle, hunted at the same time by the yelling dogs of the shepherds amid the smoke and fire, altogether presented a scene that completely baffles description — it required to be seen to be believed.

A dense cloud of smoke enveloped the whole country by day, and even extended far out to sea. At night an awfully grand but terrific scene presented itself — all the houses in an extensive district in flames at once. I myself ascended a height about eleven o'clock in the evening, and counted two hundred and fifty blazing houses, many of the owners of which I personally knew, but whose present condition — whether in or out of the flames — I could not tell. The conflagration lasted six days, till the whole of the dwellings were reduced to ashes or smoking ruins. During one of these days a boat actually lost her way in the dense smoke as she approached the shore, but at night was enabled to reach a landing-place by the lurid light of the flames.

In the mid-nineteenth century the second, more brutal phase of the Clearances began — this after the 1822 visit by George IV, when Lowlanders set aside their previous distrust and hatred of the Highlanders and identified with them as national symbols and the entire country once again approached a state of civil war.

Once again a Countess of Sutherland came northwards to visit: Elizabeth Leveson-Gower and her husband George Leveson-Gower. By now evictions were occurring at the rate of, sometimes, two hundred families in one day (this between the period 1811 and 1820) and many starved and froze to death where their homes had once been. The Duchess, on seeing the wretched tenants on her husband's estate, remarked in a letter to a friend in England, 'Scotch people are of happier constitution and do not fatten like the larger breed of animals.'

To many landlords, however, 'improvement' and 'clearance' did not necessarily mean depopulation. And neither did it mean that all parts of Sutherland, nor all those who lived there, were adversely affected. Without taking up the position of the powerful hypocritical factors and commissioners who policed the Clearances through the region, some families and certain individuals managed to maintain the small landholding they had inherited and develop this, in line with the innovations that were sweeping Scotland, to grow and extend their interests without giving up their sense of moral obligation to their communities or compromising a way of life that had defined them as long as they had been living in the region. The Sutherland family of the Parish of Rogart is an example here (see relevant sections of 'The Big Music', in the Taorluath and Crunluath movements, in particular). These families managed to make good their place in the North East and, due to strategic thinking and forethought, remained unmoved by the eviction processes that were eliminating and 'disappearing' their neighbours. As the shockwaves from the Clearances subsided, by the end of the 1800s, these same families were revered in the region and cited as examples of all that was commendable in the Highland character – strong-willed, decent and undeterred by fortune and politics. As time went on, their position in the community became, if anything, more associated with an old way of life that was enacted as if the Clearances had never happened. It was as though the brutality of that regime had only served to establish the place of decency and honour and fairness that had always been the virtues of home.

iii

Family records

There are many pieces of documentation that indicate how life was lived, particularly from the period 1850 onwards, that are available in 'The Big Music' archive. These include first-hand accounts, records of fishing; crofting rights, small documents of the Sutherland family; landholding, sheep sales etc., and notes of piping lessons, pupils. See sections in the List of Additional Materials: Archive of John MacKay Sutherland.

iv

Story of a Highland estate

It is not always the case that landholdings in the North East have been maintained by powerful, aristocratic interests that are not sympathetic to the indigenous way of life. The Grey House and holdings of Ben Mhorvaig in Sutherland, as described in 'The Big Music', is one example of private and substantial landholding in the Sutherland region that sits outwith the larger estate-owned tracts of land and occupies an independent place within Highland geography.

See the accounts of the positions and buildings of certain tacksmen and tenant farmers outlined in *The Highland House Transformed* and other relevant histories listed in the Bibliography at the back of 'The Big Music' to gain an understanding of how a prosperous class of people grew out of the traditional landholding interests in the North East and other parts of the Highlands. The Statistical Report for the Parish of Achtattan, 1823, for example, contains this quote: 'The farmers make a decent appearance, seem to enjoy the comforts and conveniences of life'; and case studies abound of small farmers who increased their holdings and social and economic position all over the Highlands by prudent management of stock and land and fair and inventive methods of land lease and rental. These methods are reflected in the kinds of houses built, their scale and detailing, though the following comment is worth noting in light of houses such as The Grey House of 'The Big Music' and a consideration of how certain class distinctions remained in place even as they were collapsed by ingenuity and private interests: 'However, although finished to the highest craft standards, the largest farmhouse remains similar in form and ornament to the smallest farmhouse. Decorative features such as columned porticoes or pediments were associated with a higher social status than that of tenant farmer and their use would have been inappropriate irrespective of the farmer's actual worth.' (from Maudlin, *The Highland House Transformed*, p. 69).

See too the story below, taken from a local pamphlet 'Melvich and Naver District', of the Dundonald Estate in the North East Sutherland/Caithness borders, for an example of a landholding with a history and background not dissimilar to that which governed the interests of the Sutherland family of Rogart, subjects of 'The Big Music':

Today, Dundonald Estate and The Big House and cottages are two independent Highland Estates that have always stayed outside the clan system of landholding in the north east and are representative of extensive though modestly represented economic interests.

The 'modern' story of the estate begins with the participation of Donald MacKay MacDonald in the Jacobite Rising of 1715 and the resulting forfeiture of land he held further south that brought to an end the essentially feudal landholding system practised in that region. At this point he retreated to the far north where he took up residence with the Donald family who had acted as foresters to the Earls of Farr from at least the 17th century – the duties of forester were to 'protect the game, to supervise timber-extraction, to conserve the woodland, and to apprehend trespassers.' During this time he secured the property known as 'The Big House' and its surrounding land and, as a result of resolving the forfeiture of 1716, was able to buy an adjoining property that later became known as The Dundonald Estate.

The next owners of the Estate were his sons, James and Duncan MacDonald, who increased the landholding to the north, including securing fishing rights extending from the Fastwater of Clear, to the sea. Papers give the year of this purchase as 1739 – however, some National Survey documents suggest 1745 is more likely – as we have surviving three letters from the then vendor Lord Naver detailing his difficulties in selling 'such choice and favoured waters such as I would prefer to keep them for myself.'

Nevertheless other records make clear that Lord Naver's intentions were to sell this portion of land so as to help 'provide' for James MacDonald's wife and son – Frances, herself a cousin of his, and 'the boy John who has always been my favourite'.

When, in subsequent years, the Estate fell on difficult times, at no point were the fishings sold for these sentimental reasons – and they remain in the possession of the MacDonald family to this day.

In general, then, we see how the Estate has been held and managed independently since the eighteenth century despite a landholding system that was, at the time of the redeployment, still essentially feudal – with the landowner himself and his sons and grandsons (John and Donald MacDonald, sons of John) continuing to act as foresters, and feuars in their own right. Along with him other feuars who managed land this way include John Farquaharson (Invercauld), Patrick Farquaharson (Invery), Donald Farquaharson (Allanaquoich).

Dundonald remains in private ownership today, though much reduced. The Big House is rented to fishing parties, and some stalking is available on the Estate.

v

Literary history

Caithness and Sutherland gave birth to a strong lyric tradition that came to prominence around the time of the Jacobite Rebellion. A large body of these songs survive and are sung today, though not always in the original Gaelic.

Poets of this era include Rob Donn MacKay, Duncan Ban MacIntyre, William Ross and Alexander MacDonald, who was present when Prince Charles raised the Jacobite standard at Glenfinnan.

The Sutherland poet Rob Donn MacKay did not take part in the rising, and his chief – Lord Reay – supported the Hanoverian side (the incumbent rulers). But Rob was still for the Prince, as this fragment shows:

Today, today, tis right for us
To rise up in all eagerness,
The third day since the second month
Of winter now has come to end;
We'll welcome thee full heartily,
With laughter, speech and melody,
And readily we'll drink thy health,
With harp and song, and dancing too.

Prolific creators or rewriters of Jacobite songs based on old models included James Hogg, Lady Caroline Nairne and Robert Burns. Burns published 'It Was A' for Our Rightfu' King', 'The Highland Widow's Lament' and a song about love called 'Charlie He's My Darling'. Lady Nairne wrote lyrics for 'Wi a Hundred Pipers' and 'Will Ye No Come Back Again?' She also wrote a more warlike set of words for 'Charlie is My Darling'.

March tunes had lyrics attached, for example 'The Sherramuir March' and 'Wha Wouldna Fecht for Charlie'. James Hogg wrote Jacobite lyrics for both of these tunes and many others. Hogg published and perhaps wrote 'Both Sides of the Tweed', a popular song known today.

Later, the work of Neil Gunn and George MacKay Brown, in particular, came to represent a way of life that is depicted in mythic, lyrical terms as well as the actual and historic. Gunn's famous novel *The Silver Darlings* and his *Green Isle of the Great Deep* are two examples on different ends of the literal/literary spectrum, both describing, to different degrees, a place that is both real and unreal, factual as well as fictional. In this, he and Brown, both, reach back to a tradition outlined above and before it, of fairy tale and Norse myth, of song and story, where the literal and invented worlds merge and blend in our imagination, become the same place.

Appendix 3A: History of the Highland North East region 1850–present

The unequal concentration of land ownership remained an emotional subject, of enormous importance to the vexed question of the Highland economy, and eventually became a cornerstone of liberal radicalism. The crofters (tenant farmers who rented only a few acres) were politically powerless, and as a result of this, it has been suggested, many had joined the breakaway 'Free Church' by and after 1843. This evangelical movement was led by lay preachers who themselves came from the lower strata, and whose preaching was implicitly critical of the established order. The religious change energised the crofters and separated them from the landlords; it helped prepare them for their successful and violent challenge to the landlords in the 1880s through the Highland Land League. Violence erupted in different regions throughout the Highlands during this period, only quieting when the government stepped in, passing the Crofters' Holdings (Scotland) Act of 1886 to reduce rents, guarantee fixity of tenure and break up large estates to provide crofts for the homeless. In 1885 three Independent Crofter candidates were elected to Parliament, which gave voice to grievances formerly silenced. The results included explicit security for the Scottish smallholders; the legal right to bequeath tenancies to descendants; and creating a Crofting Commission. The crofters as a political movement faded away by 1892, when the Liberal Party came to represent, more and more, the interests of the tenant farmers of the region. Yet, as we saw over the previous historical period, there remained certain families and interests outside the general political movement that was changing the way Highland society was being managed. Always, it is important to bear in mind the way the land, in the region of north-east Scotland, accommodated a range of economic and cultural ambitions that in turn gave much back to the community and society in terms of enlarging the sense of Highland life and expanding its horizons.

i

One particular section of Sutherland that has, since the middle of the nineteenth century, resisted the changes that were sweeping the rest of the Highlands is the land around the hills Mhorvaig and Luath, an area that has been settled, records show, since and before the mid-eighteenth century by the Sutherland family, first of 'Grey Longhouse', Parish of Rogart and environs. See the following Appendix 4: 'The Grey House' for more details of the family's history and activities throughout this period, as well as certain sections in the Taorluath and Crunluath movements of 'The Big Music'.

ii

Local maps

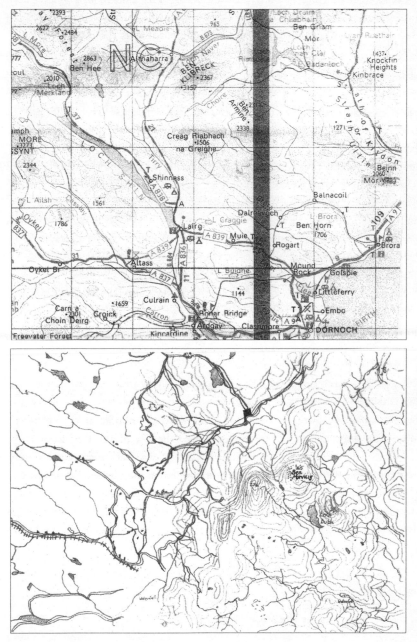

Maps indicating immediate region; incl. rivers; landfall

Appendix 4: The Grey House – history; plans; evidence

i

Site

As described in the Taorluath section of this book, The Grey House – also known as
'Ailte vhor Alech' or 'The End of the Road' – was originally a traditional Sutherland
'longhouse' or 'blackhouse', the foundations of which can still be seen to the side of the
current structure, comprising the kitchen and larders. This longhouse, of two rooms
with a connecting space to link them, was built – probably over an existing dwelling –
around the early eighteenth century and was established as a place of shelter for those
passing through the 'corridor', as it was known in the time of the great sheep droves of
the eighteenth and early nineteenth centuries, that commences inland from the north-
west of Brora and provides a route through the great hills of Mhorvaig and Luath all the
way to the markets of Lairg on the west (see relevant maps in preceding Appendices).

The site is on an elevated position at the northern end of the strath known as
Blackwater, run through as it is with one of the tributaries of the river bearing that
same name, yet well sheltered by Ben Mhorvaig at its back and Ben Luath beside it. It
is some two-thirds of a mile from the river Blackwater 'Beag' and is south-facing, well
drained, on soil that comprises Torridonian sandstone with peat depositories and of
rich mineral store. Current excavation of the site reveals deposits of granite boulders
and bone, suggesting the area was inhabited as far back as the early thirteenth century –
and though there is no evidence of similar foundations in the area, this early show of in-
habitation suggests that the site may have been one of many dwelling areas in the region.

Survey maps today mark both the 'Beag' water and the House itself, corresponding
with surviving drawings made by the first John Sutherland (1736–1793), who is recorded in 'The Big Music' as having established the House as a place where music might
be heard, and show a similar configuration of dwelling place to water, though there
are irregularities present in his representation that are clarified in the later project.
Further details pertaining to the House and its history and location can be found
in the relevant sections under List of Additional Materials at the back of this book.

ii

Construction

The current construction of The Grey House is of a substantial three-storey building of granite and lead, the east side of which has been built over the original 'Grey

Longhouse', as previously stated, and is itself an extension of what is known as 'The Old House', that is the building that was erected by John 'Elder' Roderick Callum Sutherland (1800–1871) and written of in the same Taorluath movement as above. Details of floor plans can be found, as above, in the List of Additional Materials.

Appendix 5: The Grey House – domestic history

i

How life was lived

'The Big Music' throughout contains details of the history and day-to-day life of the House from the eighteenth century onwards, see in particular 'doubling on fourth variation' and similar embellishments, Crunluath movement.

ii

The role of women

The women who married into the Sutherland family have always been known – in stories of one generation passed down to the next, or as shown in letters and journals that survive – as individuals of significant skill, intelligence and foresight. The wife of the first John Roderick MacKay Sutherland recorded in 'The Big Music' was one Elizabeth Mary MacKay, who is acknowledged in the local ballad 'The Kind Hills' by name, and noted for her beauty and thoughtfulness, and for her and her husband's hospitality in the third verse beginning:

> Elizabeth Mary said to me,
> Will you not stop for this while?
> My husband welcomes you
> to his hearth and his home
> – as do I . . .

And later:

> and the table of the House was spread then
> with a cloth as white and fine,
> and music played, music played . . .
> And she did not mind.

Her granddaughter-in-law was Anna Alexandra of Tongue (b.1807, wife of John 'Elder' Roderick Callum, 1800–1871), who kept a journal and was an enthusiastic gardener, extending the original plot of the old house and planting crab apple and plum trees in the sheltered lee of the small hill that rises from the end of the paddock at the back of the House. These fruit trees (her journal shows she took the seedlings from her native village of Tongue, a district known for its gentle climate and agricultural variety) are still in place today, growing alongside subsequent trees that were taken from them, from the main back garden of The Grey House – an area of beauty and practicality, both, established by that resourceful woman.

Her daughter-in-law, in turn, one Elizabeth Jean (b.1835, wife of John Callum MacKay, 1835–1911), established further planting to the south side of the House and was renowned for her skills in the kitchen – all her recipes remain and some are in use today by Margaret MacKay, who cooks in her kitchen. She was also a great seamstress and planned and was involved in the sewing of many dinner cloths and tray tables that are still in use – fine, fine Victorian counted threadwork and embroidery on show in the archive and still in good condition.

So, though the names of the women disappear into Sutherland, still evidence of their lives and work are present and vivid through the life of the House. In the kitchen, in the drawing room, in the Music Room – we see evidence of their thoughts and intelligence, kept in records of papers and domestic accounts. Elizabeth Clare, John Sutherland's mother, established, as has been noted in 'The Big Music', a Schoolroom at the top of the House where she educated, to a certain age, not only her own son but also those children of local farmers and workers.

The line of these women was cut, one may say, when the John Sutherland of 'The Big Music' became married to a woman who would have no intention of visiting The Grey House, much less live there – but was sewn up again when Margaret MacKay of Caithness was employed by Elizabeth Sutherland as housekeeper in 1964.

iii

The House as local primary school – including record of pupils

In 1928 the attic space under the eaves of the north end of The Grey House was converted into a single room that became known as the Schoolroom – and it was here that Elizabeth Sutherland educated her son and, thereafter, those children of the nearby lands and villages whose parents would release them for morning lessons.

The room was established as a formal teaching and educational space (though two existing photographs show that lessons were also highly creative) with a blackboard and desk (later desks) at one end and a small library and a play area at the other, where there were toys and games and also a large table that was set out for painting and glue-collage activities. A bright mural depicting the alphabet and illustrated with animals was pinned up along the long far side of the room and Elizabeth's own desk was placed at the north window, an Edwardian armchair beside it to make the most of the light, where she sat to read to her son and later the village children, or conducted lessons on a more informal basis.

This 'Schoolroom' has been written about in the local *Brora Journal* of the time – as an example of forward-thinking and enlightened educational principles that would have real effect in the community. As above, and as we read about in the Crunluath movement of 'The Big Music' and in embellishment/2b, in particular, at a period in Sutherland history when primary schools were few, the Schoolroom served a particular and necessary local function. Were it not for Elizabeth Sutherland taking in the local children of the area for lessons, it is unlikely, in many instances, they would have been educated at all – for at this time small farmers and crofters could ill afford to lose their children by sending them far away to one of the state primaries in Dornoch or Golspie, where they must board. As it was, a local farm lorry could bring them to the House in the morning, along with the deliveries, and return them to their farms later in the day.

This arrangement was started in 1934 when Elizabeth's own son, John, was sent away to Inverness to school and she found she wanted to continue those lessons she had started with him. It terminated in 1950 when the Local Schools Act demanded that all children of even the most remote Highland regions attend a regulated state primary school until the age of twelve, after which they must attend a regional high school.

The record of children who attended the Schoolroom through the above period is, then, as follows:

1934–35: John Ross; Iain Sinclair

1935–36: as above

1936–37: as above; also Helen Ross

1937–38: as above

1938–39: as above

1939–40: Iain Sinclair; Helen Ross; John Sinclair

1940–41: as above; also Jean McCaddie

1941–42: John Sinclair; Jean McCaddie'; Catriona McKay; Hector Gunn; Ishbel Sutherland

1942–43: as above; also Donald McCaddie

1943–45: as above, minus Ishbel Sutherland, but also Neil McIndoe; Jean Gunn

1945–46: as above, plus Iain Sutherland

1946–47: as above, minus Catriona McKay; Hector Gunn

1947–48: as above, plus Jamie Robb; Amelia MacKay; Katherine Sutherland

1948–49: as above, minus Donald McCaddie

1949–50: as above

iv

The origins of land use

The original longhouse that was The Grey House in the early eighteenth century was, as we have already seen, a simple dwelling built close to the land so as to escape the worst of the weather and offer, in its environs, shelter to animals and gardens as well as its inhabitants. It was made with locally farmed materials such as stone, turf, thatch of reeds, oats, barley or marram grass – usually on the worst arable land.

This was the case of the original 'Grey Longhouse', given up for tenure by the Sutherland Estates, and the land subsequently bought freehold by John 'Elder' Sutherland (1800–1871) – in both instances the land upon which the house stood (some 27 acres) regarded by the estate to be of little or no value. Thus, while its size and holdings remained modest in the period from the early eighteenth century to the mid-nineteenth century, nevertheless by acquiring the property as they did, independently, the Sutherland family were able to maintain autonomous control over their property and, as the century evolved, were able to confirm substantial land-holdings that comprised fishing, stalking and later forestry rights.

In this way, because of its locality and particular history, 'The Grey House, from its earliest incarnation as 'Grey Longhouse', was operating as though an independent concern – outwith the usual customs and fealties that accompanied the responsibilities of the independent farmer or landowner (see also Appendix 3/ii). Before the introduction of crofting at the beginning of the nineteenth century, most 'farms' on the Highland estates were run by tacksmen who paid a rent to the clan chief. On each of these there would be a small settlement whose inhabitants would pay their rents to the tacksman. No such system operated for the tenants of the 'Grey Longhouse' – who, from the beginning, sought value from the land themselves, not through renting it out but by careful management of their holdings and the extension of them in creating what became known as the 'corridor' – as detailed in the Taorluath section of 'The Big Music' and earlier Appendices. Thus the Sutherlands were able to increase their agricultural activities and prosper – while paying a modest fee to the estate – and when local crofting was formally introduced to the area, The Grey House was already established as a significant property on those lands between the hills of Mhorvaig and Luath which, even then, were still being regarded by the big estates as inhospitable, worthless ground.

So did the Sutherland family of that region escape the pressures and ignominies of the Sutherland Clearances that were elsewhere in the region stripping crofts and subsistence communities from the face of the earth. By contrast, as we see throughout the second and third movements of 'The Big Music', in the variations sections of the tune and subsequent paragraphs and doublings, the holdings of The Grey

House only became more established as time went on – with, as noted already, various fishing and stalking rights added to the original sheep-farming interests, as well as extensive developments in forestry and agriculture.

To the date of being written about, the area of grounds and land surrounding The Grey House amount to some 400 acres.

Appendix 6: The Grey House and the Sutherland family

i

History

The Vikings called the mainland south of Caithness 'Suth-r-land', or southern land, and occupied the area as far as a King David I granted a Flemish family Freskin land further south in Moray around 1130. As the power of the Vikings waned, that family acquired land further north in Sutherland and by 1235 the first Earl of Sutherland was appointed by King Alexander II. The family interests were then split – with those in Moray taking the name Murray and those further north taking the name Sutherland.

Kenneth, the 4th Earl, was killed at the Battle of Halidon Hill in 1333 fighting the English army led by Edward III. The 5th Earl was married to the daughter of Robert the Bruce and at one stage their son was heir to the throne but died of the plague. The 6th Earl built the original Dunrobin Castle. In 1651 a contingent of the clan fought with King Charles II when he was defeated at the Battle of Worcester.

There was frequent strife with the Gordon family to the south and at one stage the Gordons usurped the Sutherland earldom. In the eighteenth century the dispute over succession was heard in the House of Lords and the Countess of Sutherland was confirmed in the title in her own right. She married the Marquis of Stafford, who was created 1st Duke of Sutherland in 1833. The Duke and Duchess were responsible for the 'improvements' to the estates which resulted in the notorious Clearances and depopulation.

That period in Sutherland history resulted in many with that name being dispersed but the name is still the seventh most common in the northern Highlands and fifty-fourth in the whole of Scotland. The Sutherland family of The Grey House have been established in that part of the county that occupies the land between the hill range of Mhorvaig and Luath for many generations, however, and have not been dispersed – though most recently John MacKay Sutherland moved to London for some years. In this, he was going against the pattern of settlement laid down by his forebears who had, in unbroken succession, inhabited that particular area of the county since the early eighteenth century and before. His son, Callum Sutherland, at the time of writing, may be in the process of returning to the House to take up the place there left by his father.

The Sutherland motto is 'Sans peur' – 'Without fear'.

ii

Genealogy

The family records kept in archive detail those sons of the Sutherland family who inherited both the holdings and musical tradition of the House that had been established as early as the mid-eighteenth century, though no doubt before that date. These include a more detailed family tree and an additional 'Tree of Women', an intricate and detailed drawing created by Elizabeth Clare Sutherland in the second part of the twentieth century. In addition, at the beginning of and in the Crunluath movement of 'The Big Music', in the paper 'gracenotes/piobaireachd, its genealogy', there is presented a table of pipers at The Grey House that spans seven generations. In that chart one sees that eldest sons were traditionally named John, though in some cases, following a death, a younger son inherited.

iii

Births, deaths, marriages

For a full family tree, showing the pattern of hereditary pipers at The Grey House and the professions and status of other members of the Sutherland family, also details of marriages, illnesses and deaths – see full family records kept on file at the University of Dundee archive.

iv

Family names

As is clear from family records, there are certain names that reappear throughout the history of the Sutherland family of The Grey House: first-born sons, for the main part, take the name John, or John MacKay, with second-born sons and daughters taking the names Roderick, Callum, David, Donald, George, and Alexandra, Wilhemina, Elizabeth.

These names in turn have various 'pet' names, or alternatives, e.g. Wilhemina was always known as Bunty, the third Elizabeth was Bette, and so on. In 'The Big Music' John was called Johnnie by his mother (never his father), and, as is seen, refers to himself in later years by that name – though it is uncertain whether or not he was ever known by that name elsewhere, away from home. Certainly his estranged wife, Sarah, never called him Johnnie, nor did Margaret.

Callum, John MacKay's son, was named for his grandfather, John's father, who, though he was christened Roderick and became John after the death of his elder brother, and took Callum as his second name, was nevertheless known by John's mother as Callum – so John may have had sentimental reasons for selecting that name, rather than that it was carried by himself and his father. All through the history of the Sutherland family there is a tendency to name in this way, or to 'mark' certain family members by characteristics. Thus, the John Roderick MacKay who first established the 'Grey Longhouse' as a stop-over place for the Lairg sheep run was 'First John' and his grandson, who went himself to visit the factor of the Sutherland Estates to arrange for the leasing (and subsequent sale) of that property to himself (this, in the Taorluath section of 'The Big Music'), was always known as John 'Elder', and his son 'Old John' – although the prefix 'Old' is a local term that applies to the patriarch of any family where it is likely that a son holds the same name. John MacKay was never named this way, with the description attached. Perhaps that was because he spent the main part of his adult life in Edinburgh and London. Perhaps it was because, in that way, he had never fully belonged to The Grey House as his father and the generations before had belonged. Or perhaps, because his son was nowhere near and he barely saw him at all, there was no reason to mark him as separate from his child. They were separate enough already.

v

Family records of music kept, compositions

From as far back as the time of the 'Grey Longhouse' there have been kept records of music played and compositions attempted by various members of the Sutherland family.

In the beginning, before the easy circulation of printed manuscript, records consist of basic notes set down in a sort of chapbook that was kept in the original 'Grey Longhouse' and denotes tunes played and on what date, and some remarks. For example: the note 'I had a kiss of the King's hand' is followed by the note 'tunings, the dampe has found the bag' and 'J. played'. These are in shorthand, and hard to read – scanned versions of some of the pages are available, along with other original notes of this sort, in archive and are listed in the List of Additional Materials at the back of this book.

In addition to these papers are certain documents, letters etc. describing sections of music in canntaireachd, as may have been in custom at the time. For example, J. F. Campbell of Islay signs, 'I have often seen my nurse, John Piper, reading and practicing music from an old paper manuscript, and silently fingering tunes' (see Bibliography: *Canntaireachd: Articulate Music*, Archibald Sinclair, 1880), and certainly we have some remnants of what must have been once a comprehensive musical record kept at The Grey House that describe this practice, though the fragments left are badly damaged.

By the late nineteenth century, when the economic interests of The Grey House were prospering, there was money to purchase copies of the now-famous Angus MacKay manuscripts, all transcribed by him from the canntaireachd, which were used and played from right up to the time of John MacKay's practice – though now these have been placed in archive. In addition there are copies of the Kilberry manuscripts and reproductions of the so-called Nether Lorn and Binneas A Boreraig manuscripts and the William Ross collection. In the twentieth century the library was extended with the introduction of the Piobaireachd Society's volumes, these published regularly from 1902 until the present day, along with various pamphlets, leaflets and books containing more recent piobaireachd by John MacDougall Gillies and John MacDonald, as well as Donald MacLeod and John Callum Sutherland but excluding his last work 'Lament for Himself', which was left incomplete but is nevertheless 'finished' through the pages of this book, and is represented in extant manuscript form in Appendix 10A.

So then we understand that although, initially, the Sutherland family of pipers kept their own music for play within their own circle, at family gatherings and events, by the time of John 'Elder' Sutherland some of these compositions were notated and circulated for play by other pipers in the region, and as time went on, this practice formed the basis of the original 'Grey House School of Piping' as detailed in various sections of 'The Big Music'. Papers and records of this and the musical activities of subsequent lessons and parties form a significant portion of filed papers and booklets kept in what has always been known as the Music Room in The Grey House – these include marches, strathspeys and reels and some salutes. In addition, the works of John MacKay are kept in labelled files – Ceol Mor 1–27, 1957–79 (referred to in the Taorluath movement) – including the well-known tunes 'The Hills Always Come Back the Same', 'Stag's Leap' and 'Elegy of the Lost Son', all of which are also kept as recordings and similarly listed by number and date.

Appendix 7: The Grey House and John MacKay Sutherland – family history; business

The Taorluath movement of 'The Big Music' details the history of John MacKay Sutherland, in terms of his business activities and musical endeavours, in relation to his taking leave of and then returning to The Grey House.

In addition, the third paper of the Crunluath movement, continued, contains a time line giving details of his family life – his position in his father's family as only son bearing his father's name, and his role as husband, father – as well as indications of his education, business and musical endeavours.

The business interests contain as follows: investments in Baillie Ross; Ross Holdings; MacKay Investments; Sutherland Holdings. Also Grey House estates; additional fishing, sporting holdings; forestry; real estate, London, Edinburgh.

Appendix 8: The Grey House and the people who live there

In many respects, this section of the Appendix should sit outside the formal reference section of 'The Big Music' but is sited here for the reader's convenience, as it may be viewed that the following notes pertain more to the history and knowledge of The Grey House than to an understanding of the people who lived there permanently from the years 1964 (Margaret and Helen) and 1968 (Iain) and who continue to inhabit the House and keep watch over it, are doing so now, at the moment while you are reading this.

So is the information included here to give insight as to how the House was managed and run, from those years when old John and Elizabeth were still alive. In addition, these notes may give greater understanding of the Taorluath and Crunluath movements of 'The Big Music' – those sections pertaining to Margaret MacKay in particular.

i

Personal archive

Materials and transcripts
From the time of her (permanent) arrival at The Grey House, Margaret MacKay kept a domestic journal recording details of the kitchen and laundry, gardens and domestic upkeep – including an inventory of linens, soft furnishings and various pieces of furniture and effects, with a running commentary on the state of their repair and condition.

This detailed logbook was not kept when she first came to the House as a young girl, when she worked for one summer only as a domestic assistant, but later, when her position was made permanent, and there is evidence that Margaret updated it regularly – sometimes on a daily basis.

In these account books we can gather a pattern of daily life as is lived: the fruits and vegetables that are in season, when and how these are bottled and preserved; the seeds that are sown for flower beds and glasshouse blooms; the condition of textiles and embroideries, curtains and cushions etc. – all of which were rotated to be cleaned and mended, what rooms they were used in and indeed, how the use of these rooms changed over the years. We know, for example, how John MacKay's bedroom was moved from the first floor to the little room downstairs, with details of how this move was arranged, as well as other alterations (painting, carpentry and so on) that are not provided in the body of the text of 'The Big Music'. These records may be of interest to the student of domestic history as Margaret's notes are fulsome and often refer to her reading from earlier household diaries kept from Elizabeth Sutherland's time and before. Significantly, there is no recording in the logbook about the rearrangement of the Schoolroom at the top of the House to accommodate a double bed. In some way, it might be as though such an arrangement had never been.

In addition to journals kept, there are various transcripts of conversations, interviews, that took place between Margaret and her daughter Helen that are clearly intended to form a personal historical account – a way of placing certain facts within an objective, feminist context so as to understand more about how certain women, like Margaret MacKay, defined it seems almost entirely by their domestic capability, have a place within, say, gender studies or an understanding of the female role in literature. Though nothing formal has come of these recordings as yet, in terms of Helen MacKay editing and collecting them into some kind of history or novel or poem (save those sections used at various points of 'The Big Music' to provide a sort of 'dithis' or variation to the theme), they nevertheless provide an illuminating account of how a woman's domestic life may be described – how a mother may describe herself to a daughter, as a parent to a child; how the so-called 'invisibility' of motherhood may be made 'visible' – and someday could well form the basis of a moving and involving polemic regarding the subject of maternity and its identity and ethics. For more information on this area of study, see Lisa Baraitser and Sigal Spigel, MaMSIE (Mapping Maternal Subjectivities, Identities, Ethics), University of London. For this reason, all tapes have been labelled and numbered, with a view to providing for future research interests and general study. Included in all accounts, running through them as an ongoing theme, is the background of The Grey House and the way it provides a context – emotional as well as economic, practical and historical – for a particular way of life that is defined by living in part of the world that is far off and remote, that sees few visitors and much that is familiar, long winters and a short, sharp spring. This context may find other useful metaphors in the practice of, say, the visual and literary arts, social criticism and essay, philosophy, ethical thinking.

ii

Helen's notes and reading

Helen MacKay began keeping notes of her reading and study from as early as her time as a student at the Farr Academy, when she was a teenager, to the present day. The list is randomly kept – according to the order in which she read certain books – with a star marked alongside those titles that are of particular interest to her (and that we see written about in more detail in various school and university essays, some of which recur in her reading and research for her PhD degree and are available in archive and referred to in various papers of 'The Big Music', 'The people at the House and what they thought of him' etc.).

The pattern we see emerging from these lists is an interest in literary modernism, with a particular emphasis on the fiction of Katherine Mansfield and Virginia Woolf that is shown from early on and is developed over the years to accommodate feminist theoretical writing around both those artists and their milieu – i.e. Eliot, Pound, Joyce. Helen's interest, it is clear, lies less with placing the two artists within that other context, or finding a way of locating them either within the American or European tradition (something those men in the list above were themselves endlessly interested in defining), than with exploring the wild differences and yet similarities between two markedly distinctive yet connected writers who were outsiders, both, as women, as individuals, as practitioners.

Note: The poem to which Helen is referring in the Crunluath movement of 'The Big Music' is taken from Robert Frost and represents an aspect of her general interest in American literature that began in her adolescence and continued through to her early thirties. Other titles from this period can be seen collected as part of the same reading list referred to above.

Appendix 9: The Grey House – musical history

i

General history of music in the Highland region

The oldest forms of music in Scotland are thought by some to be Gaelic singing and harp or clarsach playing, although there is much discussion as to there being a pipe that closely resembles the Highland bagpipe as we know it introduced at a similarly early period of Scotland's history.

Certainly Scotland is today internationally recognised for its traditional music, which has remained vibrant throughout the twentieth century when many traditional

forms worldwide have lost popularity. In spite of emigration and a well-developed
connection to music imported from the rest of Europe and the United States,
Highland music in particular has kept many of its traditional aspects, and though
the musical history of the region has always been somewhat purist in orientation,
nevertheless there are certain influences of song, ballad and air that we hear played
out in some bagpipe tunes. Much has been written on the subject of the two musical
disciplines (see Bibliography/Music: Highland) – highlighting certain connections
between the two such as use of intonation, phrasing and the use of notation – where
we see how many piping ornaments mimic the Gaelic consonants of the songs.

ii
Music composed at The Grey House

The earliest tunes played at the site of what is now The Grey House will never be
fully registered, as these pieces, like so many compositions for the pipes over the
years, were passed down by canntaireachd from generation to generation, with subtle
alterations along the way, until they came to rest in the manuscript versions held in
the so-called 'Music Room'.

The tunes in particular that were originated at the first longhouse, and composed,
according to family history and local legend, by the first John Roderick MacKay
(1736–1793) are as follows:

A Small Purple Flower
Callum's Leaving
Lament for Mary, My Wife
The Far Hills

These were adapted by John Callum MacKay (1835–1911) and taught in the Study,
or Music Room, as part of the 'curriculum' for the first and subsequent 'Winter
Classes' conducted at the House in the last part of the nineteenth century and onwards, classes that were then incorporated into the more formal 'Winter School of
Piping' at The Grey House.

When manuscript paper was introduced and utilised, from around the mid-
nineteenth century onwards, following the great publication by Angus MacKay of *A
Collection of Ancient Piobaireachd* and then later the Kilberry manuscripts (see Appendix
6/v and Bibliography), all compositions could be recorded and filed. Some of these
in original form and photocopies of all extant MSS are available in archive, and are
also in the List of Additional Materials at the back of this book.

The more well-known piobaireachd of The Grey House from around this time
are:

The Long Winter
Lament for Roderick John
Farewell to the Hills

There are also a number of lesser-known airs, songs and reels composed and recorded in manuscript form.

By the time of the early 1950s, the time of the father of John MacKay Sutherland of this book, there were some early recordings made of him playing certain tunes, and many of his compositions were collated into an album published later by the Piobaireachd Society. As we read in 'The Big Music', certain marches and music for gatherings were also composed for his regiment that served in France and these folios are kept in the Library of the Imperial War Museum in London and at the Military Museum for the Highlands in Fort Augustus – all appearing under strictly numerical headings: March/1, March/2 etc.; The Gathering at Auvergne/1, and so on.

John MacKay himself, as we know from the Taorluath section of 'The Big Music', kept recordings of all his compositions on cassette – latterly, these have been transferred over to CD and were collected in the sideboard in the Music Room, beneath the whisky decanter to which Callum returned over and over on the night of his father's death.

At the time of writing, though Callum Sutherland has taken up his father's pipes, it is unknown as to whether he will compose music himself to add to the library established by his father and forebears.

iii

The Winter School

Details of the history and development of music within the Sutherland family are found all through the four movements of 'The Big Music', with certain papers, embellishments and variations given over to an exact description of classes and lessons and musical evenings that were held from the period of the mid-eighteenth century to the present day. Further details can be found in various issues of *The New Piping Times* and related magazines of the period, mid-twentieth century onwards, as well as in archive.

An interview with Callum MacKay Sutherland and a transcript of the interview with a past pupil of one of the Winter School classes may be of particular interest, the latter reproduced within the Crunluath movement of 'The Big Music'.

Appendix 10: Introduction to the piobaireachd 'Lament for Himself'

i

For a general historical introduction to piobaireachd and its musical form, see Appendices 12 and 13; also Bibliography/Music: Piobaireachd/primary and/secondary – in particular MacKay, *A Collection of Ancient Piobaireachd*; Campbell, *The Kilberry Book of Ceol Mor*; MacNeill, *Piobaireachd*.

What will be seen, the further one goes into a study of the music's origins and definition, is that the form, though reflexive in terms of its structure (see the Crunluath and Crunluath A Mach movements in particular, that are composed to show the dexterity and skills of the piper), is never so in subject. Piobaireachd has a public, social function: it is always either a salute, or a call to a gathering, or a lament, and always it is written and played for something or someone beyond the piper's playing. The Lament composed by John Callum Sutherland, therefore, that appears in its opening 'remarks'* on the first pages of 'The Big Music', is unique in that this is a Lament written for the composer himself. So the subject of the theme is the composer of it, and the subsequent opening bars that Sutherland managed to complete in the Urlar, and that can be seen in Appendix 10A/ii and in full in the Endpapers at the back of this book, indicate that there are passages in the music suggesting not only the composer's own frailty and impending death, but other themes connected with his life that would have been developed further had he been able to complete the tune.** These musical ideas include the use of a singular 'breathing' theme that is outlined in the first few bars, where the very sound of the music indicates a man who may be inhaling and exhaling his last breaths upon this earth, and then the use of 'dithis' singling and doubling upon this theme (see Glossary), a singling and doubling of the notes to indicate the presence of the composer's father and son as being part of those last moments of life.

---

* These first opening bars of the music's theme indicate the opening 'remarks' of the music laid out at the beginning of the Urlar of 'The Big Music' and also in the Taorluath section where John MacKay lies in his bed through the last hours of his life. The so-called 'breathing' sequence is clearly indicated in the repetition of these four bars.

** NB: For those who would like to hear the full version of 'Lament for Himself', it is possible to download it from a website that is being created for 'The Big Music'.

ii

Another unusual feature of Sutherland's composition is the insertion within it of a
sequence of notes at the beginning of the second line that carry the suggestion of
a theme within a theme – in this case a Lullaby, or, rather, an idea for a Lullaby*
in the repetition of the interval: 'F' to 'G', 'E' to 'A', 'F' to 'G', 'E' to 'E'. For a more
detailed account of the composition of the Urlar movement, see Appendices 11 and
12: 'General structure of the piobaireachd' and 'The form of a piobaireachd', as well
as the notes on the Urlar contained in section iv of this Appendix. This use of an
inserted theme or themes within the overall musical idea of a piece is not unlike
Wagner's use of leitmotif, in compositional terms (see Bibliography/Music: General, in particular Gilkes, *Wagner and his Leitmotifs* and Seoras, *Use of Recurring Musical
Sequencing in Nineteenth Century Composition*; also Glossary: leitmotif; gesundkunstwerk;
Crunluath A Mach), and shows how repeated use of a few notes can enhance the
overall sound of the whole, giving added depth and meaning – in this case a delicate,
haunting Lullaby that is indicated by the few notes below:

iii

As seen in Appendices 12 and 13, it is speculated that some piobaireachd music has
its basis in certain Highland songs and airs that may date back to the fifteenth
century or earlier. It is perhaps the knowledge of this tradition that worked upon
John Sutherland in his thinking about his own final composition; the Lullaby that
he had in mind being one, perhaps, that was already known to him. No records of
such a song were found amongst his papers; but his daughter, Helen MacKay, surely
discovered certain notes and writings up at the Little Hut that may have assisted her
in putting together the words of the Lullaby that appear first on p. 21 of 'The Big
Music'. Certainly the theme of babies lost or without their mothers was a common
enough one in folk song (see Bibliography/Music: Highland – Stephens, *History of
Highland Songs and Airs*, and the chapters 'Metaphor in Folk Song' and 'The Image of
the Changeling and Missing Child in Scottish Folklore and Songs') and would have

---

* The same section of music can be scanned exactly to the words for the Lullaby for
Katherine Anna that appear in the Urlar movement of 'The Big Music'.

suggested itself easily enough as a poetic idea to a mother who had herself experienced the loss, albeit temporarily, of a baby.

A scanned version of the original manuscript of the lullaby appears in the List of Additional Materials, manuscripts, in part on pp. 20–1 and 25 of the Urlar of 'The Big Music', and in full here:

(first verse)
In the small room, a basket waits,
A basket empty for no baby is there.
The mother is gone, left the room for a moment
– and in that moment he's mounted the stair.

(chorus)
You took her away,
Young Katherine Anna,
Carried her off, tall Helen's child.
You took her away, a baby sleeping
In your old arms, took her into the wild.

(second verse)
An old man taken the baby away,
He's snatched her up in his arms for to see
Her life in his, to stay his dying
but the child's not his, her mother is me.

(chorus)
You took her away,
Young Katherine Anna,
Carried her off, tall Helen's child.
You took her away, a baby sleeping
In your old arms, took her into the wild.

iv

The Urlar of John Sutherland's composition in 'The Big Music' also takes the word literally – 'urlar' meaning 'ground', to suggest the ground notes of the music, the laying out of an initial theme – but used here figuratively, to suggest the ground, the hills and landscape of his birthplace, as part of the 'colouring' or ordering of the music (see Bibliography/Music: General – Graham, *The Literal Musical*). Certain notes appear in sequence to describe this ground, as indicated by entries in the journal and in various papers gathered together by Helen MacKay that relate to this composition (see the Crunluath A Mach section in 'The Big Music'). The idea of certain notes in the bagpipe scale having certain meanings is not new, as the chart in the Last Appendix shows. That notation might match a particular place or person, so as to lend texture and a sense of narrative to the composition, is, however, not one hitherto explored by classical Highland music scholars and could provide a rich seam of understanding of certain piobaireachd sequences were it to be uncovered more fully – starting perhaps with a parsing of Sutherland's own Urlar to show, for example, certain notes for different people who feature in 'The Big Music'; also colours or objects – grass, hills, a particular burn, the fall of light in the east coast, its sea etc. See the Index of 'The Big Music' for an indication of how these themes and notes might play out in the composition and form certain patterns that may marry.

One could then go through the recurring images in the Urlar and compare these to the recurrence of certain notes as they appear in the manuscript of the music of 'Lament for Himself' (that is, as much of this as was written) that is reproduced at the end of this book. See, too, John MacKay's own paper 'Innovations to the Piobaireachd', referred to in footnotes and in the List of Additional Materials at the end of this book, and consider his ideas in the light of the completed text of that narrative.

Appendix 10A: The piobaireachd 'Lament for Himself'

i

In the List of Additional Materials we see the original manuscript that was discovered by Helen MacKay and Callum Sutherland following the death of John Sutherland at The Grey House. The manuscript, that appears here in full, in fact only represents a fragment of what was intended to be completed as a 'modest tune' – John Sutherland's phrase, as seen below in an excerpt from his notes about the composition. Nevertheless, it indicates the themes of mortality and rebirth that were to become significantly developed in the papers that comprise 'The Big Music': see especially the recurring Lullaby (as described in Appendix 10/ii above) and the reference to 'last breath taken' in the sequence of notes in the opening bars of music. Subsequent developments in the music – including the suggestion of the Leumluath idea within the second movement: a leaping off; a sense of risk – are contained within this first Urlar; see, for example, the 'drop' to a Low 'G' indicating horror and devastation (in the second bar of the second line) and the 'E' to 'A' interval that appears in the third line only that comes to fully represent the part Margaret plays in John Sutherland's life and music, and will be fully marked in the Crunluath movement of 'The Big Music' in particular. The use of singling and doubling in the extant MS shows how the themes of generation play out in the composition: the first representing his father, the great Modernist piper Roderick John Callum, from whom, during his life, John MacKay was estranged, and the second for his son, Callum MacKay, also barely known to the composer by the time of writing but whose notes are indicated in the way the composition's doubling of the theme allows him a place in the music after all. Both these themes are also indicated in the Urlar and Taorluath movements of 'The Big Music'.

ii

The excerpt from John Sutherland's notes as mentioned above:

Note: To hear how this 'modest tune' may have been developed into the full piobaireachd 'Lament for Himself', it is possible to download the finished composition, which was completed for the project of this book by an anonymous piper and composer, from a website that is being created for 'The Big Music'.

Appendix 10B: The piobaireachd 'Lament for Himself' and the Little Hut

As is described in the Urlar and following movements of 'The Big Music', most of John MacKay's creative thinking and planning took place not in the Music Room of The Grey House, as was traditional, but in a little bothy or hut he had built himself, secretly, in the hills between Mhorvaig and Luath.

This place, 'the Little Hut' as it is called throughout 'The Big Music' or 'TLH' as John Sutherland himself refers to it in his notes, became more and more a refuge for him as the years went on, a place of great privacy where it seemed the choices he had made for himself in his life – to do with being isolated and not allowing himself to be open or free with anyone, even the woman with whom he was most intimate throughout his life and who he might have allowed himself to love – played out as thoughts, ideas for music and themes in the remote and basic little hut in the hills, with its divan, its window, its desk.

The Crunluath A Mach section of 'The Big Music' contains material that was taken from the Little Hut and used for the completion of this book. It indicates certain notes, fragments of manuscript with markings and small journal extracts that may help the general reader come to know more about how the piobaireachd 'Lament for Himself' came about; how sections of it were created in manuscript or as notes for composition well before John Sutherland came to write down his Urlar in full or 'The Big Music' itself was gathered into a unifying whole. Hence, we see certain themes and ideas shown in small remarks and sections of music that may not have added up to a clear musical idea to the composer at the time, but that have a certain meaning within this book.

The idea of a secret, of great privacy being at the heart of the creative act, is of course an idea as old as poetry and time. That Helen and Callum found the Little Hut when they were no more than children and went there, that the same private place contains the scattered beginnings of every aspect of the entire story of 'The Big Music'; that everything Helen needed to start gathering her papers was already there . . . All this is as inevitable a conclusion to the elegy you have been reading as the hills themselves.

i

The following excerpt, appearing as scattered notes and taken from one of the journals found up at the Little Hut, may be of interest:

There must be a sense of 'carpe diem' about the whole – a snatching of life out of death's grip – but how? That snatching away? A sudden drop of notes to do it? Plan for this . . . ; Callum also must have a note, a small series perhaps, in the mid range, and quiet, so you might not notice the notes as a pattern at first . . . The quietest of doublings. The A Mach will be difficult – all pride, pride leading up to it . . . But somehow . . . Different. A different interpretation. As though the composition might be finished in another's hand, as though – . . . A different set of notes but they are the same.

And:

Callum's theme will only announce itself in the variations – I can't hear it in the Urlar at all. But the theme will come in all the same. It will be there in the Taorluath, from the outset, and quite clear – a branching off from the Urlar that way, you could say, in a way that seems new – but no. For the notes have already been sounded. In the repetition. That's the way to do it. So his theme might match the ambition of the repetition, yes. What I'll call the 'breathing' notes, that sound as a sequence in the first four bars . . . That repeat might also contain . . . My father. And my son.

More notes of this sort can be seen in the Crunluath A Mach movement, and are detailed in the List of Additional Materials section of 'The Big Music'.

Appendix 11: General structure of the piobaireachd

The following information is sourced from *Piobaireachd: Classical Music of the Highland Bagpipe* by Seumus MacNeill, acknowledged to be in the tradition of such writers about piobaireachd as Major General Thomason, the compiler of *Ceol Mor* in 1900, and, in the last century, the work of Mr Archibald Campbell of Kilberry. Mr Seumus MacNeill held the position of Joint Principal of the College of Piping between the years 1959 and 1974, and delivered a series of lectures in 1968 that are still talked about to this day and were most useful when gathering information for these Appendices. More details of this publication are available in the Bibliography, as are other related materials that may be of use for those wishing to further their understanding of this music's structure and content.

Like the concerto, with which it is compared, the form of the piobaireachd can be best described as a theme with variations. This is the one steady truth that can be set against it – while all other claims made about the music must be qualified and considered.

It is made up of three or more 'movements' – the Urlar, or ground, which is the laying out of the basic musical idea that will dominate the piece; the Taorluath (often attached to the Leumluath in meaning), which is a great development of that theme, a sort of branching out or leap (Leumluath translates, from the Gaelic, as 'Stag's Leap'); the Crunluath, or 'crown', which is an extravagant play of variations and embellishments upon the theme; followed by the Crunluath A Mach, in which the piper himself is describing his own virtuosity in his play – an embellishment upon embellishment, if you like, of the intricacies of the Crunluath – a fully flexible and reflexive aspect of the music on display; closing finally with the opening lines of the Urlar played again as a mark of final humility and simplicity after all that has preceded.

Within each of these movements are variations and embellishments – described in 'The Big Music' as separate but connected details of the story, and in musical detail in Appendix 12: 'The form of a piobaireachd'.

Composed especially for the music of the Highland bagpipe, it has been said of piobaireachd that the only other musical instrument that can come anywhere near its sound and quality is the human voice. This was most certainly a given in those years before 1803, before written notation was introduced, when all piobaireachd was passed down from the teacher to the pupil by singing the tune, note by note, in a method of transmission known as canntaireachd. This method today is still of much value, as singing can bring out the expression of the music in a way staff notation can only hint at.

For this reason, perhaps, it has not been the historical practice to make any great effort to write piobaireachd correctly. After all, if it is generally believed that one can only learn to play the music from one who has been properly trained to play it, who knows by heart and by memory every note of every tune that he may sing it to himself and others as well as play it on his pipes . . . Why then would the printed manuscript come to have much value from the start? One would always, in the first instance, want to hear the tune – not read – but as it sounds. In addition, collections of piobaireachd music are only intended to be of interest to pipers, since the music cannot be played satisfactorily on any other instrument. As Archibald Campbell noted (see Bibliography/Music: Piobaireachd/primary: *The Kilberry Book of Ceol Mor*), writing of staff notation applied to piobaireachd: 'It makes no pretense to be scientifically accurate, or even intelligible to the non-piper. Call it pipers' jargon and the writer will not complain.' Subsequent to his remarks, there have been perhaps a hundred tunes written without bar-lines, published as *Binneas A Boreraig* by Roderick Ross (see Bibliography), which shows how important it is that pipers are not restricted to the rigid bar-lines and time signatures of classical music when playing. It is, of course, a convenience in memorising a tune to have the phrases, or parts of the phrases, in bars, but when playing a tune, the best and most musical of pipers will bring out the phrasing and timing in their own 'time' – creating their own bar-breaks, so to speak, so as to best express the depths and mysteries of the music.

By tradition, all piobaireachd is played from memory – thus involving a considerable mental feat akin to the soloist of any classical instrument – considering especially that a tune may last for fifteen minutes or more, and is played without the prompts of an orchestra or conductor for that length of time. In order to push phrases into a suitable bar pattern, it has often been found necessary to write some notes as gracenotes and mark pauses wherever seems relevant. Occasionally a pause mark will land on a gracenote, and, as a gracenote is not supposed to have any duration anyway (it takes its time from the note following), this causes considerable confusion even among pipers.

It may well be, then, that the more incorrectly a piobaireachd is written, the better it is to be played – because the learner is forced to seek assistance from a piper who knows more than he does and who has been taught himself in the traditional manner.

The real reason, however, for not attempting to write piobaireachd accurately is that the effort to do so – when one gracenote alone can be worth entire bars of manuscript – would be tremendous, and even then the result would only be one man's interpretation of how the piece should be played. In addition, no piper really

believes that the great music can be learned without personal assistance from an
expert.

Appendix 12: The form of a piobaireachd

Piobaireachd, Ceol Mor or pibroch, as it is known in its Anglicised form, is a form
of high art, a musical genre associated primarily with the Scottish Highlands that
is characterised by extended compositions with a melodic theme and elaborate formal variations. It can only be performed on the great Highland bagpipe, with its
distinctive tenor and bass drones that sound at a particular interval so as to underlie
strangely and exhilaratingly the tune being played.

Traditionally, many pipers prefer the name Ceol Mor, which is Gaelic for the
'Great' or 'Big' music, to distinguish this complex extended art form from the more
common kinds of popular Scottish music such as dances, reels, marches and strathspeys, which are called Ceol Beag or 'Little Music'.

Here follows a general introduction to this form of music about which still
relatively little is known – from its enunciation to structure to history and known
sources of its tunes.

i

Etymology

The word piobaireachd is first found registered as written in Lowland Scots in 1719,
derived from the Gaelic word 'piobaireachd', which literally means 'piping' or 'act
of piping'.

There is some disagreement surrounding the terminology. The spelling variant
used by most dictionaries is pibroch but most who are involved with the music,
including the Piobaireachd Society, prefer the Scottish Gaelic spelling. Nonetheless,
the pronunciation of piobaireachd is usually rendered identically to pibroch (that
is, with a long i and a soft k sound for the ch, so: *pee-broch*) and in modern English-
speaking contexts both piobaireachd and pibroch are equated with Ceol Mor.

ii

Notation

Piobaireachd is properly expressed by minute and often subtle variations in note
duration and tempo. Traditionally, the music was taught using a system of unique
chanted vocables referred to as canntaireachd, an effective method of denoting the
various movements in piobaireachd music and assisting the learner in proper expres-

sion and memorisation of the tune. The predominant vocable system used today is the Nether Lorn canntaireachd sourced from the *Campbell Canntaireachd* manuscripts (1797 and 1814) and used in the subsequent Piobaireachd Society books. The Bibliography has further details of all these manuscripts and subsequent volumes.

Multiple written manuscripts of piobaireachd in staff notation have been published, including Angus MacKay's book *A Collection of Ancient Piobaireachd* (1838), Archibald Campbell's *The Kilberry Book of Ceol Mor* (1953), and the Piobaireachd Society Books, published in certain sequences from the turn of the twentieth century to the present day.

The staff notation in Angus MacKay's book and subsequent Piobaireachd Society-sanctioned publications is characterised by a simplification and standardisation of the ornamental and rhythmic complexities of many piobaireachd compositions when compared with earlier unpublished manuscript sources. A number of the earliest manuscripts, such as the *Campbell Canntaireachd* manuscripts that pre-date the standard edited published collections, have been made available by the Piobaireachd Society as a comparative resource.

Piobaireachd is difficult to transcribe accurately using traditional musical notation, and early attempts suffered from conventions which do not accurately convey tune expression. More contemporary piobaireachd notation has attempted to address these issues, and has produced notation much closer to true expression of the tunes.

Piobaireachd does not follow a strict metre but it does have a rhythmic flow or pulse; it does not follow a strict beat or tempo although it does have pacing. The written transcription of piobaireachd serves mainly as a rough guide for the piper. The expression of the rhythms and tempos of the piobaireachd tune are primarily acquired from an experienced teacher and applied through interpretive performance practice.

iii

Titles and subjects

The Gaelic titles of piobaireachd compositions have been categorised into four broad groupings. These are:

Functional – salutes, laments, marches and gatherings

Technical – referring to strictly musical characteristics of the pieces such as 'port' or 'glas', terms shared with wire-strung harpers

Textual – quotations from song lyrics, usually the opening words

Short names – diverse short names referring to places, people and events similar to those found in Scottish popular music of the period

Piobaireachd in the functional category were most commonly written for or have come to be associated with specific events, personages or situations:

Laments (cumha) are mourning tunes often written for a deceased person of note. Laments were commonly written as a result of families being displaced from their homeland, a practice that was very common after the Jacobite Rebellion of 1745.

Salutes (failte) are tunes that acknowledge a person, event or location. Salutes were often written upon the birth of children or after a visitation to a prominent figure such as a clan chief. Many salutes have been written to commemorate famous pipers.

Gatherings (port tionail) are tunes written specifically for a clan. These tunes were used to call a clan together by their chief. The tune structure is usually simple so that it could be recognised easily by clan members.

Rowing piobaireachd are more rhythmic tunes used to encourage rowers while crossing the sea.

The different categories of piobaireachd do not have consistent distinctive musical patterns that are characteristic of the category. The role of the piobaireachd may inform the performers' interpretative expression of rhythm and tempo.

Many piobaireachd tunes have intriguing names such as 'Too Long in This Condition', 'The Piper's Warning to His Master', 'Scarce of Fishing', 'The Unjust Incarceration' and 'The Big Spree', which suggest specific narrative events or possible lyric sources. There are accounts in 'The Big Music' of certain piobaireachd written by pipers of the Sutherland family that are of a personal nature or suggest a re-visiting of an idea or theme. One such example is, first, 'A Small White Flower', then 'A Small White Flower, Again'.

The oral transmission of the repertoire has led to diverse and divergent accounts of the names for tunes, and many tunes have a number of names. Mistranslation of Gaelic names with non-standard phonetic spelling adds to the confusion.

In some cases the name and subject matter of piobaireachd tunes appears to have been reassigned by nineteenth-century editors such as Angus MacKay, whose book *A Collection of Ancient Piobaireachd or Highland Pipe Music* (1838) included historically fanciful and romantic piobaireachd source stories by antiquarian James Logan. A number of piobaireachd collected by MacKay have very different titles than in earlier manuscript sources. Nevertheless, MacKay's translated English titles became the commonly accepted ones, sanctioned by subsequent Piobaireachd Society editors.

Roderick Cannon has compiled a dictionary of the Gaelic names of piobaireachd from early manuscripts and printed sources, detailing inconsistencies, difficulties in translation, variant names, accurate translations and verifiable historically documented attributions and dates in the few cases where this is possible.

iv

History

In the absence of concrete documentary evidence, the origins of piobaireachd have taken on something of a mythic status. The earliest commonly recognised figures in the history of the music are the MacCrimmon family of pipers, particularly Donald Mor MacCrimmon (*c.*1570–1640), who is reputed to have left a group of highly developed tunes, and Patrick Mor MacCrimmon (*c.*1595–1670), one of the hereditary pipers to the Chief of the MacLeods of Dunvegan on the Isle of Skye.

There is some controversy over the attribution of authorship of key piobaireachd tunes to the MacCrimmons by Walter Scott, Angus MacKay and others who published on the topic in the nineteenth century. The *Campbell Canntaireachd*, written in 1797, is a two-volume manuscript with chanted vocable and phonetic transcriptions of piobaireachd music that pre-dates the nineteenth-century attributions. It contains no references to the MacCrimmons and has different names for numerous tunes that were subsequently associated with them.

The piobaireachd 'Cha till mi tuill' in the *Campbell Canntaireachd* manuscript, which translates as 'I shall return no more', is related to a tune associated with victims of the Clearances emigrating to the New World. Walter Scott wrote new romantic verses to this tune in 1818 with the title 'Lament – Cha till suin tuille', which translates as 'We shall return no more', later republished as 'Mackrimmon's Lament. Air – Cha till mi tuille'.

In Angus MacKay's book *A Collection of Ancient Piobaireachd or Highland Pipe Music* (1838), the piobaireachd 'Cha till mi tuill' is subsequently published with the title 'MacCrummen will never return'.

v

Harp prehistory of piobaireachd

Most piobaireachds are commonly assumed to have been written during the sixteenth to eighteenth centuries. The entire repertoire comprises approximately 300 tunes. In many cases the composer is unknown, however piobaireachd continues to be composed up to the present day. Recent research suggests that the style of ornamentation in the music points to earlier origins in wire-strung Gaelic harp compositions, in particular the use of rapid descending arpeggios as gracenotes.

A piobaireachd that is considered to be one of the oldest in the repertoire appears in the *Campbell Canntaireachd* with the title 'Chumbh Craoibh Na Teidbh', which translates as 'Lament for the Tree of Strings', a possible poetic reference to the wire-strung harp. Another, more well-known, piobaireachd published by Angus MacKay with the

Gaelic title 'Cumhadh Craobh nan teud' is translated as 'Lament for the Harp Tree.' This piobaireachd appears in the *Campbell Canntaireachd* manuscripts as 'MacLeod's Lament.'

vi

Fiddle piobaireachd

Ceol Mor repertoire is likely to have transferred from the harp to the newly developed Italian violin in the late sixteenth century as fiddlers began to receive aristocratic patronage and supplement the role of the harpers.

A distinctive body of Ceol Mor known as fiddle piobaireachd developed in this period with melodic themes and formal variations that are similar to, but not necessarily derived from or imitative of, concurrent bagpipe piobaireachd, as the name 'fiddle piobaireachd' might suggest. The two forms are likely to have developed in parallel from a common source in earlier harp music and Gaelic song.

vii

Emergence of bagpipe piobaireachd

Aristocratic Scottish Gaelic Ceol Mor harp repertoire and practices are assumed to have begun to transfer across from the harp to the bagpipes in the sixteenth century. A North Uist tradition identifies the first MacCrimmon as a harper. The MacCrimmons asserted that they received their first training in a school in Ireland. Alexander Nicholson, in his book *History of Skye*, originally published in 1930, recounts a tradition that the MacCrimmons were 'skilful players of the harp, and may have been composers of its music, before they began to cultivate the other and more romantic instrument'.

There were a number of musicians across the period from the seventeenth to eighteenth centuries who were noted multi-instrumentalists and potentially formed a bridge from the harp to the fiddle and bagpipe repertoire. Ronald MacDonald of Morar (1662–1741), known in Gaelic as Raghnall MacAilein Oig, was an aristocratic wire-strung clarsach harpist, fiddler, piper and composer, celebrated in the piobaireachd 'The Lament for Ronald MacDonald of Morar'. He is the reputed composer of a number of highly regarded piobaireachds, including 'An Tarbh BreacDearg/ The Red Speckled Bull'; 'A Bhoalaich/An Intended Lament', also published in Angus MacKay's book as 'A Bhoilich/The Vaunting'; and 'Glas Mheur', which MacKay translates as 'The Finger Lock.' This piobaireachd is entitled 'Glass Mhoier' in the *Campbell Canntaireachd*. There are three other piobaireachds in the *Campbell Canntaireachd* manuscripts with the related titles 'A Glase', 'A Glass' and 'A Glas'.

'Glas' is also a key term found in the Irish wire-harp tradition, as noted down by

Edward Bunting, who uses 'glass' as a variant of 'gléis' in relation to tuning. He also lists the term 'glas' as a specific fingering technique, which he translates as 'a joining', a simile for lock. He describes this as 'double notes, chords etc.' for the left treble hand and right bass hand.

viii

Cultural ascendancy of piobaireachd

The rise of the bagpipe and the corresponding shift away from the harp and its associated traditions of bardic poetry is documented with a confronting disdain in the satirical song 'Seanchas Sloinnidh na Piob o thùs/A History of the Pipes from the Beginning' (*c.*1600) by Niall Mor MacMhuirich (*c.*1550–1630), poet to the MacDonalds of Clanranald:

John MacArthur's screeching bagpipes, is like a diseased heron, full of spittle, long limbed and noisy, with an infected chest like that of a grey curlew. Of the world's music Donald's pipe, is a broken down outfit, offensive to a multitude, sending forth its slaver through its rotten bag, it was a most disgusting filthy deluge . . .

This can be contrasted with the celebration of the heroic warrior associations of bagpipe piobaireachd at the expense of the harp and fiddle by later Clanranald poet Alasdair Mhaighstir (*c.*1695–1770) in the song 'Moladh air Piob-Mhor Mhic Cruimein/In Praise of MacCrimmon's Pipes':

'Thy chanter's shout gives pleasure, Sighing thy bold variations, Through every lively measure; The war note intent on rending, White fingers deft are pounding, To hack both marrow and muscles, With thy shrill cry resounding . . . You shamed the harp, Like untuned fiddle's tone, Dull strains for maids, And men grown old and done: Better thy shrill blast, From gamut brave and gay, Rousing up men to the destructive fray . . . '

Bardic verses traditionally celebrated the clarsach harp and made no mention of bagpipes. Nevertheless, the bagpipes gained popularity and prominence through a social need for a prominent national instrument – whether it be martial, in a period of increasing military engagements, or cultural as the instrument became grafted on to existing structures of aristocratic cultural patronage and aesthetic appreciation in the mid-seventeenth century and became the primary Ceol Mor instrument.

This is reflected in the patronage offered to a succession of hereditary pipers who were retained by leading clan families, including piobaireachd dynasties such as the

MacCrimmons, pipers to the MacLeods of Dunvegan, and the MacArthurs, pipers to the MacDonalds of Sleat.

ix

Modern bagpipe piobaireachd: early 1900s–present

In the aftermath of the Battle of Culloden in 1746, the old Gaelic cultural order underwent a near total collapse. Piobaireachd continued to be played by bagpipers, but with diminished patronage and status, and was perceived to have gone into a decline. The modern revival of piobaireachd was initiated by the newly founded Highland Society of London. They funded annual competitions, with the first being held at the Falkirk Masonic Lodge in 1781. Over the course of the nineteenth century, with the opening up of communications within the Highlands (in particular, the railways), a competing circuit emerged, with the two most pre-eminent competitions being held at Inverness and Oban, the former descended directly from the first Falkirk competition.

The orally transmitted repertoire was collected and documented in a diverse range of manuscript transcriptions mostly dating from the early nineteenth century. As noted, the first comprehensive collections were the canntaireachd transcriptions in the *Campbell Canntaireachd* (1797 and 1814) and the *Neil MacLeod Gesto Canntaireachd* (1828), collected from John MacCrimmon prior to his death in 1822. A series of manuscripts in the early nineteenth century documented piobaireachd transcribed in staff notation.

Angus MacKay's book *A Collection of Ancient Piobaireachd or Highland Pipe Music*, published in 1838, documented and presented the piobaireachd repertoire in staff notation with supplementary commentary by antiquarian James Logan. MacKay simplified many of the piobaireachd compositions, editing out complex ornamentation and asymmetries that were evident in documentation of the same compositions published in earlier manuscripts such as the *Campbell Canntaireachd*. He also specified regular time signatures that standardised and regulated a music that was traditionally performed with expressive rubato rhythmic interpretation of the musical phrasing and dynamics. MacKay's staff-notated edited version of piobaireachd became the authoritative reference for the nineteenth- and twentieth-century revival of piobaireachd, and greatly influenced subsequent modern piobaireachd performance.

In 1903, the Piobaireachd Society was founded with the aim of recording the corpus of existing tunes, collating the various versions and publishing an authoritative edition. Those normative tune settings have been the basis on which Ceol Mor competitors at the various Highland Games have been judged ever since, with the piping judges themselves being appointed by the Society.

In recent decades pipers and researchers have increasingly questioned the editing of the tunes that went in the Piobaireachd Society books, arguing that the performance style chosen favoured one piping tradition at the expense of others. Many compositions also appear to have been edited and distorted to make them conform unnecessarily to particular recognised tune structures. This standardisation of the transcribed piobaireachd tunes has made the judging of competitions easier at the expense of the ornate complexity and musicality of an art that had passed down from teacher to pupil through the oral transmission of repertoire and technique.

Independent documentation of this tradition of oral transmission can be found in canntaireachd manuscripts, chanted vocable transcriptions of the music that pre-date the normative musical scores authorised by the Piobaireachd Society and enforced through prescriptive competition judging citeria. In a belated but nevertheless constructive response to this debate over authority and authenticity, the Piobaireachd Society has recently made a range of these canntaireachd manuscripts available online as a comparative resource.

Appendix 13: The Highland bagpipe – history and anatomy

i

History

The bagpipe is, along with the harp and the drum, the oldest of instruments. It is not particularly Scottish, and indeed its introduction to Scotland may well have been in comparatively recent times when one sees representations of a similar-looking instrument on the papyrus scrolls of Ancient Egypt and set in stone on the engraved tablets of Mesopotamia.

It is unlikely therefore that it was 'invented' but, rather, more organically developed and changed through time. To graduate, say, from a one-note whistle to a more sophisticated many-note pipe takes not so much ingenuity as ingenuity and time – and it is highly likely that different versions of the instrument we now know as the bagpipe were coming into being at different places at different periods of history. Adding, first, to the simple pipe a bag as a reservoir for air, enabling the player to continue the melody while taking a breath, putting to that a drone, to provide a bass sound, adding other pipes to the solo instrument . . . And so on. After all, given an instrument able to produce first a note, then more notes around it, the invention of a bagpipe was perhaps inevitable. Shepherds and others who looked after grazing animals have long been associated with bagpipes, and no doubt the boredom of their task helped greatly in both the development of this instrument and the playing of it.

Whatever its origin, it is safe to assume that the bagpipe has been played from a very early time and is therefore as much a part of our sense of civilisation as gourds and goblets, temples, tablets and feasts.

It was brought to Scotland, a version of it, 'that instrument of war of the Roman Infantry' as Procopius described it (see Bibliography/Music: General – *Dictionary of Music and Musicians*), by those early invaders and was quickly and richly developed by the Picts and Celts as an instrument for entertainment and song – the Irish Ulleian pipe, a much lighter, 'thinner' version of the great Highland bagpipe, continues that tradition of play to the present day.

The development of all musical instruments was no doubt conditioned by two basic problems of how to sustain a note and how to make it loud enough to be heard by the audience. Less fundamental were the questions of scale and harmony, although once the instrument fulfilled the basic demands these became the chief problems and the main fields of improvement.

The bagpipe, then, was one solution to the difficulty of maintaining the flow of music. With no real effort of design, the loudness challenge was probably solved simultaneously.

How much the Romans, and their deployment of the instrument on occasions of battle, may have influenced its popularity we can only measure by the steady increase in piping culture in the centuries that followed. There is much evidence from the Middle Ages to show that by then the cult of the bagpipe was widespread, both geographically and socially. The instrument is mentioned in Spanish manuscripts of the thirteenth century and is referred to by Dante. Froissart and Boccaccio speak of it in the fourteenth century, and Chaucer says of his miller, 'A baggepype wel coude he blowe and sowne'. In the sixteenth century, Rabelais, Ronsard, Cervantes, Spenser and Shakespeare all have references to bagpipes.

And these references sound across social barriers and classes. As well as being popular at country fairs and weddings, the instrument was to be found in the courts and palaces of kings and queens. Ladies of the French aristocracy played small versions of the bagpipe, the cornemuse. Henry VIII left five sets of pipes in his collection of musical instruments at Hampton Court. The bagpipe appears regularly in English illuminated manuscripts and ecclesiastical carvings, especially of the fourteenth and fifteenth centuries, but the widespread popularity of the instrument is best heard out in the fact that today, in countries as diverse as Scotland, India, Russia, Spain and elsewhere, a version of the bagpipe is being played by those who have been taught the instrument in unbroken succession since it was first introduced there. Only in the last hundred years or so have the Scandinavian countries, as well as Holland, Belgium and Germany, followed England's example already set, for they long before gave up the playing of this unique, strange and mortal instrument that has been always too loud, so it was deemed, to be played inside. The ceilings were too low in the music rooms of the rising bourgeoisie, their cultural appetites too sated by what they thought they wanted and needed, the windows closed and the expensive carpets of their drawing rooms near glued to their floors. There was no place for the pipes in this new sealed-off world.

So, one might say, the end of the Middle Ages signalled a new way of life that was more urban than rural – social life conducted indoors and no longer on the village green. Loudness was no longer a necessary quality, sweetness and delicacy were more highly prized. Chamber music and, in time, the modern orchestra and its pleasures were to follow the new social patternings – our definition of all the aspects of what we now call Western music were thus laid down.

This way of life was exterminated with the defeat at Culloden in 1746, of course. The Disarming Act that followed proscribed the wearing of the tartan or Highland dress, the speaking of Gaelic and the carrying of arms – which was interpreted by the law to also include a ban on the playing of bagpipes. The act was not repealed until 1782 – and yet although by then it had effectively killed a way of life, it had not quietened the sound of the pipes. The colleges of piping may have been disbanded and the number of pipers diminished, but the traditional passing on of knowledge and skill continued unimpeded. Indeed, piping now received fresh vigour in the raising of the Highland regiments – and it was in this way that the music made its first real impact on the rest of the world.

So it had been rejected in earlier times as an instrument of rough irrelevance, that could not be brought indoors to be played alongside the flute and the viol; nevertheless, now it had found itself a place, this lonely, uncompromising instrument claimed by musicians who were, at heart, never entertainers but first and foremost soloists and poets. So now it had a meaning that sounded beyond the complexity of its notes and compositions. It became an emblem of a 'self', a Scotland that was in the process of trying to define itself as a single entity, its sound the sound of a people trying to claim for themselves a national identity, a sense of themselves that might make them feel not as though they were defeated but as though they might rise up again and always against oppression and unjust rule.

Perhaps this is why – from this time and through to the nineteenth and twentieth centuries – the pipes have been looked upon as the instrument of a barbaric country. For what coloniser wants to hear the music of its colony but only its own songs and tunes played? Certainly this may be why when contact was made between pipe music and the rest of music it was generally characterised by a measure of rejection on both sides, which tended further to increase the isolation of the pipers and to increase their sense of purpose.

The second reason for the Highland bagpipe's survival was that at no time did its

exponents alter the instrument to make it socially acceptable. A few players, occasionally, may have given a non-bagpipe tune to the instrument, or modified some of the
fingering, perhaps, to make a piobaireachd sound more modern, but these aberrations
were few and pass in the history of the instrument largely unremarked. Once out
of his natural environment the piper might accept that his music was different and
strange, but this did not affect his playing of it. While other pipes softened and light-
ened, the Highland bagpipe remained. Its shape and sound and make-up, the music
for which it was created, went unchanged – the same piobaireachd played in the same
way with the same sound as was played by the MacCrimmons of Skye in the fifteenth
century and earlier (see Appendix 14: 'The cultural history of bagpipe playing').

The final reason for the survival of this lonely instrument, and for its later
'popularity', comparatively speaking, is the character of the music with which it is
inextricably linked – the Big Music, piobaireachd – a form of communication so
important to Highlanders for so long that there was little chance of it being aban-
doned. As MacNeill writes: 'If all other pipe music were to fade away there would
still remain a group of Highland pipers dedicated to the study and enjoyment of
Ceol Mor.' For that, as we shall see in the next Appendix, we have to thank the legacy
of that family of musicians and poets and teachers that played down from generation to generation: the MacCrimmons of Skye.

ii

Anatomy

The parts of the bagpipe and its overall construction and shape are as complicated
and intricate as its history. An 'anatomical' representation of the instrument may
provide information as to how the various elements of the instrument come together.

Note: The pipe bag itself is the reservoir for the air that powers the reeds. This
bag is usually made from leather, although modern bags are often made from syn-
thetic replacement materials. The drones, which extend from the chanter, are in
many ways the most important element of the bagpipe. Known as 'the heart of the
instrument', they provide the sound with the clean, dulcet tones needed for its
music. The original Highland pipes probably comprised a single drone, with the
second drone being added in the mid- to late 1500s. The third, or the great drone,
came into use sometime in the early 1700s.

In the Scottish Lowlands, pipers were part of the travelling minstrel class, per-
forming at weddings, feasts and fairs throughout the Border country, playing song
and dance music. Highland pipers, on the other hand, appear to have been more
strongly influenced by their Celtic background and occupied a high and honoured
position.

The skill of playing has to be blended with the art of posture and stance. The piper's left arm should only squeeze the bag with enough pressure to feed the drones with air to sound the notes without disturbance or distortion. The bag is held towards the front of the piper's body, allowing the shorter drone to rest on the shoulder.

Modern pipes, in the early twentieth century, were made of tropical hardwoods, usually black ebony and black wood from Africa or cocas wood from the Caribbean, with decorative rings or ferrules made of ivory. Sometimes silver was used for the lower ferrules. Prior to and throughout the eighteenth century, local hardwoods were used, commonly holly and laburnum, again horn and bone being added for decoration.

Pipers, particularly teachers, were adept craftsmen as creators both of music and their instruments. Many used to make their own pipes. A notable Scottish piper, John Ban MacKenzie, who died in 1864 and was thought to be the last of these makers, is said to have killed the sheep, stitched the bag, turned the drones, chanter and blowpipe on his simple foot-pedalled lathe, cut the oaten reeds, composed the tunes and played them, all with his own hands.

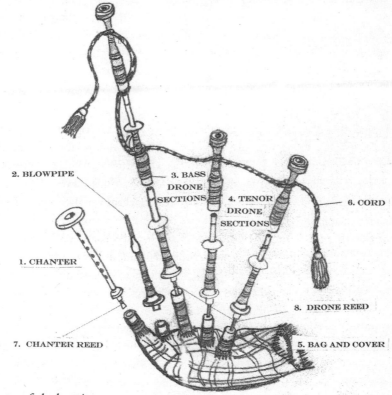

2. BLOWPIPE

3. BASS DRONE SECTIONS

4. TENOR DRONE SECTIONS

6. CORD

1. CHANTER

8. DRONE REED

7. CHANTER REED

5. BAG AND COVER

The parts of the bagpipe

Appendix 14: The cultural history of bagpipe playing

The MacCrimmons

No one who is interested in the history of bagpipe playing and piobaireachd does not know about the great musicians of Skye who perfected the musical form of Ceol Mor and composed some of the most beautiful and important piobaireachd ever to be played, including the haunting and magisterial 'Lament for the Children' – regarded by pipers and music critics, both, to be as pure a representative of its form as exists in the playing of the Big Music.

The MacCrimmons were a Scottish Highland family, pipers to the chiefs of Clan MacLeod for an unknown number of generations, who established, from the sixteenth century onwards, a piping college of music at Boreraig, where they lived, near the Clan MacLeod seat at Dunvegan on the Isle of Skye. The college was famed throughout Scotland and beyond, and pupils would be sent to study there for seven years to perfect their playing and understanding of Ceol Mor. It was, in this way, the first school of piping established in Scotland, and in the world. It was founded at the time of the great universities of Oxford and Cambridge and St Andrews, and long before any of the other schools of music we know today – and though there is nothing to survive of its walls and rooms today, it is a presence, a structure mounted at the back of any real piper or serious bagpipe student, a place they can claim as part of their tradition as they claim, too, the tradition of the family who lived there for so long.

i

History of the inheritance of piping

Over time, many pieces of piobaireachd have been attributed to the MacCrimmons, as they were one of the most famous families of hereditary pipers – along with the clans MacArthur (pipers to MacDonald of Sleat), MacGregor (pipers to Campbell of Glenlyon) and Rankins (pipers to the MacLeans of Coll, Duart and Mull). Even though the term 'hereditary' is not a native Gaelic term, it has been used, throughout the history of bagpipe playing, to imply an above-average skill or special status – as well as the sense, noted in earlier Appendices, of a tradition that is passed down through canntaireachd and close tuition from generation to generation. So in the Scottish Highlands, and in Europe itself until the Industrial Revolution, most positions were inherited, 'from the chief down to the humblest cotter', as John Gibson notes in his popular book (see Bibliography/Music: Piobaireachd/secondary). But in the case of the MacCrimmons, one is describing the great inheritance of art and aesthetics that was expressed in the manner of, say, the dynasty of Bach in Germany, or the Breughel family of painters in Holland.

This tradition – of a musical genealogy – continues to the present in that, in the twentieth century, the chiefs of Clan MacLeod instated two MacCrimmons as hereditary pipers to the clan. Despite continued debate and discussion amongst historians and scholars about the genesis of this family of musicians, there is no doubt of their inheritance and influence upon the playing and understanding of piobaireachd. The music, as they say, is the all.

ii

Origins

Certainly the origin of the MacCrimmons has long been debated. One theory, from Captain Neil MacLeod of Gesto, was that the MacCrimmons descend from an Italian from the city of Cremona. Gesto was an intimate friend of Black John MacCrimmon (d.1822), the last hereditary piper to MacLeod, and it is reputed that from him Gesto received the 'Cremona tradition'. According to Gesto, the founder of the MacCrimmons was a priest from Cremona named Giuseppe Bruno, whose son Petrus (or Patrick Bruno) was born at Cremona in 1475 and later emigrated to Ulster in 1510. On Patrick's arrival in Ireland, he married the daughter of a piping family and Gaelicised his name. Gesto's origin for the Mac-Crimmons is not taken very seriously today. According to Alastair Campbell of Airds, the tradition was 'fuelled by a non-Latinist finding the word "Donald" in a 1612 Latin charter to Donald MacCrimmon, [and thinking] that they were Italians from Cremona'.

It is generally more accepted that the surname may be of Norse origin. With MacCrimmon being an Anglicised form of the Scottish Gaelic Mac Ruimein, meaning 'son of Ruimean'. Ruimean is possibly a Gaelic form of the Old Norse personal name Hroth-mundr, which is composed of the elements hroth (meaning 'fame') + mundr (meaning 'protection').

While this name origin would seem to tie in with the MacCrimmons' association with the MacLeods and the Isle of Skye, the earliest references to a MacCrimmon (who was also a piper) appears in Campbell lands. The earliest is found in a bond of 29 November 1574 between Colin Campbell of Glenorchy and 'John Tailzoure Makchrwmen in the Kirktoun of Balquhidder and Malcolme pyper Makchrwmen in Craigroy', this being more than ninety years before the MacCrimmons are found as pipers to MacLeod of Dunvegan in Skye. Another early reference is to a 'Patrik Mcquhirryman, piper' cited in the Register of the Privy Council, vol. 5 (1592–99), in connection with a crime in Perthshire. Indeed, Alastair Campbell of Airds also speculated that the MacCrimmons were pipers to the Campbells of Glenorchy prior to the MacLeods of Dunvegan and Harris – so showing how the mists of uncer-

tainty and hypothesis surround the history and genesis of a spectacularly talented
family who have influenced bagpipe music at its very heart.

iii

Hereditary pipers

The MacCrimmons held the appointment of hereditary pipers to the MacLeods
at Dunvegan in unbroken succession for about three hundred years. Tradition
says that the first hereditary piper was Findlay, appointed about 1500, and that
he was followed by his son Iain Odhar, who was succeeded in 1570 by his son
Donald Mor.

   With Donald Mor MacCrimmon begins the real fame of the family and their
College of Piping at Boreraig that became, as MacNeill notes (see Bibliography/
Music: Piobaireachd/secondary), 'the finishing school for every good piper, the
compositions and those of their pupils reached the greatest heights ceol mor has
known'. After Donald Mor's death in 1640, he was succeeded by his son Patrick Mor,
who in turn was followed in 1670 by his son Patrick Og, perhaps the greatest teacher
of the MacCrimmons.

   Patrick Og died in 1730 and was succeeded by his sons Donald Ban, who was
killed at the Rout of Moy in 1746, and Malcolm, who composed the great 'Lament for Donald Ban' and died in 1769. By that time the whole clan structure in the
Highlands was changing and the profession of piper, which for so long had been an
honourable and full-time position, was no longer supported as a vocation. Nevertheless, Malcolm's two sons, Donald Ruadh and Iain Dubh, both seem to have been
hereditary pipers to the MacLeods. Iain Dubh died in 1822 and Donald Ruadh in
1825 – and although they had sons who might have inherited their titles, there was
no longer a college or a position to go with the title. An era had come to a close.

iv

The MacCrimmons' legends

Such was the fame of the MacCrimmon family that many myths and stories grew
up around them pertaining to their origins and the sheer magic of their music. Here
follows one such 'faerie story', by way of an example:

To receive a faerie gift is an uncertain blessing: it may bring you joy, healing or
the skill to make the most beautiful music in the world. It may fall softly and
unbidden into your life like a ray of moonlight, but it may also vanish with
the light of day if you do not keep your covenant with the Good People. Steal

faerie gold and you will have a pocketful of withered leaves by the time you get home, or, like the Scottish lad who thought he'd won a pair of bagpipes from the faeries, nothing but a puff-ball and willow-reed.

One man gifted with faerie music was Iain Og MacCrimmon of Skye in the Scottish Hebrides. Iain was sitting on a faerie hill in the west of the island, feeling disconsolate because he was not considered a good enough piper to attend a competition promoted by the chieftain, MacLeod of Dunvegan Castle. A faerie woman approached him, saying:

'Your handsome looks and sweet music
Have brought you a fairy sweetheart.
I bequeath you this silver chanter:
At the touch of your fingers,
It will always bring forth the sweetest music.'

She gave him the silver chanter for his pipes, and taught him the art of piping. Iain Og hurried off to Dunvegan Castle and won the contest over musicians from all over the Highlands, for all could tell that his music had the gift of faerie fingers on the chanter. He became the hereditary piper to the MacLeods, and from that day on, the MacCrimmons of Skye produced many generations of renowned pipers and composers. He founded a famous school for pipers at Boreraig, his home in the west of Skye, where people came from all over Scotland and Ireland to study for a full seven years.

But MacCrimmon had been warned by his faerie sweetheart that should he or any of his descendants treat the silver chanter disrespectfully, the gift for music would be removed from his family for ever. One stormy day, one of his descendants was returning to Skye from the nearby island of Raasay with the Chief of the MacLeods. As he played in the piper's seat at the prow of the chieftain's galley, the swell of the waves caused his fingers to slip. Finally, he laid down the pipes with a derogatory remark, blaming the silver chanter for his mistakes. At that moment, the chanter rose of its own accord from the galley, slipped over the gunwale and into the sea, where it has since remained. From that time on, the MacCrimmons' hereditary gift dried up, their school of piping fell into decay, and the family's fortunes declined. A lone cairn marks the spot where the school of piping stood, and it is said that the sound of ghostly piping can still be heard in the sea-cliffs and caverns of Boreraig.

The Sutherlands

The Sutherlands are an example of a more recent family of pipers that have maintained a long tradition of musicianship in the north-east of the Scottish mainland – since the early part of the eighteenth century, records show, and no doubt before that time.

This tradition reached its height in the mid-twentieth century with the famous 'Winter Classes' that were established at The Grey House, itself located on the site of an earlier dwelling that was home to a musical school of a less formal nature, when one John Roderick MacKay Sutherland, known as 'First John', first started giving lessons to local pipers and those who came from further away to take instruction from him.

Details of the family and the history of the School they established in their home forms a great deal of the substance of 'The Big Music' – and further information about the family is contained within the various movements within it, in particular in some of the variations that occur in the Crunluath section.

i

History of the inheritance of piping

Like the MacCrimmon family – though the Sutherlands themselves would never compare themselves in this way – the Sutherland family maintained an unbroken succession of pipers since records were first kept of the family's activities from the mid-1700s onwards. The table at the front of this book indicates the seven generations that lead up to the present day, although it is unknown at the time of compiling these Appendices whether Callum Innes Sutherland will take up his father's pipes in accordance with his history. There are also papers in the Crunluath movement of 'The Big Music' and various Appendices here that describe more fully the history of the family and their musical legacy.

ii

Origins

As those papers show, The Grey House itself is an important element in the description of the family's musical endeavours, representing as it does, in its various incarnations – from a traditional, modestly proportioned longhouse to a more substantial Victorian home that itself is extended – the development and growth of a musical tradition. By the time the House has reached its present state as a graciously proportioned building with a walled garden and outbuildings, with large reception rooms etc., so too has the music that emanates from it accumulated prestige and finish. Thus, he who put the finishing touches to the front and side extensions of the House was also the musician most known to pipers the world over.

Again, details of the history and story of the House and its musical associations are contained throughout 'The Big Music'. The List of Additional Materials contains further sources of information.

Appendix 15: Scottish schools of piping

i

An overview of contemporary piping schools

As indicated, the strong history of piping schools in the Highlands of Scotland has given rise to a tradition of piobaireachd being taught to pipers and musicians throughout their lives, no matter what their status or position. The MacCrimmons' school has set a precedent this way, one might say, that always will be followed – the rigorous and technique-driven Glasgow School of Piping being, perhaps, the most famous example of these in the present era.

The Highlands today are also home to a number of smaller world-class piping schools, most of which are advertised by website or in relevant publications such as *The Piping Times*. These schools, unlike the 'Winter Classes' of The Grey House, tend to run all year round in short courses of no more than a week. In addition, the Piobaireachd Society, the National School of Piping and the Army School all run their own sets of masterclasses and tutorials, and one-to-one tuition is also available on an ad hoc or timetabled basis.

An example of such a class is detailed below and is a good representation of the terms of tuition etc. that is available. This information is taken from the Wallace Bagpipes School of Music:

School dates

Spring School – 11th to 15th April

Summer School 1 – 27th June to 1st July

Summer School 2 – 4th to 8th July

Summer School 3 – 25th to 29th July

Autumn Piping School – 17th to 21st October

The daily programme will cover all aspects of performance on the Highland Bagpipe including practice routines, technique, musical expression, timing and tuning and students will be taught in small groups of similar ability for three to four hours per day, with practice time built in. The course commences daily at 9 a.m. and will finish at approximately 4.50 p.m.

Workshop topics will include such subjects as reed-making, maintenance, massed bands theory and tuning. Students are also encouraged to offer suggestions for what they may like to work on, and other activities throughout the week may include: Teachers' Recitals, Student Concert and a Pipe Band Visit.

Piping Grading Table

Level 1: Complete Beginner	No experience at all. Has not played any scales or exercises.
Level 2: Learner	Progressing towards or can play a simple tune(s). Has played some scales and simple exercises — e.g. 'G' gracenote, strikes, 'D' throw.
Level 3: Lower Novice	Able to play most movements including doublings, birls, grips, taorluaths and can play several tunes quite competently with a reasonable sense of timing. Has not yet started on pipes.
Level 4: Novice	Can competently play tunes of varying time signatures including marches, strathspeys and reels on the chanter. Is starting or has started on pipes and can perform some simple tunes. Needs assistance tuning. Developing finger technique.
Level 5: Intermediate	Working on 4-parted marches, strathspeys and reels; also can play some hornpipes and jigs. Can perform all on the bagpipe. Perhaps ready to progress to piobaireachd. Can tune pipes reasonably well or attempt to tune. Technique quite developed but needs some work.
Level 6: Advanced	Fluent with all aspects of light music. Able to play some piobaireachd on the bagpipe. Can tune pipes accurately. Perhaps ready to compete in solo competition or able to attain that standard at good junior level or beyond.

The above provides an example of one of the smaller schools of piping available today. In addition, as previously noted, there are larger national colleges and institutions affiliated with piping that conduct tutorials and classes over the year. One well-known must be the Army School of Piping (later renamed the Army School of Bagpipe Music), generally regarded as the smallest unit in the British Army. This school is now commanded by a director who is a qualified Army pipe major and who usually holds the rank of Captain or Major and is assisted by a chief instructor who is the Senior Pipe Major of the British Army.

The school forms part of the Piping and Drumming Qualifications Board, which is a collaboration among the Piobaireachd Society, the Royal Scottish Pipe Band Association, the College of Piping and the Piping Centre. Together, the Board sets a standardised piping certificate programme for students from around the world.

ii

The role of the Piobaireachd Society; College of Piping; National Piping Centre

The Piobaireachd Society was formed in 1903 to encourage the study and playing of piobaireachd and to that end has collected the available piobaireachd manuscripts and, from these and the knowledge of the existing experts and players, published fifteen books with the piobaireachd written in staff notation accompanied by notes on the sources. The Society has also published the *Kilberry Book of Ceol Mor* by Archibald Campbell, a collection of 112 of the better-known tunes. There are notes, separately published as *Sidelights* and *Further Sidelights*, that tell of Kilberry's own famous teachers and what they taught him.

The Society has published a book of modern piobaireachd and more recently new editions of important works such as Joseph MacDonald's *Treatise* (1994), The *MacArthur MacGregor Manuscript* (2001, in conjunction with the John MacFadyen Trust) and Donald MacDonald's book of piobaireachd containing twenty-four tunes (2006).

Publication of these books has helped the Society fulfil its main aim. In addition to this, the Society has now developed a comprehensive website providing sound files, manuscripts, new music, photographs and other information, all designed to encourage the understanding and playing of this music.

A sense of the atmosphere, range and type of musical activity promoted by the Society is evident in an extract taken from a report by the Society's Jack Taylor of a recent conference that is available in transcript in the List of Additional Materials section at the back of this book.

In addition to hosting events such as the one detailed above, the Piobaireachd Society has set itself, since its formation, the aim of broadening the general performance repertoire through a programme of new publications.

As previously mentioned, since 1925 fifteen books have been published, containing a nominal total of 268 tunes. We can be precise about the nominal total, as the title of each book follows essentially the same format, thus: *Piobaireachd, 12 tunes edited by Comunn na Piobaireachd* followed by *Piobaireachd, a Second Book of 12 tunes* ... and so on, with 12 tunes in books 1–3, 16 in books 4–10, and 20 in books 11–16. The real total, however, could be considered to be larger, as there is often a question of whether two pieces should be considered as distinct or as 'versions' of each other.

Nominally, each book is the work of a committee, that is, the Music Committee of the Society, to whom all questions of selection and editing were delegated. But the committee has always had other responsibilities as well, and in practice the editorial work has been undertaken by only a few people. The prime movers were John Grant and Archibald Campbell; later Archie Kenneth took an increasing part, the books from 11 to 15 being largely his. Less well known is the major contribution made by James Campbell, especially in the later books. Roderick Cannon took over in 1996. The foundation of the work was the collection of manuscripts and rare printed books which John Grant and Archibald Campbell had built up personally since they started working together in the early 1900s. These and some others acquired by the Society itself are now mostly preserved in the National Library of Scotland.

The Society's editorial policy was stated from time to time in resolutions formally adopted by the Music Committee, and in the prefaces to the various books, especially Book 1 and the revised Book 6, and in the separate 'General Preface' which supersedes the original preface to Book 1. This new preface also gives a full bibliography of sources and their present locations.

The Society writes:

The Piobaireachd Society has never had premises of its own, and this may be the reason why it has not retained an archive set of its own publications. Nor has there been, until now, any attempt to catalogue the books comprehensively. The Music Committee felt that the centenary of the Society would be a good occasion to make such an attempt with the publication of the new Bibliography. Although great care has been taken, it cannot be claimed that this Bibliography is completely accurate or comprehensive. It is in fact a preliminary publication and we hope that it will lead to new discoveries. Most books have been reprinted many times over. We catalogue here about 90 printings of the fifteen books, but less than half of these printings have actually been seen and handled by the present editor. It seems likely that examples of every edition and reprint are still in existence in one private collection or another. The Society will be very pleased to hear from anyone who knows of editions which we have not managed to locate, and even more pleased to hear of others which we have omitted altogether, or errors in the information given. If anyone would like to donate examples of the missing books they will be most gratefully accepted. They will be catalogued and added to this list, then handed on to the National Library, with full acknowledgement.

The College of Piping, established in 1944 and situated in Glasgow, is the international centre of world piping, with more than sixty-five years' experience in teaching Scotland's national instrument, the great Highland bagpipe. A registered charity, the college keeps its lessons as affordable as possible by subsidising them with profits from the college shop.

Each month the college publishes piping's most authoritative journal, the award-winning *Piping Times*. The magazine has a global monthly readership of 10,000. The college also publishes and distributes a large selection of tutor books, manuals and historical writings on the bagpipe and its music, including its Tutor Book 1, which has sold more than 395,000 copies worldwide.

In 2008 the college opened a new lecture hall, which completed the re-development of its premises and means it can now host some of the most important competitions and concerts in the piping calendar.

Also situated in Glasgow, in a historic building and with as its Patron HRH Prince Charles, the Piping Centre incorporates a school with rehearsal rooms and an auditorium not only for the Highland pipes but also Scottish smallpipes, Ulleian pipes, fiddle, accordion and drumming. There is also a museum and interpretation centre, and a reference library, as well as conference facilities and a hotel.

To that end, it is popular with visitors from abroad as well as around the UK, as detailed knowledge or skill of bagpipe playing is not a prerequisite for the enjoyment of the many facilities available – whether one is coming for performance or simply pleasure.

iii
Publications associated with teaching

Of the range of regular newsletters and journals made available to further the education and understanding of the playing of piobaireachd, and of the history of the pipes in general, the best-known and most established publications are the Piobaireachd Society's regularly updated editions of work and the monthly *Piping Times* published by the School of Piping.

When read through as a body of publications, the complete output of the Piobaireachd Society provides as comprehensive a history of the music as has ever been made available, from the famous Kilberry manuscript onwards. In addition there are many other books and recordings on piping and piobaireachd and those of particular interest to the Ceol Mor enthusiast will be *Binneas A Boreraig* and the *MacArthur MacGregor Manuscript*.

Last Appendix: 'The Big Music'

As we read in the definition that appears at the beginning of this book, piobaireachd is an ancient form of composition that may be described simply as a theme with variations, a structure of music that has gone unchanged for hundreds of years and is known to have been elevated to its status as a pure art form by the MacCrimmon family who together wrote some of the finest pieces of music for the Highland bagpipe ever known.

Piobaireachd is divided into two types, known in Gaelic as Ceol Mor, for 'Big Music', the grand and solemn laments and salutes that are played to mark formal occasions and are grave and serious in tone; and Ceol Beag, for 'Small Music', such as reels, strathspeys and marches played at weddings and gatherings and is light-hearted in mood. As the Highland bagpipes are known in Gaelic as 'piob mhor', and as a piper is a 'piobaire', so the word 'piobaireachd' may be known, literally, as pipe music – but in fact, over time, it has come to stand for the great classic music of the bagpipes, the Ceol Mor for which it is celebrated today.

The music is not easy to define or even to describe – it has been called, by some, the voice of uproar and the music of real nature and emotion. Many hear in the sound a cry that is near human – bringing to mind the ancient belief that once upon a time the pipes could actually 'speak', and that the playing of the music is nothing more than the extension of poetry recited by the bards as a way of passing down tales of genealogy and line, the story of the clan's history told in sound.

Each piobaireachd was composed for a particular purpose, breaking down into the following categories as mentioned above: gatherings, marches, laments, salutes and certain titled tunes: 'Lament for Himself', being a composition made up of the sounds and story of its composer's life, is an example of such a tune. That the individual notes of the chanter take on discrete definitions associated with certain people or themes is an idea that is present in 'The Big Music' and surely was in the mind of the man who composed 'Lament for Himself'. The following code may serve as a guide here, but only by reading the pages of the four movements of the tune that precede these Appendices, that is, the body of 'The Big Music', can one truly understand the 'lexicon' of notes that belong solely to John Sutherland of Rogart.

As it is, the code stands:

Chart of notes

Low 'G'	Note of Gathering
Low 'A'	The Tune's note
'B'	Note of Challenge
'C'	Most Musical note
'D'	Note of Battle
'E'	Echoing note
'F'	Note of Love
High 'G'	Note of Sorrow
High 'A'	Piper's own note

As we have read, in the days before written manuscript piobaireachd was composed and taught by being sung – by the teacher to his pupil – in Gaelic, with each note and inflection carrying its own word and sound. This type of instruction, known as canntaireachd, a singing-down of a tune from one generation to the next, is as detailed and fine in its oral and aural transcription as any completed manuscript on paper. My own father was taught his repertoire this way, by the great piper Pipe Major Donald MacLeod of Lewis (1917– 1982), and the method is still believed by most serious pipers to be the only true way to learn a piece of music, instruction about inflection, phrasing and dynamics being carried in the vocables themselves as well as the sheer sound of the musician's voice in conveying it.

To conclude: The basic structure of the music consists of an air with variations upon its theme. The ground – or Urlar – is the basic theme and is normally played slowly, containing within it all the major ideas of the music.

The ground is then followed by variations: the Taorluath, the Crunluath and the Crunluath A Mach – each with its own doublings and variations, and each movement also more complex and more difficult to play than the one that went before. By the final variation the composer's ingenuity and the piper's capability have been tested to the very limit.

The tune then ends, to quote the definition at the beginning of 'The Big Music', in a 'return to the Urlar's opening simplicity. Then the piper will play those same notes with which the composition began, walking away over the hill as the sound of the music fades from the air into silence and stillness takes up its watch again upon the empty page.'

Glossary

ailte	end, finish, i.e. 'Ailte vhor Alech' is 'End of the Road', one of the names given to The Grey House of Rogart
a mach	out, showing of itself, as in Crunluath A Mach; means to show the workings of a crown movement
beallach	pass, denoting height; i.e. 'Beallach Nam Drumochta' is the Summit or Pass of Drumochta
ben	behind or back; common usage
bothan	or bothy; a little hut or rough-built dwelling place
breve	long sustained note (double the weighting of the more commonly used semibreve); musical term
cailleach	old woman; witch
canntaireachd	the singing and notation of piobaireachd using vocables
chanter	the pipe of a bagpipe; traditionally made of ebony with a silver trim
ceilidh	a Highland party of music and dance
ceol beag	little music; strathspeys, reels etc.
ceol mor	big music; piobaireachd
cumha	lament; form of piobaireachd composed for funerals, death in battle etc.
crunluath	crown; the third movement of a piobaireach
crunluath a mach	a crown that shows itself in all its glory; the final variation of a piobaireachd
dithis	two or a pair; doubling of a note; musical term; doubling theme and single note repeated or played in pairs (also known as siubhal singling)
drone	the steady bass-note of the Highland bagpipe; i.e. bass drone, tenor drone etc.
dubh	dark or black; i.e. 'Dubh Burn' is Black Water or Dark River
failte	welcome or salute; form of piobaireachd composed for gatherings
gesundkunstwerk	the overall artwork; a piece of art that is all-encompassing, creates an overall experience of music, sound, image etc. that is a world unto itself
glas	particular fingering and tuning to create a 'joining' effect in the music
havering	one way or another; to be uncertain
leumluath	a variation incorporated within the Taorluath movement of a piobaireachd; also sometimes known as the 'Stag's Leap' to indicate the branching out of the tune into a new direction

leitmotif	recurring musical idea; used principally in relation to Wagner's music
og	younger; or latter; used as differentiation in family naming, i.e. Patrick 'Og' MacCrimmon was the youngest son of Patrick MacCrimmon (by contrast, 'Mor' often used to denote the elder or oldest in a family)
piobaireachd	the classical musical composition played on the great Highland bagpipe
port	musical term relating, initially, to harp piobaireachd
port tionail	music composed for gatherings
rubato	with feeling, vibration; musical term
semibreve	long sustained note of four beats; musical term
siubhal	a passing or traversing; i.e. of one set of musical notes passing from one to the other
sligheach	secret, sly; hidden
smirr	to rub over or blend; i.e. to smirr a tune is to fail to articulate individual notes; musical term as well as general use
slochd	summit; peak
strath	a long valley beween two hills; often with a river running through the centre and broadening out towards the sea
taorluath	the second movement or variation of a piobaireachd
thrawn	stubborn
urlar	ground; the first movement of a piobaireachd

Bibliography

Music: Piobaireachd/primary

Bagpipe music manuscripts in the National Library of Scotland; notated listing available from the Piobaireachd Society website at: piobaireachd.co.uk

Buisman, Frans, Andrew Wright and Roderick D. Cannon. *The MacArthur–Mac-Gregor manuscript of piobaireachd* (1820): *The Music of Scotland*, Volume 1. University of Glasgow Music Department Publications

Campbell Canntaireachd manuscripts, 1797: Piobaireachd Society website

Campbell, Archibald. *The Kilberry Book of Ceol Mor*. The College of Piping: Glasgow, 1969

MacKay, Angus. *A Collection of Ancient Piobaireachd or Highland Pipe Music*, 1838: Piobaireachd Society website

Neil MacLeod's A Collection of Piobaireachd or Pipe Tunes, as verbally taught by the McCrummen Pipers in the Isle of Skye (also known as the *Gesto Canntaireachd* manuscripts) Edinburgh, 1828: Piobaireachd Society website

Piobaireachd Society Books, Volumes 1–present: Piobaireachd Society website

Ross, Roderick. *Binneas A Boreraig: The Complete Collection*. The College of Piping: Glasgow, 1959

Thomason, Major General *Ceol Mor*, 1900: Piobaireachd Society website

Music: Piobaireachd/secondary

Anon. 'Piobaireachd and the "Winter Classes"'. Pamphlet Press, 1969

Brown, Barnaby. 'The design of it: patterns in pibroch', in *The Voice*, Winter, Spring & Summer, 2004–05

Campsie, Alistair. *The MacCrimmon Legend or The Madness of Angus MacKay*. Canongate, 1980

Cannon, Roderick D. 'The Campbell Canntaireachd manuscript: the case for a lost volume', in Joshua Dickson (ed.), *The Highland Bagpipe: Music, History, Tradition*. Ashgate, 2009

Cannon, Roderick D. 'What can we learn about piobaireachd?' *Ethnomusicology Forum*, Volume 4, Issue 1, 1995

Cannon, Roderick D. *Gaelic Names of Pibrochs: A Classification*. Scottish Studies, 2006.

Cannon, Roderick D. *The Highland Bagpipe and Its Music*. Birlinn, 1995

Cheape, Hugh. 'Traditional Origins of the Piping Dynasties'; 'Bagpipes and their Military Function', in Joshua Dickson (ed.), *The Highland Bagpipe: Music, History, Tradition*. Ashgate, 2009

Cheape, Hugh. *The Book of the Bagpipe*. Birlinn, 1999

Collinson, Francis. *The Bagpipe: The History of a Musical Instrument*. Routledge & Kegan Paul, 1975

Dickson, Joshua (ed.) *The Highland Bagpipe: Music, History, Tradition*. Ashgate, 2009

Donaldson, William. *The Highland Pipe and Scottish Society 1750–1950*. Tuckwell Press, 2000

Fraser, Alexander Duncan. *Some reminiscences and the bagpipe*. W. J. Hay, 1907

Gibson, John Graham. *Old and New World Highland Bagpiping*. McGill-Queen's Press, 2002.

Gunn, R. J. C. *Piobaireachd: Legends and History*. Piobaireachd Studies, 2008

Haddow, Alexander John. *The History and Structure of Ceol Mor – A Guide to Piobaireachd: The Classical Music of the Great Highland Bagpipe*. The Piobaireachd Society: Glasgow, 1982

Joseph MacDonald's Compleat Theory of the Scots Highland Pipe (1760): Piobaireachd Society website

MacDonald, Allan. 'The Relationship between Pibroch and Gaelic Song: Its Implications on the Performance Style of the Pibroch Urlar', M.Litt. thesis, University of Edinburgh, 1995

MacInnes, Iain I. 'Piobaireachd Society titles in need of amendment', in 'The Highland Bagpipe: The Impact of the Highland Societies of London and Scotland, 1781–1844', M.Litt. thesis, University of Edinburgh, 1988. Available online at the Ross's Music Page website

MacKay, Iain. *A History of Piobaireachd*. Piobaireachd Studies, 1976

MacNeill, Seumus. *Piobaireachd: Classical Music of the Highland Bagpipe*. BBC Publications, 1969

MacNeill, Seumus. Preface in Angus MacKay's *A Collection of Ancient Piobaireachd*, 1838: Piobaireachd Society website

McCalister, Peter. 'The Search for the Lost Volume of the Campbell Canntaireachd Manuscript', Glasgow, 2008: Piobaireachd Society website

Sinclair, Archibald. *Canntaireachd: Articulate Music*. Edinburgh, 1880

Music: Highland

Anon. *Lullabies, Songs, Airs*. Scotts Press, 1989

Clare, Merran. 'The metaphor of the changeling and missing child in Scottish Folklore and Songs', in *Caithness Research Institute of Modern Letters Journal*, Volume vi, 2003

Collinson, Francis. *The Traditional and National Music of Scotland*. Routledge & Kegan Paul, 1966.

Dow, Daniel. *Collection of Ancient Scots Music*, Edinburgh, 1776: Piobaireach Society website

Fraser, Simon. *Airs and Melodies Peculiar to the Highlands of Scotland*, 1816: National Library of Scotland

Gillies, Anne Lorne. *Songs of Gaelic Scotland*. Birlinn, 1973

Johnson, David. *Scottish Fiddle Music in the 18th Century: A Music Collection and Historical Study*. John Donald Publishers, 1984

Lowe, Susan. *Metaphor in Folk Song*. Clarendon Press, 1987

MacDonald, Allan. 'Scholarship and Research', in 'The Relationship between Pibroch and Gaelic Song: Its Implications on the Performance Style of the Pibroch Urlar', M.Litt. thesis, University of Edinburgh, 1995

MacFarlane, Walter and Daniel Dow. *Fiddle Piobaireachd*. John Donald, 1984

O'Baoill, Colm. 'Highland Harpers and their Patrons', in James Porter (ed.), *Defining Strains: The Musical Life of Scots in the Seventeenth Century*. Peter Lang Publishing, 2006

Sanger, Keith and Alison Kinnaird. *Tree of Strings: Crann Nan Teud: A History of the Harp in Scotland*. Kinmor Music, 1992

Stephens, Joy. *History of Highland Songs and Airs*. Gray Press, 1979

Music: General

Cambridge Companion to Medieval Music, Cambridge University Press, 2011

Dictionary of Music and Musicians. Grove, 1954

Donnington, Robert. *The Instruments of Music*. Methuen, 1949

Gilkes, John. *Wagner and his Leitmotifs*. Oxford Union Press, 1995

Graham, Katherine. *The Literal Musical: Synesthesia; Mimesis; Mask; Notation*. Featherstone, 2001

Seoras, A. D. *Use of Recurring Musical Sequences in Nineteenth-Century Composition*. Achavar Press, 1997

Wagner. Phaidon Classical Music Series. Phaidon, 1996

History: Highland and Scottish

Anderson, G. and P. *Guide to the Highlands and Islands* (1850). Google Books, 2009

Anderson, J. *Essay on the Present State of the Highlands and Islands of Scotland*. Constable, 1816

Barron, J. *The Northern Highlands – Agricultural Intelligence*. Ross-shire Quarterly Report (*Farmer's Magazine*, 1820): National Library of Scotland

Bruse, Jenny. *Shepherds in the Straths*. Caithness Local Publications, 2012

Carter, Ian. *Farm Life in Northeast Scotland . . . Poor Man's Country*. John Donald, 1979

Cunningham, Ian. *The Nation Surveyed*. Birlinn, 2009

Devine, T. M. *Clearance and Improvement: Land, Power and People in Scotland, 1700–1900*. John Donald, 2006

Dressler, Camille. *Eigg: The Story of an Island*. Birlinn, 2000

Dwyer, John. *Virtuous Discourse, Sensibility and Community in Late 18th-Century Scotland*. John Donald, 1987

Eyre-Todd, George. *The Highland Clans of Scotland: Their History and Traditions*. Garnier & Company, 1969

Hewitt, Rachel. *Map of a Nation*. Granta, 2010

MacDonald, Iain S. *Glencoe and Beyond*. John Donald, 2005

Maudlin, Daniel. *The Highland House Transformed: Architecture and Identity 1700–1850*. Dundee University Press, 2009

Mitchell, J. *Reminiscences of my life in the Highlands*, Inverness: MacKenzie, 1894

Mowat, Ian. *Easter Ross, 1750–1850: The Double Frontier*. John Donald, 2003

Nicholson, Alexander and Alasdair MacLean. *History of Skye: a record of the families, the social conditions and the literature of the island*. MacLean Press, 1994

Richards, Eric and Monica Clough. *Cromartie: Highland Life 1650–1914*. Aberdeen University Press, 1989

Richards, Eric. *Debating the Highland Clearances*. Edinburgh University Press, 2007

Sinclair, Sir John. *General Report of the agricultural state, and political circumstances of Scotland* (5 vols), Edinburgh, 1814: National Library of Scotland

Sinclair, Sir John. *General View of the Agriculture of the Northern Counties*, Edinburgh, 1814: National Library of Scotland

Whatley, Christopher A. *Scottish Society 1707–1830*. Manchester University Press, 2000

Whatley, Christopher A. *The Scots and the Union*. Edinburgh University Press, 2007

Wightman, Andy. *The Poor Had No Lawyers*. Birlinn, 2010

Literary: Scottish History

Christmas, Henry. 'Review of new books: Ancient Scottish Melodies, from a manuscript in the time of King James VI by William Dauney', in *The Literary Gazette: A weekly journal of literature, science and the fine arts*, No. 1150, Volume 23. Colburn, 1839

Gunn, Robert. *Neil M. Gunn and Dunbeath*. Pentland Printers, 1986

Hart, Francis R. and J. B. Pick. *Neil M. Gunn: A Highland Life*. Polygon, 1985

Lockhart, J. G. *Biography of Walter Scott*. Edinburgh, 1897

MacDonald, Alexander. *The poetical works of Alexander MacDonald, the celebrated Jacobite poet: now first collected, with a short account of the author*, Glasgow: G. & J. Cameron, 1851

Scott, Sir Walter. 'Mackrimmon's Lament', in *The Poetical Works of Sir Walter Scott*, with memoir of the author. University of Michigan Library, 2005

Literary: Piobaireachd

Gilonis, Harry. *Piobaireachd*. Morning Star Publications, 1996
McHardy, Stuart. *The Silver Chanter and other Piper Tales*. Birlinn, 2009
'The Lost Pibroch', in Brian Osborne (ed.), *That Vital Spark: A Neil Munro Anthology*. Birlinn, 2002

List of Additional Materials

Archive of John MacKay Sutherland

The following material is a sample list of papers that will be made available as a full collection kept in the Archive Department of the University of Dundee. The information was gathered together during publication of 'The Big Music' to provide background understanding of the files and inserts that had been used to form the content of that book, and they also appear in the final published version as Appendices and footnotes, contributing, too, towards the ordering of the Index and the overall arrangement of the four movements of the piobaireachd that is the story of John MacKay Sutherland and those who knew him.

Sample List 1: The Grey House – letters, notes

A range of papers and journals came from The Grey House and were filed as part of the records there, with separate folders for business and personal administration and another file box containing all musical notes and MSS that were to accompany the finished tunes that Callum was able to locate and play when he returned home to see his father for the last time.

correspondence:
1 x letter – to Piping Society
1 x letter – to Piobaireachd Society
1 x letter – to lawyer, confirming dissolution of certain London business interests
1 x letter – to wife, Sarah, re arrangements for their son
1 x letter – from his mother to him and he to his mother – from boyhood

diaries/records:
1 x page of week-to-view diary – showing London appointments
1 x page of journal entry – showing land management details
1 x page of The Grey House records – showing additions made
1 x page of The Grey House records – showing reorganisation of Schoolroom

musical entries:
1 x page of musical notes – showing details of an early composition (MS – see below)
1 x page of musical notes – showing details of a much later composition
1 x page of musical notes – showing early notes for 'Lament for Himself'
1 x page of musical diary – remarks on certain well-known tunes

1 x page of musical diary – as above and including reminiscences from competitions
1 x page of musical archive – detailing recordings made of tunes, compositions

manuscripts:
1 x example of early composition 'Lament for Sutherland' – in part (MS)
1 x example of much later composition 'Lament for Sutherland, return' – in part (MS)

accounts:
Accounts of bagpipes – sent, received
Accounts, battels – for Winter Schools, private tuition

older material:
Eighteenth-century fragments from the Grey Longhouse (these match those re-
ferred to in Appendix 6/v)
List of all early compositions – including poetry; ballads
Canntaireachd chart

Sample List 2: The Little Hut – notes, MSS

That same night, while he was listening to a recording of one of his father's piobaireachd, Callum remembered where he had seen the bulk of his father's writing and
manuscripts of new compositions and work in progress: that is, in the Little Hut up
in the hills that no one knew about except himself, his father and Helen – and to which
he and Helen went, repeatedly, when they were both young. The two of them were able
to return there after Callum's father's death and retrieve the papers that had been kept
hidden all those years. The Little Hut, it is clear, was a place of intense creativity – private and isolated. Everything we need for the story of 'The Big Music' came from this
place – from the fragment of 'Lament for Himself' that was discovered on the table
by the window to the notes John MacKay made there about Margaret, the woman he
loved and who, in so many ways, is the beginning and end of this book.

notes; MSS:
Some notes from the hut – general
Notes on the three movements of what will become 'Lament for Himself'
Preparatory MSS – for three tunes, including 'Lament for Himself'
Preparatory MSS – for Lullaby theme in 'Lament for Himself'
Preparatory MSS – for leitmotifs or variations for the above – including peat, tiny
flowers, grass

letters:
Letter to Callum – incomplete and unposted

Letter to Piobaireachd Society
Letter to College of Piping

talks; essays:
Discussion of piobaireachd 'The Return' — for *The New Piping Times*
'Introduction to Piobaireachd' — a talk given to the Royal Highland Society St Andrew's Night Gala Dinner
'Notes on Late Style' — for BBC Scotland

also available:
Full list of Sutherland compositions — these relate to those mentioned in relevant Appendices, including those by JMS, his father and forefathers

Scanned material:

A sample range of documentation appears as follows. NB: Some manuscript excerpts are also provided in relevant Appendices.

fig./one: 'Lament for Himself' — the original manuscript
(overleaf)

Of further interest:

As we know from 'The Big Music', the piobaireachd 'Lament for Himself' was never completed as a piece of music by John MacKay Sutherland but was finished nevertheless by way of the narrative that was gathered together by Helen MacKay of Sutherland as part of a project that furthered her interests in certain modernist texts — particularly those of Virginia Woolf and Katherine Mansfield. That work undertaken by her, 'The Big Music', is the tune of this book, of course.

However, since the gathering together of the papers that comprise the book, with the help and expertise of an anonymous composer, it has been possible to create a full piece of Ceol Mor that may accompany the text and indicate to the general reader the full and extended music John MacKay Sutherland may have been carrying with him in his head as he walked into the hills that day.

A website is currently being created that will give further details about this project.

Further relevant MSS:

fig./two: 'The Return' – or 'Margaret's Song'
(opposite)

Margaret's Song.

fig./three – Helen's draft of the Lullaby

> verse
> In a small room, a basket waits
> A basket empty for no baby is there
> The mother is gone, left the room for a moment
> and in that moment he's mounted the stairs
>
> chorus:
> He took her away
> Young Katherine Anna,
> Carried her off, tall Helen's child
> He took her away a baby sleeping
> In your arm arms, took her into the wild
>
> verse
> An old man taken the baby — away.
> He snatched her up in his arms for to see
> Her life in his, to stay his dying
> but the child's not his, her mother is me.
> (Helen MacKay)

Transcripts of conversations and interviews:

Amongst the wealth of domestic material that is available to the general reader, and that provides a sort of backstory to the book 'The Big Music', there is included a sound archive that comprises original recordings and interviews as well as transcripts of those conversations, preserved as verbatim accounts. The main body of this archive comprises the many taped recordings and interviews that took place between Margaret MacKay and her daughter Helen – as we have seen appearing in various sections of 'The Big Music' – and are part of an ongoing project about domestic life and maternity. Additional letters, narrative extracts, stories and notes contribute further to this work in progress.

There are also transcripts of various programmes made – radio and television. A small sample follows:

Transcript 1: John 'Bobby' Bain remembers a Big Night with Callum Sutherland presiding at The Grey House, November 1968. The interviewer is David Graham, a young piping student of the time who was compiling a list of interviews with prominent bagpipers of that era, including Donald McFadyen and Donald MacLeod.

fig./four – typed transcripts:

DG: You say you can remember some of those Big Nights they had at The Grey House back then?

BB: Oh, aye, they were grand nights then. Plenty of good music, and of course old Callum, for he was getting on by then, would be in charge so you knew it would be good from the outset. I remember there was one chap, had come over from Canada and he was staying at the House . . . well. He'd never heard so many good pipers together in one place, in one room, I mean. He said to us all [puts on North American accent], 'You guys sure do know how to have a party.'

DG: But this was educational as well, these evenings were part of the School.

BB Well, that's true, too – but some of us would just come in for the evening, you see, as a sort of recital. We'd play a simple tune for the young ones, something like – ah, you know – 'Flowers of the Forest' – and then we'd discuss it with them, the progressions and so on. Then they'd play it after us and we'd look at how they could improve themselves. So there was that – went on in the evenings, also. As well as all the drams!

DG: And there was one night in particular?

BB: Oh, in November . . . And the snow, well . . . None of us would be getting home in that weather. So Callum decided, well, he'll make it a bit of a session, you see. So we had a grand dinner in the evening – this was all arranged by Elizabeth, his wife, you know she was just marvellous at these things, just a marvellous hostess and generous . . . And so we had this very grand dinner, and then . . . The music starting after it. Callum played first, I remember that – for it set a tone. He played 'Lament for Donald MacKay'. And just . . . perfect. I remember it so well. How he played that tune, and we all know it, of course, it's such a familiar tune, but it was just as though it had been written for that room, for the moment of it being played there, you see, as though the tune had been made to be played right then, by him, on this particular occasion – oh, it was something. And the atmosphere in the room . . . There would have been about eight of us gathered . . . Well, you could barely speak afterwards. Is what it was like. As though a kind of a spell had been cast. And then, that was played, and the next one got up, and the

next — and we all got up — like that — one after the other —
but with barely a word spoken between us and we played . . .
you know, various tunes, the big tunes 'Lament for the
Children' and so on, all the big tunes . . . We just played
them through, all of us, like in a row, and no words between
us . . . And do you know? Not a single wrong note? Misplaced
note? Just the fingering, everything . . . Perfect. Perfect.
And then the last one of us finished and it was like . . .
Well, it was like a dam breaking then. All of us talking,
roaring! After the silence and the music, suddenly, there we
were — back to earth again — and, oh, the party started then!
The whisky came out. That was a night. We finished when light
broke . . . And of course, well, by the end, the whisky had
taken over from the music by the end, there — but before, the
night before . . . Well, nothing could take it away . . . the
magic, you see, of that first tune, and the eight tunes that
came after it, one after the other, coming out of the silence.
It was something. All of us gathered together and quiet like
that, I tell you . . . It was something, all right. I'll never
forget it. That particular night.

Transcript 2: Postman Roddy George recollects various aspects of local life for
a BBC Scotland radio programme *In the Day* that was broadcast out of Glasgow
between the years 1972 and 1974. The following is excerpted from a broadcast made
in September 1973:

BBC: And you would have seen a lot of things back then you
wouldn't see now.

RG: Oh, yes, because folk would invite you in, you see. When
you were only delivering once a week, it was a big occasion,
the post coming like that. And there was this one house, 'The
Grey House' it was called, and it was way up, oh up Rogart
way, but miles and miles down a dirt road, a private road,
you know, and oh the place was remote . . . And the post they
had! This was the Sutherlands — and they had the Piping School
up there, you know, everyone knew about the School, and they
took a lot of post, international post. I'd arrive there — oh,
with a bagful of letters and parcels — for it would be music,
you know and reeds . . . And people would be sending him pipes
for to have a look at, and this from all over the world . . .
People sending him things from all over the world. So I'd go
in there, I'd see Mrs Sutherland and she'd give me a cup of

tea, and Margaret would, for she helped out around the place,
with helping to run the School and all the concerts they had
and so on . . . And, oh, I was like Father Christmas with all
the things I had for them in my bag, and this was maybe once
a week, once a fortnight. It was a lovely house, a lovely
atmosphere, if you like. A family, you see — and you'd go in
with the post and you'd be part of things. There was a wee
girl there, she was the daughter of the housekeeper, Margaret,
and I've things for her also, you see, for she was doing some
of her lessons by distance — this was in the days before they
had set up proper transport and so on and the little ones in
these remote places did some of their lessons at home
. . . And I remember this one time she was running around
the place shouting 'I'm not going to school! I'm not going!'
and I arrived, you see, with some book or other for her to
study, and her mother said to her, 'Well, the school has just
arrived for you!' — for that was my role, in a way, to bring
everything in . . .

Further material available:

Sections of various letters — including courtship of Callum and Elizabeth — also
samples of scanned 'originals' of some letters dating back to Victorian times. Also
accounts of clothing, personal items bought, stationery, books etc.

Many records of domestic life at The Grey House — some dating from as early as
the mid-eighteenth century — are available for perusal at the University of Dundee
archive. These records include recipe books and notes, a Visitors' Book that keeps a
file of all house guests — including those who attended various Schools and recitals,
programmes of recitals — house plans showing additions and improvements etc.

An example of the above is shown below:

fig./five – plans of the house showing extensions and additions.

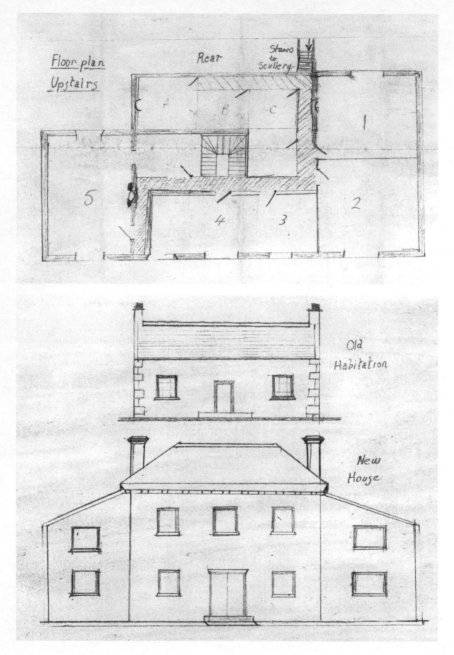

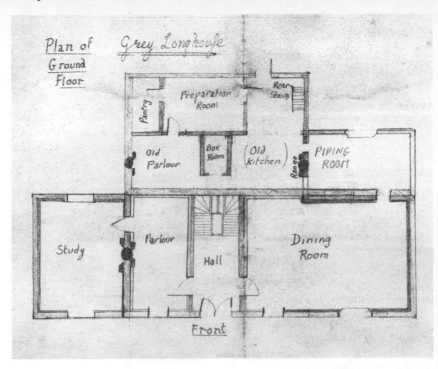

The following are available in archive:

Land acquisition papers and legal documents

Pages from recipe books and related notes

Pages from Visitors' Book; also list of all piping pupils and some recital programmes; also examples from Elizabeth Sutherland's journal 'Recollections of The Grey House'

Home improvements and decorating papers – including wallpaper and fabric swatches

Garden journals and related letters

Linens inventory

Books and examples of work and drawing from the Schoolroom

fig./six – photograph showing Schoolroom at The Grey House

Additional musical information

'Innovations to the Piobaireachd'
by John Callum MacKay Sutherland, The Grey House, 1997
(from an address given to the Piobaireachd Society by J. C. M. Sutherland, July 1974)

To those of you unfamiliar with some of the developments
taking place in the playing and composition of certain Ceol
Mor tunes, I have been asked to give a brief description.
These developments are by no means sudden or unexpected.
Those of you who were familiar with my own father's style
of playing will know him to be a player always alert to the
various possibilities of execution within a composition.
Indeed there are those who would say that my father never
played the same tune twice – that there was, to quote his
own word for it, a certain 'heuristic' approach to his
playing that meant he could only 'find the tune', again
to use his own expression, by 'playing into it', thereby
allowing certain notes and phrases to find their own
individual expression.

   It is with this approach in mind that I have gone to my
own pipes – viewing them and the traditional tunes also as
a 'means to an end', that is, as a base from which one's own
musical interpretation may grow and flourish.

Now there will be many among us, purists and traditionalists both, who will be against this method of play, first set down formally, in papers given, and so on, in books and lectures, by my father and now taken up, one may say, by the son! Yet I would say to those men that there is nothing so wayward about this approach — when we consider the historical tuition methods of the bagpipe that were always conducted via canntaireachd, a musical method that is in itself somewhat modernist, 'heuristic', if you like, in origin. For when a tune is sung to a pupil, the day it is sung, the mind and the mood of the singer, whether it is hot or cold . . . All these details and circumstances will come to colour the tune in particular subtle and sometimes dramatic ways. So it is impossible for a piece of music to be sung in exactly the same way twice — no matter how the traditionalists may long for such order in life! — in the same way might it be with our playing of that same tune.

It was this kind of thinking, then, that led to me developing my own composition work in certain ways that might allow for the 'mood' or 'change' in a tune to be more apparent — which is why, as many of you in this room will know, I have gone to some of the great German classical music composers for instruction, to learn from them, how emotion and a certain 'story', if you like, that we might allow the tune to sing, may come to dominate the overall texture of a piece, rather than its notes and structure.

This is not to say, of course, that some of our greatest traditional tunes do not have such a story to them, such emotional force. We all know the power of the Ceol Mor compositions and it would be presumptuous of me in the extreme to suggest I am doing something new here. No, it is my aim simply to bring to the fore certain practices employed in my own work — the use of leitmotif, in particular, that repetition of certain phrases or musical ideas throughout a piece that work to build up an emotional landscape in a piece as first defined by Wagner, or the use of suggestion as first introduced by Beethoven, where a theme may be hinted at but not fully allowed in to the tune until later, creating a present and past in a piece, and so on — to bring these forward for your attention as ways of extending the reach and depth of my own compositions, to give them some power and force that the arrangement of a theme with its Taorluath and Crunluath would not otherwise allow me.

Call me musically bereft, if you like, that I have not
the great imagination of a MacCrimmon that I need to rely on
such devices! You would be right — my own scattering of notes
across the page would not suffice. But add to that scattering
some repeat, some simple recall of a past theme, or the
merest change of an embellishment to bring about a shift in
atmosphere . . . Then I have a piece I can be pleased with,
that might give me pleasure to play, that, as we hope with all
musical endeavour, might bring pleasure to others.

In conclusion, therefore, my argument would be that there
is room for both approaches in our play, that our repertoire
is solid enough, is established and formal enough, to allow
for the arriviste! Permit me, then, to play for you now one
such new arrival — a tune I have been at work on over this
past year. I have entitled it 'As the Deer Come Down from the
Hill'.

Taken from a report, by Jack Taylor of The Piobaireachd Society, of a recent conference:

We were gifted with a number of speakers all attending to the theme: 'Piobaireachd
and the Imagination: Applied and Research-based Approaches' and there could be no
doubt that it was a subject with rich implications for the scholar and musician alike.
The overall ethos of the conference was one of imaginative and scholarly investiga-
tion of a musical form that remains as complex and rich to us after many years of
study as the day when we first arrived at it, chanters in hand, music in our heads.

Now for the details . . .

Keith Sanger tends to spend his time in the National Library of Scotland — and
there he found papers telling of the pipers of the Breadalbane Fencibles, with particular emphasis on John MacGregor. The Fencibles began recruiting in 1793 — and
John wasn't too keen to join, as he didn't have a bagpipe. Perhaps the incentive to
him of having the regimental pipes to play, together with the promise of adding
land to the family smallholding, was enough to persuade him. In any event he soon
had his own pipes, as he won the prize pipe at the Highland Society competition
that year. The regiment had a poet, too, and pipers won't be pleased to know that he
was paid fifty per cent more than the pipers.

Jim Barrie's presentation entitled 'Select Features of the Cameron Style' had received the accolade of a prior editorial in *The Piping Times* hinting 'what is all the fuss
about?' Jim started by saying that his father often said that the old pipers in Scotland
all played in almost the same way, except for preferential differences, and finished

with a quotation by Duke Ellington – 'If it sounds good, it is good.' In between, in the Piobaireachd Society's first PowerPoint presentation, he skilfully showed, with musical examples from Robert Reid, Andrew MacNeill, Willie Connell, Willie Barrie, Jim Barrie and Robert Brown, just what the differences, however small, are. What is not in doubt is that these nuances can significantly alter the musical impact of a tune. Jim showed this very well in the evening with his fine playing of 'Marion's Wailing'.

US piper Derek Midgely and Crieff man Craig Sutherland put their playing forward for dissection by Andrew Wright in a repeat of last year's successful master-class. Andrew showed how they might improve their performances – a plate of soup came into it somewhere – and he indicated how much difference little changes can make to musical effect. Derek left with some new ideas about how he might present 'Lament for Patrick Og' and Craig was given pointers about balancing the phrases in the rarely heard 'Lord MacDonald's Lament'.

After dinner Society ex-treasurer Donald Martin had gathered eleven volunteers to play. Instructed by Donald to lead from the front, Jack Taylor started it going with the 'Vaunting', including a presidential tuning pause. We then heard 'Sir James MacDonald of the Isles' (Walter Gray), 'Battle of Auldearn' (Rae Bell), 'Too Long in this Condition' (John Shone), 'Corrienessan's Salute' (Bill Witherspoon), 'Mac-Dougall's Gathering' (Peter MacAllister), 'Marion's Wailing' (Jim Barrie), 'MacKay's Banner' (Alan Forbes), 'A Glase' (Rory Sinclair), 'Hiharin Odin Hiharin Dro' (John Frater), 'Macrimmon's Sweetheart' (Alistair McQueen).

On Sunday morning selected tunes set for this year's senior competitions were demonstrated by Bill Witherspoon (nameless Angus MacKay MS, 'Red Hector of the Battles', 'Pretty Dirk', 'Sister's Lament') and Andrew Wright ('Aged Warrior's Sorrow', 'Old Woman's Lullaby' (Campbell Cainntaireachd setting), 'Park Piobaireachd 1', 'Salute to the Birth of Rory Mor MacLeod'. Both players had done their homework, and, as well as playing beautifully, gave thoughtful analysis about the music and its construction. Word on the street was that Bill's pipes were the best at the conference.

The AGM was next. All office-bearers were reappointed by acclamation. John Shone tendered his resignation from the General Committee and was thanked for his contribution. John Frater was welcomed in his place. The meeting heard that the Society is in a healthy state, largely due to the success of the website, and that the General Committee is generating ideas about how we can use our resources to further our aims. The sound clips on the website are a very popular feature and the meeting was informed that the Music Committee had decided to expand these further by adding tunes not already included, and by including, in a separate section, 'alternative styles', such as those gained by interpretation of the Lady Doyle manuscript and other recent research.

The president closed the meeting by thanking all office-bearers for all their hard work.

Periodicals, journals, relevant publications

The Piping Times
The New Piping Times
Piobaireachd Society *Newsletter*
Local Dunbeath/Tongue publication: *Piobaireachd in the North East*

Finally, to complete the account of additional information available in connection with this book, an example of a fully written-out piobaireachd appears here – the famous 'Lament for the Children' taken from the original Angus MacKay edition of *A Collection of Ancient Piobaireachd* . . . (1838).

fig./nine: fully scored piobaireachd
(opposite)

50

No. 49.

8:, 8, 8.

The Lament for the Children

PATRICK MOR MACCRIMMON

I GROUND

II VAR. 1.

III VAR. 2.

IV TAORLUATH. V DOUBLING. VI CRUNLUATH. VII DOUBLING

(TAORLUATH AND DOUBLING)

(CRUNLUATH AND DOUBLING)

Abbreviations used

S = *Singling*. D = *Doubling*. T = *Taorluath*. C = *Crunluath*.

Index

NB: The above is a partial index only – to serve as a guide to the general patterning and 'sound' of the narrative. A fully referenced index is available in archive.